A Question of Honour

A Question of Honour

EMMA DRUMMOND

LONDON
VICTOR GOLLANCZ LTD
1991

First published in Great Britain 1991
by Victor Gollancz Ltd,
14 Henrietta Street, London WC2E 8QJ

Copyright © 1991 by E. D. Books

A CIP catalogue record for this book is available
from the British Library.

ISBN 0 575 05069 1

Typeset at The Spartan Press Ltd,
Lymington, Hants
and printed in Great Britain by
St Edmundsbury Press Ltd, Bury St Edmunds, Suffolk

A Question of Honour

Chapter 1

Nothing could be heard but the crackle and roar of the huge log fire as the assembled members of the family gazed at the figure standing at the head of the long polished table. General Sir Gilliard Ashleigh made full dramatic use of the suspended moment at the end of the speech he made on each such occasion. Then he continued in the deep voice used to commanding and being obeyed.

'Ladies and gentlemen, we shall now honour in customary manner the memory of Lieutenant Vorne Ashleigh, hero of Khartoum.'

Every man present, from octogenarian Great-uncle Harry down to the baby-faced subaltern at the far end of the room, leapt to his feet then turned to a large portrait hanging above the oaken fireplace. They raised their glasses, held them steady for a silent count of three, then drank a toast. The ladies remained seated, gazing at the tablecloth, until the men slowly resumed their seats in that room where the painted eyes of past generations of Ashleigh warriors stared out from gilt-framed portraits around the panelled walls. Sir Gilliard was the last to sit. It was due to pride rather than age that he did so. The Ashleigh family could boast numerous acts of gallantry on the battlefield, but none so great as the one they were remembering tonight.

On 22 January 1885, Vorne Ashleigh, Sir Gilliard's handsome, dashing grandson and heir, had laid down his life in an heroic attempt to prevent the fall of Khartoum and the murder of General Charles Gordon. Each year a memorial dinner had been held at Knightshill, home of the Ashleighs for the past three hundred years. At these dinners Sir Gilliard always related how his grandson, arriving in Khartoum with dispatches from the relief column advancing with ponderous leisure, had found the situation more desperate than his own commanders had guessed. He had immediately volunteered to disguise himself in native garb and face once more the dangers of both the desert and the fanatical followers of the religious tyrant known as the Mahdi, in a bid to carry back a starkly bitter command from Gordon to make all haste to reach the stricken city. Had that communiqué reached its destination, Gordon, Khartoum and the entire Sudan might have been saved, but Vorne Ashleigh had been betrayed by tribesmen he had trusted and regarded as friends. Three miles out from Khartoum he had been set upon by his companions and left for dead with multiple knife wounds. Yet he had somehow dragged himself a further mile and a half with his vital dispatch, before loss of blood and the agony of his mutilations had brought death on the lone and level sands beside the Nile. When discovered, the body had been identifiable only by the sealed communiqué still strapped to its bloody torso.

Occupying a distant grave like so many of his forebears, the family hero could only be honoured by marking the anniversary of his death each year in the old house that should have been his inheritance. Sir Gilliard expected every able member of the family to attend, along with officers of the regiment served by Ashleighs throughout twelve generations. Heavy snow had today blocked the road up from Dunstan St Mary, the village at the foot of the heights on which Knightshill was set. Those who lived a good distance from Wiltshire had arrived yesterday with the intention of staying a week. If the severe weather continued they would be forced to remain longer. The old general welcomed the prospect. The company of other military men was so stimulating.

During the subdued murmur which followed, the head of the family surveyed those around him. At the foot of the table his second granddaughter presided as hostess. A sensible, high-principled woman of twenty-seven resigned to spinsterhood because of a deformed left foot, Charlotte fulfilled her duties admirably. Midway down the table sat his elder granddaughter with her pious husband. The romantic and determined Margaret had married a handsome clergyman who had caught her youthful fancy, thus breaking the military tradition of the family. The Reverend Philip Daulton was virile in appearance, but his strength was directed into good works and prayer. Sir Gilliard barely tolerated the man, and reminded Margaret of his disapproval of her choice whenever a chance presented itself. The boy and girl of the union were attractive enough children, but young Timothy was unlikely ever to take up arms against any foe but the heathen.

On each side of Margaret were Sir Gilliard's ageing sisters and their military husbands, several of whom were unlikely to be present next year. He sighed. If only his sisters had been brothers. If only he had had more than one son. The thought revived pain which each year seemed to intensify rather than diminish, although he had long ago forgotten the face of a young girl who had briefly entranced him before producing his child only to abandon it and run off with an Italian poet. Lady Caroline Ashleigh's desertion of the infant while her husband was in India caused a sensation.

As a young officer with ambition, Sir Gilliard had survived public humiliation and inner wounds by devoting himself to his career from then on, never allowing himself to grow close to a woman and regarding with contempt those of a passionate nature. The pain he now felt more deeply as time passed was caused by the fear of losing that to which he had devoted his whole life: the glory of the Ashleigh family.

Roland had grown to manhood at Knightshill during the many years of foreign service which had prevented Sir Gilliard from really knowing his son. No sooner had the young man become a subaltern in the West Wiltshire Regiment than he had fallen victim to a seventeen-year-old with large adoring eyes and a great need for male protection. Clarissa Ashleigh had met with her father-in-law's approval on just one count: she was a breeding mare of the first order. Roland sired eight offspring before dying at Knightshill from wounds received in the second war against the Afghans. The dutiful son had done all that was expected of him and departed from the world without ever seeing the lusty babe born in his absence.

When that child was four years old, the widowed Clarissa married an American rancher and sailed for her new home. Her five surviving children had remained at Knightshill after a one-sided battle with Sir Gilliard. He remembered vividly the day on which a woman had exchanged five children for a loud, cigar-smoking braggart from the New World. Life at Knightshill had been better without her, for he then had full control over three grandsons whom he determined to fashion in his own image. Vorne had been twenty-three and all a man could wish for in an heir. Blond, sturdy, as sharp as a blade, filled with military élan and admirable immunity to feminine wiles, the youthful officer had been a source of immense pride to a soldier whose warring days were over. Then he had sailed to the Sudan with his regiment and never returned. Lieutenant Vorne Ewart Roland Ashleigh had died a hero's death, but Sir Gilliard's hopes and dreams had died with him. This dinner tonight highlighted the fact once more.

Sir Gilliard glanced over several more cousins until reaching the blond youth in evening dress seated on his left. The youngest of his four remaining grandchildren, Valentine Ashleigh already possessed all the dash, virility and fervour of the man they were remembering tonight. A mere infant at the time of his mother's remarriage, the boy had been 'adopted' by the fifteen-year-old Margaret who still treated her young brother with maternal fondness. But this senior schoolboy was a strapping six-footer, with a wayward streak, and determination bordering on stubbornness. At seventeen, he was impatient to follow in the footsteps of the heroic brother for whom eager worship presently flushed his handsome face. Sir Gilliard noted it. Despite several rebellious outbursts during lectures on his progress at school, the boy was as keen as mustard. All he needed was strict discipline to lick him into shape. The West Wiltshire

Regiment would provide that, after a spell of conscientious study at Oxford to compensate for schooldays devoted to the development of his physique. Until Valentine had been tamed, drilled and converted into a young officer prepared to obey any order, the element of fear would always be present, Sir Gilliard acknowledged, for on this boy would probably rest the honour and future of the Ashleigh family.

With that premise heavy within him, the grand-patriarch turned to the person seated tonight at his right hand. Vere Ashleigh wore no expression of reverence to match that of young Valentine. At twenty-five, the heir to Knightshill was an unbearable disappointment. Possessing something of the family good looks, Vere was far too slender and his bearing was not in the least soldierly. With his mother's colouring of light brown hair and greenish eyes, the young man who had never expected to inherit the Ashleigh estate and fortunes had been an invalid since birth. On the point of following a brother and two sisters to an immediate grave on entering the world, Vere had rallied enough to survive the initial dangers. Only a very protected childhood, great caution during adolescence, and the country air necessary to those of delicate health had ensured his reaching manhood. He was no true Ashleigh. He had also inherited his mother's diffidence, her gentle, shy smile and her love of pretty things; an undoubted misfit in a line of strong extrovert men. Sir Gilliard could not depend on an heir with inherent weakness. It was vital to ensure the continuation of the line with the birth of a male infant before Vere succumbed to a certain early demise.

Shifting his gaze to the strikingly lovely young woman beside his grandson, the elderly man's soul warmed with thankfulness. Annabel Bourneville had swept Vere off his feet six months ago, and the Ashleigh rubies had been placed on the girl's finger at Christmas. One fear remained. Could a man of less than robust constitution sire a male child? Sir Gilliard had asked Dr Alderton and been reassured, yet he would not rest until proof had been given. An early marriage was vital.

Vere was growing restless. He longed for the opportunity to have Annabel to himself. Even with the Ashleigh rubies on her finger he found it hard to believe he had won this beautiful girl. Edward Bourneville's unconditional agreement to the engagement had been a delightful surprise, because Vere had been frank about his history of illness when applying for his permission to marry his eighteen-year-old daughter.

Fever had ruled Vere's life. It had prevented his following the path through public school, university and the regiment favoured by Ashleighs through the ages. Educated by a tutor at home, he had grown to maturity directing his thoughts and desires along lines which were anything but martial. Love of the natural beauty and wildlife around Knightshill led him to spend much of his time roaming with sketchbook and pencil. He had accepted the physical limitations forced upon him by losing himself in the study of art treasures and the cultures of past empires, by reading poetry and prose, and listening to music.

Deep interest in expression through paint and brushes had led the adult Vere to the salons of well-known patrons of the arts. There he had been introduced to the Bohemian life enjoyed by others who did not conform to accepted standards. Amongst these men, their models, mistresses and friends, Vere had found a rapport lacking in the warrior atmosphere in which he had been brought up. In the studios of professional artists and sculptors he had found the opportunity to paint nudes, both male and female, but these canvases were never shown to his family. In this unconventional world of artists he had found confidence as a painter and as a man. Several affairs with models possessing heavenly features, but very earthly desires, had revealed that his constitution in no way inhibited his ability as a lover.

Contentment had burst into unbridled joy last summer on being introduced to the daughter of a distinguished Anglo-French banker. Golden-haired, oval-faced, and blessed with a gracefulness that made her every movement a delight, Annabel was a girl whose morals were as angelic as her features. When deeper acquaintance had revealed that she was gentle, compassionate and wildly romantic, Vere had had no doubt that he had found his lifelong partner.

Glancing now at the girl seated beside him, Vere marvelled once more at the miracle which had overtaken him. Annabel had never looked more vital. There was a soft blush on her cheeks and such fire in her deep violet eyes, he longed for this meal to end so that he could tell her how much he wanted her. When his hand sought hers under the table she turned to him, her face excitingly aglow. Yet it seemed to Vere that her gaze looked beyond him to something out of reach. For an uneasy moment he sensed that she was in another world, a realm he could not enter. Then he dismissed the thought as too fanciful. This whole ritual smacked of unreality. He was probably the only Ashleigh present who was immune to the dramatic hero worship.

As he was about to ask Annabel where her thoughts were centred, his sister Charlotte rose to lead the ladies out to the sitting room and Vere resigned himself to endure what he knew would follow. It was the same every year and the pattern ran true to form tonight. Sir Gilliard opened the conversation by expressing his impatience over the progress of the campaign in Egypt.

'They need a stern fellah behind 'em to whip 'em all into action,' he declared. 'How that upstart Kitchener came to be given command I dare not think. Licking the right boots, I shouldn't wonder. However, having licked 'em, why don't he get on with the job? He's fiddle-faddling with the construction of a railway when he should be pushing on to Khartoum. By God, it's taken this confounded government eleven years to mount an avenging campaign! Now Kitchener's dawdling beside the Nile as if he had all the time in the world. In my day . . . '

Vere allowed his mind to wander. He knew little of his hero brother. Eleven years had separated them, and his own frail health had kept him in the sickroom for much of the time. An active extrovert personality had restricted his older brother to occasional brief visits, with cheery encouragement for the invalid to get well soon, before departing on his own lusty affairs. It had been Margaret, three years Vere's senior, who had read him stories and played nursery games when beguiling warmth outside had beckoned irresistibly. Vorne had seemed an adult man to eight-year-old Vere when he came from Oxford to attend the funeral service for their father. During that brief visit, Vere had first become aware of the meaning of inheritance and its great importance to his grandfather. The tall, laughing brother had been unusually serious when explaining that the death of their father had created changes. Vere had been more dismayed than anything else over the ruling that he must take great care of himself, as he was now the second in line. It had seemed too much for a bewildered boy to contemplate the possible loss of both his grandfather and a hearty brother so soon after that of his father. Fear of being left all alone in the world had given him nightmares which soon induced a bout of the dreaded fever, prolonged by fretting over Vorne's having asked him to avoid being ill. The responsibility of being the second in line had seemed almost unbearable.

Vere had become Sir Gilliard's heir at the age of thirteen. By then deeply and passionately fond of Knightshill, and knowing that he would not be obliged to leave it for university or the army, the adolescent boy had thrown himself into learning all he could of farming and estate management. He now employed a good steady man as bailiff, and the estate thrived as it never had under a succession of absent soldiers. He was proud of Knightshill, loved every acre, every tree, every living creature on his land. With Annabel as his wife, he would be a monarch in the perfect kingdom.

'It's a damned clever piece of work, you have to give him that,' said Great-uncle Harry breaking into Vere's thoughts. 'It's not often a commander finds the only means of going forward is to build a confounded railway first.'

'Kitchener's an engineer,' pointed out John Howard, one of Vere's second cousins, whose face was almost as red as his jacket by now. 'Railways are his forte.'

'Even so, it's a damned clever piece of work,' insisted Great-uncle Harry. 'We'd have given our best pair of boots for a train during the dusty march to Jalalabad. I well recall Percy ffrench-Martin saying to me at the time . . .'

The resonant voice went on to recite a story Vere could have told from memory. Closing his ears to his elderly relative's booming voice, he studied his companions critically. Most of them wore the uniform of the West Wiltshire Regiment. Margaret's husband always excused himself from the drinking of port, and Annabel's parents were laid low with influenza, so Vere was conspicuous as the only man in evening dress. Young Val did not count. He was metaphorically wearing a scarlet jacket. Aside from the great-uncles and their male offspring, six officers of the West Wilts had come from their headquarters in Salisbury and planned to put up overnight at the Stag's Head Inn. If the bad weather continued they might be obliged to extend their stay, although military men would probably refuse to be defeated by a solid wall of snow, Vere told himself ruefully. They would doubtless mount a concerted attack on it and tomorrow evening would see them in Salisbury relating their victory to brother officers.

Young or old, each of these men followed the snail's pace progress of the Anglo-Egyptian force presently making a show of strength along the banks of the Nile. The serving officers made no secret of their disgust at being left at home. The West Wilts had formed part of that relief column eleven years ago: one of its officers had become the hero of the hour. They, more than any others, should be given the privilege of repossessing the city and avenging the murders.

Vere did not understand them. Why did men long to face heatstroke, thirst, epidemics and violent death? He naturally hoped his own courage was sufficient to cope with such things should they ever be forced on him, but any man who claimed to be in despair over being denied such experiences must surely be a little crazy. After hearing yet another of his relations deplore the fact, he could stay silent no longer.

'You could transfer to any one of the regiments in Egypt, Miles. You'd be in the thick of things then.'

'Transfer!' choked his cousin, dropping cigar ash down his medal-covered jacket. 'Leave the West Wilts!'

'Just my fun,' said Vere, smiling to suggest that he had not expected to be taken seriously. The Regiment was sacrosanct. Let no one dare to joke about it.

Miles frowned at Vere as Sir Gilliard remarked testily, 'Reinforcements will be required shortly. The West Wilts will be out there by the time we hold the Waterloo Ball, mark my words. No man lays a railway across the desert then walks away to leave it to the natives.'

'Hear, hear!' roared another of the second cousins with drunken enthusiasm. 'The damned Dervishes can't run a railway.'

'They've been living quite successfully in the Sudan for centuries,' Vere pointed out. 'What would such people want with trains?'

'That's not the point, old chap,' argued his inebriated relative. 'They've got 'em now, haven't they?'

'To hell with the trains,' interjected a beefy major from Salisbury. 'Up the Nile in boats. *That's* the best method of reaching Khartoum. Unless they advance soon, the river'll be too low. Can't navigate some stretches at certain times of the year, you know. When we were there in 'eighty-four there was no end of a to-do at one cataract. I recall old Jimmy McKenzie trying to . . .'

Vere's mind wandered again. He had also heard *that* story before. Forbidden to indulge in cigars because of his weak chest and allowed just one glass of port, he sipped it contentedly and thought about his valuable orchids. The hothouse at Knightshill contained many rare species brought from the East by past Ashleighs who had soldiered there. By extending the area of glass it should be possible to increase output sufficiently to supply florists in London as well as in the local area. He liked the notion. Orchids were exotic, curious plants. In bad weather he often sat in the hothouse to paint the blooms which produced such unexpected, exquisite combinations of colours. He had presented a pair of his orchid water-colours to Mrs Bourneville at Christmas, and she had been charmed by the delicate detail of his work. He would speak to his bailiff, John Morgan, about the idea. They could work it up to a very profitable extent within a year.

'Have you taken *that* into account, young man?' accused Great-uncle Harry looking pointedly at Vere.

There was a brief silence while everyone lolling at the table gazed in expectation of receiving an intelligent comment from him. On what? Just as he was about to murmur a non-committal, 'Well, not entirely, I confess,' his grandfather spoke in harsh tones.

'It's no use discussing military tactics with that boy, Harry. You must have seen that he's been totally inattentive since the ladies left the room.' He scowled. 'We had better join them, I suppose, or risk facing accusations of neglect.' Rising to his feet reluctantly, he addressed all his guests. 'We can continue our discussion in the morning. I doubt any departures will be possible even if no further snow falls. We are under siege, gentlemen, and can use the fact to good account, hey?'

Vere watched them all leave the table in various states of unsteadiness and wondered if the ladies would not be better off on their own. Sir Gilliard's tall figure led the procession. At eighty-seven he was not in the least bowed and could drink any guest under the table. A proud man all his life, he never spoke of his faithless bride. Whether or not the young Gilliard Ashleigh had adored her, Vere did not know, but the army had subsequently become his grandfather's ruling passion. Vere had long ago given up trying to be what Sir Gilliard wished his heir to be. Only by donning a scarlet jacket could he do that.

Entering the salon, Vere told himself the most wonderful girl in the world loved him for what he was and that was all he desired. He would take her away from all these warriors for a while. Her tranquillity would be a relief after the discussion he had just endured.

He found Annabel in a small group near the fire, the one silent person in a chattering quartet. She jumped when he touched her arm. 'Did I startle you? Forgive me,' he said, enjoying the faint colour that crept into her cheeks at the sight of him. Turning to his aunts and cousin, he added, 'Please excuse us,' then took her arm and headed for the parlour at the far end of the room. It was cosy and dim there, with only the light from a fire and one low lamp to provide the romantic atmosphere he wanted. Kicking the door shut, he then drew her close.

'I've been longing for that interminable meal to end so that I could have you to myself, darling. I almost kissed you at the table.' He then demonstrated his lack of patience very thoroughly.

'Vere, please behave,' she protested breathlessly, pulling free of his arms and turning away.

'I can't. I want you so very much.'

Her response was unexpected. Walking slowly to the fireplace she turned to face him. 'I had no idea of the true nature of this family anniversary. It hardly seems right to . . . to break the solemn mood of the evening.'

Taken aback because *he* had not indulged in the solemnity to which she referred, he then realised that tonight was her first experience of the Khartoum Dinner. The ritual was too melodramatic, in Vere's opinion. He supposed Annabel must have been overwhelmed by it, so he moved forward swiftly to take her hands in his.

'You mustn't let Grandfather's dramatic speech and all that military fervour upset you. No one knows the truth about my brother's last moments: it's mere conjecture on the part of those who discovered his body. Grandfather has embellished the tale with an old soldier's passion for the kind of glory he can never personally recapture. My family and the regiment indulge him every year because they respect and admire the old boy. When he dies, so will this rather macabre anniversary dinner. I promise you I have no intention of continuing it.'

Her hands lay unresponsively in his as she gazed at him in disbelief. 'I can't accept that you are serious, Vere.'

Perturbed by her coolness, he explained. 'Eleven years have passed since Vorne died.'

'Most heroically.'

'No one would deny that, but I believe it possible to honour his memory in a less ostentatious manner.'

Annabel drew her hands free of his clasp and walked to sit in a chair before the fire, gazing at the glowing embers as if in a world of her own. Vere was bewildered by her change of mood. He hesitated while an antique clock ticked heavily in the sudden silence, realising he had been a fool not to have prepared her for tonight's ritual. Blood and battlefield gallantry were subjects for military messes and gentlemen's clubs only. His old aunts, second cousins and sisters were inured to them but this gentle creature who delighted in beauty, as he did, could only be upset by what she had just experienced. He was on the point of kneeling beside her to offer reassurance when her next words halted him.

Studying the flashing cluster of rubies on her finger, she asked in faraway fashion, 'Would this ring have been given to Vorne Ashleigh's bride?'

Disconcerted, he answered rather stiltedly. 'Over the past two hundred years, all wives of Ashleigh heirs have worn it until their first-born sons became engaged, or until the next male in line did so. My grandmother had enough conscience to leave the ring here when she absconded, and my mother surrendered it on remarrying. It's been in the bank vault since then.'

Her eyes were dark and unfathomable when she looked up to ask, 'He had chosen no one?'

Knowing instinctively to whom she referred, he shook his head. 'My brother was too carefree a person to take on that responsibility at an early age. He was more concerned with living life to the full.'

Gazing down at the ring again as if mesmerised, Annabel eventually said, almost to herself, 'So young. So splendid. So fearless. How *unutterably* tragic!'

To Vere's consternation he saw tears begin to shimmer on her cheeks. Annabel appeared to have forgotten his presence.

When Charlotte led the ladies to the more cheerful atmosphere of the plum-and-gold sitting room, Margaret made her way up the branched staircase to check that her children were sleeping peacefully. Nanny was ironing their clothes when Margaret entered the familiar suite and went through to the large room painted blue and white, which Timothy and Kate still shared. As she looked down at their faces rosy with sleep, she told herself both children possessed that mixture of charm, self-confidence, and obstinacy which was the hallmark of the Ashleighs. They betrayed little evidence of their Daulton heritage, and she frowned as she recalled the scene which had occurred when she had come earlier to kiss them goodnight. Although Nanny had settled them to sleep, Timothy had sat up swiftly at his mother's entry, his blue eyes wide and shining.

'Mama, Uncle Vorne was very, very brave, wasn't he?'

'Yes, darling,' she had agreed.

'Why did those men put knives in him?'

Margaret had sat on the edge of his bed, knowing the boy would not be content until they had been over the story again. 'Uncle Vorne had something they wanted, so they decided to hurt him to persuade him to give up the important message he was carrying.'

'But he didn't give it up.'

'No, dear.'

A sleepy Kate in the other bed had said in matter-of-fact tones, 'If they had only asked him very politely, he would have given it to them. Nanny says it's rude to take things without asking first.'

Margaret had smothered a smile. 'In this case your uncle couldn't have given them what they wanted, no matter how politely they asked. He was in the service of the Queen. Only she could have given him permission to hand it over.'

'Did she *want* him to be hurt by knives?'

'She wanted him to be brave enough to do his duty. We all have to be brave enough for that.'

'I shall be,' Timothy had declared. 'I'm going to wear a red coat like Grandfather and all those other gentlemen tonight. Val says he's going to have one soon, because all Ashleighs are soldiers. Except Uncle Vere.'

'I expect he's glad he won't have knives put in him,' Kate had reasoned from the pillow.

'Yes, I expect so,' Margaret had agreed with a sigh. 'Go to sleep now.'

When she was half-way across the room, Timothy had asked, 'Is the Queen angry with Uncle Vere?'

Turning, she had replied, 'Her Majesty understands that we all do our duty in different ways. Vere does his by running the estate and by looking after us all.'

'I want to do mine by wearing a scarlet coat and being very, very brave. I want the Queen to give me a medal to wear on the coat . . . and I want my name to be Ashleigh,' he had added fiercely.

'That can never be, darling,' she had told him on a sigh.

It had ended the cross-examination. Timothy's obsession with military matters made Margaret uneasy as she crossed the nursery where past generations had dreamed their dreams – the boys of martial glory, no doubt, and the girls of happiness ever after. It had been an unbroken pattern through the ages, until now.

As an only child her father must have been lonely in this huge, high-ceilinged nursery. Perhaps that had led him to fill it with numerous offspring. Or his eight children could have been the natural outcome of deep love for a woman of charm and vivacity.

Margaret remembered her father's death vividly. Vere, Charlotte and herself had been summoned to the bedside by their nineteen-year-old brother urgently summoned home from Oxford. She had been inconsolable for a week after seeing the coffin lowered into the earth and covered over as if Father had never existed, but the blow of her mother's remarriage had been even greater. Margaret had been introduced to a large handsome man with a loud voice, who told her he intended to take his new wife to a plantation in America. Her weeping mother had explained that they were all to remain with Grandfather at Knightshill, and that Margaret must look after her brothers and sister in Mother's place.

It had seemed a tremendous responsibility to a girl of fifteen, yet little had changed. Charlotte and Vere had continued to be coddled by Nanny as the invalids of the family, so Margaret had spent most of her time with the baby for whom she had felt almost maternal pride since his birth. A faint smile touched her mouth. How hotly indignant Val would be if he knew she still thought of him that way.

Walking through to the rooms she occupied with Philip, Margaret went to the mirror to tidy her glossy light brown hair and felt an ache growing in her breast. At twenty-eight she still retained the bloom of eager youth. The Ashleigh looks, with which she had been more generously endowed than her sister, continued to draw glances of admiration wherever she went, yet she could just as well be a copy of Nanny for all the effect she had upon her husband. The beauty which once had set him alight no longer touched his heart or senses.

Turning to the window, she gazed at the snow-driven night with a matching chill in her veins. The shock of her mother's abandonment, followed by Vorne's murder a year later, had heralded a breakdown from which it had taken months to recover. Dr Alderton's remedies had not been as effective as the arrival of a handsome new curate. Hopelessly romantic by nature, and seeking a rock to cling to, Margaret had swiftly and passionately surrendered to a man offering understanding and solace. Philip Daulton had also offered irresistible excitement to a young girl starved of love. Dark-haired, dark-eyed and filled with ecclesiastical fire, the young churchman had soon been filled with fire of a more basic nature than his calling demanded. Margaret had responded to it so eagerly,

Philip had been obliged to approach Sir Gilliard for permission to arrange a marriage before their passion got out of hand.

Badly knocked by the tragic deaths of his son and his eldest grandson within a few years of each other, and having only shallow interest in the women of his family, the elderly general had put up no more than token resistance to the union.

Across the snow-blanketed knot-garden and the lawns beyond, great soft flakes drifted down as Margaret saw in her mind's eye the bridal veil which had floated around her on the day she had pledged her obedience and her loyalty to someone who had already possessed her heart. Those first years had been ecstatic, for Philip had been an ardent, hungry lover. Bearing his two children had been an extension of the union which had brought her total fulfilment. Until three years ago, she had confidently believed Philip shared her feelings.

The change in him had been frighteningly sudden. A visiting missionary on sick leave from Africa had seduced him with words and visions, so that he became ruled by a vastly different passion from that day on. Like a man in the grip of fever Philip had pursued his new love, abandoning all else along the way. He no longer preached, he dictated. The loving husband and father had been subdued by an overriding crusade to save the heathen souls of the world. Timothy and Kate were now seen as mere vessels of his life's mission. Their young minds were being filled with the implacable creed of salvation. He no longer saw Margaret as a lover, friend and soulmate, but as a disciple of his new all-consuming work. The love which had once been the gleaming core of her existence was dying slowly and humiliatingly. She dared let no one know the truth, least of all the man who was driving as many knives in her breast as natives had in that of the lone and helpless Vorne Ashleigh.

The youngest person present in the salon sought relative solitude in a corner by a window. The Khartoum Dinner always affected Val so deeply he found it difficult to resort to chit-chat with aunts and female cousins once he left that room so full of military ambience. All the women seemed interested in was getting to know the girl who would soon be one of the family, and the future mistress of Knightshill.

Val had arrived home for the Christmas vacation to be told Vere would be spending it at Richmond with his fiancée and her family. He had thought the engagement rather sudden, but he was glad for his brother. Annabel was very pretty and seemed fond of him. The poor devil had missed out on so much but, to his credit, he had never complained. Neither had he shown resentment of Val's freedom to follow family tradition and do his utmost to enhance Ashleigh military distinction. It was probably a good thing for Vere to marry and have children. As next in line, Val had no wish to run the estate when Grandfather died. His heart was set on pursuing excitement and the thrill of battle in foreign lands. So, aside from the loyal bond of brotherhood, he wished Vere a long and happy life with a clutch of sons to succeed him.

Turning his back on the room, Val gazed from the great square sconced window overlooking the gravelled driveway which led from a wooden bridge over what had once been a moat. Snow lay deep and untouched as huge flakes continued to drift down to add a further layer. No one would be able to leave the house due to the blocking of the lane from Dunstan St Mary. *Cut off, with supplies running low and with the relief force bogged down while the enemy lay in wait outside the walls of the bastion!* What action would he take? He saw the scene clearly: men gazing at him with complete trust and confidence as he gave his orders, himself unafraid as he outlined their plight and committed them to an heroic last stand.

As he gazed in fanciful manner from the bright room into the night beyond, the snow became sand. What had General Gordon's last thoughts been as he had faced that horde swarming over the stronghold of Khartoum with fanatical hatred in each heart? Could he possibly have cursed Vorne Ashleigh for failing in his desperate mission? Surely not. He must have known an Ashleigh would sacrifice all to do his duty. Val sighed. He had been six when news of Vorne's death had reached Knightshill. All he knew of the family hero was a vague recollection of a tall laughing man in a red coat, who had swung him in the air and called him a fine little fellow. That must have been shortly before Vorne had sailed to Egypt, the last time the family had seen him.

Ashleighs had died on the battlefield before; many had been wounded. A few had performed individual deeds of daring, but no other had offered his life for a mission which had entailed making his way across hostile and waterless land, where torture by the elements could be as agonising as that inflicted by native captors. The West Wilts had honoured Lieutenant V. E. R. Ashleigh by hanging on the wall of its Headquarters Officers' Mess an artist's impression of that incredible final crawl after being left for dead, with the vital message from Gordon still secretly strapped to his body. His murderers were pictured making off with the empty dispatch case. The gallant former pupil was mentioned on Chartfield's Roll of Honour and an illustrated account of his heroism which had earned a posthumous D.S.O. hung beneath. Val was inordinately proud to be Vorne's brother, and intensely aware of the obligation to match up. He intended to do so, but in his own way.

He turned back and gazed around the room. The scarlet jackets of Great-uncles Harry and Bartholomew, of the male Howard, Flinders and

Carlton-Jay cousins, and of Sir Gilliard himself, fired him with excitement and deepened the yearning which had caused him to choke back a sob of pride during the toast to a man he would give anything to have known.

'Well, my lad, how are your studies progressing?' asked a voice at his elbow, reducing the eager warrior to a schoolboy.

Val turned to one of his second cousins, whose nose and cheeks were now as red as his coat. Herbert Flinders was the son of Sir Gilliard's sister Maud, and Val disliked him because he was a military prig.

'I'm captain of the rugger team now, and Stroke in the rowing eight. My friends are counting on my winning the fencing prize next term, if not the Waycliffe Cup for sportsman of the year. I'm up against some impressive rivals for both, so I don't take either for granted,' he added frankly.

'Mmm,' grunted Herbert. 'Your grandfather's strictures have done no good whatever. I ask how your studies are progressing and you reply with tales of sporting prowess. Acquiring muscles won't help you pass examinations.'

Val scowled. Last term's report had made him the butt of many acid comments from Sir Gilliard over the Christmas holidays. He was not a dunce, it was simply that sport took up so much of his time. Spending hour after hour with books held no appeal for him, but racing down a frosty field to score a try or bending his back and revelling in his own strength as he pulled an oar was exhilarating. If he was voted captain of the cricket team this summer, as he hoped, he did stand an excellent chance of being awarded the Waycliffe Cup. He would pass his exams by the skin of his teeth, but take far more pride in the sports trophy. Boundless energy burned within him. He grew restless when inactive, loved the camaraderie of team games, the physical well-being induced by exhaustion and aching muscles. He was happy only when using eyes, wits and limbs in punishing physical activity. It was this trait which had led him to a decision he would allow no one to force him to change.

'A chap can't swot all the time,' he said defensively. 'I won't shine in the exams, but so long as I pass no lower than last year I'll be all right.'

Herbert shook a reproving finger at him and tut-tutted. 'That's not the attitude to take, Valentine.'

Val disliked his cousin and he hated being called Valentine, so he retaliated defiantly. 'It's the only attitude I've got, I'm afraid.'

Herbert's beady eyes registered affront at this retort from a mere boy. 'You'll have to change it, if you expect to go up to Oxford then into the West Wilts. They won't accept duffers.'

'I'm not going to Oxford, nor am I joining the West Wilts,' he confessed impetuously. 'I'm planning to put my name down with a cavalry regiment and go straight to Sandhurst.'

The slight lull in conversation meant that his words reached a group of other middle-aged cousins to their right. They turned in surprise, as if expecting a stranger somehow to have braved the snow to enter their midst. John Carlton-Jay, son of Sir Gilliard's second sister, took a step towards them.

'Did I hear aright, young Valentine? An Ashleigh in the damn cavalry? It's unthinkable!'

Val bridled. 'What's wrong with the cavalry?'

'Everything. They're all brawn and no brains. Well-known fact,' he drawled, fingering the badge of his own infantry regiment.

Herbert tittered. 'Just suit our young cousin, John.'

Another officer cousin sauntered up to join them. 'What's all this about horse-soldiers? Been embroiled in yet another damn-fool caper, have they?'

Val fired up in defence of the *arme blanche*. 'Where would our army have been without the charges of the light and heavy brigades at Balaclava? How would Wellington have managed at Waterloo without cavalry to rout the enemy? And what of Roberts's fate in Afghanistan if his entire army had been on foot? The mounted regiments more often than not go in to clear the way for infantry, thus taking the brunt of the fire.'

'Is that what you plan to do, young fellow-me-lad?' asked Peter Howard, with a knowing wink at his companions. 'You've always been the kind of horseman who thinks with his backside.'

Val was furious at this injustice. 'At least mine will be on a charger in the thick of battle, not on a chair behind a desk in Horse Guards like yours is.'

'Come along, gentlemen,' said a chiding female voice from the edge of the group, as Margaret came between two of her cousins. 'I can't allow you to neglect us, especially after spending so long with your port and cigars.' Glancing around at them all, she then asked suspiciously, 'What are you up to? Young Val looks like a stag surrounded by snapping hounds.'

'Just been ribbing him a little,' said John airily. 'Fellow can't take a joke, apparently.'

'I can when it's genuinely funny,' said Val, glad of his sister's interruption of this concerted attack by second cousins all nearing retirement. They lacked imagination and treated him as a juvenile – despite his height which enabled him to face them eye to eye.

Margaret slipped her arm through his, saying, 'At a gathering designed to honour one Ashleigh and congratulate another, I'm surprised that you should join forces to bait a third who is certain to be the most distinguished of them all.'

Unwittingly, she had played right into their hands. Peter nudged Herbert with his elbow as he said, 'Ah . . . by charging the enemy on his trusty steed and thus making things simple for we foot soldiers, I understand.'

'Oh look, a joke's a joke,' Val growled.

'Does the old man approve of this?' asked John, in his affected voice.

'Approve of what?' demanded Margaret.

'The boy has aspirations to wear a fancy hat and go to war leading a mounted squadron. It seems the West Wilts will not do for him.'

Great-uncle Harry, bored by a monologue from one of the female Howards, turned on overhearing the last sentence and asked for clarification. 'Who's this pernickety fellow you're discussing, hey? The West Wilts not good enough for him indeed!'

Val's heart sank. The whole thing was getting out of hand. 'I didn't say that,' he protested.

'Young Valentine has his sights set on becoming a Hussar, or some such fancy soldier,' Herbert told his father. 'No need for studies then, d'ye see.'

Sir Gilliard's brother-in-law looked horrified. 'A *Hussar*! You mean those damned fellows in indecently tight trousers, and coats covered with gold lace? Must be mad – or the boy's sickening for something. Christmas is the time for fevers and rheumatism. I know. Had experience of both. Best put him to bed.'

Margaret put her hand on her great-uncle's sleeve, saying soothingly, 'Take no notice of this nonsense. Herbert, John and Peter are merely having an overlong joke at Val's expense.'

'A joke?' exclaimed Esmé Howard waspishly, joining the group. 'The last time my brother Peter deigned to laugh was when I slipped and fell at the Russian Ambassador's feet. I thought he'd never stop.' Darting a glance at the culprit, she went on to say, 'He'd had far too much port on *that* occasion, also.'

Sir Gilliard appeared, drawn by the liveliness of the conversation in that part of the room. In a convivial mood now, he asked, 'Who is the blackguard guilty of indulging in an excess of port, eh? Come on, own up, sir . . . and don't all speak at once,' he added with a chuckle.

Great-uncle Harry pointed at Val. 'Too young for port. Thought so all along, but not my place to say. Should have left the table with the ladies. I see what it is now. Not ill, just inebriated. Bad business, Gilliard, bad business. Only a boy, you know.'

Sir Gilliard, splendid in his scarlet jacket hung with medals, frowned. 'Have you been misbehaving, Valentine? I thought you could take a glass of port like a gentleman.'

'Grandfather, there's been a misunderstanding,' explained Margaret quickly. 'Val is perfectly sober, and if anyone has been misbehaving it is these "gentlemen" who gain amusement by joining forces against an unequal foe. I think it's time we asked Charlotte to play for us all, and forgot this silly nonsense.'

Sir Gilliard regarded her with irritation. 'The boy is almost eighteen and well able to speak in his own defence, Margaret. I'm surprised he allows you to cosset him like young Timothy when he should be man enough to handle his own problems.' Rounding on Val, he asked sternly, 'What have you done to cause a "misunderstanding" between so many people? Why should Colonel Flinders imagine you to be either unwell or not fully in command of yourself?'

Such instant reversal from geniality simply because it was he who appeared to be at the centre of the affair made Val's defiant spirit rise immediately. He had intended to announce his plans at the end of the school year, at an appropriate time, but his cousins had mocked something so very dear to his heart he was driven to defend it now.

'What I did, sir, was to reveal to Cousin Herbert my intention of signing up with a cavalry regiment and going straight to Sandhurst,' he said, in a voice which had gained unmistakable assurance through his having captained so many sporting teams. 'The only misunderstanding tonight is that no one appears to realise I meant what I said.'

The room had grown silent save for the crackle of the fire. Val was aware that all heads were now turned in his direction. Vere murmured in the ear of the girl in white satin beside him before coming across to stand a little behind their grandfather. The sensation of being one against a hostile horde pumped further defiance into Val. A man must be prepared to speak up for his beliefs no matter how great the opposition.

'I don't want to waste time at Oxford when I could be already gaining my commission.'

Sir Gilliard fixed his immensely blue eyes in a stare designed to wilt subordinates. 'Your intellect has never been a source of pride to me, but to prattle such nonsense and claim it as fact indicates a fool. I suggest you retire before you cause further offence.'

'Grandfather!' exclaimed Margaret. 'A mountain has been made from a molehill. No one has been offended.'

'*I* have,' averred the old general in most damning tones. 'It is not the first time a member of my family has revealed a lack of common sense and loyalty – as you should know, my girl.'

'That's not fair!' cried Val in defence of his sister. 'We each have the right to do as we wish with our life.'

'The voice of heedless youth! A mature man recognises his obligation to put duty before self.'

'I intend to do my duty, sir,' declared Val heatedly, 'but I'll do it best at the head of a squadron of cavalry.'

22

Into the silence, Vere spoke with his customary quiet tone. 'Are you truly set on this, Val?'

He nodded, hoping his brother's lack of military involvement would allow him to understand. 'I'm counted among the best riders in the county – you'll support that, Vere – and I'm never happier than when I'm around horses. I've studied military tactics in all the great battles, and the part in them played by the cavalry fascinates me. I want to be on the move in war,' he insisted fervently. 'I want to be able to see the whole picture, be mobile. I want to ride out and challenge the enemy, not wait in static squares until he approaches so close I'm forced to fire.' He turned back to appeal to Sir Gilliard. 'I won't be putting self before duty because both demand that I take my place in the Queen's service. I'm impatient, sir! I can't wait to gain my commission, and I'll emulate my forebears to the extent of dying on the battlefield, if need be. Surely it makes no difference which colours I serve, so long as I do it with Ashleigh honour?'

Sir Gilliard's features displayed the determination which had led the men of his family to perform many acts of courage, and he spoke as if to his grandson alone. 'There is no honour in a man who rejects his heritage. Your family has served a brave and famous regiment through twelve generations. Tonight we are here to honour one of its most heroic officers. That you should speak on such an occasion of there being no importance attached to which colours you serve wounds me deeply. Is it that you are afraid of not matching up to your dead brother?'

Colour flooded Val's face at such an inference, and he almost choked on his words. 'I believe I have courage enough for most things. It would have been easy to avoid your anger tonight by allowing you to believe I wasn't serious about joining a horsed regiment. I have never been more serious. My admiration for the West Wilts is deep and steeped in family history, but I am so totally drawn to the cavalry it's with them I shall serve my country best.'

The old man did not raise his voice: his words were enough to crush this minor uprising by an ill-matched foe. 'Cavalry regiments are expensive. At the end of the next school year your allowance will cease, unless you inform me that you intend to take up your studies at Oxford. I shall use my military influence to ensure no cavalry colonel will ever accept an application from you for a commission in his regiment. Attempt to flout me, boy, and you'll live to regret it. You'll serve your country with the West Wiltshire Regiment, or not at all. Is that clear?'

Chapter 2

Morning brought blue skies and a breathless hush over the landscape. After an evening which had never recovered from the unfortunate family confrontation, all but the elderly wanted to escape the house. The snow lay too deep to venture far, but Benson had set his twin sons to clearing paths along the terrace as well as through the rose-garden, which caught the best of the sunshine. It was to this spot that Vere led Annabel after they had watched the Daulton children starting a snowman on the flagged terrace. Vere thought the sight entrancing: two small, rosy-cheeked figures in bright coats, scurrying back and forth with pails of snow to tip on the growing mound. A splendid subject for a painter talented in the art of capturing movement on canvas. He was not. The beauty he yearned to copy was walking beside him.

Happiness was almost a pain within as he guided his fiancée along a path banked high on each side with glittering frozen snow. The air was still and chill, intensifying his sense of elation. Annabel looked stunningly lovely this morning. In a coat of sapphire blue trimmed with grey fur, and a hood which revealed a glimpse of hair as shimmery-gold as the morning sunshine, she made all his senses sing. Silenced by the perfection all around him, Vere rejoiced that she seemed as enchanted by it as he.

From the rose-garden Knightshill looked solid and impressive. The house rose to three floors, the main rooms being situated on the first two. At the top were the servants' quarters and various attic stores. Today, sunshine glinted on the multi-paned windows, and warmed the stone to a more mellow grey than that shown by the stark cold light of the previous few days.

As they walked arm in arm, their breath frosting in the cold air, Annabel finally broke the silence. 'How magnificent this place is! When I saw it on that earlier occasion there were beautiful autumn tints everywhere, but an afternoon call is scarcely long enough to give an impression of Knightshill's full glory.' Glancing up at him with laughing violet eyes, she added, 'Especially when it was the son of the house Mama and Papa had really come to inspect.'

He smiled back. 'They knew me well enough. I was rarely absent from your home in Richmond throughout the summer. Did they really think I would be so different in my own environment?'

'Perhaps.' She looked away towards the house again. 'I'm trying to imagine what it was like all those years ago.'

'You don't have to imagine it, darling. Numerous paintings in the picture room show its development through past generations of Ashleighs.'

She shook her head as she studied the east wing rising up to cold blue skies. 'Not that far back. Just a decade or two, when you were all children. Tell me about it, Vere.'

'You should ask Margaret. She's the eldest now, and can probably remember more about it than I can. I'm afraid I spent more time in the sickroom than anywhere else.'

She glanced up briefly. 'Yes, of course.'

'I didn't mind too much,' he assured her. 'It meant that I missed birthday parties and picnics, but enforced convalescence provided the opportunity to read to my heart's content. I probably went through our library twice over, although half the volumes in it must have been incomprehensible to a boy of that age.' He squeezed her hand. 'While my brothers and sisters were outside having adventures, I was having far more exciting ones in the land of imagination.'

'Weren't you ever conscious of being . . .' she hesitated before choosing her word, 'deprived?'

'I sometimes longed to run around, play games with the others. When the Goose Fair was held at Winklesham I naturally pleaded to be taken there. Although Lottie had to forgo many things because her leg was in an iron, even she was allowed to go to the Goose Fair. Yes, I suppose I felt deprived at times like that,' he admitted, as they turned towards the sun at the far end of a garden in which the iced rose trees were no more than glistening spikes. 'Most of the time, I was highly contented. I had no desire to attend school when I could have a tutor to myself and learn twice as fast. I enjoyed my brief spell at Oxford, however, because individual tuition was readily available.'

'And the Regiment?' she asked, gazing at the sun.

He gave a wry smile. 'Can you imagine me in a red coat, shouting orders and reliving old wars with men who have nothing better to do? No, darling, you'll never have to sit at home with our children while your husband is in India, China, Africa or any point east of Dover, as most Ashleigh wives have. I've great plans for Knightshill. Grandfather is loath to make changes, but when the estate is mine I shall lighten the atmosphere by inviting artists and intellectuals here. Painters, musicians and men of letters. The old house will echo with music and song, not endless martial reminiscences.' He stopped and turned to face her. 'How soon will you come to live with me here, my darling?'

25

It was a while before she responded. 'We've been engaged three weeks. It's a little early to press me for a wedding date.'

'Not when a man's as madly in love as I am.' He took her gloved hands in a fierce grip. 'Sir Gilliard and your father approve an early marriage. What about July? That would give your parents six months for preparations.'

'Not July, Vere. Spring is the traditional time for weddings.'

'May?' he suggested eagerly.

She nodded. 'That will give us fifteen months in which to arrange everything.'

With a sinking heart he realised she was suggesting the spring of next year. He did not understand. Annabel was not the type of girl to indulge in provocative teasing, so she must be serious. Sick with disappointment, he challenged her. 'Is there some special reason for delaying so long?'

'Engagements frequently last for several years. Fifteen months isn't very long.'

'It's an eternity,' he declared heavily. 'I don't know how I'll be patient until then.'

Slipping her hand beneath his arm she urged him to walk on. 'You must have learned patience in the sickroom, Vere. I can hardly bear to think of you shut inside while your brothers chased about these lovely acres, growing healthy and strong. Poor little boy!'

'I was far from unhappy,' he insisted, trying to accept the unwelcome delay to their union.

'How like you to say that, my dear. You have so many virtues, so many admirable qualities. I suspect Valentine knows little of them,' she observed. 'What will become of the young rebel?'

He shrugged. 'He could hardly have chosen a worse time to defy Grandfather, but the members of my family become extremely tiresome where military matters are concerned. How lucky I am to have the perfect excuse to duck out of the Ashleigh obligation to serve the colours.'

Annabel stopped and put a hand on his arm in a gesture of comfort. 'You need not adopt a pretence with me, Vere. I well understand how deeply you feel your inability to follow in your dead brother's footsteps, and I would be blind not to have noticed Sir Gilliard's disappointment. It must add salt to your wounds.'

Vere was totally disconcerted. What had he said or done to suggest that he had been an imprisoned invalid gazing enviously from his window at his brothers at play? He felt no resentment; he suffered no wounds. As he studied the face he longed to paint on a madonna, enlightenment came. He had met and courted her in London. Although he had spoken of the childhood illness which prevented his following tradition, it was not until this visit to Knightshill that the girl he loved had experienced the extent to

26

which the military dominated the Ashleighs. Warmth raced through him as he drew her close in swift sympathy.

'My dearest girl, that wretched business last night upset you more than I guessed. The whole family in scarlet jackets covered with medals, and no conversation other than military balderdash! Then Val creating an unnecessary drama which was elaborated into a matter almost of life or death. I apologise on behalf of them all. It wasn't the best time to be introduced to my relatives,' he said with a wry smile, tucking her hood closer around her head with cherishing hands. 'And you're quite wrong, darling. I was never a "poor little boy" watching enviously from a high prison window. I have never adopted a pretence with you. I never will. Your sense of compassion is one of the myriad reasons why I adore you, but it's misplaced in this instance. The very last thing I would care to do is follow in Vorne's footsteps.'

She stiffened in his arms. 'It is?'

'Certainly. My brother was a very dashing sort of fellow, never happy unless he was up to his neck in a risky caper. When he was at home it was impossible not to be aware of his presence. His voice and footsteps seemed to echo all about the house – so did his laughter. You've seen his portrait. That smile enabled him to persuade others to do just as he wished.' He laughed lightly. 'A saucy devil, apparently. My clearest memory of him was when he came on leave prior to sailing for Egypt. He was full of excitement at the prospect of going into battle. I recall thinking his attitude dreadfully bloodthirsty. I didn't understand how he could bear to leave all this.'

Pausing thoughtfully, his appreciative gaze took in the ancient, noble lines of the house, the stables and orangery, the formal flower-beds and snow-decked shrubbery, the tree-covered slope which protected Knightshill from north winds. Then he glanced to the east, where the Ashleigh herd grazed high meadows during summer before going down to winter quarters on the perimeter of Dunstan St Mary. Studying the southern aspect where the ground dropped away gently to provide good growing land, he considered the rows of hothouses where orchids flourished. This would all eventually be his. On this land pheasants ran out, startled by his cantering horse, and scarlet berries rioted amid Old Man's Beard in the hedgerows. Here, the sun spangled dew-covered webs early in the clear mornings, and hares boxed on the open hillsides when March delirium touched all who revelled in its promise of summer.

His gaze returned to the delicate face uptilted to his, and he said softly, 'At Knightshill a man can be at peace with himself, with the world. No, darling, the very last thing I have ever wanted was to follow in Vorne's jaunty martial footsteps.'

'Is that why you intend to discontinue the annual dinner to honour his memory? Do you disapprove so much of his desertion of his home?'

Vere had forgotten the statement he had made last night. It had been an attempt to comfort her clear distress wrought by his grandfather's dramatic recounting of the heir's imagined last desperate hours.

'All Ashleigh heirs have left home to go to war. Sir Gilliard did, and my father. Of course I don't disapprove. Their chosen profession demands that they follow the drum. I have never regarded their absence as desertion. We've always had an excellent bailiff to run the estate.' Circling her with his arm he suggested they move on. 'You'll be growing chilled if we remain here much longer. Let's go to the terrace. The children have almost finished their snowman and will seek praise for their efforts.'

They began walking slowly and he returned to his original subject. 'Eleven years have elapsed since Khartoum fell. Vorne was such a merry, exuberant fellow I believe he would prefer to be remembered that way rather than as helpless and alone in a barbarous land, facing death in the knowledge that he had been betrayed by those he had counted his friends. The annual dinner is really held to satisfy Grandfather's desire for the military drama he misses so dearly. Would you agree with that opinion?'

'I'm ill-qualified to speak on the subject, Vere,' she commented in cool tones as they climbed the steps. 'I wonder if you would accept the ruling of a soldier on a matter concerning an art gallery?'

Margaret called out cheerily, 'You're just in time to add the finishing touches, Vere. I'm afraid he's a little lop-sided.'

Shaking off a ridiculous feeling that Annabel had just reproached him, Vere went forward to examine the figure resembling the tower at Pisa. Kate slipped her hand into his and begged him to make the snowman stand as straight and tall as Great-grandfather.

'Well, let's see,' he began, taking in the earnest expression on her face flushed by the chill, and her exertions. 'You and Timothy fetch another pail of snow each. Perhaps I can then do as you ask.'

The child scurried off with her brother. Vere discarded his gloves and squatted, picking up the garden dibber which had been used to make features and a series of indentations for buttons down the front of the figure. It was hardly a sculptor's knife, but it served well enough to create a more symmetrical shape with the aid of additional snow brought by the children. Contentment flowed through him again. What more could any man want? The sun was warm on his face as he laughed and played with Margaret's children, on the terrace of a home he loved almost as deeply as the girl who had promised to marry him next May. Perhaps the time would pass more swiftly than he feared. He was eager for her; eager for their own children. With Annabel and their infants round him, his cup of happiness would surely overflow here at Knightshill.

'How on earth did you do it?' asked Margaret from behind him. 'We spent an hour making something which resembled a toppling mound. With a few deft strokes you've turned it into a work of art.'

Vere laughed as he began to carve a walking-cane in the figure's left hand. 'A work of art it surely isn't, but "Mr Frost the snowman" he might now claim to be.' Glancing away from his chilly work, he said to the boy, 'You surely don't expect your friend to stand out here without something to keep him warm.'

The fair-haired child was ready, as Vere had known he would be. Rushing to the conservatory, Timothy returned with a battered hat, a long woollen scarf, a pair of spectacle frames and a pipe.

'Here you are, Uncle,' he cried, his breath clouding around him. 'Benson gave us these when we told him what we planned to.'

'Good old Benson,' Vere declared. 'What would we do without him?' Stretching out both arms to draw the children close against his sides, he said in low tones, 'Shall we ask Miss Bourneville to dress him in the hat and scarf? I think she'd like that.'

Two pairs of eyes studied him consideringly. They were being asked to make a tremendous concession to this stranger who was apparently going to marry their well-loved uncle one day.

'He's *our* snowman,' Timothy pointed out possessively to his sister.

Kate's rather prim little face puckered into an expression of uncertainty as she gazed back at him. 'She's a very pretty lady.'

'What's that got to do with it?'

'Everything, of course! When a lady is very pretty, gentlemen have to do whatever they ask.' Turning to Vere, she added, 'That's what the princess said in the story you read to us.'

'She was a horrid princess,' her brother reminded her, with explosive disgust.

'Only at the beginning. When the prince showed her how greedy and selfish she was, she was very, *very* sorry. Papa says it doesn't matter how wicked a person has been so long as she repents and asks God's forgiveness.'

'She didn't ask God, she asked the prince,' said the pedantic Timothy. 'He forgave her, then married her and they lived happily ever after.'

Vere smothered his amusement as he broke into the discussion. 'I'm going to marry Miss Bourneville and live happily ever after. That's why I'd like to ask her to dress Mr Frost.'

'Was she once as greedy and selfish as the princess?' asked the boy.

29

'Gracious, no! She's kind, thoughtful and very good,' he said firmly. 'Unfortunately, she hasn't anyone of her own to help with the building of a snowman.'

'Poor lady,' said Kate sadly. 'Is she one of those abandoned souls Papa says we must help?'

Unable to control himself, Vere bowed his head to hide the tears of laughter. Losing his balance as one boot slid on the packed snow, he sprawled full length. With the sun warm on his face and everything right with his world he lay on the ground laughing joyously until he realised faces were staring down at him wearing astonished expressions. Sobering, he scrambled to his feet.

Margaret smiled across at Annabel. 'How quickly grown men lapse into their boyhood.'

Brushing snow from his coat, Vere said, 'I was never able to do such enjoyable things during my boyhood, Margaret, so don't scold me now that I can.'

Annabel touched his arm, and he glanced up to see concern on her face. 'Are you all right, Vere?'

'I've never felt more splendid.' Circling her with his arm, he added teasingly, 'I'm perfectly sound in wind and limb now, you know. It's my heart which is so vulnerable . . . and I was hoping for a speedy cure.'

'What about Mr Frost's hat and scarf?' demanded an impatient boyish voice.

Dragging his attention from Annabel's faint flush in response to his words, he declared, 'How remiss of me to forget our snowy friend. Falling down put him right out of my mind. Will you ask Miss Bourneville, or shall I?'

'You,' growled Timothy.

For the next few moments they all indulged in the merry business of putting the finishing touches to the figure Vere had turned into a commendable sculpture. Charlotte then tapped on the glass of the conservatory to indicate that she had brought a tray of hot chocolate. The adults were soon settled in basket chairs set around the heated area enhanced by plants brought by successive Ashleighs from all parts of the world. The children went up to the nursery for hot milk and biscuits. As he sipped his chocolate, Vere asked where everyone was.

'The ladies chose to take breakfast in bed,' Charlotte told him. 'They'll probably decide to remain there because the men are holding some kind of military post-mortem in the smoking room, and will certainly continue it throughout the afternoon.'

'Oh, lord,' said Vere. 'I suppose the pattern will go on until the snow clears and they have no excuse to stay. Philip's not with them, is he?'

'He's taken the snowshoes and set out in a bid to reach the mission hall for a meeting,' Margaret said dully.

He grinned at her. 'Not a man to let an act of God prevent him from doing the Almighty's work.'

'Vorne used to enjoy the snow,' she said in a definite change of subject. 'He'd get the toboggan out on the slopes behind the house at the first opportunity. How he never broke an arm or leg I'll never understand. He was completely fearless. Benson would attempt to talk him out of it, but you know how persuasive he could be when he was determined, Vere.'

'So you've often said. I had little personal experience of it.'

She began to chuckle. 'Lottie, remember the time he coaxed Mr Rundle into allowing him to take Cissie and Flo out in the dog-cart?' After explaining to Annabel how the Rundle girls were strictly watched over by their widowed father, she continued, 'He decided to take a short cut across the stream, but the wheel hit a stone as he charged through it and both girls were thrown in. Vorne had the effrontery to wring from their father a commendation on his bravery in rescuing his daughters from a watery grave. Poor old Rundle had forgotten drought had reduced the stream to a mere trickle.'

The sisters laughed over the escapade and Vere joined in. Stretching contentedly, he continued their mood by relating the cause of his own earlier laughter whilst building the snowman.

'Philip is certainly impressing Kate with his teachings,' he concluded. 'Tim seems more sceptical.'

'The boy's mind is filled with dreams of a uniform and military glory,' she said with a sigh.

'Of course it is. He's surrounded by such things. The old man sees no other profession for any Ashleigh.'

'He's not an Ashleigh . . . much to his regret.'

'He's a boy who'll grow into a man. That's all Grandfather considers,' Vere warned. 'Although he's too young to attend the dinner, he knows very well why the entire force of sabre-rattling relations descends on Knightshill each January. The old man must have told him the gruesome details a dozen times over, and there's barely a room in the house which doesn't reflect soldiering. What chance is there of a boy being lured by piety when battlefield heroism is represented so strongly as the only guiding star?'

'Philip believes a firm hand and strong moral teaching will overcome any wish to don a scarlet jacket.'

'Let him say it again in ten years' time when Tim is as eager as Val for one. They'll be empty words by then.'

Vere fell silent. His own children would be reared on a diet of learning and culture which would endow them with a wider understanding of the world than that gained in the Church or Army. He turned towards Annabel, but she was gazing from the window at the orangery totally lost in her reverie. From her three-quarter profile Vere could see her lips were parted, as if in a smile of enchantment. Whatever her thoughts, they were very pleasant. Could she be looking into her future with him and their children?

Realising that Charlotte was studying him he raised his eyebrows at her quizzically. His sister smiled. She had also noticed Annabel's transition to some place other than here. The elder by eighteen months, Charlotte had shared some of Vere's early restrictions. The heavy iron she had needed through childhood, to correct a deformity in her left leg, had been abandoned in adolescence. She now wore a boot with a four-inch sole on the withered foot, hidden by her long skirts, although her slight limp could not be disguised. Even so, a slender figure, a natural curl in her light-brown hair and a pair of large, lustrous hazel eyes gave the lie to her own belief that spinsterhood was her clear destiny. She gave no man the opportunity to draw near her and, when Margaret married, she had slipped naturally into the position of lady of the house at Sir Gilliard's decree.

Closer to her than to his other sister by age and temperament, Vere knew their physical limitations had always set them apart from the rest of the Ashleighs. They both had a deep love of nature and country life. They would often ride over the estate and surrounding hills in search of birds, butterflies or wild flowers. Then Vere would sketch whatever caught his fancy while they sat together to eat the picnic Charlotte had prepared. She was the perfect companion for such outings. She knew the art of sitting in relaxed silence while he captured on paper the beauty of a China Blue, a field mouse or a green woodpecker. In one respect, however, their personalities differed greatly. Vere was an incurable romantic; Charlotte was precise, matter of fact, and quite unforgiving of those who failed to live up to her rigid standards. She never spoke of the mother who had deserted them all through hopeless passion for a man she had known only a few months. Charlotte had no time for romantic love. She had never experienced it so had little patience with those who succumbed and behaved, she claimed, like moonstruck fools. It was probably a good description of himself, Vere thought wryly, but his sister did not know what happiness the state brought its victims.

Annabel was still gazing dreamily at the snowy vista when she suddenly broke the short silence. 'There's your young brother. He looks very dejected.'

'He's been in the stables most of the morning,' Charlotte said crisply. 'If there had been the slightest chance of his taking a horse out, I truly believe he'd have gone careering over the hills with no thought for his own neck or that of the beast.'

'Probably wanted to keep clear of the house,' murmured Margaret. 'I

32

can't say I blame him after the whole family turned on him last night. Poor Val.'

'*Poor Val!*' exclaimed Charlotte in derisory tones. 'You've always been far too indulgent with him, Margaret. He's wayward and thoughtless. What's more, he sets out to charm people into allowing him too much freedom for a boy of his age.'

'You're wrong,' retaliated the one who had practically mothered him. 'I'll agree he has many of Vorne's qualities, but he's as yet unaware of their persuasive powers. He uses them unconsciously. Vorne was a devil. He knew from a very early age that he was irresistible when he chose to be.'

Charlotte continued her theme. 'I can't understand why Val made such a statement on an occasion which the family regards with such reverence. It was almost as if he *wanted* to cause discord.'

'He wouldn't do that,' declared Vere. 'He's always as thrilled by the Khartoum Dinner as Grandfather is, and he looked positively wretched for the rest of the evening. Of course he didn't do it deliberately.'

'I admired his courage in staying until we all retired,' Annabel put in softly. 'After being so severely censured, most of his schoolboy contemporaries would have sought privacy.'

'Yes, they would,' agreed Vere warmly. 'How very perceptive you are, darling.'

'Hardly that,' she said, with a faint smile. 'I did not know your elder brother, but from what you have revealed of Vorne's personality it seems clear Valentine is cast in the same mould.'

Vere got to his feet, smiling back at this girl who had just shown she already regarded herself as one of the family. 'It was all a storm in a tea-cup. I can't see that it makes any difference which regiment he joins, so long as he serves it with honour.'

'I agree,' said Charlotte, putting a different slant on his words. 'The Ashleighs have always officered the West Wilts, and so should Val. He can be just as heroic with them as he can with the cavalry. It's simply his latest attempt to be individual.'

'He is,' Vere pointed out mildly. 'We're *all* individual. Just because our name happens to be Ashleigh, none of us is obliged to be a copy of another.'

Annabel stood up beside him, her eyes shining with fervour as she said swiftly, 'But, my dear, don't you see that that is exactly what he *does* want to be? Knowing *you* can never emulate Vorne Ashleigh, the obligation now rests upon him.'

By the end of January all that remained of the snow were tiny patches in the most shaded corners of the northern slopes around the house. The Howards, the Flinderses, the Carlton-Jays had all gone home, and Val had returned to school. Annabel was still at Knightshill due to the protracted bout of influenza afflicting both her parents. Vere was delighted to keep his fiancée at his side, but other members of his family were growing a little thoughtful. Margaret and Charlotte eventually brought their feelings into the open during a drive to the village on a morning when the sun popped in and out of racing white clouds.

'As Vere's involved in discussing lambing arrangements with John Morgan, I asked Annabel if she'd care to accompany us,' Charlotte began, as she guided the mare along a lane the beast knew very well. 'He hasn't deserted her often during her visit and I thought she'd welcome an outing. She said she preferred to stay at home.' With a sigh, she added, 'Well, the old place will be hers before long. It's as well she loves it so much.'

Margaret glanced over her shoulder as the trap swung round a turn in the lane. From here, Knightshill looked every bit the splendid old house built to last for centuries by men who had had a hand in the shaping of their nation and also played their part in making Wiltshire a prosperous county. She loved her home; loved the grand lines of the house with its twin gabled wings flanking the main building, and its heavy fortified door with the great, wide, multi-paned window above it. That window was famed throughout the country. Architects and historians came just to examine this feature known locally as 'the Great Window', and it was mentioned in the ancient history of Dunstan St Mary, which was kept in the library of the Vicarage. The window gave a profusion of light to the first-floor ballroom. Each year, the Ashleighs held a Christmas Ball on the second Saturday in December, and another in June to celebrate the victory at Waterloo in which three generations of the family had fought with Wellington.

Margaret turned back to regard her sister. 'You always knew you'd have to retire gracefully when one of the boys married, Lottie. If Vorne had been a little less fond of the ladies, we might have had a young widow on our hands now.'

'That would have been an unenviable position for any woman. Knightshill wouldn't have been her own family home, so Annabel would naturally supplant her. I shall at least have a right to continue living here when she arrives as a bride, even though she will naturally take over as mistress of the house.'

For a moment or two, the cheerful ring of trotting hooves on the surface of the lane was the only sound to disturb the country silence. Then Margaret said what she felt she must.

'I suppose we both still have a right to regard Knightshill as our home when Vere marries, but that's because the house is Grandfather's. When he dies, it will be different. Vere and Annabel will then own everything. Have you considered our position when that happens?'

Her sister kept her gaze on the lane ahead. It was clear the question was unwelcome to her. 'Grandfather has been the head of the family from my earliest recollection. It seems inconceivable that one day he'll be gone. I have considered the future, and always hoped I could still fulfil a useful purpose here if and when Vere took a wife.' She gave Margaret a brief glance. 'He's never been strong. At the back of all our minds has been the thought that Val was more likely to inherit Knightshill. Happily, it seems we have all been too pessimistic. Vere is the perfect heir for such a valuable estate, and I believe Annabel will prefer to manage without my support. I must begin to consider where I shall go when the time comes.'

'You'll come with us, naturally,' Margaret declared. 'Philip will doubtless find a small house near the mission, but there will be room for us all. We've been the only females in a house full of soldiers and heroes since Mama left. It's created a bond which can never be broken. *Of course* you'll come and live with us.'

Although Charlotte smiled, her voice was still bleak. 'It might not be for some time yet. Grandfather vows he'll see in the new century.'

'I have no doubt he will,' Margaret responded, gazing with pleasure at the gentle green countryside surrounding them. The trap then ran beneath the stone arch which still stood to mark the boundary of Ashleigh land. A wall had once enclosed it but the years had destroyed all save a few crumbling sections, and the acreage had changed so often during the past century it had never been renewed. The village came into view as the trap clattered over the stone bridge spanning the same stream Vorne had recklessly crossed, tipping the Rundle girls from the dog-cart. The level was high today after the melting snow.

Out of the blue, Charlotte asked, 'Do you think they're really suited?'

'Vere and Annabel? They appear to be very fond of each other.'

'He's more than *fond*,' exclaimed her sister disparagingly. 'He practically worships her.'

'Vere has a sweet, loving nature. And the girl is very lovely.'

'I think he's extremely foolish to kneel at the shrine of someone he's known for only a few months.' Charlotte sighed. 'However, one has to acknowledge that he has never looked so fit. If nothing else, Annabel has done wonders for his constitution.'

Margaret knew only too well what had given their brother the spring in his step and the sparkle in his clear green eyes. Vere was so uninhibited with kisses and endearments, it was plain he was no novice to passion. Margaret guessed he had conducted discreet affairs during his many trips to London. Had his mistresses resembled the perfect Annabel? The wedding was planned for next May – a date almost certainly of the bride's choosing – and Margaret wondered how a man so mad for his girl would manage to wait that long. Knowing from personal experience how persuasive the voice of temptation could be, she felt Vere's constitution could suffer a severe setback before many weeks passed.

'Miss Bourneville appears to do wonders for Grandfather's well-being, also,' she commented, as the mare dropped to a walking pace on entering the village square. 'They spend so much time together in the armoury or going through the family history, he seems to have taken on a new lease of life.'

'No one has shown such intense interest in the things he loves so dearly – at least, not for a long time.' Charlotte drew the mare to a halt and prepared to climb from her seat to tie the animal to the post. 'I can't decide whether or not her interest is as genuine as it seems.'

Margaret took up the basket from the seat beside her. 'It's genuine, there's no doubt of that . . . which is a great pity.'

In the act of securing the mare, her sister threw her a questioning look. 'Why a pity?'

She stepped down to the cobbled path before replying across the width of the trap. 'Surely it hasn't escaped your notice that all Annabel's questioning leads back to just one subject – Vorne Ashleigh, the hero of Khartoum.'

It was the kind of morning Val loved. Dawn was breaking as they set off for their run through the copse and over the hills surrounding the school. Frost nipped at his cheeks and bare legs as the boys strung in easy fashion along the valley where mist hung haphazardly over any marshy patch. They were the sportsmen of the upper school, those to whom physical development was infinitely more important than academic laurels. The Saturday dawn run was a regular ritual.

At the end of the valley lay the copse through which paths led to the top of Cartwheel Hill. One meandered in gentle curves to the summit; the other offered a shorter much steeper route. In the early days of term they took the easy way up. Once they were back in shape, they chose the more testing uphill run. The three miles across Cartwheel Hill were level and easy-going, which enabled them to recover from the strain of the climb. The view from the top was worth every grunt of pain, every protesting muscle. It might be too misty today to make out the Dorset hills and valleys stretching in successive ridges as far as the eye could see, but there were sure to be rabbits, partridges and a few early lambs to gladden the eye as they passed.

At the point where the valley began to fill with trees stood a thatched house owned by a farmer named Bartlett. His daughter Jessie was only sixteen but very experienced after encounters with senior scholars, and

Clive Jepson was currently augmenting her wisdom on the subject of sex. She was waiting for him by the edge of the copse.

They approached, and Clive veered towards her leaving the rest to continue on their way. Val glanced over his shoulder in time to see Jessie eagerly accepting a comprehensive kiss accompanied by exploration of what lay beneath her bodice. Val turned away with a grin. His friend would soon have to decide whether he preferred sexual or athletic conquest. He could not have both. Girls were too demanding on a fellow's time and strength.

Val had made his decision on the subject last year after a tentative dalliance with Flossie Marchant, who served in her uncle's bakery in Tetherbury. He had advanced as far as telling her she was very pretty, when she took matters into her own hands by asking him to help her lift a heavy tray because her uncle was ill. Once in the bakehouse, she had made it abundantly clear what she expected by pursing her mouth and closing her eyes. Val had kissed girls before, in an experimental, pristine manner, but Flossie had been so clearly available he had decided to take the experiment further. No sooner had he fastened his mouth to hers and begun to slide his palms over her chubby buttocks in a tight shiny skirt, than a fury with hands like vices – later identified as Flossie's aunt – had descended from nowhere to drag him away. Her outraged complaint to the school had led to Val being forced to offer an embarrassing apology. A lecture from his housemaster on respect for the weaker sex had followed, and Tetherbury was put out of bounds to him for the remainder of the term. Geoffrey Manton, the sportsmaster, had light-heartedly advised him to reserve his energies for the games field. His friend Clive had regarded the affair as no more than a minor setback. From his greater experience, he had declared Val to have been a fool to close with the girl on her home territory.

'Always lure them to neutral ground before commencing action,' he had advised with a wink. 'I should have thought that basic tactic would be known by a fellow from a family steeped in military glory.'

Val had taken Geoffrey Manton's advice. Being elected captain of a team was more exciting than kissing a girl, anyway. He would probably get around to it more seriously later on, but he had more vital things to concentrate on now.

The copse closed around him as the track began to wind through denuded trees, now and then relieved by dark green holly or a graceful pine. In summer, this area provided juniors with plentiful spoils on their nature rambles. It was also a favourite haunt of older boys who had managed to get hold of alcohol or a willing girl. Val had made himself quite drunk on several occasions when his friends had indulged in defying rules,

37

but the effect it had had on his sporting performance during the following days had made him decline to indulge again. It had been cheap, sour-tasting stuff, and he preferred wine from the cellars at Knightshill.

The path forked. The leading boy veered on to the right-hand route which would give them an easier run. Val knew this gentle climb would still be a challenge, so he began to breathe a little faster and deeper in order to cope with it. He was nicely warm now despite the low temperature. The ascending run was a test on muscles and stamina, but he was extremely fit and could cope with it easily. More than anything, he was determined to build a body which could endure the greatest hardships imaginable. The success of any soldier must depend on his physical resistance to exhaustion, sickness and pain. No matter how great a man's courage, an epidemic, heat, thirst or a frail constitution could bring about his collapse before a shot had been fired. Vorne Ashleigh had known that. Only a superbly athletic physique had enabled him to crawl a further mile and a half after sustaining wounds which would surely have killed any average man instantly. A superb body, and personal courage of the highest order. The opportunity to gain the first was in Val's hands now. He would only discover the second when he donned that coveted uniform.

Breathing even faster as he neared the top of the hill, Val thought of the brother he knew only by his exploits. Vorne had been Head Boy of the school in his last year, and he appeared in sporting as well as scholastic pictures which hung around the walls of the main hall. Racquets champion of 1879 – the year of Val's birth – he had also been a member of the cricket team and rowing eight, going on to gain his rowing blue at Oxford in addition to a decent classics degree. His brother's reputation with women had only been hinted at in Val's presence, but Vorne had been a handsome and popular fellow with a wide, winning smile, so he thought it not surprising that girls had been very taken with him. While Val knew he would never be Head Boy, there was every chance of his winning the Waycliffe Cup along with other sporting trophies this year. If he did, he would equal the school record presently held by a boy who was now one of the leading peers of the realm. Val wanted that record desperately, almost as much as he wanted to join the cavalry.

Conscious of the ache in his legs after the climb he broke from the trees to head across the easy stretch atop Cartwheel Hill, brooding on his problem. Time and again, he had cursed his relations for baiting him into mentioning something which was no concern of theirs, and his own temper, which had flared when he should have had the sense to control it. There could hardly have been a worse time or setting for his grandfather to hear of his plans. Even so, Val had been unprepared for such violent opposition from the old man. Without money he could not afford a commission in any regiment, especially the mounted ones. Even if he managed to borrow against a legacy due on his twenty-fifth birthday, his grandfather had enough influence to persuade any cavalry colonel to reject an application to join his élite body of officers.

Running smoothly along the crest stretching away into the mist, which now had a faint gilding as a weak sun tried to break through, he remained lost in thought. He was bursting with life and energy, aching with eagerness to use both to the full. He yearned for that elusive place at the head of a mounted squadron. The ache in his legs settled in the rest of his body as his grandfather's words returned. He could not think how he had managed to see the rest of that terrible evening through, except that it had been an act of defiance born of his dead brother's courage. Surely an old man's will should not be such a formidable adversary that failure should be accepted without a fight?

'Not still fretting about that set-to with your grand old man, are you?' panted a voice, and Val glanced round to see that Clive had fallen in beside him.

'Good lord, your stamina is extraordinary!' he exclaimed with surprise, and not a little envy. 'I thought you'd push on back to school to recover in blissful solitude.'

Clive made a face. 'That girl was set on far too much for a morning like this. She had no notion what cold weather can do to a fellow's performance. I've persuaded her to come to the roller-shed after dinner instead.'

Val thought the wooden shed, where their groundsman kept the tools of his trade, hardly more conducive to sexual philandering on a chilly February evening.

'You're not intending to do the whole thing, are you?' he asked curiously, as they reached the end of the hilltop run and began the descent.

'Perhaps.'

'Be careful.'

Clive laughed breathlessly. 'She's a fast little piece who knows what's what. Girls like her always do. It's the virgins you have to worry about. Steer clear of them, at all costs.'

Val studied his closest friend. Dark floppy hair, dark eyes and a complexion which betrayed his Italian ancestry, he could not truthfully be called good-looking. Yet he clearly had a way with girls and an intense interest in them which Val found difficult to understand. Clive was destined to enter the Diplomatic Service after taking a degree in languages. Already fluent in French, Italian and Spanish, he would study Russian, Pushtu and Mandarin at university. Not for this budding ambassador the urge to defy his set destiny. He blithely accepted what was expected of him and used his superfluous energy in punishing physical activity. Whether or not seducing Jessie Bartlett came into that category, Val did not know. He had only eased that particular urge in the usual manner, so the act of coupling with a female remained a mystery to him. Was it really as compulsive and satisfying as male lore proclaimed? It would have to be truly spectacular to outdo the thrill of galloping across the hills at home, bending low for greater speed, the thunder of hooves filling his ears and the warmth of the animal's body between his knees as they raced in perfect accord through the growing dawn. Yearning again became an ache within as he saw himself racing, sword drawn and shouting encouragement, across the desert sands towards the white-robed enemy.

'Thought of a solution,' Clive offered jerkily, breaking into his thoughts once more.

'To what . . . Jessie Bartlett?'

'There's only one solution to *her*,' came the ribald reply, as Clive skirted a fallen branch lying on the broad way down to Tetherbury village through which lay their destination. 'Why don't you go abroad, join a Prussian regiment? Only snag is, you'd have to grow a frightfully large blond moustache. How long d'you think it would take you?'

Val found no need to shave, as yet, and he scowled at his friend as he wiped perspiration from his face with the towel slung around his neck.

'I've never heard a more idiotic idea! The Prussians are even more aristocratic than we are. To enter their cavalry regiments a man has to be a count, at the very least, with a line stretching back for centuries. How would I fool them into taking me on? Besides, suppose they went to war against us. What would I do? Tell them my name was really Ashleigh, not von Aschenheim, and would they mind awfully if I changed sides?'

'All right, all right, I merely offered a possible solution. If you're so damned keen to become a Hussar or Cuirassier, or whatever, I didn't think it mattered to you which army you were in.'

'Of course it matters,' cried Val, ducking his head to avoid an overhanging branch. 'What d'you take me for? I'm an Englishman through and through. Not a mongrel like you,' he added, to get his own back for the gibe about his lack of beard from this boy whose dark stubble had to be removed every week.

Clive immediately jostled him so that he ran straight through a deep puddle. Mud came up to cover him in a fine shower. As he wiped it away from his face, his friend's smooth voice said, 'I still can't see why it matters so much which regiment you join. If all you want to do is to die heroically, like a good Englishman should, whichever coat and trousers you're wearing at the time is surely unimportant.'

Passing the village baker's shop and keeping his gaze resolutely ahead, Val ran on in silence. The last mile was always the worst. Thoughts

40

invariably dwelt on the shower, clean clothes and breakfast awaiting. After eating, he supposed he must put in an hour on the Latin prep he had delayed for so long. He had organised a practice session for his rugby team at eleven-thirty, and after lunch Geoffrey Manton was taking the school eight and the reserves to the river for speed trials.

Amid groans and exclamations of exaggerated relief the runners entered the main gates of the school, then headed along the gravelled drive which edged the rugby field with its many pitches. The school stood out against the dark trees, an impressive stone structure with a chapel at one end to break the austere lines with its square tower. Although it hardly resembled Knightshill, it always reminded Val of his home because it had that same appearance of inviolate antiquity.

In the washroom they all stripped off and stood beneath the deluge of water. As Val towelled his hair dry, Clive reopened their conversation about his future.

'You're damned lucky. Unlike some poor souls who're forced into a family business when they long to become an actor or couturier, the Ashleighs can't wait to install you in the army with a lifetime of glory awaiting you. But you have decided that only by dressing in a fancy get-up which is too tight around the arse and too high in the collar will you ever be happy. What's wrong with the family regiment?'

Val's hands stilled, and he sighed. '*That's* what's wrong with it. The whole damn family has been in it. My ancestors have distinguished themselves with the West Wilts since it was raised as a private band of volunteers by the local noblemen. From my first day at this school I've been known as Vorne Ashleigh's brother. Wherever I go in this building I see reminders of his achievements. Sometimes it almost seems as if his ghost walks beside me. If I go up to Oxford I'll find the same thing there. If I join the West Wilts, it'll be even worse. I shall be simply the latest Ashleigh in a long line of them. It won't be just Vorne, it'll be Grandfather, Father and a collection of distinguished soldiers whose reputations will govern my life. I'll always be Roland's son, or Gilliard's grandson, or Vorne's brother!'

His friend's dark eyes regarded him shrewdly as he shrugged on his blazer. 'Go on.'

'I feel . . .' Val searched for words. 'I feel smothered by obligations. I'm immensely drawn to and excited by the skill of *mounted* warfare. I have to be on the move – you know me well enough – and I haven't the patience to wait, with men in static ranks, for the enemy to fire first.' He frowned. 'I'm terribly afraid I'd order a premature advance and kill my troops unnecessarily. I *know* I'd make a bloody awful infantry officer, but they're all set on my becoming one. I've got to get out of it somehow.'

'There's always the Prussian army.'

Val wrapped his wet towel around Clive's face with the advice to consider a career other than diplomacy, then they headed towards the dining hall and breakfast.

After eating, they sauntered along to their rooms on the upper floor. Two more of Val's friends fell in beside them to discuss the depressing prospect of extra Latin lessons after Easter, but their progress was halted by a voice from one of the rooms whose door stood open.

'Hey, Ashleigh, I've got some news for you.'

Val stopped, then moved across so that he could talk to a studious boy named Fanshawe, also from a military family.

'Don't tell me Manton has cancelled the trials this afternoon,' he said. 'We need the practice.'

The lanky occupant stood up and came over to him, filled with suppressed excitement. 'This'll interest you much more than rowing, believe it or not. I had a telegram from home this morning. My father and brother are coming here at two o'clock to say cheerio before they sail for Egypt. Their regiment is to join Kitchener in the Sudan. It looks as though he's all set to strike out for Khartoum despite orders to hang back for a while.' Fanshawe's long face was aglow as he added, 'I'd give my right arm to be going with Father and Peter, but I bet you'd give even more for the chance to get back at your brother's murderers and enter the fallen city in triumph.'

Chapter 3

Margaret sat at the breakfast table studying her husband as he read a religious broadsheet lying beside his plate. Even this pleasant morning hour had been stolen from her by the Word of the Lord. Philip was hardly aware of her presence while he ate porridge from a Wedgwood bowl and absorbed the contents of the latest pamphlet from mission headquarters.

Knowing that she must tackle him on the thorny subject, Margaret attempted to draw his attention. 'Philip, it will be Timothy's eighth birthday next month.'

'Yes . . . quite so,' he murmured, still absorbed.

'We should write to the headmaster of Misleydale to let him know Tim will be joining them in September.'

Her husband's gaze came up to meet hers – lustrous brown eyes which had once seen her as the light of his life. 'I'm sorry. Joining *who?*'

'His preparatory school. Grandfather put his name down soon after Tim was born. All Ashleigh boys go to Misleydale.'

'Our son isn't an Ashleigh.'

'He's a son of the family.'

'A son of the Daulton family.'

'Philip, it's one of the best prep schools in the country. He's a very bright boy who should be given every opportunity to learn.'

The pamphlet lay forgotten as Philip leaned back in his chair, his handsome features hardening. 'I'm teaching him all he'll need to know for the work awaiting him. There is no question of your domineering grandparent fashioning the future of my children. My son will never lift so much as a hand against a living soul. He will follow me in serving mankind to the exclusion of all else. So will Kate. They are *not* Ashleighs, Margaret.'

'They still have to be educated,' she countered, 'and Timothy should be given this chance to learn from the best teachers.'

'So that he can join the family regiment and kill his brothers on earth?'

'Vere hasn't. He's a man of peace, like you. But he uses his excellent brain to enhance the beauty of the world for mankind to enjoy.'

Philip stirred his tea, his mouth twisting. 'You've chosen a poor example. Your brother has been totally unable to think clearly since setting eyes on that girl he has chosen to marry.'

'Even a clever man can be rendered foolish by love, Philip . . . as you well know,' she added with passion.

His voice was even harsher because of her unwelcome reminder of their earlier relationship. 'There is only one love, the love of God.'

The familiar pain of rejection began. 'What of the love of our fellows?'

'The one stems from the other.' His lean face beneath crisp dark hair took on an expression of irritation. 'Why do you choose to fight me? If you would only join me in the Lord's work you would find greater fulfilment than any you have yet known.'

'I did join with you in the Lord's work,' she cried. 'I found fulfilment as a curate's wife. Helping you with parish matters, decorating the church, visiting the sick and dying, collecting garments for the poor – all this gave me a wonderful sense of purpose and devotion. When I had the children I was then also able to advise and comfort mothers less fortunate than I. These things fulfilled me because I undertood those I sought to help. The people of the parish are all known to me, the church has always been a part of my life. I know about the sick and dying. Vere was an invalid for many years, and I was present when Father breathed his last. The family has always helped the poor.' She tried pleading with him. 'Can't you see why this new path of yours bewilders me so? I know nothing of the black people of Africa, or of their ways. I can't visit them or write them words of comfort. They speak a different language, they wear hardly any clothing, they practise very cruel customs and apparently worship one of their own number who holds them in fear of being cursed or horribly afflicted. In addition, they hate anyone not of their own tribe and kill in the most hideous fashion those who offend them. Even Dr Benedict suffered at their hands, because he had given a baby medicine to cure it of a fever. The witch doctor claimed he was trying to take the child for the god he worshipped, and the father was ordered to kill the white man. Dr Benedict survived only because the spear missed his heart by an inch.'

'The Lord was watching over him. Good triumphed over evil. Surely that much must be obvious to you?' returned Philip heavily.

'But the tribe then drove the missionaries away and burned down their hospital,' Margaret reminded him. 'Philip, I have tried to feel compassion for these alien people. I have tried to be concerned over their barbarous behaviour . . . but I can't rid myself of the notion that our interference might simply be making their lives a great deal more difficult. When you were the curate at Dunstan St Mary the help and comfort we gave was so evident and welcome. I've yet to be persuaded that school books, modest dresses, medicines they dare not accept, and disciples who are seen as an evil threat are really providing help and comfort to these people half a world away.'

Giving his wife a look of deep despair, Philip got to his feet. 'You still have not recognised that we do the work God instructs us to do, without question. It is not for us to expect to be told of the purpose of our endeavours. That He has shown us the way is enough.'

Margaret also stood. 'He has not yet shown *me* the way,' she confessed through a tight throat. 'You're so certain about it all, Philip, but I have terrible doubts. Why?'

'Because you are a somewhat selfish woman,' came his cutting reply. 'Attending local parishioners gave you a sense of satisfaction in your own goodness. Organising a bazaar results in the receipt of humble appreciation from all concerned. In short, Margaret, you require a reward for practising His work. When you can act as His disciple, even though you are cursed or threatened for doing so, then your doubts will flee. You must be wholehearted in what you do.'

'I'm wholeheartedly your wife! I'm wholeheartedly the mother of our children!' she cried. 'Isn't that enough to earn your regard?'

The dark eyes which had once been lively with love darkened further with disparagement. 'Can't you even do that without expecting a reward?'

'Yes. I've continued to do the former for the past three years and there's been little by way of return for my devotion,' she reminded him.

Her words left him completely untouched. 'If you spent more time helping me you would understand how blessed we are to have been chosen for this work. The people you claim not to understand are no more than children. They have to be taught to fear God and love their brothers. They're children, Margaret,' he repeated. 'You understand Timothy and Kate.'

'Our children are *civilised*!'

'Because we have taught them to be. If man were left to his own devices there would be no civilisation. The scriptures show us the way, and we have been called to enlighten those who cannot read His words. No other consideration must be allowed to interfere with this.'

Philip was implacable. It was impossible to reason with him. 'So Tim is to be denied his place at Misleydale?' At his brief nod, she asked stonily, 'You will write to the headmaster with an explanation?'

'Sir Gilliard will have to do that. He is responsible for putting my son's name forward.'

'With your approval, as I recall.'

'I was not then aware of my true purpose in life. Both children will devote their lives to the work of the Lord. They will have no need of anything else.'

'How do you know that?' she cried passionately. 'How can you assume a child of five and a boy of eight will have no need of anything save your restrictive creed? Kate is hardly old enough to understand relationships, much less her own mind. She quotes your dicta as she quotes Nanny's, without knowing the true meaning of her words, and she has grown almost afraid of the father who used to smile and play games with her. Tim is naturally filled with longings to follow family tradition. All small boys have their dreams.' Inspired, she added, 'You once told me you were determined at the age of ten on captaining a tea-clipper. If your father had thrust goodness and piety down your throat, and forbidden you to speak of your ambitions, you would probably have run away to sea at the first opportunity. Your inflexibility will drive our son away.'

Philip grew angry. 'You are becoming hysterical. I have no time to listen to such nonsense.'

'*Make* time!' She crossed to confront him as he turned to leave. 'Our children must be given freedom to do as they wish with their future. You had that freedom.'

'You think Ashleighs have it?' he challenged in disparagement. 'Each man of them has his destiny decided at conception.'

'It's what they want, all the same.'

'Is it? Vere is regarded with contempt because he enjoys frittering away his days with orchids and painting. Valentine has even been forbidden to join a different regiment. Do you call *that* freedom, eh? The Ashleighs are not gods, Margaret, as you seem to believe. There is only one, and we are all here due to His mercy as His disciples. Remember that!'

After he had stormed out Margaret stood for a long while in the room used for meals when the family dined alone. Each time she attempted to reach the man she could not believe no longer existed beneath the zealot, the exchange merely drove them further apart. Was he right in claiming she was selfish? She certainly could not surrender everything for the sake of distant tribes. Her children must not be drawn into his world, yet how could she help them?

Walking to the french windows which overlooked the terrace, her heart grew bleaker still. If she did as Philip suggested, would it bring a return of the happiness they had shared? If she hid her doubts and pretended to share his fervour for his heathens, would he love her again? If she abandoned her family and all it stood for, if she led her children into the path he was determined they should take, would it be her bounden duty? At the back of her mind she had always known that when Grandfather died, his heir would own Knightshill and set up his own family here but she had never faced the prospect of no longer being a part of it. When Annabel became mistress of this lovely old place, she would not want sisters-in-law beneath her roof.

Charlotte had been reassured by the invitation to live with the Daultons, but Margaret now realised Philip would never agree to it unless her sister joined him in his relentless mission. Pressing her clenched fist to her mouth in distress as she gazed out at all she had known and loved since childhood, she finally acknowledged that her passion was spent. The man she had loved no longer existed. How could she live with Philip when Knightshill ceased to be her home? There would be nothing left.

'Have you already had breakfast?'

She spun round to find Charlotte in the room. 'Yes, a while ago!'

'Sit with me and have another cup of tea,' said her sister persuasively, her shrewd eyes assessing Margaret's expression. 'Do you have a headache?'

'I slept badly,' she returned evasively. 'Kate had a chesty cough. I was conscious of her restlessness and worried about her condition, remembering how Vere used to lie night after night coughing until he was sick.'

'Poor little boy,' agreed Charlotte, putting an egg in the silver coddler and lighting the flame beneath it. 'Kate has a slight chill. Nothing to worry about.'

'I hope not.' Trying to compose herself, Margaret prepared the spirit kettle once more. How could she ever adjust to a life divorced from all this? What was to become of her and her children when Grandfather died?

Taking her egg to the table set with starched linen, Charlotte asked, 'Has Philip retired to the library already?'

'He intends to drive down to the mission hall early. The area superintendent will be arriving later today for an important meeting concerning the Eastern races. Philip had to prepare some papers on the subject.'

Charlotte pulled a face. 'Don't mention it to Grandfather at dinner tonight. He will give his opinion of the Eastern people he fought to the gates of Peking, and I cannot think that it will match that of the mission members.'

Margaret took the teapot to the table and poured from it into two cups. Forcing a smile, she murmured, 'The family firebrand, but what would we all do without him?'

When they eventually left the table the morning was advanced enough for them to encounter John Morgan walking through from the formal garden at the rear of the house. The estate office was a small room leading off the Great Hall at the foot of the branched staircase, and the sisters might not have noticed his presence if he had not hailed them. A man in his late forties, John held a unique position at Knightshill. Neither servant nor equal, he could best be described as a respectful friend. Having known him since childhood they all called him by his first name, but he addressed them as Mrs Daulton, Miss Charlotte, Mr Ashleigh and Master Valentine.

Skirting the staircase they approached the door of his office where he stood awaiting them. After exchanging greetings, John looked at Charlotte. 'I'd be glad if you could spare me some time to discuss arrangements for the orchids. With Mr Ashleigh away visiting Miss Bourneville again, the matter has become pressing. I did try to speak with your brother before he left, but he made an excuse every time and finally patted me on the shoulder telling me he had every faith in my judgement.'

Charlotte smiled. 'We all have that, John.'

'A fine bailiff I'd be if you hadn't,' he said gruffly. 'I can get them packed up and off, but I'd like you to show me which you want kept for the house. The early varieties are ready for cutting, and these orders from London must be attended to by Monday.'

'Let's go now,' said Charlotte, then glanced at her sister. 'Come with us and help me decide which to keep. They're all so lovely I find it hard to choose.'

'I'm not much better than you at making a firm decision,' she said as they all moved off.

It was hot and humid in the glasshouses containing the delicate flowers which commanded good prices from the Bond Street florists they now supplied. While the sisters wandered between rows of plants which were perfuming the air, John stood chatting to Benson, the head gardener. Margaret was aware that John's attention kept wandering to the slender figure in dark green trimmed with lace walking beside her. Twenty years older than Charlotte, it was plain he had been in love with her for some time, yet Margaret appeared to be the only one who had noticed. A big, broad, country-bred man with fresh cheeks and light-blue eyes, he had done well from humble origins. Bachelor John wore good-quality breeches and boots, with a jacket in quiet good taste, and his manner was very pleasant. He would make a fine husband for the right woman . . . but not if her name was Ashleigh.

The orchids were selected, and John said, 'It's not that I can't get on with my work in his absence, but it's so unlike Mr Ashleigh to be away during lambing. There's the annual fatstock sale coming up next week – he's not missed *that* for the last six years – and he promised to tell me whether or not to buy Gifford's Hereford bull. The beast will go elsewhere if we delay much longer. Do you know when your brother is likely to be back?'

Charlotte shook her head. 'Not for a while, I imagine. I think you should accept what Vere said about having faith in your judgement. You must buy the bull if you think it'll be a wise move, John.'

His deep country voice expressed a warning. 'Gifford's asking a tidy sum.'

'If the animal is worth it you'll be making a good investment.' Putting her hand on his arm in the gesture of one who had known him when she was a child and he a young man, Charlotte added teasingly, 'I'll take the responsibility for your decision, and bear the brunt of my brother's wrath if it's the wrong one.'

John gave his great baritone laugh. 'Mr Ashleigh has the best temper of any man I know. There'll be no wrath for anyone to bear, Miss Charlotte. Howsoever, that bull is a real good'un and we'll do well to get the beast.'

The pair left the hothouse, and Margaret followed several yards distant. Watching them as they strolled through the spring sunshine talking of the orphaned lambs John had in his cottage to hand feed, she reminded herself that her sister would also lose all she knew and loved when Vere became owner of Knightshill. He would never turn out his sisters, but Annabel had bewitched him. She would know just how to ensure that she was the sole woman in the house. Only then did it occur to her that one day Val, too, would no longer be able to regard this place as his home. But he would have the army. She and Charlotte would have nothing.

Halting to look out over sloping meadows where sheep and lambs called to each other, Margaret offered up a silent prayer. It was not for the distant

48

heathens, however. She asked God to allow Sir Gilliard Ashleigh many, many more years of life.

The gallery was crowded but not all the visitors were serious patrons of art. Many of the men in sober morning attire, who escorted partners dressed in gowns designed to attract attention and outdo any rival, were there merely to be seen. The artists and devotees of things aesthetic could be identified by their more flamboyant dress, although Vere looked conventional enough in a grey cutaway coat and dark trousers. A large clove carnation in his buttonhole and a waistcoat of dull rose-coloured brocade betrayed his preference for a little colour, but he was cast into sartorial shade by the man beside him as they shouldered their way through the crowd more intent on gossip than on viewing the exhibits.

Gilbert Dessinger was a theatrical designer. A stocky man of medium height, with a full red beard and prominent amber eyes, he cut an unmistakable figure this morning in a coat of bottle-green plaid, black trousers and a satin waistcoat in astonishing stripes ranging from orange to plum. He was a man who liked people for what they were and expected others to accept him on the same terms or to keep out of his way. Vere admired and respected Gilbert, as he did many other creative men. His own extensive knowledge of antique art, particularly French and Chinese, had been useful in giving Gilbert advice on authentic interiors for several historical stage dramas. A close friendship had grown between the pair, and Vere always lodged at the Dessinger residence when in London. He had been there for the past ten days.

They halted before a small exhibit displaying a motif intended for the illustration of a title page in a book. The subject should have appealed to Vere's love of natural countryside beauty, yet his thoughts were elsewhere as he gazed at the decorative design, which combined trailing leaves, a full moon and draped field mice.

'Well, my friend, what do you make of all this extraordinary nonsense?' asked Gilbert in booming voice, his words betraying his own opinion of *Art Nouveau*.

Dragging his attention back to his surroundings, Vere summoned a smile. 'I find the concept exciting. I shall certainly try it myself.'

'Remind me to cross your name from my list of friends. Can't stand fellows who disagree with me.'

They walked on, arguing light-heartedly over whether or not *Art Nouveau* was pure art or mere affectation. Then Gilbert drew Vere to a corner where a corridor linked two salons. 'For someone who declares this concept to be exciting, you seem remarkably full of melancholy, dear boy.'

49

'Sorry,' Vere apologised lamely, conscious of how far Gilbert's resonant voice travelled.

'It's your beloved's *mama* who has been afflicted with a chill, not the goddess Annabel herself,' Gilbert pointed out, deepening Vere's unease at being so transparent. 'You did all a decent fellow should on receiving Miss Bourneville's note this morning – exceeded the simple obligations of a betrothed man, in my opinion. A swift note of understanding and commiseration to your fiancée – immediately dispatched to Richmond by your own fair hand – was more than handsome. Ordering flowers for the invalid and her dutiful daughter was overdoing it somewhat. The lady is not upon her death bed, and I suspect Miss Bourneville was not reluctant to leave a scene she no longer appears to enjoy.'

Vere stiffened. 'I'd be glad if you'd refrain from speaking of her in such a public manner. What has occurred is not one of your damned stage dramas, I'll remind you.'

His friend nodded sagely. 'So the truth has finally penetrated your rose-tinted spectacles.'

'What truth?'

'That the lady is human, not divine.'

'I find that remark offensive,' Vere snapped, and began to walk away from the man who was forcing him to hear what an inner voice had been trying to tell him in vain. His path was blocked by a large man in morning suit, who escorted an elegant woman in a mulberry velvet coat with a matching hat set at a beguiling angle on her silver hair.

'Ashleigh!' cried the man in delighted tones. 'My dear fellow, I'm relying on you to speak in praise of my efforts here. Lady Mawson declines to be impressed, but I expect from you the opinion of a man of sound judgement.'

Vere gave a slight bow as he clasped Lady Alicia Mawson's extended hand. 'My judgement is so sound, Sir Crispin, it advises me never to contradict a lady.'

The woman laughed lightly. 'Spoken like a gentle man. You'll notice that I deliberately separate the two words, for it's rare these days to find someone who is both gentlemanly *and* gentle. You are almost a phenomenon, Mr Ashleigh.' Slipping her hand through the crook of his arm, she coaxed him back to the salon he had just left. 'Come and persuade me that there is *some* merit in this gaudy technique, if you can. I warn you I am quite set against it.'

Captured by the most beguiling widowed hostess in Bohemian circles, Vere swallowed his anger and made a commendable attempt to pass on his enthusiasm for this new decorative art which purists were reluctant to accept. Lady Alicia Mawson listened attentively to his comments for around twenty minutes, then stopped walking and smiled disarmingly.

'You once very kindly allowed me to see some of your own delightful Wiltshire water-colours, so I understand why you are so taken with a style which often combines floral and countryside themes. However, charmed though I am by your company, I cannot say you have seduced me into changing my opinion. I still regard it as *Art Bourgeois!*'

Vere laughed. 'My dear Lady Mawson, you will have half London renaming it by the end of next week.'

'Dear me! Do you consider that I have *such* influence upon society?' Taking his arm again, she began heading for the main entrance of the gallery. 'I hear Miss Bourneville had been obliged to attend her sick mama in Richmond.'

He glanced at her in surprise. 'I only had the news myself at seven this morning.'

'Ah,' she said, 'I am quite well acquainted with her aunt, who divulged the information last night. Such a dutiful daughter, and so very easily distressed. Mrs Gateshead confessed to me that her niece has been decidedly out of sorts lately, and believes the girl to have been over-anxious for her parents' health since their serious bout of influenza at the start of this year. A great pity. Miss Bourneville should be shining with happiness over her betrothal, but appears *distrait* and subdued. It must be a source of great concern to you, Mr Ashleigh.'

Vere said nothing. He could not walk away from Lady Mawson as he had from Gilbert, but he found her words equally unwelcome. He endured a further thirty minutes of conversation with other acquaintances, then escaped to the sunshine of that March morning. Hyde Park was golden with daffodils but, for once, he was not reminded of Wordsworth. He saw nothing but a face of immense beauty and violet eyes which no longer shone with love for him. He walked blindly, swinging his silver-topped cane at squirrels he usually fed with biscuit. His happiness had clouded since Annabel's visit to Knightshill. She had begun somehow to retreat from him after he had placed the Ashleigh rubies on her finger. Not only had she delayed the wedding longer than he had expected, she had spent too much time with his grandfather, poring over family history.

He had been so restless since her return to Richmond, he had begged her to arrange a visit to her aunt in Chelsea so they could spend some time together away from his family. Now he admitted that the past fortnight had not been the bliss he had expected. Annabel had developed a headache at Gilbert's party last week and returned home early, refusing to allow Vere to stay with her more than ten minutes. At the opera on Thursday, she had been silent and seemingly distracted by a noisy set of Artillery officers in another box. When Vere had declared he would go round and request better behaviour from them she had stopped him, saying they were probably *en route* to Egypt and must be excused their high spirits. Everyone was talking of the Sudan expedition. Annabel appeared to find the topic of immense interest, to the extent of upbraiding him because he clearly preferred to fill his days with frivolous expeditions and his evenings with lavish entertainment at parties or theatres. When he had explained that all his arrangements had been made in an attempt to please *her*, she had apologised so warmly his sense of disappointment had evaporated. However, at a gala performance of a new ballet two nights ago, she had totally disconcerted him by confiding to friends during the interval her opinion that men who pointed their toes and moved with a grace more suited to a female were creatures to be pitied. He had been driven to protest that male dancers required great physical strength and stamina to perform as they did, to which she had replied teasingly that she was greatly relieved his own health prevented him from emulating them for she had no wish for a pirouetting husband. Everyone had laughed, but Vere believed the answer to her changed attitude lay in that sentence. Clearly, all the talk of his sickly childhood had persuaded her that she had promised to marry a man who would swiftly leave her a widow. Once they were alone in the carriage, he had assured her of his fitness and swore she could expect a lifetime of happiness as his wife. Her response to that had banished all his doubts and sent him home in a highly charged mood.

In truth, he was in a fever of impatience to marry her. A further twelve months of waiting seemed intolerable. He was unable to concentrate; he no longer found interest in running the estate. Annabel had stirred in him some kind of mild madness which only calmed when he was with her. Wanting her induced actual physical pain, and restraint was taking its toll. For the first time in his life he became short-tempered and intolerant. Those things he had enjoyed with great zest suddenly seemed less beckoning; he began to experience doubts where once he had been assured. He was overwhelmed by a curious feeling of inadequacy. From the moment he had read Annabel's note this morning, he had been silencing a voice which whispered that her mama's chill was a welcome excuse to cut short a visit she was not enjoying.

Vere halted to stare at bare willow branches curving over the water. The pattern was perfect for an *Art Nouveau* motif. Annabel used to be an admirer of beautiful things. She had always enjoyed an evening at the opera or the ballet. Through Gilbert's theatrical connections, Vere had been fortunate enough to escort her to the first night of the latest Savoy opera – such a glittering occasion, and his girl had shone more brightly still! What had gone wrong? Why had she allowed him to kiss her so possessively two nights ago, then departed for Richmond leaving a note to be delivered twelve hours later? Lady Mawson had known last night of Annabel's return home. He had not. Could she be right in her claim that Annabel was overly solicitous since her parents' illness in January? It would explain her behaviour, yet she had not been excessively concerned with their welfare during her visit to Knightshill. He had admired her meticulous but calm exchange of correspondence with her aunt, who had remained at Richmond after Christmas to care for the invalids. No other solution to the painful situation occurred to him as he stood lost in thought. Her loving response after the ballet surely proved her feelings for him had not changed, yet she definitely no longer enjoyed the things they had shared with pleasure.

Making a swift decision, Vere turned and headed for the Dessinger house. Arriving there, he instructed the valet to pack and summon a cab. Scribbling a note to his host, he left it on the tray by the door and went out to the waiting hansom, instructed the driver to take him to Waterloo, then sat back feeling happier than he had since reading Annabel's note. His love for her was so deep it could overcome any fears she had.

Vere was known at the hotel for he had lodged there on many occasions during the summer. He ate a light lunch, then took the pleasant riverside walk to the Bourneville home. It was an elegant modern house, in contrast to Knightshill, yet Vere appreciated the charm of white stone, long windows and wrought-iron work in the form of mock balconies and decorative railings. The approach to it was a delight to his eye. A mass of flowering cherry and almond trees suggested a bridal canopy, and fallen blossoms turned the path into a perfumed carpet. His spirits rose at the thought of seeing his love, then concern dampened them once more as a curve in the path revealed two carriages at the foot of the steps. A doctor here? Visitors for an invalid more ill than he imagined? Guilt arose because he had suspected his fiancée of using a slim excuse in order to leave London. Mrs Bourneville must be in a serious condition. On being greeted by Robson, Vere enquired after her health.

'Madam has a slight chill, sir. She is resting in her room today.'

'Is the doctor here?' he asked, handing over his hat and cane.

'No, sir. The Master and Miss Bourneville are entertaining visitors in the drawing room.' He gave a polite smile. 'Are you expected, Mr Ashleigh, or shall I ask Miss Bourneville to receive you here?'

'Yes, please do so,' he said swiftly. 'I wish to speak privately with my fiancée.'

The man crossed the hall to enter a room on the far side of it. As he opened one of the double doors the sound of laughter came from inside the drawing room, where large bay windows gave a view of lawns sloping to the river. The voices sounded overwhelmingly masculine. These visitors were certainly not here out of concern for the invalid.

53

Any uneasiness he felt was immediately dispelled when Annabel came quickly towards him, her hands outstretched in greeting. She looked outstandingly beautiful in a dress of deep pink silk with soft frills at the throat and wrist, and the hair ornament of artificial roses and pink pearls placed just above her right ear highlighted the delicate blush in her cheeks. Vere's heart turned over as he realised how deep his fears had been, and how desperate he was to give her the Ashleigh name, which would banish them instantly.

'Vere, why didn't you tell me you meant to come?' she greeted warmly. 'Such beautiful flowers! Mama was overwhelmed by your consideration. But to send no message with the bouquets! I was uncertain what to think.'

With Robson hovering, Vere could do no more than kiss her cheek and hands. But her apparent delight at his arrival set his happiness soaring once more. 'I began a letter, then realised I must offer personal support. How is Mrs Bourneville?'

'Very vexed that she has been obliged to ask me to deputise for her during the visit of her oldest and dearest friends. So tiresome that a slight temperature should spoil such a particular occasion, but a rest now will enable her to join us at dinner tonight.'

Vere was taken aback. 'She is not seriously ill, then?'

Annabel's eyes widened in surprise. 'Did you imagine she was?'

He took her arm. 'Can we find a little privacy?'

'Later, my dear,' she promised. 'You'll dine with us, won't you? Let me introduce our guests. They'll be delighted to meet someone of whom Mama has written so enthusiastically in her letters to Scotland. They know you're here and I promised to bring you to them immediately.'

He allowed himself to be led across to the drawing room, even though he had a greater desire to be alone with Annabel than to be pleasant to her parents' oldest and dearest friends. However, it was enough just to be with her after the misery of the earlier part of the day. There were five people in the spacious room, decorated in cream, gold and strawberry pink. Edward Bourneville stood as they entered and came across to Vere wearing a welcoming smile.

'This is a most pleasant surprise, my dear fellow. We had not believed you would be free to join us. How fortunate that your commitments allowed you to do so after all.'

While Vere tried to understand the implications of these comments, his future father-in-law led him across to a stout woman in dark blue on a settee near the window. A tall grey-haired man – presumably her husband – rose from his seat beside her as they approached. Vere dutifully greeted Sir Marcus and Lady Selina Reeder, who both regarded him from head to foot as though assessing the value of a Highland bull, while they congratulated him on his good fortune in winning the daughter of their valued friends.

'I had such high hopes of dear Annabel one day becoming *my* daughter,' Lady Selina told him in a thin reedy voice. 'However, Sir Marcus was obliged to take up his duties in Scotland when his dear father died, so the children grew up as relative strangers.' Giving a curiously girlish titter, she glanced to her left. 'I believe the boys now wish they had not been so remiss when I suggested they should come to Richmond whenever an opportunity occurred. Isn't that so, my dears?'

Vere turned to study 'the boys', introduced as Lieutenants John and Frank Reeder of the Seaforth Highlanders. Sturdily built with fresh faces, dark curly hair and dark eyes they presented a picture of such vigour the room seemed too small for them.

'Congratulations!' declared one, gripping Vere's hand with his own and pumping it heartily up and down.

'Fortunate man,' agreed his brother, repeating the pumping action. 'We're very envious.'

'Come now, gentlemen,' protested Annabel laughingly, 'after the enthusiasm you've been displaying for the adventure ahead of you, I doubt either of you envy poor Vere anything.' She looked up at him to explain, 'John and Frank are sailing for Egypt at the end of the week. Sir Marcus and his wife travelled down to wave them off, and they've all agreed to stay with us for a few days. It's so disappointing that Mama should be indisposed.'

'Yes, very disappointing,' murmured Vere, speaking for himself. He had hoped to be alone with Annabel. With this beefy family around the prospect was slim.

They all sat and John Reeder said, 'Annabel has already told us Vorne Ashleigh was your brother. You must be very proud of such a courageous man.'

'Yes,' agreed Vere, still confused by the situation in which he found himself. Annabel was radiant; her sick mother hoped to join them for dinner. Why, then, had the visit to Chelsea been terminated so abruptly with no more than a vague note of apology?

'Sir Gilliard Ashleigh holds a memorial dinner on the anniversary of his grandson's death,' Annabel told the visitors. 'It's a tremendously stirring occasion. When every male member of the family turns to Vorne's portrait in a silent toast to his courage, one finds it difficult to hold back the tears.'

'Dear me, yes,' murmured Sir Marcus. 'Very moving.'

Annabel turned to Vere. 'The Reeders naturally assumed you were also on your way to the Sudan, but I explained that you were . . . that it was not possible for you to go,' she finished demurely.

'Don't worry, Ashleigh, we'll avenge your brother on your behalf,' Frank Reeder assured him warmly. 'Those devils will be given a taste of punishment they'll never forget.'

Vere looked at the man's broad honest face and heard himself saying, 'Vengeance is pointless, in my opinion. It always comes too late to prevent the original act of aggression. Slaying any number of men in the Sudan now won't bring my brother back or lessen the agony he suffered eleven years ago. I have no yearning to avenge his death, Mr Reeder.'

Silence followed his words, and Annabel flushed darkly as she stared at her lap. Her father broke the moment by asking how long the voyage to Egypt would take, but conversation seemed forced and Vere was miserably aware that Annabel refused to look at him. After forty-five minutes, he rose saying he must return to his hotel to dress for the evening. When she made no sign of intending to see him to the door, he asked pointedly if he might speak to her on a private matter. She then had no option but to accompany him from the room. They walked together in silence until he had taken his cane and hat from the table near the door. Then he turned to her, saying desperately, 'I believe I have upset and offended you. It is the very last thing I wish to do.'

She released her breath in a long sigh as she considered her reply. Then she faced him, and her expression made him feel even more wretched.

'It is your great misfortune to be the only Ashleigh cursed by ill-health. Your family understands that. I understand it. Everyone who knows you understands it. Through no fault of your own you cannot fulfil your rightful destiny. To fill your lonely convalescent hours you developed an interest in those few pastimes an invalid can indulge with perfect safety. I admired you for that. I shared your enjoyment of beauty and grace and gentleness for their own sake, and also because I wished to compensate you for all you had been denied.' She took several paces from him in agitation before turning determinedly. 'You have one great fault, Vere. I do not admire the manner in which you seem deliberately to denigrate those things you can never have. It is most unworthy and hurts very deeply those who are closest to you. Your dismissal of Frank's vow to avenge your brother's savage murder cut so cruelly into my feelings, I wonder how I managed to hide the fact. It was insulting to Frank, and unforgivably wounding to me.'

He moved towards her. 'Annabel . . . darling, *please* . . . '

'No, Vere, you must allow me to finish,' she said coldly. 'I went to stay with my aunt at your request, but while the whole of London talked of Kitchener's expedition to recapture Khartoum you persistently chatted of ballet dancers, the Impressionists, Sir Arthur Sullivan's latest score or how early the cherries have bloomed this year. It's as if . . . as if you regard your brother's great sacrifice as of no account.'

'*No!* How can you think that?' cried Vere in deep distress.

'I had not realised the truth until I visited Knightshill and saw how you callously disregarded the traditions your family holds so dear. The Khartoum Dinner is to be immediately discontinued when Sir Gilliard dies, you declared.'

Vere caught at her, held her resisting body by the waist. 'I explained why I believed Vorne would not want to be remembered in such a manner,' he said urgently. 'I think I also once said my family could become tiresome when military matters were being discussed. But I do *not* callously disregard their traditions, I swear to you.'

'Then why do you go out of your way to undermine your grandfather's pride so heartlessly?'

On shifting sand, and unable to believe this was the girl he knew and adored, he shook his head. 'I don't understand.'

'Isn't it terrible enough that the man who should have been his heir was stabbed by a dozen knives and left to die alone and despairing, with no word of comfort from those who loved him? Isn't that terrible enough, without you emphasising your own inadequacy at every opportunity?'

His hands dropped to his sides leaving her standing stiffly two feet from him. She could have been two yards, two miles, two *years* away, he felt so desolate.

'Please go on,' he murmured through a dry throat.

'We – we all understand why you can never be another Vorne, but is it necessary to be cruel enough to – to – to *brag* of it?' She forced herself to add, 'You surely can't have failed to notice your grandfather's expression when you bring out your little paintings of mice or poppies, especially when visitors are present?'

With blow piling upon blow he heard himself say, 'I suppose I *have* failed to notice it. You had better enlighten me.'

With growing passion, words tumbled from her. 'His face is full of derision. His eyes betray pain, because the man who must now represent a distinguished heroic family is proud of nothing more than creating pretty pictures. Is it your deliberate intention to break an old man's heart and mock the valour of your ancestors, or do you really believe your small talent for splashing colour on paper makes you their equal? If you do, you are not the person I believed you to be. You are merely a pygmy among giants.'

Everything became clear with those words; confusion turned to acute painful perception. From the depths of his anguish he heard himself say, 'It was the Khartoum Dinner. You changed from that evening on.' Swallowing hard, he accepted the unacceptable. 'You have allowed

57

yourself to be seduced by a ghost, Annabel. You've fallen in love with Vorne Ashleigh.'

Edward Bourneville returned the ring of clustered rubies to the bank used by the Ashleigh family on the day after Annabel wrote a formal note terminating her engagement. In his heart Vere knew it had only lasted the four weeks between Christmas and the Khartoum Dinner. Vorne had taken Annabel from him on that night. He returned to Knightshill in a state of numbness, realising how totally his chosen bride had ruled every aspect of his life.

His late-afternoon arrival fortunately coincided with family activities which kept them busy enough not to spot the carriage approaching the house, so Vere was able to go directly to his rooms without being waylaid and questioned by his sisters. His valet was not expecting him, for which Vere was glad. He stood at the window for a long, long time still in his coat. It was not due to the absence of a fire; he was simply lost in a labyrinth of unhappiness. But word travelled fast in the domestic hierarchy. His valet arrived with a maid carrying a bucket of coal at his heels.

'Notice of your return failed to reach us, Mr Ashleigh,' exclaimed Stoner, giving his master respectful benefit of the doubt over his unannounced arrival. 'Foster will soon have a fire going, and I've arranged for tea to be taken to the small parlour which is nice and warm.' He eased the overcoat from Vere's shoulders and took it across to the wardrobe. 'Did you have a good journey, sir?'

'No tea, Stoner,' he ruled wearily. 'I'll have a brandy to warm me up while the fire catches. You can unpack later.'

The balding, thin-faced man who had once served Vorne stopped in his tracks. 'A *brandy*, sir?'

'That's what I said,' he told the valet with unusual sharpness.

Stoner hesitated. He might have taken advantage of a long-standing relationship between servant and master in order further to question the astonishing request for spirits at four in the afternoon, but the girl was still at the fireplace where there was more smoke than flame, at present, so he permitted himself a sigh of disapproval before departing. There were no decanters in these rooms, as there always had been when Vorne occupied them. Brandy had to be brought up to someone forbidden to indulge in serious drinking.

Returning to study the view from his window, Vere was unaware of the young maid's polite words on her departure. He needed the brandy to steel himself for the inevitable interview with his grandfather. It would be one of the most difficult confrontations of his life. Yet, when Stoner returned with the brandy balloon on a tray containing a decanter and the small spirit heater used to warm the glass, Vere told him to take it away again. A pygmy among giants, she had called him. False courage would not make him taller.

'Is anything wrong, sir?'

'Where is my grandfather, Stoner?'

'In his quarters taking tea,' the man replied, using the military term always used to describe Sir Gilliard's suite.

'Tell Clunes I shall be along just as soon as I have washed away the dust of my journey.' He turned towards his bedroom. 'I'll ring for you when I'm ready.'

Ten minutes later, he made his way to the rooms always occupied by the owner of Knightshill, taking the route through the west wing, the ballroom and the art gallery to avoid any risk of encountering his sisters. Their rooms were on the other side of the house. The master suite comprised four rooms above the vast library and picture room, where it commanded sweeping views of the estate and surrounding villages. Vere had imagined himself here with Annabel so many times it deepened his sense of loss as he nodded acknowledgement of Clunes' greeting, then stepped across the rich carpet to where Sir Gilliard sat enjoying his tea.

'So you've decided to return, have you?' he commented. 'Sit down and have some of this excellent toast. It's exactly how I like it – hot, plenty of butter and a good thick layer of relish. Introduced to it in India, y'know. Fond of it ever since,' he added in his customary reminiscent manner. 'Sit down, sit down! After absenting yourself on no more urgent business than to attend the opening of the latest of those damned libellous comic operas, you can surely spare me a little of your time.' Casting him an impatient glance as Vere remained standing, he growled, 'It's no use pleading urgent estate matters. Morgan has run the place so well during your absence it's perfectly clear he could do so until kingdom come and you'd not be missed. *Sit down, sir!*' he commanded.

'I wish to speak to you on a subject of great importance,' Vere told him. 'I'd be glad if Clunes would leave us.'

Sir Gilliard wiped butter from his white moustache with a heavy linen napkin, raising his bushy eyebrows. 'Don't tell me you've rushed back here to say the Queen is dead! By God, the nation will go to the dogs in the hands of that licentious son of hers.'

'*Please*, sir, may I speak to you privately?' urged Vere with mounting desperation, knowing his grandfather's fondness for teasing those who displayed uncertainty or nervousness.

The white eyebrows rose higher as the elderly man said crisply, 'You may go off-duty, Clunes. I'll take my usual sundowner in the library.'

'Thank you, sir,' said the former West Wilts corporal, leaving the room by the door to the adjacent bedroom.

59

If Vere had any suspicions of the man eavesdropping he did not allow them to worry him. The news would be public knowledge very soon and speculation would be rife. He had bombarded everyone with his happiness; he must accept that they would participate in his misery. *A pygmy among giants.* Here was the tallest giant of all. No, Vorne was even taller. Was it any wonder Annabel had made a comparison and found her future husband wanting? Facing the proud, autocratic head of his family Vere knew he must make some show of Ashleigh courage now.

'Miss Bourneville has returned the rubies, sir. She feels unable to fulfil her promise to become my wife. I think I need not tell you how . . . *disappointed* I am.'

Sir Gilliard studied him for some moments with inscrutable silence. When the late sun suddenly broke through cloud to gild the heavy antique furniture and cast bright light on a face which had seen wild areas of the world and witnessed the savagery of mankind, Vere saw disdain dawning on it.

'Despite your high-flown flummery, I deduce that what you are telling me is you have lost the girl.'

'Yes, sir.'

'Then get her back, you young fool.'

'That's impossible.'

'Pah! Are you a man, or not?'

Vere remained silent.

'I'm set on that match, d'you hear? So is Bourneville. She was more than happy during her visit here. Should have set an earlier date for the wedding. Instructed you to do so.'

'The date was set by Annabel. I couldn't persuade her to change it.'

'Then what did you do or say to bring about this nonsense?'

Nothing would draw from Vere the fact that the personality of a man long dead seemed infinitely more fascinating than his own to the girl he adored. A living rival would have been less humiliating. In view of his refusal to answer, Sir Gilliard rose to take up the implacable stance well known by members of his former regiment, and by his family. His shrewd blue gaze pierced Vere painfully.

'Didn't overstep the mark with her, did you?'

'Of course not,' he protested, with all the heat of his frequent struggles against doing so. 'I thought too highly of her.'

'There's no need to tell me *that*. The entire family saw you behaving like a moonstruck cowherd whenever she was near. Commented on it to me. Saw it as weakness – which it was. Because of it you've mishandled the affair, failed to measure up to what was expected of you.'

'I'm well aware of that,' Vere said tonelessly. 'I came to give you the plain facts, that's all. What caused Annabel to cry off is my concern alone.'

'Ho, is it, sir?' The General's voice rose to the level he used during court martial proceedings. 'Nothing you do is your concern alone, it is the concern of all those associated with you. The future of this family and the perpetuation of its glorious tradition of service to the crown will rest in your hands when I die. It is a dictate of birth that you should step into the shoes of your splendid brother for as long as the good Lord spares you. We have had to accept that you are unable to do your obvious duty, but you have now failed in the one direction open to you. What you did to cause that young woman to reject you is *not* your sole concern because it has put paid to my expectations of a son to succeed you. You are a dismal failure, sir.'

'No more than Vorne, in that respect.'

Sir Gilliard's cheeks flushed with anger. 'Your brother was strong and lusty. There was no necessity to sire a son at the first opportunity.'

'There was *every* need,' cried Vere passionately. 'A military firebrand, he was in greater danger of an early death than I. So is Val. Perhaps *he* should take a wife at the end of term, and produce a male child as a safeguard.'

Stiffening to his full, formidable height, his grandfather said, 'You're growing impertinent! Valentine is a schoolboy of no more than eighteen.'

'Who will be obliged to step into my shoes when I fulfil every expectation of dying ignominiously of fever!' With words, Vere released the anguish within him. 'Vorne dedicated himself to his beloved career. Val will do the same. If he survives its demands long enough to marry, he will raise progeny merely through the careless satisfaction of nature's demands. The siring of a son is only so vitally essential to you in *my* case because you see it as the only way I can serve family and country. If I were wearing a scarlet coat out in the Sudan right now no one would give a damn about my procreative abilities. Being an officer in the West Wilts is sufficient distinction for any man. For one who is not, the only compensation for his failings is to become a stud stallion, it seems.'

'*That's enough!*' thundered Sir Gilliard.

'Yes, I daresay it might be,' continued Vere, as angry as his grandfather. 'But you would have been disappointed even in that, because I had no intention of regarding Annabel as a breeding mare. I wanted her for my wife because I love her, not because I was obliged to produce more Ashleigh boys for the West Wiltshire Regiment. I wanted her to share with me this wonderful old house and its productive acres. I wanted any children we might have to be raised here in the freedom of a home filled with love and unrestrictive beliefs.' He gave a great sigh in an attempt to

61

bring his alarming outburst under control. 'Unhappily, I misjudged Annabel's feelings.'

'You've misjudged a damn sight more than that, sir! You have a duty to me and to your heritage, and you'll not fulfil it by growing orchids for Bond Street beaux to present to their mistresses in the chorus-line. John Morgan can run Knightshill very handsomely on his own, so you're not needed in that area. As for water-colours, poetry and *comic-operas*, they are pastimes for effeminate fools who try to cover their inadequacies with high-flown mumbo-jumbo suggesting that their intellect is greater than those of us who see with unblinkered eyes.' He pointed an unwavering finger at Vere. 'Your duty is to produce a son with the least delay. Dr Alderton assures me that you are capable of doing so.'

Seething inside, Vere exploded. 'My God, you've discussed *that* with Alderton? My virility is my own affair!'

'You're an Ashleigh. It's the concern of your family,' came the harsh response. 'Now then, whatever it is you've done to cause this setback you must make good. Bourneville wants Knightshill for his daughter, so there'll be little opposition there. Your duty, sir, is to win that girl back and wed her swiftly. I want to hear no more about it being impossible. Get yourself to Richmond without delay and set an early date for the nuptials. Have I made myself clear?' he asked, as if reprimanding a junior officer who should rightly be chastened and obedient.

Vere was no junior officer and had no empathy with military ways. In addition, he was in the grip of an anger completely foreign to him and, therefore, out of control.

'You've made yourself more than clear,' he managed, starting to shake with the force of his feelings. 'I'm to marry as soon as possible and devote myself to ensuring that my wife swiftly produces a son. I may then allow myself to expire, having done my bounden duty to the Ashleighs. Very well. I'll take to the altar the first female willing to accept the bargain. The vessel is unimportant, of course, it's the life that pours from it which matters to you. I'll give you your male child, but not by Annabel Bourneville. There is no question of making good the rift between us.'

Rising easily to deal with lingering insubordination in a truculent young offender, the old general adopted his fiercest expression to add force to the voice of overriding authority.

'Don't be arrogant with me, sir. I'll tell you where you went wrong. A female needs to look up to a man, not have him constantly on his knees before her. She needs authority, dominance, an air of unassailable strength. All the girl had from you were calflike glances and a succession of fripperies tied in pretty ribbons. Small wonder you lost her.'

The shaft went right home, shattering the last of his pride. 'I'm not the first Ashleigh to lose the woman of his choice, as we're both aware. But I've at least done it *before* I married her.'

The colour drained from Sir Gilliard's face as he stared at Vere as if seeing him for the first time. 'Get out,' he said with difficulty. Then, as Vere hesitated, his voice rose to the familiar roar. *'Get out!'*

Chapter 4

The Waterloo Ball held annually at Knightshill was always a splendid affair. The Colonel and officers of the West Wiltshire Regiment attended along with many other military men invited by Sir Gilliard. The Ashleigh family was there in force, with one exception. June examinations always prevented Val from being present. He had been sorry to miss the martial aspect of the occasion in the past, although dancing held little interest for him. This year he was glad of the excuse to be absent. During the Easter vacation his grandfather had made a great many pointed remarks which told Val the ultimatum given in January had not been forgotten.

Margaret always looked forward to the ball. She loved the gaiety, the colour, the grandeur of an evening when the ballroom of the house was filled with couples dancing to music played by a full orchestra hired for the occasion. The guest rooms were all occupied for several nights and the old house came alive with lights and laughter. Although the gardens were illuminated by lanterns, there were dim bowers where lovers could dally for as long as convention permitted. It was a gala event reported in society magazines and in the columns of newspapers.

This year, Margaret had less enthusiasm for the extensive arrangements prior to the ball. Timothy's eighth birthday had come and gone. Philip's refusal to allow him the place reserved for him at Misleydale had caused bitterness. Sir Gilliard had cursed and thundered to no avail. The Reverend Daulton was no Ashleigh to be ruled by the head of the family, and her grandfather had confessed to Margaret his fear that the family was breaking up.

'That boy of yours has a right to all I can offer him. I could make something of the lad,' he had declared morosely. 'It's too late for the others. One can do nothing but dabble with paints and recite pretty verse. The other's a young rebel. They invariably destroy themselves. So will he.

63

The only one of any worth was taken before his prime. It's the end of a line, my girl. I never thought to see it. *Never!*'

Margaret worried over the old man's state of mind. The end of Vere's short engagement had precipitated a quarrel of such ferocity the pair were no longer speaking to each other. If Sir Gilliard was upset by it, it was nothing to the way it had affected Vere. There was a dismaying decline in his well-being, and Charlotte vowed Annabel's rejection was slowly killing their brother. He had no zest for life, no interest in the estate, no enthusiasm for the things which had once delighted him. Moody and withdrawn, it seemed the sunshine of his temperament had been banished by black clouds of depression.

The sisters were unclear as to why Annabel had returned the rubies. The story circulating society was that Miss Bourneville felt a strong sense of duty towards parents whose declining health demanded that she should devote herself to them in the coming years. Whether or not this ludicrous story was believed Margaret and Charlotte had no idea, but they could not see *that* girl sacrificing all marriage to Vere would give her merely to pamper parents who were more robust than he.

Margaret was also worried about Val. During his vacation he had confessed his unfaltering determination to join the cavalry by any means open to him. Her warnings had fallen on deaf ears, and she was afraid of the consequences if he dared defy a force as powerful as Sir Gilliard.

By the evening of the ball, some of her usual excitement had bubbled up. She had searched her sewing-box and found some antique lace with which she had trimmed a gown of midnight-blue stiff silk she had not worn for several years. It looked well on her, for her figure was as slim and shapely as when the dress had been made. Sitting at the mirror after Louise had dressed her golden-brown hair in an upswept style which emphasised the daringly low neckline of the ballgown, Margaret took from its velvet case the single sapphire on a gold chain which had been her coming-of-age present from Sir Gilliard. The pendant was the most valuable of all her jewels, many of which she no longer wore because Philip preached against the sins of vanity and self-adornment in the presence of the children. Tonight, she would be guilty of the sin and revel in it.

She fastened the chain so that the huge sapphire flashed like blue fire just above the point where the rich silk curved across her breasts. Dabbing perfume on her skin with the stopper from a crystal bottle, she then took up long gloves and a velvet purse before rising to study her reflection. The dress hung in folds of light and shade from her waist, adding elegance to a figure taller than usual for a woman. The jewel enhanced the whiteness of her skin, and the shining piled hair emphasised eyes which suddenly glowed with the vivacity Philip's neglect had slowly driven from them. She smiled at the young woman before her, welcoming her temporary return. For a few hours she would be Margaret Ashleigh once more, a young girl with not a care in the world. How wonderful to dance and laugh, putting her worries aside for a while.

She left the bedroom to cross the sitting room with a rustle of long skirts, then was halted by Philip's entry from the upper landing. He remained by the door, slowing closing it behind him, staring at her with an expression akin to shock. In the peculiar silence that followed, Margaret started forward again.

'Lottie will be waiting for me,' she said briskly. 'Some guests have already arrived.'

He crossed to her as if she had not spoken, staring at the sapphire like a man compelled to approach it. When his gaze lifted to hers, there was hunger in dark eyes which had seen her as no more than his disciple for too long. Her heartbeat quickened with inexplicable apprehension. This man was her husband; he had been her lover. Why should she suddenly feel afraid?

When he reached for the blue stone lying between her breasts, moving it slowly so that it caught the light, Margaret had to master an urge to step away from the lingering caress of his fingers.

'I wear it so seldom, these days,' she said, striving for lightness. 'Tonight seems the perfect occasion to show it off.'

'The bauble of Jezebel,' he breathed. 'The fire of carnal temptation.'

Her throat grew dry. 'What nonsense, Philip. The pendant was a present from Grandfather, as you well know.'

As she stepped round him towards the door, he caught her arm to swing her roughly back to face him. '*The fire of carnal temptation.* You mean to go out there and flaunt yourself before men wearing the scarlet jackets you all revere, press your body against theirs without shame,' he accused, his face starting to work with passion. 'That's all you've ever wanted, isn't it?'

His assault was that of a man possessed. What had once thrilled her was now loathsome. His mouth was wetly repulsive as it closed over her own, then travelled down her throat, across her shoulders, and slowly over the rise of her breasts. Instinctive resistance turned to fear as he demanded something she was appallingly unwilling to give. His strength increased to overcome hers born of the neglect and wounding words of the past three years. Saliva began to trickle from the corner of his mouth as they grappled with growing ferocity against the far-off strains of the first waltz played by the hired orchestra in the ballroom.

There were no murmured endearments, no teasing caresses, no gentle compulsion to surrender as he half-carried, half-dragged her back to the bedroom and threw her on the counterpane. An act which had once bewitched her now became one of savage violation which seemed to serve as punishment for his own unwelcome desire as much as for what he saw as her wantonness. During the ordeal, her devotion which had turned to despair darkened to hatred so acute it burned as deeply into her soul as his frenzied passion burned into her body.

It was over as violently as it had begun. Philip flung himself from her with a deep gasp of anguish, gripping his hair as if he intended to pull it out in atonement for his sin. He walked the room in demented manner, treading over the torn ballgown he had tossed to the floor. Time passed. Margaret struggled to ride out the storm tide of humiliation for the physical weakness women could never conquer. Gradually, however, she found a new strength as it occurred to her that Philip would regard what he had just done as a greater sin than any ordinary man would consider it to be. His weakness was vastly more humiliating than hers because he had broken his own rigid commandments. He could never preach to her again, never claim that he was an instrument of God whose life must be devoted solely to the heathen. He had surrendered to human weakness of the vilest form and she would never allow him to forget.

When she felt strong enough she dragged herself from the bed and took another dress from her wardrobe. Then she tidied her hair with icy fingers. The gold chain had broken when Philip had tugged the sapphire from around her neck, so she fastened a triple row of pearls in its place. When she crossed the sitting room he was standing by a wall, his hands spread wide, his head bowed as if on a cross. He appeared to be sobbing in silent anguish. She passed him and left the room, pausing only briefly to take a deep breath before walking towards the sound of gaiety knowing she would never be the same after tonight.

Vere stood by the renowned Great Window which reflected light from several hundred candles. He had attended the Waterloo Ball for the past six years but had never been so conscious of his attire. It was an over-whelmingly military occasion. The colourful uniforms with gold buttons and epaulettes, the spurs on polished boots, the loud authoritative voices discussing past battles and future victories in the Sudan all seemed so right in this house of warriors. Yet the heir apparent was a weakling who painted pretty pictures of mice and butterflies.

His gaze lifted across the whirling dancers to fix on the tall straight figure in the familiar uniform of the West Wiltshire Regiment. Sir Gilliard would be a soldier until the day he died and would not give up life without his greatest ever battle to hold on to it. Since Annabel had lifted the veil from Vere's eyes, he had watched his grandfather closely and seen the derision of someone who could not accept a man who failed to reach Ashleigh standards. He believed it was also in the eyes of most people tonight when they looked his way.

The scene with Annabel haunted him night and day. He had been so easily able to accept his own limitations, it had blinded him to evidence that others could not. His conscience tormented him whenever he thought of his intention to discontinue the Khartoum Dinner as soon as his grandfather was in his grave. Would he also have ceased to hold this annual ball to celebrate a famous victory won when that same old warrior had been a mere five years old? Possibly.

For some weeks he had been wandering moodily around the estate by day, tossing restlessly at night. The idyll was irrevocably over. Annabel had been right. He *was* a pygmy among giants. The truth robbed him of the small delights he had enjoyed and left an abyss at his feet. A true Ashleigh would stride across it; he had either to fall to the bottom or attempt a perilous struggle to reach the far side. In losing Annabel he had also lost the ability to make decisions, to think clearly. The weakling that he was allowed the days to drag by while the abyss widened.

Charlotte came to him, bringing him back to the present. Her fond smile ill disguised her concern, but he could not summon one in return for his favourite sister.

'It's growing uncomfortably hot, Vere. I've instructed Winters to open all the doors to the terrace so that it will be cool when we eat supper. I can't imagine why Margaret hasn't put in an appearance. People keep asking where she is.'

'Perhaps Philip is being difficult. He sees sin in almost everything lately,' Vere observed.

'I don't think Margaret shares his enthusiasm for his work, do you? She puts on a brave face to fool Grandfather, but the life seems to have gone out of her lately. Philip used to be so popular in the parish, but he's all fire and damnation now. Margaret once generously offered me a home with them when you . . . ' She broke off, colouring slightly. 'I couldn't contemplate residence in that man's house when Grandfather dies.'

'You don't have to. Your home is here,' he told her brusquely, then he added words which took him completely by surprise, because it seemed the elusive decision had at that moment been made by him. 'Val will be roaming the world with a sword in his hand. He'll need you to run the place for him.'

'Val? But Knightshill is yours.'

He shook his head slowly. 'I don't belong here. It's a house for a line of warriors. Even its name smacks of chivalry, and I'm not even a knight at heart, you know.' Glancing away at the military roundabout before him, he said, 'Look at them all! Gallantry partnering fair lady. Knightshill was built for that. Young Val won't chase the heroic old shades from these rooms or drown the echoing battle cries with sweet music and poetry.' He looked back at her. 'You'll be here to preserve the air of dignity within the house, and John Morgan will run the estate with diligence and affection. When Val comes home briefly, between wars, he'll find his home exactly as it has always been.'

Charlotte gazed at him in distress. 'Please don't say such things. You're the first Ashleigh for generations who loves this place as a true home, and who takes a pride in its surrounding acres.'

He regarded her in silence, uncertain how to continue. The decision to leave Knightshill might have been made, but he had no notion how to put it into effect. Standing irresolute, his attention was caught by the appearance of his other sister who hesitated by the door from the art gallery to search the ballroom with a rather wild gaze.

'There's Margaret, at last. She looks agitated. Perhaps one of the children is unwell.'

Charlotte turned to look. 'She's dressed for the evening so the problem can't be too acute, but why is she wearing that beige dress when she spent hours stitching lace on the blue silk everyone admires?' She began moving away. 'Now she's finally here she can dance with some of the guests who arrived too late to fill their cards. That's the trouble with military affairs. There's always a surplus of gentlemen.'

A surplus of uniformed heroes, Vere caught himself amending silently as he watched the scarlet and blue and gold kaleidoscope pass before his brooding gaze. The thought remained with him as he considered the resolution which had come to him out of the blue a moment ago. The scarlet jackets spun round faster and faster as the waltz reached its frenzied conclusion, and loud, authoritative voices rose on all sides to beat at his brain.

'I well recall the plight of the 10th at Sebastopol . . . ' 'came up on their left flank and took 'em totally by surprise . . . ' 'never seen so many damn Zulus as there were on that ridge.'

As if mesmerised, Vere began to make his way between the couples strolling from the centre of the ballroom, and walked through the broad upper corridor towards his own rooms in the west wing. Reaching them, he went to his writing-desk and drew forward several sheets of notepaper. He felt amazingly calm while composing two letters in concise terms. There must be no doubts or misunderstandings. Time was short and he was desperately impatient for action. When the letters were sealed he rang for Stoner and instructed him to arrange for them to be taken down to Dunston St Mary immediately. Vere remained at his writing-desk lost in thought. The letters would be collected early in the morning. By late

68

afternoon they would arrive at their destinations and he could expect swift replies. The sensation of being in the hands of destiny invaded him. He had cast the dice. Let them fall where they would.

The end of term cricket match was almost over when the players walked from the field for the tea interval. Chartfield had knocked up a good score against Sherborne, thanks to a true captain's innings by Val, and the twenty runs needed to win were certain to be gained by the remaining six batsmen before close of play. Although the two schools were great rivals, there was a lively atmosphere in the tea tent as the boys did justice to the sandwiches and cakes set out for them.

Val sat beside Clive, chatting with friendly enthusiasm to some of the Sherborne team. The main topic of interest was where they all planned to spend the long summer vacation. One of their rivals was going to Nice, another to Venice. A third hoped to accompany his mother to Cairo where his father would take leave from Kitchener's army and join them for a month or two.

Clive was to be a guest at Knightshill, for which Val was glad. Margaret had written to tell him Vere was very depressed after his broken engagement, and had quarrelled with their grandfather. They were no longer on speaking terms. It sounded remarkably unlike his good-natured brother, so Val could only think Annabel Bourneville had upset him very deeply. The tone of Margaret's letter had been predominantly gloomy, so Val was thankful he would have a cheerful companion to leaven the censure he was certain to receive from Sir Gilliard over his examination marks. This year's results were the worst he had ever had. He was already far enough in his grandfather's black books on the subject of his future military career, which the old man erroneously thought settled.

The burning ambition to join the cavalry was partially to blame for Val's poor scholastic performance. Constant scheming on how he could defy Sir Gilliard's formidable influence in military circles had kept concentration at bay during study periods. At the end of his next school year he must either follow the course appointed by past generations, or take battle for his right of choice. He was not afraid to fight, but what hope did a single unarmed man have against an entire battery of artillery? Yet Val sensed that his own will was as strong as that of his grandfather, so the only tactic to adopt was to negotiate a ceasefire, then resort to reason. However, with the old man in a black mood over Vere's affairs, it seemed a ceasefire and resorting to reason were unlikely during the summer break.

Patience was not one of Val's virtues, so the prospect of waiting until Christmas had only caused further lack of concentration on necessary evils such as Latin and advanced mathematics. His tutors had issued warnings followed by an ultimatum. Unless considerable work was undertaken during the vacation to catch up with the rest of his classmates, he would find himself relegated at the start of the new school year. More than one master had hinted that a little more physical effort in pushing a pen across sheets of blank paper rather than passing a ball across the greensward would be sound tactics, but this advice came from academics who looked upon sportsmen as Philistines. Geoffrey Manton, the sports master, held the opposite view. He had awarded his most versatile athlete the coveted Waycliffe Cup for the sportsman of the year. The only shadow over Val's golden glow of achievement was that cast by an old warhorse who wanted a reincarnation of Vorne Ashleigh, rather than a young man determined to flash his own individual brilliance.

The players were back on the field after tea and Val was sitting in the roped enclosure with the rest of his team when Geoffrey Manton approached. 'Dawkins has just come with a message from the Head. Your brother is here to see you, Ashleigh.'

Val was astonished. '*My* brother! Are you sure, sir? Young Ashmead was expecting some of his family down to the match.'

'The Head wouldn't make a mistake of that nature. You'd better cut along to his study.'

Certain there had been confusion between his name and that of the junior member of the team who had invited every relative he possessed to witness the game, Val got to his feet reluctantly.

'Tell them to slow down a bit. I want to be back in time to see the winning stroke.' Pulling on his blazer, he added, 'I still believe there's been a misunderstanding.'

'If that's so, I want you back pronto. It's a captain's privilege to receive the congratulations of the defeated team.' Manton grinned. 'If it *is* your brother, drag him back here with you. Your eighty-one runs gained us the match, so he should welcome the chance to witness your triumph as you take the Schools' Cup from Sherborne.'

Val shook his head. 'Vere doesn't know one end of a bat from the other. He's the brainy one of the family. If I had half his intellect I wouldn't be under threat of relegation next year.'

Keen to return as soon as possible, Val ran across the grassy area which pupils were forbidden to cross except during fire drill. The hero of the hour should be allowed to go where no mere schoolboy could! He cursed Jeremy Ashmead's numerous kith and kin, especially this brother who had arrived when the game was practically over. Dr Keening was among those who had suggested that Val should devote less time to sporting activities next year, so he was unlikely to appreciate the importance of the moment. He would apologise profusely to this visiting relative then oblige Val to take the man

70

down to Ashmead, who had scored only a feeble number of runs due to nervousness beneath the eyes of his whole blasted family.

He reached the Headmaster's study after taking the main steps two at a time. However, he stopped to smooth down his unruly hair with his hand and to straighten his blazer before knocking.

When he entered, Vere rose from a leather chair and turned towards him. Surprise turned to shock as Val took in his brother's appearance. His good-looking face was haggard and drawn, and there was a perceptible stoop to the shoulders of this man of twenty-five. It could mean only one thing. Sir Gilliard was gone.

Val turned cold. He had never known his father; Vorne was merely an elusive memory. Mother had gone to America when he was only five. His sister Charlotte had always been distant and disapproving, more attuned to Vere's artistic personality. When Margaret married, his close relationship with her had changed. The one enduring figure in Val's eighteen years had been his grandfather. Despite head-on clashes with the unyielding old general, Val admired and respected him. He could not imagine Knightshill without that impressive upright figure.

'Hello, Val,' his brother said quietly. 'I'm sorry to interrupt your match.'

'It doesn't matter,' he replied diffidently. 'I've had my innings.'

Dr Keening walked from behind his desk. 'I'll show you to my sitting room, Mr Ashleigh. You can talk privately there.'

Val followed them to the familiar room in a state of mounting consternation. Vere looked so ill! All thought of cricket and silver trophies fled as he grappled with the implications of this visit, and he was not aware that Dr Keening had gone until Vere suggested he should make himself comfortable while they talked. Sitting heavily in a chintz-covered chair, Val stared absently at a bowl of cream tea-roses on the polished oval table while faint sounds of cheering reached him through the open window.

'This is not easy to say,' Vere began. 'It'll come as something of a shock, I'm afraid.'

'It doesn't matter,' Val muttered again. 'We knew it would happen eventually, didn't we?'

'I certainly didn't. The decision was a sudden one. Hence there was no time to let you know I was coming today.'

He frowned up at his brother. 'What decision?'

Vere sighed. 'I've come to say goodbye and to get a few things straight with you about the future.'

'What?'

'I've joined the militia. After brief training I've been promised a commission in one of the regiments serving with Kitchener. I'll be in Egypt before Christmas, ready to march on Khartoum.'

71

Val was horrified. '*No!* He couldn't demand that of you even on his deathbed.'

'Whose deathbed?'

'Grandfather's.'

'Good lord, is that why you think I've come?'

'He isn't dead?'

'It never occurred to me that you would . . . No, Val, Grandfather is hale and hearty.'

Driven to his feet, he said, 'Look I can't make head or tail of this. What's going on?'

A maid in a black dress entered with a tray containing tea and biscuits. They were silent until she left, then Val joined his brother standing at the window bay and saw just how ill and drawn he looked in the glare thrown by late-afternoon sun on the wall outside.

'What's all this about going to the Sudan?' he demanded thickly. 'You'd never survive the rigours of the desert and military campaigning.'

'I've come to tell you of my intentions, not to discuss them with you,' Vere said firmly. 'Someone of your determined disposition must allow that each man is entitled to do with his life what he wishes.'

'But it's madness,' he protested with heat. 'I can't think who would agree to give you a commission so that you can commit virtual suicide. Why are you doing it? *Why?*'

'I'm giving you Knightshill and the responsibility for upholding the honour of a great family. You'll do the job far better than I.'

Deeply disturbed and upset, Val said urgently, 'Margaret wrote that you had quarrelled with the old man. Doesn't he realise the enormity of what he's asking?'

Green eyes swivelled to look directly at him. There was a haunting sadness in them. 'I've left my affairs in order, so you'll find no complications when the time comes. Take care of your sisters, and don't neglect the old house too badly while you fight your wars.'

It sounded so much like a concluding remark, Val seized his brother's arm to hold him there. 'You can't come here out of the blue with an announcement like this and refuse to answer any of my questions. It's not fair on a chap. All this nonsense about giving me Knightshill. I don't want it. Anyway, it's not yours to give until Grandfather dies.' He ran a distracted hand through his hair. 'Dammit, Vere, you can't go off like this.'

'It's the family tradition.'

'But you're different.'

Vere sighed. 'Therein lies the answer to all your questions.'

'No, it doesn't. *It doesn't,*' he argued hotly. 'It confounds them. What have we all done to make you so desperate?'

Vere studied him for a moment. 'I wasn't expecting this reaction. I imagined you'd be my champion.'

'In deliberately courting death?'

'Isn't that what every soldier does?' He frowned. 'Perhaps I should have obeyed my first instinct and written to you, as I have to the girls, but I felt I owed you the courtesy of telling you in person, as you'll be my successor. I also wanted to see you again before I left.' He paused for a moment before adding, 'We've seen less of each other than if we had been nearer in age, and differing interests widened the gap, I suppose. I should have been a better brother, Val, but my affection for you is mixed with admiration for the qualities I know are beneath your youthful impetuosity.' His hand gripped Val's shoulder. 'Follow your star, however thorny the path. I've a feeling you'll be the greatest Ashleigh of all.' His arm dropped to his side as he turned away. 'God go with you.'

Before Val knew it, Vere had left. Confused and upset, he stayed where he was as he heard Dr Keening bid his brother farewell. What had made a gentle, laughing person consider such action? Surely even Grandfather would not be so ruthless as to drive a man to this extreme? Although he loved the old place as the secure home he had always known, Val had never craved ownership of Knightshill. Vere had just given it to him. His sisters were both older even than Vere, so could surely take care of themselves. Margaret was married, and he could not imagine Charlotte heeding a schoolboy brother bidden to take care of her.

Deeply unsettled by this abdication of someone whose life was bound up with Knightshill, and by the feeling that he had seen his brother for the last time, Val left the room to cross the old stone flags to the school's entrance. What madness had sent Vere seeking death?

As he walked slowly over the forbidden grass, Val suddenly saw an explanation of the extraordinary affair. The whole family had known Vere was unlikely to reach old age because of recurring fever and constitutional weakness. Had Dr Alderton given his brother a limited time to live? It would explain the broken engagement to someone he had clearly loved, and it would make sense of this bizarre decision. If Vere must die, what better way than to do so in true Ashleigh style? Tears sprang in his eyes. Poor old Vere had had the most rotten luck to miss out on all he should have enjoyed from life. This courageous gesture would ensure that he would be for ever inextricably linked with the hero of the family in the desert wastes around Khartoum.

Rounding the corner of the cricket pavilion Val saw the teams leaving the field to signify the end of the match. As his fellow players, plus as many schoolboy spectators as could get near him, thumped him on the back in congratulation, all manner of emotions beset him: pride over their victory, sadness at the parting from Vere, elation at being the hero of the day, and the burning fervour of being an Ashleigh. As he stepped forward to receive the cup as captain of the winning team his imagination turned him into the commander of a victorious army. *Nothing* would prevent his enlisting and going to Sandhurst next year. He would gain a commission in the cavalry somehow and follow his splendid brother at the first possible opportunity. The call to arms could not come quickly enough to satisfy the yearning Vere's sacrifice had instilled in him today.

The weather had been stormy since Vere's departure. Both facts darkened Margaret's life further. Since the night of the Waterloo Ball she had struggled to maintain a pretence where her marriage was concerned. She had slept on the couch in the nursery for the few hours remaining after the guests had departed, and had arranged for a bed to be placed in Philip's dressing room on the following day. Telling him what she had done when he returned home in the evening, Margaret had met with total silence. Into it, she had added the information that the marriage existed only on paper from that day on, and that Philip could expect no help whatever from her in work which had turned him into a violent hypocrite. His silent acceptance of her ultimatum was a relief, although she was certain guilt and remorse were so overwhelming him he needed to pay the heaviest penance to be able to face his colleagues at the mission. Keeping her family in ignorance was not too difficult because Philip had withdrawn more and more over the past three years.

The question of the children was more problematic. Philip had the indisputable right to make all decisions on their upbringing, and Margaret knew he would insist on their being absorbed into mission work. He had already begun tightening his demands on their time, as if to show her he meant to have two disciples out of three. Timothy had been denied his place at Misleydale and would not be allowed to go to Chartfield either. Yet he longed to follow in the Ashleighs' distinguished footsteps. Her son was as headstrong and determined as Val, and would surely defy his father when the time came. Would Philip resort again to violence to gain his own way?

Dogged by the desire to help her children, Margaret finally decided to ask Vere to give them secret lessons which would supplement the religious teachings which replaced all else. On the point of approaching him with a proposal she hoped would also help him through the misery he was suffering, Charlotte had come to her in the greatest distress over a letter their brother had posted in London. To Charlotte, Vere had sent his deepest affection and thanks for the many ways in which she had shared his pleasure in their surroundings. He begged her to understand and forgive him for not offering a personal farewell. *It would have been too painful,* he had written, *and you would have tried to stop me – you and Margaret, my beloved sisters.*

The letter sent to Sir Gilliard had been brief. It expressed regret over words spoken at a time of personal anguish, and asked that they be considered unsaid.

The sisters were shattered. Sir Gilliard could not hide the fact that he was moved, but his eyes shone with pride rather than sadness over what they saw as their brother's sacrifice for the sake of a girl who had broken his heart. Knightshill was quieter and sadder now, even though Val had arrived for the summer vacation with Clive Jepson. To everyone's amazement, especially Sir Gilliard's, Val spent much time studying in the library with his friend, which seemed indicative of the changes which had overtaken the old house. It was now apparent just how much Vere had enlivened the place with his constant comings and goings, his music and his enthusiastic accounts of what had occupied his days on the estate. John Morgan quietly accepted the increased responsibility but turned increasingly to Charlotte for nominal approval of his decisions. She spent much of her time riding across the estate, even in the stormy conditions they had suffered recently, and had taken over Vere's supervision of the orchids.

Margaret had no such outlet for her troubled spirits. Her sister was best left to ride out her sorrow in the meadows and lanes where she had spent so many happy hours with Vere, John Morgan now providing rock-like companionship. Recalling how Philip had once provided it at a critical period in her own life, Margaret left them well alone. Her only joys were her children, but the certainty that they were being slowly wrested from her made her seek ways of counter-balancing Philip's influence.

She cornered Val one morning when the sun made an appearance after ten days of wild weather more suited to early spring. Her young brother was looking a little heavy-eyed, she thought, so she was pleased when he announced that he and Clive were going to ride out over the hill to Leyden's Spinney.

'The pool should be full after all the rain,' he said enthusiastically. 'We're going to take a picnic and swim.'

'Be careful,' she warned, as a mother would. 'John vows that pool is bottomless. Young Willie Chance almost drowned there last summer.'

Val made a face as he brought a bowl of porridge to the breakfast table and sat beside her. 'Willie Chance was eight and hardly a competent swimmer. Credit me with more sense and strength than he had.'

'You've more strength, but I'm not so certain about your common sense. Lottie wasn't very happy last evening when you raised the subject of the

Sudan crisis at the dinner table. Grandfather went into full spate on the campaign and you know how upset she is over Vere.'

'Lottie's never happy with anything I do,' he stated, eating heartily. 'We're not very compatible. I honestly don't think it's my fault, do you? It's always been her and Vere, you and me. I can't be held responsible for Vere's actions. He's a man, entitled to arrange his own life.'

'And his death?' she asked quietly.

Her brother slowly put down his spoon, and his broad, good-looking face took on the familiar expression of defiance. 'That, too. Vorne must have known his chances of getting through with that communiqué were pretty slim, but *he* didn't hold back. If Vere feels he must follow in those footsteps, he has every right to do so.'

Margaret studied him. 'Are you still hoping to arrange *your* life by joining the cavalry?'

'Oh, yes,' he said, taking up his spoon again. 'Haven't worked out how yet, but I've a year to do it in.' He grinned. 'Clive insists that I should change my name to von Aschenheim and enlist in the Prussian Army.'

Margaret laughed. 'He's a nice boy, and his influence over you must be strong if he can tie you to a chair and make you study during your holidays.'

'It's not Clive but old Keening who's responsible for that,' Val admitted, finishing his porridge and going to the sideboard for bacon and eggs. 'He's threatened me with relegation unless I catch up. That would delay my entry to Sandhurst by twelve months.'

Margaret watched him fill his plate then carry it back to his seat. Why was he behind with his school work? Was he chasing the girls in Tetherbury? More likely, were the local girls chasing him?

'Why haven't you been working, Val?' she asked sternly.

He was no child to be chastised. Giving her a saucy glance he said, 'Stow it, Aunt Meg,' (his special name for her), 'I'm not young Tim. I'd never have won the Waycliffe Cup if I hadn't devoted my time to sport.'

'You shouldn't have.'

'Why not? I'm good at it.'

There was no answer to that so she changed the subject. 'I had intended to ask Vere to give the children some extra tuition on basic subjects. I suppose it's pointless asking you to do so if you're working hard to avoid relegation.'

'I thought old Philip had taken on the job of teaching them.'

'He hasn't the time to cover every subject as fully as he would like.'

Val's clear blue eyes challenged her. 'Too much emphasis on God?'

'Perhaps,' she heard herself say tonelessly.

A frown now accompanied the candid gaze. 'Is everything all right? I must say you've been rather quiet lately.'

'Have I?'

'I suppose it's Vere going off like that,' he reasoned, returning to his bacon and eggs. 'The whole place is quieter without him. Funny, isn't it? He was the most placid of all the Ashleighs, yet Knightshill seems to have gone to sleep since he left. It takes a fellow's absence to make one realise what a strong presence he had.'

'My word, you've grown astonishingly perceptive,' marvelled Margaret, glad he had left the subject of her relationship with Philip. 'You're right, of course. We're all so used to military bluster and bombast we didn't realise the power of gentleness.' She sighed. 'What do you think about the prospect of giving Tim and Kate a few lessons?'

His blond head nodded assent because his mouth was full. When able to speak, he said, 'I'll rope Clive in. He's brighter than I am on most subjects and a blessed genius when it comes to languages.' Pushing away his empty plate, he got to his feet. 'I'll go up and drag the lazy blighter out of bed or we'll never get started for Leyden's Spinney.' He smiled at her with warmth. 'I'd invite you to join us but we'll probably swim in the buff, and you'd be shocked.'

'You can't do that!' she cried. 'You're no longer little boys, Val.'

The smile changed to a delighted laugh. 'If you could see your expression, Aunt Meg.'

She laughed too. 'Devil! Vorne used to delight in teasing people, and I was one of his victims all too frequently. Being eight years younger, I couldn't give *him* a good hiding, but you'd better look lively, my lad. My advanced years entitle me to administer punishment.'

Scampering to the door like an overgrown puppy, he laughed even more boisterously. 'You'd have to catch me first. Your advanced years would prevent that, ma'am!'

He was going through to the hall when she sobered to call after him. 'About the lessons for Tim and Kate. There's no need to say anything to anyone else.'

Poking his head back into the room, amusement still dominated his expression. 'Right-o. Philip'll find out sooner or later, though.' With a broad wink, he added, 'He's on such good terms with the Almighty, news of his wife's activities are certain to reach him through heavenly means.'

The silly little joke upset Margaret. She sat with a cooling cup of tea and reflected that many things upset her lately. Was she becoming a real 'Aunt Meg' – a humourless, disapproving matron? The sunshine outside taunted her. It had heralded a day of seductive summer glory yet she was indoors seeing nothing but bleakness ahead. All at once, Val's vitality and youth found an answering call in her. She rose swiftly to cross to the french windows and fling them open. The scent of dew-covered roses in the morning heat wafted to her with beguiling strength. She stepped outside

77

and felt the sun on her face. Drawn by the beauty before her, she descended the steps to the rose garden where the perfume was so heady she felt giddy with it.

Roaming the path aimlessly she found the dazzle of colour so vivid it hurt her eyes and made them water. Only when the leaden weight inside her breast grew unbearable did she realise that she was crying with the pain of all she saw around her. Val had called her Aunt Meg for years. It was a sign of affection, so why should it have bothered her today? Leaving the roses she wandered on through the knot-garden to the shrubbery at the rear of the house. More scented beauty greeted her as she approached trailing jasmine, orange blossom, camellias and nodding lilies. Full summer! The tender, susceptible plants of spring had blossomed to their greatest glory. Then they would fade and die.

Putting her hand to her breast in an attempt to ease the deep ache which had settled there, she halted among the orange blossoms and closed her eyes against the sight. But their perfume taunted her even in her gilded darkness. She was like these plants. The vulnerable girl had blossomed into a woman of considerable beauty, yet she was fading long before autumn came. Neglect, lack of warmth needed to maintain growth and the cold wind of early winter were all destroying her prematurely.

The prospect was so frightening she opened her eyes and began to walk very fast through the fragrant shrubs until she broke through to the slope beyond, where they used to toboggan as children. Holding up the skirt of her yellow dress she strode up with great energy, as if proving to herself that she was only twenty-eight and in no danger of fading. Tears still edged onto her cheeks as she climbed away from the man who had fed the seed of her womanhood, brought it to fruition, then trampled on it.

Breathing hard she reached the summit and turned to look back at a scene she had known and loved all her life: the ledge on a green hillside where the grey stone splendour of Knightshill rested in a surrounding tapestry of flowers, lawns, glasshouses, meadows and dark, glossy pines. Beyond that lay the village of Dunstan St Mary, beside the bright gleam of the river which wound its way through Wiltshire and thence to the Dorset coast.

Sitting on the summer-green grass, Margaret leaned back on her arms as she thought of Vere's solution to intolerable unhappiness. Loving all this perhaps even more than she did, he had gone away knowing he was unlikely to return, because he had lost a girl whose heart had never been wholly his. Knightshill had seemed empty without the love he had believed would last for ever. So it now seemed to Margaret. Yet she could not leave. She was not a free spirit to go in search of release from the pain and humiliation of a passion grown cold. Her children were being inexorably weaned from her, yet she was trapped here by their existence. Trapped in a travesty of marriage, with the rest of her life stretching before her like a black funeral ribbon. Lucky Vere! His act of desperation was viewed as heroism by society but if she were to emulate it she would be dubbed wanton and heartless. Yet her despair was as great, her unhappiness as intolerable.

Ashleigh men traditionally left their wives to bring up their children in loneliness here, and were not condemned for it. She had felt secure because Philip was not a soldier whose duty would take him from her. How could she have known her husband would be taken whilst remaining at her side? It was lonelier than being deserted, worse than being supplanted by another woman. A mistress she could fight. God she could not. He was her enemy, so she could no longer pray for help. Vere might be going to certain death in the Sudan but, in that moment on the hill above a house which had witnessed the loss of her hopes, she envied him the desolation of the endless sands.

Chapter 5

Throughout the long journey to the Middle East Vere remained as aloof from his fellow passengers as conditions allowed. To a young man of artistic nature, who had never been allowed to undertake the Grand Tour which those of his social standing regarded as the essential complement to their education, the trip should have proved a delight. But there was no lightness in his spirits, no peace within his heart. By day, he sought whatever isolation could be found from those surrounding him. By night, he tossed restlessly in sleeping-cars or cabins.

The steamer docked at Cairo amid the noise and pandemonium usual at foreign ports, as natives vied with each other to serve passengers in any capacity which would earn a few coins. Many of those aboard were familiar with the ways of Egypt, so were not taken in by these persuasive rascals; newcomers were mostly met by residents who also knew the ropes. This left a few innocents abroad who had no welcoming expert to guide them. On these a veritable rag-tag of humanity descended.

Vere watched this pantomime from the port-hole of his cabin. Normally, it would have amused him, but his glance flicked over the scene then returned to study the curious reflection in his full-length mirror. For some while he stared at the stranger who stared back at him with angry confusion clouding clear green eyes. It was the first time he had put on these clothes since collecting them from his tailor; he had no choice now but to wear them constantly. Yet even in this starched khaki suit with a high collar, bright buttons and polished leather straps, the man in the mirror looked no more than elegantly graceful. Search the image though he might, there seemed no resemblance between it and the portraits of fierce, stalwart Ashleighs whose burning gaze challenged all visitors to Knightshill. A warrior's uniform had failed to transform him into one and only a fool would have believed it to be possible. Sighing deeply, he put on the khaki pith-helmet. His pale face looked even whiter beneath its jutting brim, his expression more desolate than before. A mockery of a soldier, this!

A sharp knock sounded on the louvred cabin door. Snatching off the helmet, Vere crossed to open it. Waiting outside was a dark-haired bull of a man whose powerful frame was encased in immaculate khaki and whose volatile face was impressively darkened by days in the desert sun. Vere's heart plummeted further. *Here* was a soldier; *this* was a potential hero. A far cry from the slender artist he had just seen in the mirror.

'Right cabin, I see,' boomed the perfect warrior with a smile as devastating as Vorne's had been. 'May I come in?'

Vere simply stood aside. The cabin seemed crowded with this man in it.

'God, it's stifling in here! No wonder you look done in,' the other commented, as he gazed around at the several trunks ready packed. 'Good man, you've had the sense to start early and steal a march on most of the passengers. I've a porter waiting outside. More trustworthy than most but still a rogue, of course. National trait.' He smiled again, blue eyes dancing with vitality as he proffered his hand. 'I'm Steadman.' Practically crushing Vere's fingers with the strength of his grip, he added, 'It's an honour and a privilege to welcome an Ashleigh to Egypt.'

'Thank you,' said Vere quietly.

'Must be a particularly emotive moment for you, arriving here to avenge your brother. Can't wait to get down to Khartoum, no doubt.'

Vere was spared an answer. Striding to the door his visitor roared two incomprehensible words. A man in off-white loose garb sidled in, bowed several times, then gave a brown-toothed grin whilst assuring them both they need have no worries when he, Jaffir, was in charge of removing their baggage from ship to shore.

'Lying hound!' countered Steadman heartily. 'If these trunks had no padlocks, your pilfering fingers would be reaching inside them the moment our backs were turned. Get them down to the carriage at number four post right away. If we're kept waiting longer than five minutes, there'll be no *baksheesh*, understand?' Turning to Vere, he asked, 'Ready to leave this floating oven, old chap?'

'Yes, quite ready.' Taking up the pith-helmet and the swagger stick which the military tailor had assured him was *de rigueur* in Egypt, Vere prepared to follow the young officer who had come to conduct him ashore.

The heat of the sun assailed him as they left the shade of the deck to walk down the gangplank onto Egyptian soil, as his brother had thirteen years before. Was it an emotive moment? Not in the way Steadman imagined, for his thoughts were only for the girl whose worship of the lost hero had defeated his own passion for her.

'Not that we'll be in Khartoum yet awhile,' said Steadman over his shoulder, reverting to a subject Vere thought had been abandoned. 'Damn slow affair, this war. When have you ever known an army to build a *railway* in order to reach the enemy?'

Still lost in further recollection of that fateful quarrel with Annabel, Vere made no comment as he clattered in heavy boots along the wooden ramp. All along the road leading to the jetty waited carriages with fringed canopies, reserved by those meeting passengers from the steamers. Reaching number four post, Steadman poked the sleeping driver of the carriage with his cane to stir him to action. Full of profuse apologies, the Egyptian tumbled to the ground and bowed his passengers aboard.

'Lazy tykes, the best of them,' commented Steadman, indicating that Vere should climb in first. He followed, causing the sprung vehicle to tilt sharply beneath his weight. Settling heavily in the seat he grunted with effort, then explained why.

'I was up at six this morning, Ashleigh, and I also missed out on my afternoon slumber while waiting for your steamer to come in. Debilitating in this climate, you know.' Letting out another grunt, he went on, 'Yes, a damn slow war. Everything's slow in this part of the world, except the propensity of the native to relieve one of cash or belongings. Be on your guard or you'll lose all you own before you're aware that it's missing. The staff at the hotel can be trusted – we none of us live in barracks because it's a hell-hole never intended to house European officers – so you can relax in your accommodation. Most of the clubs you'll frequent are scrupulous on that score, also. Keep your eyes skinned anywhere else, however.' He leaned toward Vere in confidential manner. 'One word of advice about the ladies of the town. If you've a penchant for brown skins there are one or two accommodating creatures who are safe to visit, but better by far to mingle with the European community for a week or so. You'll find invitations coming your way from the most surprising sources. *Delightfully* surprising sources, old chap,' he added with a wink.

81

Not liking the trend of the conversation, Vere turned to study the long tree-lined avenue along which all manner of traffic was toiling. As well as carriages like the one in which he was sitting there were ox-wagons, laden mules, carts hauled by mangy horses, and smart barouches. His eyes ached in the brilliant light, his head ached from the pounding heat and his heart ached with the futility of what he was doing. What a fool he had been to imagine that simply by following in his brother's footsteps he would take on a heroic mantle. A man was born to be what he was most fitted for in life, and he was an observer of field mice and wild orchids, a dreamer who could be brought to the edge of tears by an aria, a symphony or a girl so lovely she symbolised perfection. He was courting further humiliation by this ridiculous gesture.

'Didn't tread on sore toes a moment ago, did I?' asked the robust voice beside him.

He turned back to the true soldier. 'Eh?'

'Not a married man, are you?'

He recalled the conversation. 'No.'

'Even the best of us needs a little female companionship in a hole like this,' explained Steadman. 'Military men are much favoured due to their habit of popping off suddenly to inaccessible places. No troublesome entanglements, no risk of being pestered long after the excitement has waned, d'you see?' He grinned. 'There's none so endearing to the ladies as a uniformed hero about to go to war. Short, infinitely sweet . . . then adieu!'

The trunks arrived upon the shoulders of two skinny urchins who were under the command of Jaffir, the man exhausting himself with no more than the responsibility of directing his underlings. Vere swallowed the protest on his lips. These were the ways of the country. No word from him would change them. With a flood of abuse, accompanied by gesticulations with his sinewy arms, Jaffir supervised the stowing of Vere's baggage at the rear of the carriage. Cursing roundly, Steadman threw the boys some coins before thrusting what he considered to be an adequate sum into the man's eager palm. With a jerk the carriage moved off. Vere's head began to thump even more as the jolting vehicle made its way from the banks of the Nile to the centre of Cairo. He soon realised what heat truly was. Without the breeze from the river to stir the air, the streets were stifling. They were also noisy and odorous. Listless, infinitely depressed, he gazed at the passing scene while his companion talked ceaselessly.

'Funny kind of war, however one looks at it. Everything depends on the Nile. It's the only way to reach way down into the Sudan, and even then one has to consider the level of water each month. Kitchener has got himself some gun-boats, which did sterling work during the advance on

Berber. The Dervishes don't like 'em in the least,' he observed with a grunt of laughter. 'The cannon aboard can blast 'em to kingdom come as soon as they get within range, so their access to water is severely restricted. Fatal to be denied water out there, of course. Our naval boys proved pretty smart in getting their cumbersome vessels through the cataracts intact. Seen them at all, Ashleigh?'

Vere realised that he was being asked a question but had to have it repeated.

Steadman's patience was commendable. 'Been up the Nile before, have you?'

'No.'

The dark head nodded. 'Ah. Couldn't recall where the West Wilts served after the Gordon Relief Expedition was abandoned. Knew you were too young to have been out here with your renowned brother, but some regiments stayed in Egypt after we withdrew from the Sudan. Thought you might have joined yours out here for a while.'

Vere said dully, 'The West Wilts returned to their home station in 'eighty-six. I understand they're extremely frustrated at being overlooked for this punitive action.'

'Natural enough. Feelings ran high when the relief force was ordered to retire and abandon Khartoum without making some kind of attack on the Mahdi's men. Made us look a trifle feeble, to say the least.' His dazzling smile broke out. 'I daresay your brother officers in the West Wilts were damned green when you negotiated this secondment to get out here.'

'I'm not here on secondment,' Vere confessed. 'I've never been a member of the West Wilts.'

Here was a statement to confound even the garrulous Steadman. He stared at Vere in silence for almost a minute. Then he said in hushed tones, 'Good lord! The Ashleighs have always . . . well, good lord! You're actually one of *us*?' he asked incredulously.

'That's right. I suppose you could call me the new boy.'

'New boy? You mean . . . you mean you've only just joined?' came the even more incredulous query.

'Yes. I'd be glad if you could show me the ropes.'

The handsome, sun-darkened face was a picture of bemusement. 'Show you the ropes?' he echoed faintly.

'Unfortunately, I only had time for brief basic training and to arrange for the tailor to make my uniforms before I left England. I've no idea what's expected of me,' Vere explained. 'I'd be glad of a pointer or two.'

Struggling against a state remarkably similar to shock, Steadman eventually recovered enough to reach up and tap Vere's pith-helmet with his silver-topped cane.

'We *never* wear these in town, old chap. I would have mentioned it right away except that I imagined it must be a West Wilts tradition. Nor do we sport breeches and riding boots when we're not on a horse. As for that ornate sword dangling at your side, I'd advise you to keep it hidden until you reach your hotel room. They're only worn here for ceremonial occasions and it might be thought a trifle warlike if seen on an officer arriving fresh from the steamer. Don't want to upset the Gyppies do we? They won't be aware that you're a . . . a new boy.' He sighed heavily. 'Good lord!'

It was not until three days after his arrival that Vere was summoned to meet his commanding officer, Colonel Winterton. The senior man had been up to Abu Hamed and had now returned with the news that the Mahdi's successor, the Khalifia, was preparing to send out a force to recapture nearby Berber and slay the infidels to a man. This news provided Kitchener with justification for a full-scale Anglo-Egyptian advance on Omdurman, the Khalifa's capital on the banks of the Nile facing the ruins of Khartoum. Then Gordon would be finally avenged in the eyes of the world.

Colonel Winterton was elated and in very good humour to meet his new subaltern. Any grandson of General Sir Gilliard Ashleigh was a welcome addition to his regiment, particularly when it was on the brink of attacking the Dervish hordes. First-class junior officers were worth their weight in gold when waging war in conditions of incredible difficulty and danger. A youngster with a cool head, who was brimful of confidence and military swagger, could hold together a motley platoon simply by personal example in adversity. Yes, an Ashleigh was more than welcome to the regiment. That he was here to avenge his brother would add further dash and courage to the young man's performance, without doubt.

The Adjutant did not feel inclined to pass on to his colonel the information volunteered by Colin Steadman regarding their new officer. He hoped fervently that Steadman was wrong, and decided to let their commanding officer make his own judgement of Second Lieutenant Ashleigh. When the new arrival presented himself in the marble-floored outer office cooled by overhead fans, he looked unusually pale but otherwise unremarkable to Captain Moore. Many of the more aristocratic officers were inclined to be indolent in their bearing, although excellent soldiers. The Ashleigh family had an impressive background, so maybe this slender, hesitant man fell into that category. The Adjutant consoled himself with the thought as he conducted the young officer to Colonel Winterton's office.

The meeting lasted longer than normal on such occasions. Captain Moore saw it as an encouraging sign, yet Ashleigh appeared paler than ever when he left, and Colonel Winterton was uncharacteristically subdued during the subsequent discussion on the outcome. Keeping his wild thoughts to

84

himself, Captain Moore received instructions to arrange passage for Mr Ashleigh on the next steamer to Abu Hamed.

'No point in giving him a command here,' declared the grey-haired Colonel. 'He'd no sooner settle in than he'd have to go. Been ill recently, I gather, so I've given him leave until the steamer departs.' Clearing his throat noisily, he threw light on his extraordinary action. 'I promised Forrester one of my junior officers when I could spare someone. An abominable plague struck down half his regiment last month. He's now short of three subalterns. Ashleigh's just the man for him, I believe. Yes, just the man.'

Vere returned in one of the canopied carriages to the hotel overlooking elaborate gardens. He was more than ever convinced that he had made a grave error in using the family name and military connections to gain what he wanted. No longer even sure that he did want this, it was clear that Vorne's reputation, together with the deeds of gallant ancestors, had imbued Vere in other men's minds with qualities he did not possess.

Colonel Winterton had baffled him completely. Warmly welcoming at the start, the man had grown quieter and quieter during their conversation, ending it with the astonishing news that he planned to send Vere on loan to one of the advance regiments. On the point of confessing that he felt unequal to such an assignment, Vere had remained silent. He had journeyed to Egypt in an attempt to become what an Ashleigh should be, and here was the perfect opportunity to prove himself. If Winterton and the rest believed him to be another Vorne, then let that impression stand until the prevalent plague in Abu Hamed claimed him as a victim. It was reputedly felling even the strongest and toughest, so a man with a weak constitution was hardly likely to last long.

With such thoughts filling his mind as he crossed the vast marble vestibule of his hotel, he instinctively stepped aside when a figure suddenly blocked his path. The man moved to the right also, forcing Vere to halt in slight irritation over this deliberate obstruction.

'Many apologies, sir,' said the man courteously. 'I have been awaiting your return, Mr Ashleigh, waiting for a considerable time.'

Vere frowned at his accoster. An Egyptian in a quality lightweight suit could only be a member of the hotel staff. No other local resident would know him by name.

'You could have left a message at the desk for me.'

The man smiled sadly. 'Written messages have a way of never reaching their destination, I have found. Better to come in person, sir.'

'Is it so urgent that we must discuss it here? Surely you have an office which would be more private.'

'Dear me, Mr Ashleigh, I would not ask a gentleman of your standing to put himself to the trouble of visiting my premises. However, I must first discover whether or not the information I was given is correct. Are you, sir, the kinsman of Lieutenant Ashleigh, late of the West Wiltshire Regiment?'

Astonished, Vere nodded. 'Did my brother stay in this hotel?'

The man indicated a group of leather chairs presently unoccupied in a nearby alcove. 'Please, may we sit here while I explain the purpose of my visit?'

'Your *visit*? You're not a member of the hotel staff?' Vere grew annoyed. 'What is this all about?'

'I am Benjamin El Habib, owner of an establishment known only to gentlemen of discretion like your brother, sir.' He put out a hand in elegant invitation. 'Please, let us sit here for a moment.'

Acutely conscious of people glancing curiously as they passed, Vere found himself doing as the Egyptian requested. Lost in a labyrinth of conjecture on how this man came to know that a relative of Vorne's was in Egypt after all these years and to trace him to this hotel, a curious feeling arose of walking in his brother's footsteps far more literally than he had expected. It was as if that laughing, boisterous young man in a scarlet coat was beginning to reach out from the past to him.

'I haven't much time,' Vere said firmly, once they were settled in the leather chairs. 'Please explain your business as briefly as possible.'

The Egyptian gave his sad smile as he took from his pocket an envelope addressed in thick black handwriting. 'This was returned to me twelve years ago by an officer of the West Wiltshire Regiment, with the information that your honoured brother had entered paradise outside the walls of Khartoum. When I heard yesterday that Second Lieutenant Ashleigh had arrived in Cairo, I — '

'How did you hear?' he interjected crisply, feeling the past growing even nearer at the sight of that envelope.

'In this city one hears everything,' came the smooth reply. 'Sir, please believe that I would not have approached you over a trifling sum. But a man must thrive, and a gentleman like yourself would surely wish to honour the memory of his brother by settling a debt which has stood against Lieutenant Ashleigh's good name all these years. A generous man, your kinsman, sir; generous, robust, a lover of all those things which men of virile personality enjoy. When he departed so suddenly from Cairo, an oversight on his part meant that his debt remained outstanding.' Another sad smile accompanied the presentation of the envelope. 'My polite reminder reached Metemma too late. It has been a great burden all these years to know that a brave man entered paradise with this stain upon his soul, sir. I am overjoyed that you have this chance to remove it.'

In a daze, Vere slit open the envelope to read the contents. The date at the top of the note couched in courteous terms was 4 September 1884. The sum outstanding was staggering. Staring at the figures for some time, he tried to collect his thoughts. If the envelope had not been stained and evidently well travelled, judging by the many mail-office stamps upon it, he might have suspected that date. As it was, he found himself accepting the story, realising as he did that El Habib had kept it sealed, just as it had been returned to him, for all these years. Hope sprang eternal in the East, apparently.

He glanced at the olive-skinned face. 'I only arrived here three days ago. Before I can consider settling this extremely large debt I must make enquiries about the *bona fides* of your establishment, and about your personal veracity. I'm sure you'll appreciate that.'

'Of course,' said the Egyptian with grave courtesy. 'I hope you will honour me with a visit to my premises one evening. That account might suggest your brother was a loser, Mr Ashleigh. On the contrary, he was very lucky at the tables, if a little reckless. His liking for wine and the other attractions of my establishment reduced his fortunes made on the fall of the dice, and only a run of bad luck just before he left Cairo was responsible for this unfortunate situation.' El Habib rose to his feet. 'When a gentleman plays for very high stakes, his fall is the harder.'

Vere stood up, unsettled by the encounter. His family had spoken of Vorne's zest for life, his penchant for pretty women. It should not be surprising that he had patronised a discreet casino where a man could later relax with a hired companion. Many officers probably did the same. Yet that uneasy feeling of meeting up with a brother who was little less than a legend was creating a cold sensation at the back of his neck.

'I will wait to hear from you, Mr Ashleigh,' said the other, with a slight bow. 'The diversions of my establishment are naturally available to you without an introduction from another member, sir.'

He walked away through the criss-cross of men in uniform or lightweight suits, and ladies whose pale dresses trailed the ground, leaving Vere holding an envelope which had come to him across the years from those far distant sands covering the body of his brother.

Within the next three days, eight separate tradesmen sent in accounts outstanding from thirteen years ago. Vere soon realised that by accepting the first in the hotel vestibule, he had opened the floodgates for every shopkeeper to present Vorne's bills for settlement. Deeply worried by the situation, always having been meticulous in dealing with his own accounts and those of the estate, he pondered on the best course to take. Something about El Habib had impressed him; the poignancy of that much-travelled envelope had urged him to wipe that slate clean. But bills left at the reception desk for him by the unknown managers of local emporia were different. There was no way of proving or disproving these claims, and his funds would not stand payment of such large debts. If Vere had asked the advice of anyone who knew the Middle East, he would have been told to ignore the bills and to threaten to put out of business any man who persisted in bothering him. He kept his own counsel, however, and, like any country squire who had never before left England, took the problem seriously.

It was in the firm expectation of seeing yet another bill that he slit the seal of an envelope delivered to his room by the bell-boy four days later. Before he opened the folded sheet, however, he detected a much sweeter perfume than the indefinable smell of Cairo which pervaded the other communications he had received. Frowning slightly, he studied the brief note written in a delicate tracery of ink on paper.

I have returned to Cairo this morning and hasten to write to you of my delight in hearing that Vorne's brother is here. Do, I beg of you, visit me at your very earliest opportunity.

The letter was signed Floria, Contessa Pallini.

The cold sensation at the back of Vere's neck increased. What connection was there between this woman and his brother? Surely she was not also owed money by a man slaughtered so many years ago? Yet why else would she be so anxious to see him? He sighed heavily as he walked to the window to gaze out over the palms towards the wealthy district given as the address of the sender of this note. The Contessa had not enclosed a bill; neither had she accosted him in the vestibule. The note suggested a personal summons. Tapping the letter rhythmically against the palm of his hand as he thought the matter over, he told himself he would be gone in two days. This was surely one problem he could easily avoid.

With that resolution made, he sat at the desk to go through the pile of bills. A morning visit to the bank had resulted in a decision to settle just two or three, those he judged to be the most genuine. Writing the appropriate cheques he sealed them in envelopes to be delivered after the steamer had sailed. Putting a match to the remaining papers, he then caught himself hesitating to burn the perfumed note. Against his better judgement he read the words once more. Who was Contessa Pallini? If she was owed money by Vorne it suggested she had been a resident of Cairo for at least twelve or thirteen years. The scented paper teased his nostrils. He was intrigued despite an inner warning voice. His departure from Cairo was imminent. Why not burn this with the rest?

An hour later he alighted from a carriage outside an impressive pink-washed mansion with dark-green shutters, whose only concession to local architecture was the honeycombed screen running around the outside of the first floor to protect the verandas from the glare of the sun. Apart from that, it could be an Italian villa he was visiting. Standing for a moment or two at the foot of the flight of steps, he found his neck prickling with ice once more. A spectral image of that laughing handsome fellow whose portrait was toasted each year at Knightshill seemed to appear on those steps just above him. Shaking the fanciful notion from his head, Vere trod up towards the door telling himself he had been crazy to come.

A good-looking young servant in the usual white suit and fez let him in, then took Vere's card on a silver tray through a series of inter-connecting salons before finally disappearing behind double doors. Five minutes passed before he reappeared to bow and request Mr Ashleigh to follow him. To Vere's surprise the man led the way up a curving marble staircase to an open doorway on the first floor. Ushering the guest inside a cool, dim room, the servant then discreetly withdrew, closing the doors behind him.

Vere's reservations fled as he gazed around a room containing works of art worth a fortune. On the walls were a number of Impressionist paintings which he was drawn to study with the greatest appreciation. The gilt-legged Florentine furniture was further enhanced by pure cream rugs. Along the far wall stood an antique glass-fronted cabinet containing some of the finest and most exquisite glassware he had ever seen. He walked across to it eagerly and forgot all else as he took in the beauty ranged along the various shelves.

'So you are his brother,' said a voice from behind, making him jump nervously. Turning, he saw a woman dressed in a flowing cornflower-blue boudoir gown who stood only a few feet inside the room. Brown hair dressed high on her crown then cascaded in a shining fall almost to her waist, which emphasised the generous curves of bosom and hips. Amber eyes gazed almost apprehensively from an exciting face which betrayed her Italian heritage with its deep cream flawless skin. Around her neck hung a long rope of large lustrous pearls, an adornment whose beauty was worthy of its wearer. The perfume which wafted from her was that which had scented the letter. Excitement flooded Vere as he studied the incredibly sensuous attraction of a woman who would inspire any artist. In that moment, he realised he had not once thought of Annabel since receiving an envelope which had remained sealed for twelve years. Now the remembered pain of her contempt returned.

'My dear, you have no notion how relieved I am,' his hostess said in her softly accented voice, as she walked towards him. 'There is a faint family resemblance, of course, but if you had looked very much like him I should have found it too painful.' Reaching him, she added, 'Thank you for coming. I longed to see you, yet somehow dreaded the meeting. He was so . . . so very dear to me.'

To Vere's consternation her eyes glistened with tears. This spectactular woman was certainly not about to ask him for money, but an emotional confession might be equally disturbing. Vorne Ashleigh had left debts of a personal nature in Cairo, that much was already clear from her approach.

'Your note took me by surprise,' he began tentatively, unable to recover swiftly from the unexpectedness of this encounter. 'My brother was eleven years older than I. We saw very little of each other, and I knew nothing of his friends outside the family circle. If you . . . if you hope to talk of him, I'm afraid I can contribute little which would be of interest to you.'

Taking his hand, she urged him towards a brocaded sofa set beside a mosaic table. 'I can contribute a great deal which will be of interest to *you*. Come, sit here with me. We shall have coffee and I shall tell you of the man you did not know. Poor boy,' she declared, echoing Annabel with those words. 'To have had such a brother and know him only as a stranger! That is very sad.'

She rang an ornamental bell before turning to draw him down to the seat beside her. 'Vere is a romantic, poetic name. It suits you well, my dear. Pale, graceful, eyes full of dreams! You find life difficult, strewn with thorns, yes?'

He gazed back silently. This woman to whom Vorne had been so very dear was far too frank, too perceptive for him to feel at ease in her company. This entire encounter was unsettling. He was again being compared with his heroic brother and was certain to be found wanting. He longed to leave, yet the curious sensation of meeting up with the past kept him there.

'You are very young, as was he,' she said softly. 'Twenty-four. So full of life, so sure of himself, so *rascally*,' she added with a sigh. 'Vorne Ashleigh could be the devil incarnate, at times, but it was that satanic streak which made him irresistible.'

The servant brought strong black coffee which he poured into two cups of delicate French porcelain, before withdrawing as silently as he had come. The Contessa handed a cup to Vere, then sat with her back very straight in a pose as graceful as it was regal. Through the thin layer of crêpe-de-Chine beneath the lustrous pearls he could see the cleft which emphasised the fullness of her breasts. She would be a wonderfully erotic nude model for any artist's brush. He pondered the whereabouts of Pallini. He would surely not approve of his wife entertaining men alone, dressed as she was now. With a determined effort, Vere tried to get to the purpose of this meeting.

'I've already discovered that my brother was very well known in this city. Please tell me why you asked me to call on you, Contessa.'

Her eyes widened in surprise, then registered amusement. 'I wished to offer you my hospitality, of course. But you must not break my heart as that wicked boy almost did.'

Vere slowly lowered his cup to the table as he recalled something the garrulous Steadman had said to him in the carriage ride from the jetty. *Invitations from delightfully surprising sources.* This woman beside him had been Vorne's mistress!

'I'm leaving on Thursday's steamer,' he said carefully, knowing that he could never take a woman his brother had seduced. Even in passion he would doubtless not match up to the hero of Khartoum.

'Poor boy,' she said again, genuine regret in her words and expression. 'To meet so briefly, then to lose you to the desert!' Rising swiftly, she walked to the doors opening to a veranda where she stood gazing at something beyond his vision. 'I hate it. I fear it. It is like the ocean. It takes men and devours them, then flows onward as if they had never been.'

Something in her voice touched him. Beneath her outward serenity lay dark memories connected with the endless sands, he felt certain. Compulsion drove him across to her side. Far in the distance, over the miscellany of trees, domes and minarets, he could make out the tip of a pyramid. The sands began at its foot and went on to eternity. He shivered involuntarily, and she turned to him. There was now a hint of desolation in her eyes.

'Such are the great forces of nature, one either fears them or finds them inexplicably fascinating. Mountains, oceans, deserts – all are places which uplift or destroy.' In a lightning change of approach, she tucked her hand through the crook of his arm and led him up to a Monet he had admired on entering. 'I saw you studying my collection of glass when I came in. You have the air of a man who appreciates beautiful objects. What is your opinion of this, my dear?'

On firmer ground, though still disturbed by the encounter, Vere began to discuss the painting with a woman who proved as knowledgeable as he on the subject of great masters. As they moved around the room to study pictures, glass and porcelain time passed unnoticed by him. Instructed to call her Floria, Vere was drawn to her by cultural rapport. Born in Italy of wealthy parents, she had married Pallini at the age of seventeen, she revealed. Her husband had been obsessed with the treasures of ancient Egypt. On an archaeological expedition during the second year of her marriage, he had gone into the desert never to be seen again. The entire party had vanished without trace. She had been left a probable widow at eighteen. Unable to remarry until proof of her husband's death had been found, she had been persuaded to accept the protection of a hopeful suitor. It had been the greatest decision of her life for her protector had inevitably moved on, and his friend had then become her lover. Others had swiftly followed. Now, she used her reputation to her own greatest advantage.

So relaxed were they in each other's company by then, Vere heard her confess to enjoying the company of the many men who treated her with greater understanding and devotion than the husband she had known for so short a time. She went on to express her respect for Vere's knowledge of Italian art, music and literature. When she declared that he must have visited her country on many occasions in order to possess such wide knowledge of it, he found no embarrassment in telling her he had never before left England, and why.

Her amber eyes then studied him with concern. 'You are now well? You have been cured?'

'Certainly,' he lied. 'Why else would I be here?'

'But you are not a soldier, my dear, you are a man of peace,' she accused. 'Why are you doing this?'

'To avenge my brother.' It was what everyone believed so the words came easily.

With her expression clouding, she hesitated before saying gently, 'Vorne would not wish for that. He was a man who did not care for others to . . . to draw too close, you know. He lived life to the full, but he . . . ' she shrugged expressively, ' . . . he used his friends for that purpose while remaining untouched himself. Vorne Ashleigh was a flame to which we moths were helplessly drawn, knowing that we stood in danger of being burned.' Putting her hands on his upper arms she looked deep into his eyes. 'Don't allow yourself to be destroyed for his sake, I beg of you. You are the more worthy man.'

He was unable to accept that. 'My brother was a hero.'

The smile which touched her mouth held a trace of her former sadness. 'A man may be a hero in two ways: with a sword in his hand and a loud cry on his lips, or quietly with a cry in his heart.'

Her perception was too dangerous. He moved from her clasp saying he should leave. She followed him.

'Now that we understand each other so well, will you not stay, my dear?'

Knowing what she was offering, he shook his head gently. 'I have a great number of things to do before Thursday.'

'You are going up to Abu Hamed then on to Omdurman? Don't look surprised. It is all over Cairo that the British mean to annexe the Sudan at last.'

He nodded slowly. 'Yes. I imagine that's where I'll be going.'

'Poor boy!' With those reminiscent words she began to unwind the rope of gleaming pearls from around her throat. With it clasped tenderly in both hands, she looked up at him with sudden emotion. 'Vorne gave me these on the night before he left Cairo for Khartoum. The day after we learned of his death, the jeweller arrived on my doorstep demanding payment or the return of the pearls.' She smiled mistily. 'It was typical of the man I had allowed myself so foolishly to love. I could not bear to surrender them, so I paid. All these years, I have worn them as a reminder of him.' Pressing the warm necklace into his hands, she said, 'Take them. If you ever return from the desert, give them to the girl who has driven you to do this.'

Dumbfounded, he stood holding the cascade of milky pearls as she put a finger up to caress his mouth with a light touch.

'Quietly, with a cry in your heart,' she said softly. 'It is so very obvious, Vere Ashleigh.'

The steamer pulled away from the jetty amid the usual noise and excitement. A number of military men were aboard, all keen to reach the advance force at Abu Hamed. Mostly, they stood together talking of the great battle which must lie ahead of them. One officer remained in the stern alone, watching the city growing smaller on the horizon. The numbness which had ruled him since leaving England was melting. He wished now that he had seen the wonders men through the ages had travelled here to view – wished that awareness had returned sooner. Floria Pallini had reawakened him to cultural beauty too late. Regret flowed through him. He would not return to Cairo.

For some time he remained alone, watching the brown waters of the Nile eddying past him as the paddles churned the depths with throbbing power. In Cairo, he had learned some unsettling facts about the man he had come here to emulate. Vorne Ashleigh had been a reckless gambler, an uncommitted friend and a careless lover. But he had also been a man not easily forgotten by those he had encountered. Following in such footsteps was proving more revealing than he had imagined. Perhaps he would learn more in Abu Hamed than how to become a soldier and a hopeful hero.

Chapter 6

The tented camp at Abu Hamed housed a military community with none of the comforts or entertainments of Cairo. Spread along the banks of the river within firing range of the protective gun-boats, the row upon row of pointed white tents were hardly a welcoming sight to Vere as the steamer came slowly alongside the jetty serving the town which had been stormed two weeks earlier. His heart sank. The meeting with Colonel Winterton in

Cairo had been awkward enough; here, among battle-hardened men, he would be excruciatingly inadequate. Yet again he wondered what had possessed him to take this crazy decision. Far from showing he could emulate the Ashleighs, it would merely highlight the fact that it was impossible.

As he walked diffidently along the broad avenue between tents, followed by several native porters humping his trunks which looked all too obviously new, Vere felt as conspicuous as a poodle amid massive-shouldered aggressive bulldogs. Starched khaki and a pith-helmet with an extended neck shield were universal wear for the British troops, while the black Sudanese and brown Egyptians sported the fez with their uniforms. To the rear of the camp were the horse lines and compounds containing camels. The smell arising from this area hung over the whole camp to add to that of the Nile and the nearby walled town. The heat of early afternoon only served to intensify the heaviness of the atmosphere. A few soldiers were moving around the tents and these meticulously saluted Vere, obliging him to return the courtesy. This he did by touching the peak of his helmet with the stick he carried, because he felt unequal to the curious business of snapping his hand up to the region of his right eye then snapping it back to his side. Military antics did not come naturally to an artist, he had discovered.

He had been told by a colossus of a corporal that he would find Major Forrester's adjutant at the end of a line of administrative tents. He was sweating profusely by the time he neared one with the canvas sides looped up to allow free passage of whatever air there was. The occupant was evidently in a bad mood. His censure of a hapless culprit could be heard some yards away. Vere was briefly reminded of his grandfather on hearing the well-bred roar of authority.

'Get out of my sight, damn you! We have enough poisonous creatures in this God-forsaken hole. I don't need you to add to their number.'

As Vere drew level, a small white-robed Sudanese hurtled into his path, salaamed as he scurried backwards, then raced off towards the river. Vere frowned as he dipped his head beneath the canvas to enter. A sweating, middle-aged man with a red face bedecked with an equally red moustache and matching bushy eyebrows gave him belligerent head-to-toe scrutiny.

'Well, what do *you* want?' he challenged.

Unused to such treatment, Vere bristled. 'A little civility, for a start.'

The other's jaw dropped open, his eyes widening as if the two actions were somehow linked. 'You *insufferable* pip-squeak! Who the hell do you imagine you're speaking to?'

'Not Captain Ford, I imagine,' Vere replied crisply. 'I was told the officers of the regiment I've come to join are extremely affable and undoubted gentlemen. I must be in the wrong tent.'

Driven to his feet, which revealed him to be several inches shorter than Vere, the officer's wrath vied with curiosity. 'Where've you come from?'

'The steamer.'

'From Cairo?'

'Colonel Winterton sent me on attachment.'

'Good God, we didn't expect anyone this swiftly.' Wrath triumphed over curiosity. 'It's obvious why. I always knew Winterton was a sly old fox. He'd never send anyone of any value to himself when he hopes to see action shortly. If we're driven to taking in subalterns like you, we'd be better off under strength.'

'We?' queried Vere, disliking this man more by the minute. 'You really *are* Captain Ford?'

'I am – and you'll do well to abandon that manner before you regret it. We don't suffer prigs or upstarts in this regiment, and you appear to be both. What's your name?'

'Ashleigh.' Greatly goaded, he added, 'My brother was killed out here in 'eighty-six while trying to reach the Relief Force from Khartoum.'

'Vorne Ashleigh of the West Wilts?' the man queried slowly. 'You're *his* brother?'

'That's right.'

Ford's expression changed dramatically. 'My God, Winterton has sent us one of his best men.'

'I'd like to settle in,' Vere told him hastily.

'Yes . . . yes,' murmured Ford, clearly thrown by the discovery that a hero's brother had turned up without warning. 'Our officers' lines are the fourth row of tents to the south. I'll arrange for a groom to see to your horses.'

'I have no horses.'

'No horses? But . . . I mean . . . *no horses?*'

'I came directly from England and I was only in Cairo a week.'

'You came on direct attachment from the West Wilts. Very understandable, Ashleigh. Want to be there when we enter Khartoum, of course.' When Vere wisely remained silent, he went on, 'No problem about quarters. Carter and Moynihan are on their way to the hospital in Cairo and unlikely to need theirs for a month or more. Choose whichever of the unoccupied tents you fancy. I'll tell Major Forrester you've arrived when he gets back from Berber tonight, and I'll detail a batman to unpack your gear.' The shiny red face was startlingly transformed by a smile as Ford thrust out his hand. 'We're delighted to have you with us, Ashleigh.'

After momentary hesitation Vere shook his hand, but said nothing due to nagging regret over using Vorne's reputation so blatantly. If this objectionable man had not annoyed him so much he never would have.

Although it had eased the situation with amazing speed, the news would soon spread and the inevitable disappointment in him would be correspondingly speedy.

With the two porters trailing behind him he sought the empty tents he had been offered and found one of the two right at the end of the row Ford had mentioned. Telling the porters to put his trunks inside it, he then paid them off far too handsomely, if their expressions of disbelief were anything to go by. It was stifling under the canvas so he began fastening the sides back as Ford had done. While engaged in this he grew aware of someone watching him. His neighbour was lying on a camp bed, peering from beneath canvas which he had raised with one hand.

'I wouldn't advise that. You'll have everything covered in sand in no time at all.'

Vere's hand stilled.

'Besides, small urchins from the village will gather for the entertainment of watching your every move. We all avoid being at the end of the lines if we can. It's almost impossible to prevent pilfering. The little beggars nip in and out so fast they're seldom caught.' The face still indistinct in the shadows turned towards Vere's brand new trunks. 'Haven't brought anything of value with you, I hope.'

He had brought *everything* with him. Only the rope of pearls had been left behind. The bank had instructions to return them to the Contessa on his death. After Ford's belligerent attitude this man's cheerful pessimism increased Vere's sense of being a disastrous misfit. No one had told him what to expect here. He realised too late that he should have left a great deal of his baggage at the hotel in Cairo.

'Come to join us for a while, have you?'

Startled from his thoughts, Vere turned to see that his neighbour was now standing just outside the entrance of the next tent. He was a little shorter than Vere, with dark, tightly curling hair and lively eyes. Deeply browned by the sun he presented the relaxed, solid image of a man in his true element as he stood nonchalantly in shirt and breeches sizing Vere up.

'Yes.'

'Poor devil!' The man grinned. 'Someone in Cairo had it in for you, that's plain.' Closing his eyes in mock ecstasy, he added, 'Beautiful women, five-course meals, chilled wine, fans to cool the air, orchestras playing softly, fountains in the courtyards and, best of all, *comfortable beds.*' His eyes opened again. 'What did you do to earn the punishment of being sent here?'

Warming unexpectedly to this approach, Vere said frankly, 'I arrived from England just at the time Colonel Winterton had promised to send

96

a subaltern to replace some of yours who were ill. It must have seemed logical to send me on instead of one of his regular officers.'

'Poor devil!' the other said again with a sympathetic smile. 'Straight from England to Abu Hamed. Some introduction to the Middle East!' He paused before adding, 'Look, it'll be a while before your batman arrives. Come in out of the sun and have a drink while we get acquainted. I can probably put you wise on the situation here so that you'll feel less of a fish out of water.'

Even that was an understatement of how he presently felt so Vere was happy to accept the man's offer of hospitality. Once inside a tent fitted out with all manner of rough conveniences his would not have, he was invited to make himself at home. Sitting on a folding canvas chair, Vere took off his helmet and unbuttoned the starched tunic thankfully. His host turned from his search in a small lockable cabinet and proffered a glass containing a stiff brandy and soda.

'I'm Ross Majors, by the way.'

Vere took the drink. 'Thanks. I'm Vere Ashleigh.'

'Not one of the . . . no, can't be. They're all in the West Wilts.'

Knowing he would have to confess, Vere shook his head. 'Not this one.'

'You mean . . . '

'I'm Vorne Ashleigh's brother.'

A whistle through his teeth expressed the other's reaction to that news, but some infallible instinct, fortified by a gulp of the brandy and soda, led Vere to confide the truth.

'I'm afraid I'm not another hero,' he finished ruefully. 'I'm not even a real soldier. I've no idea what's expected of me here.'

Ross Majors' square brown face took on a thunderstruck expression as he sat on the bed with his drink untouched, watching as Vere downed his in several more gulps. 'How the devil did you manage to get a commission and join a regiment out here?'

With his head starting to swim, Vere said, 'A name like mine will get a man more or less anything he wants in military circles. I used it quite ruthlessly to persuade those in high office to sweep aside formalities and rush the whole thing through. I enrolled in the militia one day, began a month's training the next. My grandfather's political and military connections turned blind eyes, waived certain procedures and moved men with unaccustomed alacrity to ensure that I achieved in a very short time what normally takes a great deal longer. It seems the publicity value of having a hero's brother rushing to the colours to avenge a horrendous murder outside Khartoum was too good to forgo. The slow progress of the campaign out here is not to the British public's taste, so any incident which suggests that we are fully in control is eagerly exploited.'

97

After a pause, Ross said, 'You must have had damn strong reasons for doing it.'

'Yes. But I didn't take into account that the mere mention of the Ashleigh name, especially in this part of the world, instils in everyone the belief that I'm a crack officer. It was first made apparent to me when I came upon a mammoth named Steadman, who met me off the ship at Cairo. Your Captain Ford has just made the same mistake in thinking the regiment fortunate in welcoming an Ashleigh to its ranks.'

Still looking thunderstruck, Ross said, 'A crack officer would hardly be only a second lieutenant at your age. Have you really had no more than a short spell of training with the militia?'

'That's all. A man with my background should have absorbed a great deal of military knowledge, but I confess to perpetually closing my ears to anything martial in the belief that it was acutely melodramatic.' He sighed. 'In theory, the notion of donning uniform and sailing for the Sudan was splendid. In practice, I think . . . '

'Even in theory it was madness,' pronounced the man who had somehow become his friend in a matter of minutes. 'You're short on stamina, ignorant of military leadership and lacking in sufficient guile to survive long in this exacting profession.' Taking Vere's glass to refill it, he then said, 'There are two types of officer, you know. Excellent soldiers, and those who bluff everyone into thinking they are. You will have to join the latter category. Being called Ashleigh gives you a head start in *your* bluff.' He refilled his own glass. 'What did you do before this?'

'Do?' The heat and the brandy were affecting his wits.

'What was your profession?'

'I ran the estate, and I suppose you could call me an amateur artist. I paint and sketch rather well.'

Ross burst into loud gusty laughter. 'Oh, my lord, this gets more and more unbelievable. I now understand *exactly* why Winterton sent you to us. The old devil! A Pre-Raphaelite bearing a sword. How rich. How bloody rich!'

Having downed the second drink Vere caught himself laughing, too. He had never viewed what he was doing as humorous. Now it seemed to be exquisitely so. 'You should have seen the range of expressions which crossed Ford's face. He began by calling me an insufferable pip-squeak and ended by saying how delighted he was to welcome me to the regiment. That word "Ashleigh" worked like magic.'

Ross sobered as he sank back on the pillow of his canvas bed. 'We have to keep that magic intact with concentrated bluff, until you've learned enough to maintain their belief in your excellence with true military efficiency. I'll teach you the ropes concerning command of a platoon, and keep an eye on your comings and goings. If they give you Carter's men, Sergeant Withers will really command them whilst treating you with fatherly respect. But Moynihan's platoon are a tough bunch led by a sergeant who loses no chance of putting officers in awkward positions. Lord help you if Forrester hands you over to *them*.'

'Why is a major commanding a regiment?' Vere asked, not a whit worried about being given Moynihan's platoon due to blissful ignorance of the pitfalls of junior command.

'It's only temporary. Colonel Meers is in Alexandria on an official mission. Reggie Forrester is a decent fellow normally, but he's trying to cope with too much here as well as riding back and forth to check the small advance force already at Berber. Only just back on his feet after a dose of fever, he's chasing his own tail in his attempts to make his mark in Meers' absence. Leaves him somewhat short-tempered. We're used to him, but I'll stick close to your side when you meet him in Mess tonight so that you won't ruin the bluff.'

Feeling very strongly that he would also like to stretch out on a bed right now, Vere studied his reclining neighbour for some moments. Then he asked, 'Why are you prepared to do all this for a perfect stranger?'

Ross turned his head to answer. 'Fellow officer, and all that. Might want you to save my life one day soon.' His grin then softened the seriousness of his words. 'Besides, your arrival promises an element of relief from boredom. There's nothing else to do in Abu Hamed other than sleep or go down with fever. I've done the latter and recovered. Now, if you'll excuse me, I'll indulge in the first. Chin, chin, Ashleigh.' He closed his eyes, leaving his visitor to depart rather unsteadily.

In his own tent Vere found a soldier of around his brother's age unpacking various items from the smart trunks. Although tall, the young lad did not possess the powerful physique Val had cultivated. Neither had he the air of assured determination characteristic of that distant schoolboy. Even so, Vere felt drawn to the batman who announced himself dolefully as Private Perkins.

Smiling encouragement, Vere said, 'My name is Ashleigh.'

'I knows that, sir, and I begs Captain Ford as to not give me this duty.'

'You didn't want to serve me?'

The thin pale face twitched nervously while eyes the same colour as the Nile studied the tent rather than Vere. 'No, sir.'

'I see.' Nonplussed, he said, 'I'm sure I can persuade Captain Ford to give you some other duty. No man should be made to do something completely onerous to him.'

The eyes swung to confront him. 'It's not owner – . . . what you said, sir. No, not that.'

'Then what?'

The corners of the thin mouth turned down miserably. 'A gentleman like yourself, sir, should 'ave the best.'

'And Private Perkins is not?'

The lad shook his head. 'Mr Moynihan give me what-for quite reg'ler. Says I'm no better than them blackies what come up from the town.'

'Two of them carried these heavy trunks of mine all the way from the steamer this afternoon and did the job to my complete satisfaction. I see no reason why you shouldn't do the same, Perkins,' Vere told him forming a swift opinion of the absent Moynihan. 'Suppose we give it a try for a day or two.' Seeing the young soldier's doubt, he added, 'Would you consider the proposal?'

Frowning in perplexity, Perkins said, 'I can't *consider* nothin', Mr Ashleigh. I gets me orders.'

'Ah. In that case, I order you to forget all this nonsense and do my bidding. I have a notion we shall get on extremely well.'

Perkins did not appear to share that confidence but understood direct commands. He nodded in resignation.

'I'd like you to take yourself off and leave me to have a nap. Come back in one hour to make tea. I like it strong with plenty of sugar. I also like two biscuits with it. You'll find a tin of them in that other trunk. After the tea I shall require water to wash myself. Do you know where to acquire it?'

'Oh, yes, sir, *corse* I do.'

'Good. While I'm endeavouring to take some kind of bath, you can remove from my baggage those things I shall need here. I shall send the remainder back to Cairo on the next steamer.' He smiled at the serious face regarding him. 'I rushed out here from England with no time to organise things properly.'

''Spect they'll send you into Khartoum first, as so they should.'

Vere let that pass. 'How old are you, Perkins?'

'Jest a bit past eighteen.'

'I have a brother of that age at school in England. He'd give anything to be out here as you are.' He sat on the side of the bed which Perkins had already set up. 'Cut along now and let me rest.'

Before he drifted into sleep Vere had time to reflect that he had just come across two examples of military men who were vastly different from the old warriors who visited Knightshill. Ross Majors seemed eminently sensible about his chosen profession and the members of it. He also appeared to have become a potential friend, something Vere believed would never be possible between himself and an army officer. Perkins was so much the complete opposite of Val, it seemed providential that the unpleasant Moynihan should be too ill to need his batman. Here was a boy in uniform who seemed as unsuited to the life of a soldier as the officer he had been detailed to serve. One more thing he contemplated before surrendering to slumber. He had just downed two brandies, something strictly forbidden by Dr Alderton. He had enjoyed them – had enjoyed drinking companionably with Ross Majors. As he was unlikely to survive long in this hot, disease-ridden country, it no longer mattered if he flouted the restrictions he had suffered for years in order to live as long as possible. From now on he could do exactly as he pleased. A tremendous feeling of freedom washed over him as his eyelids closed in sleep.

The Officers' Mess was a make-shift affair in a large tent. The moment Vere entered with Ross he was surrounded by men eager to shake his hand and discuss the campaign. A year had already passed since the punitive expedition was launched, and Khartoum was still more than two hundred river miles away. Vere was asked for his opinion on this sloth-like advance. As he had none he looked to his new friend for help.

'It's the same as ours, only more so,' said Ross. 'He can't wait to march into Khartoum and raise the flag.' He called for the steward. 'What'll you have, Ashleigh?'

'I think I should sign for this,' Vere said, wondering if he should offer drinks all round.

'Rule of the regiment that no man pays for liquor on his first night in Mess,' Ross told him.

Vere was bombarded with questions concerning his own regiment in Cairo. On hearing that he had been with them a mere week, he was then asked about the West Wilts. On firmer ground, he found he was able to recount word for word some of the anecdotes told around the dining table at Knightshill. His listeners found them hilarious, to his own mystification, so he was the centre of a ring of boisterous young men in thick scarlet mess jackets and strapped blue trousers when Captain Ford pushed through them to announce that their acting CO was on his way. A general stiffening of posture served as respectful acknowledgement from subordinates, who chorused a return greeting when Forrester said, 'Good evening, gentlemen.'

Vere experienced surprise as he studied the new arrival. Tall, muscularly graceful, with hair as pale as the sands around them, Reginald Forrester was one of the most beautiful men Vere had ever seen. The bone structure of his face was Grecian. His eyes were an arresting, dreamy blue-green as they glanced round the tent until meeting Vere's across the space of several yards.

'He's superb,' Vere murmured to his companion. 'I wonder if anyone has ever done a nude study of him.'

'Thank your lucky stars *I* happened to be the one to overhear that,' said Ross quietly. 'Anyone else would gain a very dangerous impression.'

Vere glanced round. 'What?'

'Subalterns should *never* voice a desire to see their commanding officer naked!'

'But he's the answer to an artist's prayer,' Vere explained. 'He shouldn't be doing this. Any man can be a soldier. What a waste.'

Ross sighed heavily. 'Your bluff won't last beyond an hour if you think along those lines.'

'I'm an artist. I can't prevent such thoughts.'

'Then don't put them into words, for God's sake,' came the plea as Forrester began crossing toward them. 'Let me do the talking.'

Forrester's smile was worthy of him and increased Vere's sense of artistic admiration of the man.

'Ashleigh, I speak for the entire regiment when I say we are very aware of our good fortune in having you on attachment to us,' the god-like creature said warmly. 'Colonel Winterton knew a moment of rare generosity in sending you straight up here, although Abu Hamed is hardly salubrious, especially to a man straight from England. You won't care for that, I know. Anxious to get up to Khartoum, of course. Well, progress might be slow but there'll be no turning back until we reach the city.' The charming smile returned. 'If we're lucky enough to have you still with us then, I promise to see that you're one of the first to enter.'

'That's very good of you,' Vere murmured, appreciating the misplaced generosity.

Forrester drank gracefully from the glass Captain Ford handed him, then asked, 'How's Peter Carlton-Jay?'

'You know my cousin?' queried Vere in surprise.

'From many years back. He once hoped to marry my sister.'

'If your sister is as beautiful as I imagine she must be, I'm not surprised Peter was unsuccessful. He's something of a silly ass, like most of my military cousins,' he confessed.

The smile faded. 'All in the West Wilts, aren't they? A crack regiment.'

'Great pranksters, the West Wilts, sir,' put in Ross smoothly. 'Ashleigh has been telling us the most hilarious anecdotes. They fight hard and play hard. Famous for it.'

Forrester nodded. 'See what you mean, Ashleigh. I once had the privilege of meeting your grandfather. Very impressive man; difficult to forget. It was in 'eighty-six. He was still very cut up by the death of your brother. Found it difficult to come to terms with a tragedy which robbed him of his heir.' Taking another graceful sip from his glass, he added, 'Your surviving brother's something of an invalid, I understand.'

As Vere opened his mouth to correct the statement, Ross exclaimed, 'Sergeant Rutter is trying to catch your eye, sir. Dinner is served, I believe.'

'Ah, good.' Forrester turned away to signal his readiness to eat. 'Shall we take our places, gentlemen? After the rations served up to me in Berber even *consommé Abu Hamed* followed by *Boeuf au Nil* will taste like Ambrosia.'

General laughter greeted this local joke and the officers took their seats at the long table covered in a starched white cloth, set with silver and crystal. Ross grabbed Vere's arm to ensure that they remained together, and placed him strategically at the end of the table so that no one sat on his right.

With a plate of soup before him Vere studied his new friend. 'We can't keep this up the whole evening.'

'I realise that,' said Ross heavily. 'You'll have to get drunk as quickly as possible. That's something they'll expect of an Ashleigh. Meanwhile, I'll work out the best way of making you into an acceptable officer.'

'That's impossible.'

'Start drinking,' commanded Ross,' and stop looking at Reggie Forrester in a manner which could be disastrously misconstrued.'

When Perkins woke him Vere felt decidedly ill. His head was full of cobblers hammering tiny nails into his skull, and his stomach ached. The white glare of the canvas hurt his eyes, so he shut them again.

'Go away,' he groaned. 'I shall stay here for a while.'

'There's tent inspection afore breakfast, sir, and it's already seven. I got your washing water ready, and the shaving things laid out. There's a nice cup o' tea beside you. I hopes that's the way you likes it.'

'What I like is to be left alone. Just go away.'

'Do as he says, Perkins,' instructed a hearty voice. 'Come back when we leave for tent inspection.'

Vere opened one eye and saw a man in immaculate khaki standing beside the bed. His face looked freshly shaven and glowing with energy. His thick black curls had been damped into place, and his expression was one of resignation.

'Haven't you been drunk before?' Ross asked.

'Doctor's orders restrict me to a small glass of wine and one of port. You can't get drunk on that.' He closed the eye again.

'In that case, why aren't you dying?' came the blunt question.

'I am. Believe me, I am,' claimed Vere.

'Rot! You're suffering no worse than any man after his first night with the regiment. Get on your feet. Tent inspection in twenty minutes and I'm sorry to tell you you've been allocated Moynihan's platoon. Sergeant Box will be out to test you to the limit. If he finds you wanting he'll never give you a moment's peace of mind.'

Through the fur lining his mouth, Vere said, 'Of course he'll find me wanting – more than any officer he's ever come across.'

'But your name happens to be Ashleigh, and therein lies your greatest chance of pulling off this bluff.'

Vere opened both eyes and winced as he asked, 'How?'

Ross held out the cooling cup of tea. 'Being the brother of a man who performed an act of great heroism in this area gives you certain advantages. We lesser mortals have to work hard at being competent officers, but men in your position are allowed to be arrogant to the point of eccentricity. It's almost expected of you. You will be forgiven practically anything because of that name of yours.' He thrust forward the cup. 'Come on, drink this.'

'My stomach would revolt.'

'That's the idea. You'll feel better once that's happened.'

The next fifteen minutes were little short of purgatory, but by the end of them Vere was clean, freshly shaven and dressed in the uniform he still found so alien. Ross then offered him a glass containing a small amount of a cloudy white mixture.

'My own form of pick-me-up. Drink it!'

While Vere obeyed, Ross advised on how best to deal with Sergeant Box. 'He is expecting you to be a top-rate officer, cool, competent and very conscious of your own consequence. You told me yesterday you're fond of opera and have advised on set designs for theatrical productions, so you must know a bit about acting. Get out there and *act*, man. Treat Box to a performance which will fool him into believing you to be another hero in the making.' Seeing Vere's doubtful expression, he added urgently, 'You reversed old Ford's attitude very swiftly yesterday. Do the same thing again. Make the inspection as if the whole business is a tiresome bore and treat Box to a few languid responses designed to put him in his place. If you're faced with anything you can't cope with give the man a charming smile and say, "Carry on, Sergeant, I have every confidence in you." He'll be flattered and you'll be off the hook.' Ross picked up his own helmet as a bugle was heard nearby. 'That's the call to prepare for inspection. Come on.'

Vere donned the heavy helmet in resignation. Walking with Ross along the sand liberally sprinkled with tufts of coarse grass, he asked himself again what an artist was doing here. He was of no use to these people and the sooner they realised it, the better. Ross had even spoken yesterday of possibly relying on him for his life. Vere Ashleigh could do little to save his own, much less that of any other man in battle. They had a right to be warned.

'Here are your platoon's tents,' Ross said quietly. 'That's Box waiting for you by the first one. Go to it – and remember, you're an Ashleigh.'

Vere hesitated as Ross walked on, but those last words touched him in a way they never had before. He had come here to play the part everyone wished him to play. He had heedlessly donned the costume worn by the hero of the piece, so he surely owed his audience a performance. He definitely owed his family his best effort. If he could never equal their glorious endeavours, he could do as much as possible to avoid casting the shadow of failure over them.

Treading down the broad path between two rows of tents, he fought the pounding in his head while recalling what Ross had told him to do. Reaching Sergeant Box he halted and touched the peak of his helmet with his cane in acknowledgement of the NCO's smart salute. Unbidden came the amusing thought that the name suited its bearer very well. On legs thick enough to bear any weight, the Sergeant's torso was as broad as it was long, a rigid military pose squaring the outline encased in immaculate khaki. A bushy dark moustache and fierce protruding eyes completed the image of a man reputed to dislike weakness in those of higher rank. Vere was not in the least intimidated by him. The finer agonies of insecurity suffered by excessively keen subalterns were unknown to this Pre-Raphaelite with a sword.

In the manner he always used towards tenants and employees, Vere smiled and said, 'Good morning. How are things with you?'

Box goggled. 'I beg your pardon, sir?'

'Have you any particular problems?'

'Er . . . problems?'

It was clearly the wrong approach. 'My name is Ashleigh, by the way.'

'Oh, yes, sir, I was informed that you had taken over from Mr Moynihan, in a temporary capacity. May I take the liberty of welcoming you to this regiment? I think you'll find it definitely on a par with the West Wilts, sir.'

Remembering Ross's advice, he merely nodded. 'I have every confidence in your judgement.'

Box was not certain how to respond, so Vere suggested they begin the inspection. There was nothing to it. All he had to do was enter each tent, which housed six men, glance at the items set out on each palliasse, note the general tidiness and ensure that the rifles were clean and in working order. While he did this the occupants of the tent stood to rigid attention gazing at some point several inches above Vere's shoulders. He bade them good morning on entering and murmured that everything was satisfactory as he left. The whole business was taking no time at all. However, in the last tent but one there was a noticeable difference. Five of the mattresses bore kit laid out in perfect order. On the sixth was an untidy pile which suggested it had all been dumped there only a few moments ago.

'Whatever has happened here?' he exclaimed, pointing with his cane at the muddle.

'*Baxter!*'

Vere jumped as Sergeant Box unexpectedly roared the name right beside his ear. A boy stepped from the line of men. He was white-faced and had clearly been in tears not long ago. To Vere's consternation the young lad was shaking with fear. The tough characters who shared the tent stared innocently at that abstract spot on the canvas roof. It was all too plain what had happened. On the verge of acting instinctively, Vere hesitated. He had never attended school and had only managed two months at Oxford before illness had overtaken him once more, but he had heard Val's tales of ragging which sometimes reached the point of cruelty when the victim was particularly weak or sensitive. He had also heard of similar instances in military ranks. One fact had impressed itself upon him. To sympathise or to attempt to help only worsened the plight of those who suffered.

To give himself time to think, Vere stepped over to the boy. 'What's your explanation for this?'

The boy looked ready to faint. Vere was appalled. How could a trivial thing like this make anyone so dreadfully afraid? What would happen when the boy faced his enemies if he was terrified of his friends?

'*Answer the officer!*' roared Sergeant Box.

'None, sir,' stuttered Baxter hoarsely.

'Perhaps I can suggest one,' said Vere with a smile. 'When your friends here overturned your mattress on hearing me enter the neighbouring tent, there was insufficient time for you to set all your things out neatly again.'

The boy said nothing and the other five still stared innocently ahead.

'Well, I'm sure it won't happen again,' he said, and turned away.

Box stopped him outside, squaring his chest until the buttons on his tunic were ready to pop off. 'You didn't inspect the rifles, Mr Ashleigh.'

'It was pointless. They're certain to have done something to his,' Vere told him, loudly enough to be heard by those inside.

'But we're on stand-by here, sir,' argued the other, getting into his reputed stride. 'If we're attacked and those rifles are not in perfect order . . . '

'The men trying to fire them will be killed, Sergeant. By their own hand, not that of the Dervishes. The choice is theirs. If they prefer to play games rather than keep their rifles at the ready, that's their affair.'

'I beg your pardon, sir, but it's the affair of the whole regiment,' Box claimed in superior tones, his eyes bulging even further. 'Each man of us relies on the other.'

'Tell that to them, not me,' said Vere calmly.

'Does that mean you don't intend to issue no reprimands; *nothing*?'

'I hope they've just overheard me indicate what silly fools they all are. If they continue to be while they're on stand-by, they'll meet the fate they deserve. They don't need a reprimand, just a grain more sense,' he concluded. 'Now, shall we see this last tent?'

Everything was in order and they were soon outside with the inspection completed. Aware of the Sergeant's new hostility, Vere caught himself viewing the attitude with impatience. It increased when Box announced that

106

he would have to mention Baxter's kit in his written report, which Vere would have to sign.

'What do you wish me to enter in the column provided for noting officers' actions, sir?' he asked with aggressive pointedness.

Anxious to get away and ease his throbbing head, Vere said, 'You can only enter *nil*. When I sign it, I'll add a note to the effect that I'm disgusted to see a young lad reduced to shivering terror over something so trivial. Is this *really* what an army does when going to war?'

Box's jaw dropped open in disbelief, but Vere was well into his theme. 'Respect is not born of fear, you know . . . and when men are suffering – even dying – in order to reach Khartoum and restore our prestige, I find it ludicrous to make a fuss because a poor devil's belongings were thrown in a heap this morning. *There are more things in heaven and earth,* man.' Realising too late that he should have concluded by telling this experienced warrior to carry on because he had every confidence in him, Vere heeded Ross's other observation on eccentricity being allowed the brother of a hero. 'Do you read Shakespeare, Sergeant? He has much to say which is worth heeding. Well, I'm for breakfast now.' Touching his helmet once more with his cane, he walked off as fast as the cobblers in his head would allow him to.

Perkins turned in astonishment when Vere entered. 'Lor', sir, you've finished quick! Mr Moynihan took a good old time with tent inspection, and none of the others is back yet.'

'None of the others has a head like mine,' Vere told him mournfully. 'Nor a mouth as dry. Rustle me up another cup of tea, there's a good lad.'

'There's breakfast in the Mess in five minutes,' Perkins told him.

'I can't face that.'

'They all says that, sir, but they manages it all right. My ma always had it that a belly wot's been awash with ale needs something solid to settle it.' Aware that he had spoken without thinking, the boy hastened to add, 'She was talking about my pa and his mates, a 'corse.'

Vere sat on the bed and watched the lad preparing tea with the spirit kettle. 'Do you miss them, Perkins?'

'Not so much now as at first.'

'You get letters from home?'

The thin face glanced his way. It was tinged with a red flush. 'They can't read nor write, sir.'

'What about you?'

'Not much,' came the low admission.

This seemed a tragedy. 'I could teach you to read well enough to absorb most books. There's a whole wealth of knowledge contained in them which you are being denied. Opening that world to men is surely more important than obliging them to lay out their possessions each day for no apparent purpose.'

Perkins busied himself with the tea and made no reply. Vere studied him with curiosity. There could hardly be a boy more the opposite of Val than this one. 'Do you like this life?' he asked eventually.

Perkins came over to him with the tea. 'It's as good as any, Pa says.'

'What do *you* say?'

He hesitated. 'It gets lonely.'

'*Lonely?* In a large regiment?'

'You can be more lonely with lots around you than in an empty field, sir. In a field there's no one *can* talk to you. Here there is, and if as they don't, it seems worse.'

Vere smiled. 'You're a philosopher, Perkins.'

'Well, I'm sorry, Mr Ashleigh, but that's how I thinks,' said the lad, having no idea what a philosopher was. 'I told you at the start you needs someone better'n me to look after you.'

'That's probably true, but I'm quite happy with the arrangement so far. We agreed on a trial of two or three days' duration, I believe.'

Perkins' long face grew apprehensive. 'I can't *agree* to nothing, sir. I gets me orders.'

'What if you receive orders to go into battle?'

'It might come to that, Mr Moynihan says, after they took this place.'

'You'd go, if ordered?'

'*Corse,*' Perkins said, surprised at being asked such a question. 'I'm as much a soldier as all the others.'

'You wouldn't feel afraid?'

'Well, I might . . . but I'd still go. They'd expect it of me.'

'Yes, yes,' mused Vere. 'They always expect it of one.'

Ross burst in without ceremony to confront him. 'Well?'

'I survived, as you see. Will you join me?' He held aloft his cup and saucer.

'No, I'm going for breakfast. Leave that and come with me. Then you can give me the full story.'

Vere got to his feet. 'Mrs Perkins maintains a belly that's been awash with intoxicating liquor needs something solid to settle it. I expect she's probably right.'

'Who's Mrs Perkins?' asked Ross, as they went out into the sunshine.

'A great sage, I imagine – which is more than Sergeant Box will ever be.'

'The regiment requires him to be a good fighting man, not a sage,' Ross commented brusquely. 'When we took this town he led Moynihan's platoon in a successful assault, instilling confidence in every one of them. He's a first-class soldier.'

'I'm sure he is,' Vere murmured. 'If only he were not quite so serious about the fact.'

'When you're facing a horde of Dervishes you *have* to be serious about it. You'll discover that before long.'

Vere remained silent. The likelihood of his ever facing the enemy was extremely slim. Fever would claim to him long before then.

The bluff lasted a mere two days. Despite Ross's vigorous efforts, nothing in the world could disguise the fact that Vere was a novice at soldiering. What had been accepted as eccentric casualness from a man with no need to prove his worth was gradually seen in its true light. That Vere was the invalid grandson of Sir Gilliard and not the younger brother came as unwelcome news to Major Forrester, who was unsure whether he was more furious with his subaltern or with Colonel Winterton for burdening him with this sickly liability. The officers showed resentment at being duped by ignoring Vere when they could. Sergeant Box gave him no mercy and only grudging respect for the rank he held. Able to make life difficult for a youthful, timid or inexperienced officer, he did so to the utmost. Only Ross and young Perkins remained stalwart. This at least entailed being looked after devotedly by his batman, and having a very friendly neighbour.

Although he forged a deep bond with Ross over the following weeks, Vere grew increasingly depressed. His antipathy to things military remained. So much of what he was obliged to do each day seemed pointless. Inspections, parades, marching back and forth, NCOs roaring orders to make others perform like automatons, paperwork, complaints, punishments – that last seemed the most pointless. According to the rule-book, Vere was obliged to order a man to march up and down in the full force of the sun for half an hour because he had neglected to clean his boots, or had been late on parade, or had answered back to a rhetorical question put by his sergeant. Alternatively, the accused might have his pay withheld, or be given short rations as a punishment for something Vere considered unimportant. In severe cases, he learned, it was possible for a man to be lashed to a gun-wheel without water for an entire day. He found that utterly barbaric. When he said as much in the Mess, adding that British armies appeared to be little more civilised than the Dervishes, tight-lipped silence ensued for a long while.

Ross was prepared to listen to his views, but could not accept them. In frank and friendly manner he pointed out that Vere had always lived as an individual, that the communal life of school or university was unknown to him, but he must accept that rules were essential when large groups were formed and that those who broke them must be punished. On each occasion, the professional soldier asked him why on earth he had felt driven to take such calamitous action. Vere never gave an answer.

He walked often beside the river after the heat of the day, alone and yearning; yet it was not for the girl he had once adored that he longed, it was for the soft green of the hills, the sound of sheep calling to each other on misty mornings, and a grey stone house where there were books, a hothouse full of exquisite orchids, and peaceful contentment for an aesthetic soul. Leaving all he loved had been easy when a girl and an old man had destroyed his pride by dubbing him a pathetic failure. As the hurt inflicted by their words gradually faded, the deeper pang of the loss of his heritage settled within him. His thoughts were forever turning to Knightshill, to those golden days when he had cantered through the meadows with Charlotte, captured on paper the beauty of creatures and flowers rioting there, and lain on the sweet grass beside her in perfect spiritual accord. He recalled the delight of playing with Timothy and Kate, reading stories and teaching them about the gentler things around them. It was astonishing how much he missed that pair. Margaret's maternal attitude toward the family, John Morgan's bluff, courteous friendship, Stoner's devotion, and old Benson with his twins, who cared for the grounds as if they were their own – all these Vere increasingly missed.

Whenever he thought of Val there was a subtle difference. Remembering his brother, flushed and fiery in cricketing clothes during their farewell, Vere regretted that he was unlikely to witness the boy's certain glorious destiny. He saw Val in so many of those around him, so the sense of alienation was not so pronounced. Similarly with Sir Gilliard, and it was the echo of their quarrel which drove Vere to endure life ordered by blasts on a bugle. Annabel's derision no longer troubled him but the sense of failure did. He had made a quixotic gesture so that his family could record that he had died in the right uniform, yet he was still obstinately alive in conditions which should have finished him off swiftly.

He began to drink heavily, which earned him a modicum of respect from his fellows. As it was the panacea for his unhappiness he availed himself of it as often as possible, but there were even rules governing inebriation in this khaki society. While it was seen as a desirable accomplishment on the right occasion, it was considered a failing in those who indulged it to suit themselves. Major Forrester took Vere aside and warned him to pull himself together before the regiment lost all respect for him. He continued to drink.

One afternoon in the middle of January, Vere was making his round of the camp as Officer of the Day when he stopped beneath some palms where there was a view of the Nile and the myriad craft toiling up and down its reaches. It seemed even hotter than usual. His head had started to spin and he was sweating heavily. Taking off his pith-helmet he dabbed his face and neck with his handkerchief. *My kingdom for a horse?* He would give it for a cool breeze to lift his damp hair and to enable him to breathe more easily. There was nothing but burning heat, and the sand beneath his boots was shifting dizzily as he stared through aching eyes. Regretting the several glasses of wine with his lunch he knew he had broken the rules yet again. The Officer of the Day was required to be sober and able to carry out his duties. Second Lieutenant V. R. O. Ashleigh was in no state to do anything but return to his tent. He could not, of course. There were rules governing *that*.

Ramming the helmet back in place, he left the shade of the tree. The sun beat into his back to burn like hot coals. He would now give his kingdom for a glass of water. A hundred yards on he found it difficult to walk over ground which rose and dipped violently. A hundred yards more and he keeled over to lie while blood pumped through his veins like thunder. Feet pounded the ground to halt beside him. The faces peering down seemed to triple in number as he gazed back helplessly. The shakes had begun and he knew what it meant. He had lived with fever since childhood and this particular variety was a killer.

It developed with lightning speed. By nightfall he was so ill the regimental padre came to ask if there was any service he could render. Answering was beyond Vere, so the man gripped his hot hand and promised to do everything possible. When the padre asked the doctor in an audible aside what the patient's chances were, Vere already knew the answer. Now the moment he had courted was here he realised he did not welcome it. There was so much he should have done, so many things he could have said before eternal darkness arrived. He had left no loving farewell letter to his family and it was too late for one now.

The burning convulsive hours passed in torment of mind as well as body. No more music to delight his ear, no beauty on which to feast his eyes, no lyrical words to enrich his intellect. Never again to feel the cool Wiltshire breeze through his hair as he galloped as a free man; never to hear the first lark of the year singing high above him. Never again to hold a newly born lamb! Cohesive thought deteriorated into snatches of reality between long periods of unconsciousness. Childhood memories mingled with visions of trailing orchids, ballet dancers, rows of old men in scarlet jackets, fields of wheat golden beneath autumn sunshine, and a myriad sketches of mice and poppies. Faces floated in and out of the visions. Kate asked him to make a snowman, but it was too hot for that. She accused him of no longer loving her. A stern voice insisted that he should have a son. The boy came, but a girl with the face of a madonna fled from him screaming that he was a pygmy. Vere apologised to the girl; he apologised to the stern old man who turned his back. Then he apologised to a schoolboy whose face was full of strength and determination, knowing he must take over all responsibility. The blond boy smiled and said, 'It doesn't matter.' But it did. It *did*.

Ross Majors went to the field hospital soon after dawn. The Medical Officer had remained there all night. He looked weary as they walked together to the patient who was muttering incomprehensibly and fighting the restraints which tied him down.

'He should never have been allowed to come out here, Ross. He's totally unfit for this life, mentally as well as physically.'

'He twisted arms galore, and silly buffers in high places were loath to offend an old general who was highly regarded by Her Majesty during his days at Horse Guards. It was unthinkable to refuse a commission to a member of a family so revered in military circles.'

The medical man sighed. 'God knows why the young fool embarked on this madness. It's as if he wanted to commit suicide.'

Ross shook his head. 'I think he was mistakenly trying to measure up to his famous brother.'

'The only way he's going to emulate Vorne Ashleigh is to die in the Sudan on January the twenty-second, I'm afraid.'

But even in that Vere was a failure. He was still alive on the twenty-third.

Chapter 7

Colonel Meers arrived back in Abu Hamed in late February. He bore exciting news. The Khalifa was making a move, at last. From his stronghold at Omdurman he had sent out up to sixteen thousand men under the command of a troublesome emir named Mahmud. Their target was reputed to be Berber, presently held by a token force of Kitchener's army. Reinforcements had arrived from England, so it seemed certain a major battle would take place a hundred or so miles forward of this present position, where the River Atbara led off from the Nile. All that was wanted was the order to march.

Two days after his return, Colonel Meers called to Major Forrester as the junior man was passing his tent just before sundown. 'Can you spare me a moment, Reggie?'

'Of course,' said Forrester, removing his helmet as he turned to duck beneath the canvas entrance. 'Are we off?'

'No, more's the pity. Will you take a drink? Good. Help yourself. I've told Corcoran to take himself off for an hour because this is a damned delicate matter which I don't care to have spread all around camp.'

Forrester had been expecting this and groaned inwardly as he sat in a camp chair with his glass filled. 'We'll have to move soon, or Mahmud will take Berber and settle in while we sit here.'

This attempt to forestall what was coming did not succeed. Colonel Meers fixed him with a fierce stare and asked, 'What are we going to do with Ashleigh?'

'Send him back to his own regiment.'

'We can't. Winterton's men have already set off from Cairo.'

'That's all right, then. He can join up with them when they reach us.'

'They won't. They're going straight through to Berber,' the Colonel growled. 'Now, look here, Reggie, I want to know why you didn't tell me of the problem the moment I arrived back. I also want to know why the fellah wasn't returned to Winterton long before this.'

Knowing he could not avoid this tricky interview, Forrester played the only card he had. 'The man was ill with fever. Very ill. It was touch and go.'

'So I heard. Why was he allowed to stay here long enough to catch the fever?' The questioning was growing more probing as the level of liquid in the glasses lowered, and so did the sun. It was the time of day for frank conversations conducted in reasonable manner. The same things said when the sun beat down in full force could provoke tempers and make enemies of friends.

'We were short of subalterns and he had been sent on attachment.'

'He's bloody useless.'

Forrester sighed. 'So we discovered.'

'And?'

'And you weren't here to have it out with Colonel Winterton. In addition, he's the brother of a man who died heroically at Khartoum. All manner of tricks were played to get him out here.'

'I heard *that*, too. I wish to God those desk-wallahs in London could be sent out for a taste of what we're facing. It's quite enough without nursemaiding an influential nincompoop who wants to put on uniform and be there when we put the flag back over Khartoum.' He drained his glass, and motioned Forrester to pour another for them both. 'Well, what's to be done?'

'I've no idea, sir. Carter and Moynihan are back, so we're up to strength. We don't need Ashleigh.'

113

'Who does?' came the heavy question. 'Hell and damnation! Winterton will have to answer for this when the opportunity presents itself. I'm in an impossible position. Put a step wrong where this man is concerned and the wrath of Horse Guards will fall on me. When we receive orders to advance, I've no choice but to take him with us. He's a liability, a thorn in our sides. It's a bad thing to allow troops to see an officer make a fool of himself. Undermines morale. They have to respect and trust those who lead them.'

A brooding silence fell. Dusk made it impossible for them to see each other clearly, but neither man moved to light the lamp. After the blinding glare of the sun this soft twilight was very pleasant; too pleasant to end prematurely.

After a long sigh, Colonel Meers asked, 'Is there *nothing* he can do with reasonable competence?'

Forrester thought deeply. 'He's a talented artist.'

The angry bellow that would have greeted this at midday was mellowed to a grunt by the softness of the hour. It was followed by silence so Forrester decided to elaborate.

'During his convalescence he did some impressive drawings of young Majors, his batman and several of the urchins who persist in clustering around the perimeter. He's now inundated with requests for likenesses to send home to families in England. I do believe the fellow could set up in business here. In the most unexpected way, he's earning respect from the men who recognise his talent.' He took the theme a step further. 'As you know, soldiers have little time for those who do not conform. They can treat them very harshly. However, if the outcast can play a good tune on a whistlepipe when they're feeling low, or can dance a jig, or can tell entertaining stories to ease boredom, then he's treated with rough affection. Ashleigh appears to have won them over with his sketches in the same fashion. The officers are proving rather more resistant, but the man has a greal deal of charm. If one forgets his imposture and his name, it is very easy to like him.' He added with slight diffidence, 'He asked if I would consent to sit for him. My features are apparently the perfect subject for a pen portrait.'

Into the resultant silence, Colonel Meers said, 'Reggie, you're a fool!'

The perfect features turned pink as Forrester regretted his minor boast. He had been flattered by Vere Ashleigh's request, but, not a vain man by nature, he now felt very uncomfortable. However, his companion had forgotten the subject in the excitement of pursuing the facts to a satisfying conclusion.

'That's it! You've provided me with the perfect solution.'

'I have?' he asked in bewilderment.

'We shall be advancing very shortly over terrain unknown to us. If someone could travel ahead to make sketches of the physical features we can expect to encounter, and villages *en route*, it would be very useful.'

'You're proposing to send Ashleigh off on his own, to make sketches?' Forrester asked incredulously.

'He can *ride*, can't he?'

'Certainly, very well. He's also a most proficient marksman.'

'There you are, then.'

'But he's a complete novice to campaigning,' Forrester protested. 'The man has no notion how to bivouac or look after himself in such conditions.'

'We'll send a Sudanese with him. Someone who'll play mother and who knows his way around the area.'

'Why not send the Sudanese on his own, in that case?'

'Damned fellow wouldn't make sketches, would he?' glowered Meers. 'No, it's a splendid scheme. Absolutely splendid.'

Appalled at the prospect of sending into the wilderness a man so inexperienced, but nevertheless seeing it as a way out of the predicament, Forrester asked how the notes and sketches would reach them.

'Ashleigh will put them on the steamer when he reaches Berber . . . where Winterton and his fine boys will be waiting to have him back in their ranks.' A gusty sigh of satisfaction punctuated that sentence. 'How *very* fortunate that the fellah can draw.'

Forrester pursed his lips. 'What about Horse Guards? How will they react to such a move?'

'With full approbation, Reggie, with full approbation.' A chuckle reached him across the darkness. 'Came out here to emulate his heroic brother, didn't he? We're giving him the ideal opportunity to do so.'

'What if he meets a similar fate?'

'Oh, the sketches are not so vital we can't advance without 'em . . . and *they* can happily give the man a medal, which will make everyone feel vindicated.' Rising to his feet, Colonel Meers added, 'Thank you for sparing me a few moments of your valuable time. I think the problem has been most satisfactorily resolved, don't you? See you in the Mess later, Reggie.'

As Forrester took up his helmet to go, the other man put a hand on his sleeve to say confidentially, 'I'll leave you to handle it. As the fellah seems so taken with you, you're the best one to ensure that he understands what's wanted and sets out without delay.'

Gritting his teeth, Forrester departed into darkness broken only by lanterns and fires dotted around the camp. Pride had led to an ignominious fall!

★

The sensation of treading in Vorne's footsteps returned strongly in the wild, awesome expanses of the Sudan, as Vere travelled slowly towards Berber with a white-robed Sudanese guide. The man cooked their food and selected each night's resting place along a route which was never dangerously distant from the life-preserving waters of the Nile. Communication between them was mostly by sign language, but each exchanged the respect travellers of the desert observed in a land where survival frequently depended on help from one's companions, and neither man was unhappy with the long silences. Vere actually welcomed them. Why he had felt no affinity with his brother at Abu Hamed he was unsure. Perhaps Vorne had never been there. No one had approached him with recollections; no debtors had presented thirteen-year-old bills. But if there had been nothing to learn about the dead hero in that place, there had been much to learn about himself.

Views once held so staunchly had begun to waver. The belief that cultural sophistication gave him greater understanding of life than those who dragged themselves across inhospitable lands to wage war was erroneous. Soldiers not only understood it, they saw life passing before their eyes. A brain filled with the wonders and philosophies of the world was no substitute for personal experience of them. The men around him had seen peoples and lands he had only read about; they had gained understanding of cultures and religions by witnessing the rituals. How much fuller that brand of education than his own!

At Abu Hamed he had discovered how isolated he had been for most of his life. Knightshill had been a bastion retreat. London had been the centre of his universe. Ross Majors had early pointed out that he had been denied the lessons of communal living learned at school or university. Vere now saw that he had also been denied the opportunity to assess others with an unbiased eye. His judgement was suspect because he acted on sight and sound rather than from experience. His eye was that of an artist, dazzled by beauty, splendour, or drama, seeing only what he wished to see in each case. His ear was that of an aesthete, closing against anything discordant, unfamiliar, or unwelcome. The extent of his ambition had been to turn the home of a hundred past warriors into a place where he could float in the peace of sweet sounds, and sweeter visions, for the rest of his days.

For the rest of his days. He had not cared to consider how many they might be, but they would all have been squandered. It had taken a girl with the face of a madonna and the heart of a susceptible adolescent to show him how small he was. It had taken a proud old man with full knowledge of the scope of human endeavour to shame him into leaving his small, safe, fragile, beautiful world. In so doing, he had discovered some astonishing things. It was possible for Vere Ashleigh to find friendship with the type of man he had formerly disliked; it was possible to earn the respect and camaraderie of such men by being himself. An imposter they would not tolerate; a producer of life-like pen-portraits they had taken to their hearts. At Abu Hamed he had learned a sobering truth. If he had remained at Knightshill for as many years as the Almighty granted him, he would have died knowing less of life than the merry, gallant, twenty-four-year-old Vorne, whom he had counted a fool for leaving behind his inheritance to rush to this land full of eternal discovery.

He gazed around at the distances stretching in three directions, leaving the comforting proximity of the river in the fourth. It was barbaric, yet thrilling. Beauty was not necessarily soft and sweet, pure and untouched: the rural delights of Wiltshire entranced him, but the desert had a more profound effect upon his senses. Sunrise and sunset were so awesome they echoed the timelessness of eternity which made man and his endeavours unimportant. The killing heat of midday, during which his guide insisted that they rest beneath shade, assaulted those beneath more effectively than any warlord. A silent enemy! The curious mirages which deluded the eye completely fascinated him. While he understood the reason for the phenomena, he nevertheless allowed them to excite or intrigue him into hoping they were reality. It was a struggle to make sketches of such an area without turning them into artistic impressions. A regiment did not want pretty pictures to guide their marching progress.

Each time he thought of the purpose of this bizarre journey, Vere turned his mind from it. The unbelievable had happened in that he had recovered from a virulent fever known to have killed others. He had flouted Dr Alderton's rules on alcohol, adequate rest and diet, surviving in spite of it. The man who had been a friend as well as medical advisor would be horrified if he could see his former patient now, yet he had been riding through this austere terrain and sleeping on the floor of the desert for days without dire consequences. Was it a miracle, or had everyone at Knightshill been too protective? Was it possible that the guise of an invalid, which had been cultivated from those early years, no longer applied? Had he grown strong with full manhood? He had come to the Sudan in the belief that he would meet his end here, not in battle but at least wearing the uniform which would uphold Ashleigh pride. Now he must face the possibility of actually being slain by the enemy. It was from this prospect that his thoughts always turned very swiftly. He did not believe that he was afraid to fight, but something within him recoiled from the act of killing.

Hatred was unknown to him. He had always loved his fellow man – found him occasionally irritating, perhaps, but lived in peace with him. On reflection, he admitted that Captain Ford and Sergeant Box had aroused an emotion rather stronger than irritation in a temperament unused to quick responses. Conversely, Ross had prompted feelings of friendship deeper than those he had enjoyed in England. This all took him back to the fact that his life had been very narrow. His friends had been artists or local residents sharing a common interest in country matters. His cousins and Sir Gilliard's military guests, Vere had avoided whenever he could. Here, he was obliged to mingle with all types of people. The garrulous ox-like Steadman in Cairo, and the enigmatic El Habib who had kept for twelve years a letter to a man dead that long. And Floria Pallini, who had loved a man enough to pay for the expensive pearls he had given her on parting. Reggie Forrester, who resembled a Greek god but thought of nothing but the coming orgy of killing in revenge. Young Private Perkins, who had powers of observation he was unaware of possessing because lack of intellect prevented full understanding of what he saw. All these varied characters had left a deep impression on Vere. He was finally meeting mankind face to face. He had no desire to destroy it in battle.

He presently welcomed the state of having left one place and not yet arriving at another. This transient peace was exactly what he wanted in order to come to terms with his metamorphosis. The task he had been given well suited the man he had been for twenty-six years; the journey allowed another persona to emerge from the artist in his own time. So Vere made his sketches while gradually becoming acquainted with a man who was stronger, mentally and physically, than the one who had counted himself a failure. As the days passed, sometimes glimpsing distant mounted enemy marauders and occasionally coming upon a village which had been devastated by them, this new Ashleigh began to face the unexpected challenge of surviving to enter Khartoum with the army of retribution. What would he do then? When he had departed from Knightshill he had abdicated in favour of young Val, never expecting to return. Could he go back and continue as before? He pushed the problem away. He was still travelling, and Khartoum was a long way off. Only when his boots were clouded with the dust of that ruined city could he make a decision on his future. Before that, he must seek out his brother's grave at Metemma. Maybe he would find the answers to questions he had not yet asked himself when he stood beside it.

Berber was a town of dirty stone buildings and narrow streets, with a market straggling through smelly, twisting lanes and the usual quayside squalor where almost anything could be bought or sold. But there were also larger houses with overgrown courtyards owned by merchants or men of learning, who attempted to teach those who could afford an education of sorts. Before the Dervish garrison had fled several months earlier they had reigned by terror, taking what they wanted on pain of death. The British-led Sudanese troops, which had arrived hot on their heels, were welcomed as temporary liberators. When regiments of white men began assembling in Abadia, a village twenty miles from the town, the residents believed their troubles were over for good. The several voices which warned of misplaced optimism thirteen years earlier were shouted down. However, when reliable reports that a vast Dervish army led by the Emir Mahmud and Osman Digna, ruler of the feared 'fuzzy-wuzzies', had advanced to camp just south of Berber where the River Atbara broke away as a tributary of the Nile, those warning voices rose with renewed force. Could these red-faced soldiers in clothes the colour of Nile mud defeat a horde of some fifteen thousand men of the country? That a great battle would soon take place around the village of Atbara was evident. Who would emerge as the victor was not. Those who could prepared to leave Berber at short notice.

Vere found the regiment whose badge he wore, but which he hardly considered as his own, when he rode into the tented camp at Abadia. Reporting briefly to Captain Moore, the adjutant who had arranged his attachment to Abu Hamed, he rode on to Berber immediately. The steamer was due and he wanted to get his sketches to Reggie Forrester without delay. Moore did not attempt to stop him, which was as well since Vere still considered himself to be under orders from the man he had had no opportunity to draw before he left. At the jetty he found the usual pandemonium and no little panic. Word had gone round that the steamer carried Dervish warriors who had slaughtered all the passengers and taken over the vessel. Vere pushed his way through to the dispatch office and was pleased to see a British officer with a Sudanese sergeant on duty.

They exchanged greetings, then Vere told Lieutenant Harmesworth why he was there. 'They're certain to be setting off from Abu Hamed shortly and they'll need all this information.'

'The more the merrier,' agreed the young man with hair bleached almost white by the sun. 'It's been damned nervy up here knowing Mahmud is on his way north to meet us, and all we have here is one battalion of Sudanese. There's no greater comfort than a few British regiments nearby.' He looked keenly at Vere. 'Did you say your name is Ashleigh?'

'That's right.'

'No relation to — '

'Look, I must register this package,' he interrupted hastily, moving toward the office manned by a local official.

He filled in the necessary papers, signed them, then handed over the fat envelope, sealed as Forrester had directed, for the box set aside for military baggage.

'Rest assured, Mr Ashleigh, that your communication will be quite safe on our vessel,' the man told him.

Why did the accompanying burning gaze make nonsense of that assurance, Vere wondered uneasily. He moved off and approached Harmesworth again.

'I suppose there's no truth in this rumour that the steamer has been seized by the Dervishes, is there?' he asked with a frown.

'Not a scrap,' said the other breezily. 'We have spies out and they all report that the entire enemy force has settled beside the river with every sign of staying put.'

'Then why are you here?'

He gave a broad grin. 'To persuade the populace there is nothing to fear. Only a bally fool would stand here with just a sergeant if a boatload of Dervishes was about to arrive.'

Vere knew this was a typical example of military understatement, so he commented on the curious demeanour of the dispatch clerk. 'It was as if he had no intention of putting my package aboard.'

'Don't worry, Ashleigh, they all look villainous. They adopt that threatening expression to impress their importance on anyone requiring service from them. It's a responsible post which they mostly fulfil admirably. But they can all be bribed, of course.' He gave a short laugh. 'Who can't, in this part of the world?'

'If that includes your spies,' Vere commented slyly, 'you might actually *be* a bally fool standing here with just a sergeant to meet a boatload of Dervishes.'

As he rode away from Berber through the motley criss-cross of native Sudanese and those itinerant foreigners who find their way to places offering anonymity, Vere asked himself why he had made that parting dig at someone who had been perfectly friendly. By the time he reached Abadia he had the answer. He was becoming one of them without realising it. To cover fear, apprehension or uncertainty the soldier resorted to exaggerated light-heartedness. He now realised both he and Harmesworth were worried about that steamer, but it arrived and departed without incident. Vere supposed the young blond officer had returned to the garrison much relieved. For himself, he watched the steamer pass on its way to Abu Hamed and wondered about the fate of his packet. There had been something about the look in that official's eye which still bothered him.

When he joined the officers he had never met before, their reception as he entered the Mess tent was one of universal curiosity. Steadman made his clear by his immediate approach. Still looking the epitome of the perfect warrior, he spoke with the same hearty energy Vere had encountered on that first day in Cairo.

'Archie Moore said something about your coming up from Abu Hamed alone. Not true, is it?'

'No.'

'Ah, *thought* not.'

It was said with such smug satisfaction, Vere smiled inwardly. 'I had a good Sudanese guide with me . . . and a baggage camel.'

Steadman's blue eyes clouded with bewilderment. 'But . . . I mean . . . never crossed desert before, have you?'

Vere's smile broke through. 'No. It was an interesting experience.'

'*Interesting experi* . . . Why didn't you come on the steamer to join us?' Steadman challenged suspiciously.

'I couldn't have spied out the land and made sketches to send back to Reggie Forrester.'

'*Sketches!*'

'I'm the only artist the Ashleighs have ever produced. Hopeless at soldiering, but pretty damn good at drawing pictures,' he said in Colin Steadman's brisk military manner. 'By the by, old chap, I *did* find invitations arriving from unexpected sources in Cairo, as you predicted. Don't know what I'd have done without your invaluable advice. I think I've even learned which uniform to wear for each occasion. My Sudanese guide was very impressed with my Mess Dress at sundown each evening.'

'*Mess Dress!*' Steadman goggled. 'In the middle of the desert?'

Vere put a hand on his arm. 'A joke, old sport, a joke.'

At that point they were joined by several others who all seemed somewhat sceptical about the journey he had just made. It was plain they knew all about the Ashleigh who had joined their regiment in Cairo, only to be shunted off on attachment to another because he was a liability. This did not tie in with his story of having undertaken what they knew to be a hazardous lone mission across terrain known to be patrolled by breakaway groups of enemy tribesmen. As they discussed his journey, Vere found all tendency to levity fading. Either Forrester had been unaware of the presence of the roaming marauders or he had deliberately failed to warn of the danger they presented. Perhaps he had not wanted to scare him unduly. Yet Vere was now familiar enough with military ways to know that risks were seldom minimised. They might be pointed out with light-hearted bravado, but not omitted altogether. He had seen those bands of distant horsemen, but had not considered himself to be in danger. Fortunately, they must have been too intent on greater targets than a solitary pair of travellers they could not easily identify.

He allowed Forrester the excuse of not knowing the true situation, but worried about the growing respect of those around him. It suggested that he was lucky to have arrived in one piece. When Colonel Winterton arrived, Vere's unease was compounded by his words just before dinner was served.

Winterton, a short, round man with grey hair and moist eyes, which gave him a melancholy air, seemed less than pleased to see his subaltern.

'Ah, you're back, are you?' he greeted rather testily. 'Heard you'd come into camp then gone straight on to Berber. Some vital dispatch to send on the steamer, Captain Moore said.'

'Not a dispatch, sir. My sketches made *en route.*'

'*Sketches!*'

Vere was tiring of this reaction. It was as if what he had done was something rare. 'Pencil impressions of the landmarks and villages along the way to Berber, to aid their march. I wanted to get them on today's steamer because they're wanted urgently by Major Forrester.'

'Well, he won't get 'em.' It was said with the snappiness of a bad-tempered terrier. 'They marched out of Abu Hamed two days ago. Heard it on the telegraph. Can't think why they'd need *sketches*, anyway. They've half a dozen excellent Sudanese who know the area intimately.'

'Colonel Meers had only just returned to Abu Hamed. Perhaps he was unaware of the presence of the Sudanese guides.'

'Perhaps.' Winterton sighed. 'Now you're back with us I'll have to find something for you to do, I suppose.'

Vere said nothing. He was deeply disappointed that his painstaking work would be wasted. He also knew Reggie Forrester must have been aware of the presence of guides even if Meers had not. At the back of Vere's mind hovered the suspicion that the whole business had been no more than a means to return him to what was supposed to be his regiment. He suddenly recalled those endless reminiscences over the port at Knightshill. Snatches of them stood out in emphasis now. *'Sent old Waldegrave off on a wild goose chase to get him out of the way for a while . . . the silly fool nearly got us all killed so they gave him a forward outpost to command and he was a casualty almost immediately . . . Only thing to do with a useless fellow like Fosdyke was to invent a solo mission and send him off on it.'*

Vere retired to his tent depressed and dispirited. This military life was a succession of short periods during which he strove to adjust, only to find everything changed again. Cairo had produced shocks concerning his brother, Abu Hamed had shown him it was pointless to pretend to be what he was not, the desert had brought him the prospect of surviving to return to the home he had never thought to see again. Tonight, he felt an unwelcome stranger among men he must now live and fight with. Strangely, he wanted the companions he had had at Abu Hamed. He had grown used to them, even liked them during his convalescence. He missed Ross, who had taken him for what he was right away. His neighbour here was a foppish youth, with a laugh like the bray of a mule, who was presently entertaining several friends very noisily in his tent. Sitting at the entrance to his own, Vere gazed at the stars and wished himself back in the desert with his silent companion. How much better men would deal with each other if they were unable to speak, he mused. The minute words were exchanged a companion became either a friend, an enemy or a bore. If he, himself, were nameless and mute he would probably fare a great deal better in this curious communal life.

He was awoken by his new batman just as the sun was turning the sky yellow. Private French was the complete opposite of young Perkins. A man who had soldiered through several campaigns with the regiment, including the one which had failed to reach Khartoum in time to save it, he was sardonic, efficient and well suited to his profession. Vere sensed straight away that French would take him over given the chance, so he determined to show the man how it must be between them. Glancing at the cup beside his bed he studied his batman shrewdly.

'I haven't yet told you how I like my tea, French.'

The monkey face broke into a smile. 'I've been looking after gentlemen like yourself for long enough now, sir, as to know their little preferences.'

'Other gentlemen aren't like me,' Vere pointed out, swinging his feet to the ground. 'Everyone is different, which means that each of us has an individual taste in tea. Mine is for a strong brew with plenty of sugar. I also like two biscuits with it. Please sort that out for me while I wash.'

French's smile vanished. 'That *is* strong, sir, and there's three spoons of sugar in it.'

'Good.' He stretched. 'How about the biscuits?'

'There wasn't any in your baggage.'

'I've been crossing the desert for ten days. No chance to replenish supplies. But I'm confident a man of your great experience could coax a few from the Mess sergeant.'

'It's not that easy,' French said obstinately.

'Ah. A fierce character, is he? I won't ask you to brave the lion in his den.'

The man drew himself up. 'He's no lion, that he ain't. I can get biscuits from him any time I like.'

'Well, I'd be very glad if you'd get some for me. Returning to routine after that long, lonely journey will be much more enjoyable with a biscuit or two.'

'You wasn't in the desert on your own, was you?' asked French with awe.

'I had a Sudanese guide.'

'But there's Dervishes out there, sir.'

'I know. We spotted some,' he said as nonchalantly as he could, reaching for the tea. 'Ah, this is just as I like it.'

'Right, Mr Ashleigh, I'll be back with a supply o' biscuits soon as you can say "fuzzy-wuzzies". I'll make sure you gets a couple every morning.'

During the next thirty minutes the pair walked around each other warily, but at the end of that time a relationship satisfactory to them both had been established. As he had not yet been given a platoon to command, there was nothing for Vere to do before breakfast. He decided to walk around the perimeter of a camp larger than the one he had left, and liable to continue to grow as regiments arrived in the build-up.

He left his tent and walked the few yards to the perimeter path, worn by the constant treading of boots. He was restless and needed exercise before facing what he was certain would be a difficult day. Beneath a nearby palm stood a man whose sharp-featured face and red tarbush proclaimed him to be Egyptian. Vere was surprised: only persistent mongrel pedlars of pornography or begging urchins dodged the guards to linger around military camps at dawn and dusk. This man had the bearing of an upper-class merchant despite the tattered quality of his suit. That he was in this predominantly Sudanese area suggested the cause of his poverty. At the time of the Mahdist purge many Egyptians caught in towns and villages saved themselves from murder by declaring loyalty, surrendering every possession as proof of it.

'Mr Ashleigh!'

He turned in surprise as his name was spoken by the man beneath the tree.

'I regret to trouble you, sir, but may I ask if you are one of the family of Lieutenant Ashleigh who passed this way thirteen years ago?'

Instantly on his guard, Vere hesitated. All he need do was to deny it and go on his way. If he did he would be troubled by a sense of guilt; if he did not he would almost certainly be presented with a sheaf of bills.

'Who are you and how did you know I was here?'

The man moved forward, bowing his head in greeting. 'I am Ahmed, a man of learning who has suffered much at the hands of the savages.'

'One of the very many who have. How did you know I was here?' Vere demanded.

'You sent a packet on the steamer yesterday.'

'The man in the dispatch office is a friend of yours,' he concluded, finding the explanation for the burning gaze which had unsettled him. He knew this part of the world well enough now to be unsurprised by the way news travelled. Still wary, he added, 'It's common courtesy to approach the guards so that an officer can be asked if he is able to receive a visitor. A man of consequence, as you claim to be, doesn't sneak into camp and wait under a tree in the manner of a villain.'

Dark eyes hardened despite an ingratiating smile. 'The matter is of a nature which requires delicacy, Mr Ashleigh. I was certain you would not wish to discuss it before the guards, or even before your honourable friends.'

Believing this smooth, hostile man to be another of Vorne's creditors, he still debated whether or not simply to walk away, for his brother's debts would soon exhaust his present funds. On the point of concluding the conversation by disclaiming knowledge of the other Ashleigh, Vere saw the man raise a beckoning hand. From behind the cluster of palms came a woman of uncertain age who must once have been strikingly beautiful. Beside her walked a boy of around eleven or twelve. Vere's stomach tightened as instinct told him this concerned no cash debt.

'Sir, are you of the family of Lieutenant Ashleigh who passed this way thirteen years ago?' Ahmed asked once more.

Vere made no answer as he stared at the boy whose skin was fair for an Egyptian and whose eyes were a vivid blue. Dear God, what kind of man had been this unknown brother, this crowned hero?

'I see by your expression that you recognise the delicacy to which I referred, Mr Ashleigh,' said a soft voice beside him. 'Believe me when I say I would not have approached you if the matter had not been urgent.'

Vere faced him. 'Urgent?'

The ingratiating smile reappeared. 'Allow me to explain, sir. At the time of the Mahdi I lived in Metemma with my wife and daughter. I taught those who wished to learn of the world, and lived in a house with a courtyard as befitted my position. The British soldiers came on their way to Khartoum. They dallied there too long, as the world already knows.' The hardness in his eyes intensified. 'It seems the girls of Metemma were too beautiful.'

'Go on,' invited Vere dully.

'When I heard Khartoum had fallen I left my home and took my wife and daughter to one of the boats leaving for safety. It became overcrowded and sank. My sick wife did not reach the bank. Deeply saddened, I took my daughter by the hand and began to walk. We reached a village and were told that Berber had fallen and the steamer carrying Europeans and Egyptians from Khartoum had been captured by Dervishes, who massacred them. From that time on we wandered, begging for food and sleeping where we could.'

Vere believed every word of the terrible story. He had heard others even more appalling related by officers who had been out here longer than a year.

'The child was born in a deep cleft between rocks,' Ahmed continued. 'I insisted on leaving it there when we moved on, but when I slept that night she returned for it. At the next village, a woman whose child had just died gave us shelter. We remained there for many years, and the boy grew.'

'Why didn't you attempt to return to Egypt?' Vere asked. 'It must have been possible by some means or other.'

There came the shrug of the shoulders typical of these people. 'I could not go back. A youthful indiscretion.'

'You could have sent your daughter and child.'

Again the shrug of the shoulders. 'I held her in too much affection to let her go, sir. She cooked and worked on the land.'

'So what are you doing in Berber?'

'We came to escape the Khalifa's purges several years ago. But it has been difficult. I have been forced to teach the creed of Mahdism, for which I receive a bowl of grain. My daughter earns what she can. I am ashamed for her, but we must live. There is also the boy to consider. The son of Lieutenant Ashleigh.'

Now it had been put into words Vere immediately challenged it. 'There's no foundation for that belief. He could be any man's son.'

Ahmed's manner changed dramatically. 'My daughter was pure until an Englishman used her for sport,' he said with bitter anger. 'Why else would I leave the fruit of foreign seed in a cave to die?'

'Your daughter cared enough to go back.'

'That one was disobedient and foolish. She wept when he left for Khartoum, but I did not know why she wept until she could no longer hide her disgrace.' He turned to indicate the boy. 'Look at him, Mr Ashleigh, and see that he is the son of your kinsman.'

Vere knew it in his heart. There was something about the shape of the face and the blueness of the eyes which vaguely resembled Val, despite the black hair. The boy was striking. Vere's skin began to creep as the full impact of the situation hit him. He had told Sir Gilliard in anger that he would sire a son by any woman to give him the desired heir. Here was one ready made. This honey-skinned boy was an Ashleigh, yet the son of the dead heir was living in poverty while his mother sold herself in order to live!

Hating himself, Vere murmured, 'Blue eyes suggest that the father was probably European. Beyond that there is no proof of your claim.'

Ahmed beckoned the woman closer. She came with her gaze fastened on Vere's face as if she could never see enough of it. It made him feel even sicker. In her outstretched hand she held a small leather coin purse. Tooled in gold upon it were the letters V. E. R. A. *Vorne Ewart Roland Ashleigh.* Margaret and Charlotte had often spoken of how their brother laughingly claimed their mother had wanted a daughter named Vera when he was born. His spirit was presently so close Vere could feel its very presence.

Looking at the woman whose face mirrored her sad life, he said, 'He was killed near Khartoum. They buried his remains at Metemma. He was my brother.'

The man beside him let out a gust of satisfaction. 'The Lord is good, the Lord is merciful. His hand guided you here at our hour of need.'

Vere turned to Ahmed. 'This has been a shock. One for which I was totally unprepared.'

'It *has* been a shock,' agreed the Egyptian. 'When Ramesh spoke of the officer Ashleigh sending a packet on the steamer, we thought he had returned. I saw at once that you were too young, but there is that about you which told me you were a kinsman. The boy has that same look.'

At a loss, Vere said frankly, 'History is repeating itself. We shall all be moving on very soon for Khartoum. There will be heavy fighting. I can't guarantee that I shall be back.'

Ahmed held up his hands. 'No, no, sir, that is not why we are here. There will be much bloodshed. The Khalifa claims the British will turn and run as they did before the Mahdi.'

'Why *are* you here?' Vere demanded.

The ingratiating smile was back. 'You are a gentleman, sir, a man of some substance. We, on the other hand, are living from day to day.'

'You're after money?'

'For the boy,' came the swift interjection. 'Only for the boy, Mr Ashleigh.'

Vere did not know anyone who had been obliged to buy off the family of his brother's bastard, so he had no notion what this would cost him. A damn sight more than a gambling debt, he guessed.

'I quite understand that you wish to educate the boy, send him and your daughter to Egypt so that he will have a better life. It will be easy to arrange that now the Nile is safe to travel. It will take time for me to transfer a suitable sum from England to my bank in Cairo. Meanwhile, I will give you what I can spare for now and arrange for an adequate sum to be given to your daughter each month, even in the event of my death in action.'

Still shaken by this bizarre encounter, Vere had forgotten he was dealing with people of the East, who did not think the way he did. Ahmed gestured the woman to bring her son nearer. When the boy was standing right before Vere, Ahmed took the lad's shoulders in a firm grip.

'Study him well, sir,' commanded the silken voice. 'Is he not *beautiful*? Many men find him too beautiful to resist, and I have been offered a tempting sum by the owner of a popular establishment.'

Vere turned cold again. 'You'd sell your grandson!'

'A man sometimes has to sell even his soul in order to live. The boy would eat well and have a roof over his head even when the Dervishes come. They have great fondness for pretty boys.' His hand ruffled the dark hair of Vorne Ashleigh's son. 'If we could but persuade the brothel-keeper to forgo the income the boy would bring, and still have enough left to take the steamer north . . .'

'How much?' Vere asked harshly.

127

Ahmed pushed the boy roughly towards his mother. 'A trifling sum to a gentleman, I assure you. If your brother had not been so unfortunately struck down I'm persuaded he would not hesitate to help us. It must be a source of great satisfaction to you to do so on his behalf, removing the stain on his mortal soul.'

Afterwards, Vere was troubled by conflicting emotions. The family had undoubtedly suffered along with most residents of the Sudan during the past thirteen years, although it was in no way his brother's fault that they had. He supposed they had a moral right to ask for his help, and he certainly felt a sense of responsibility towards the Ashleigh who could never claim an inheritance rightly his by blood but not in law. Ahmed had asked for an impossible sum. Vere had agreed to pay him half the amount, which was probably twice as much as he had hoped to receive. Yet the horrible certainty grew in Vere that the boy was doomed anyway for the brothel.

During the next few days, he remained deeply troubled. He had probably been a fool to respond to the man in the first place. There must be hundreds like that boy in every part of the world. Soldiers sought their pleasure where they could, then moved on. Doubtless there had been other Ashleigh bastards through the ages. He had been a fool to become involved with this one.

Yet a hand appeared to be guiding him along a predestined path full of astonishing revelations. Vorne had expended his irresistible personality on heedless pleasure which took no account of those he encountered. He had lived on credit, used his considerable charm without compunction and treated the deep feelings he aroused with a carelessness bordering on contempt. Floria Pallini had loved him enough to pay for the pearls; Ahmed's daughter had loved him enough to retain that coin purse rather than sell it. With a heavy heart, Vere accepted that his brother had been a military hero, but a man of little honour. An entire family had been raising glasses to his hallowed memory every January for thirteen years.

Within the next month troops arrived by barge, steamer, horse and camel until the environs of Berber were filled by a force comprising not only the Anglo-Egyptian regiments, but some of the finest men in the British army who had been rushed out from England with no chance to acclimatise. It was plain to everyone that Kitchener was planning to attack Mahmud's army, which was giving no sign of making the first move in a bid to claim Berber. Excitement mounted.

Walking through the camp one evening at the start of April, Vere heard his name called. He turned to see Ross Majors approaching. They shook hands warmly.

'It's good to see you,' Ross declared with his wide smile. 'What a hell-hole this is! I was glad to leave Abu Hamed, but I think my joy was misplaced. Dear God, what a march! We did it within a week, you know.'

Vere was astounded. 'That's some feat!'

'*Feet* being the significant word,' his friend said with a laugh. 'I have never felt more thankful for my horse. The men suffered, I'm afraid. Even the redoubtable Sergeant Box keeled over with an overdose of sun.'

They walked together, in relaxed fashion, chatting about their separate experiences since they last met. Vere did not speak of the blue-eyed boy who still haunted his conscience. Instead, he mentioned the drawings he had been sent to do.

'I put them on the steamer, but Winterton said you had set out two days earlier. They were rather good. I'd like to have kept them if I'd known they would never be used. What do you suppose will happen to the packet?'

'It'll be sent back up here. First, there'll be no end of a performance during which it will be handed to a series of officials who will put a stamp on it, then direct it to some office ill-equipped to deal with the problem. There, it will lie around for days because no one will wish to take responsibility for a decision on what to do next. Finally, some un-suspecting Englishman will have the packet thrust on him as he boards a steamer for Berber. We'll have reclaimed Khartoum, set Kitchener up as Governor-General, and gone home before those drawings turn up here. The whole business will then be reversed by the dispatch office.'

Vere grimaced. 'You know the East.'

'So should you, by now.'

'I'm learning.'

Ross slowed. 'My tent is the third along this row. After dinner, come along for a real chat. Are you still defying your doctor and imbibing?'

'Yes, very definitely.'

'Good. How about Reggie Forrester?'

'I still think he should pose nude.'

Ross laughed. 'That's my man! A Pre-Raphaelite with a sword. How do you view the coming battle?'

'With great dread,' Vere admitted.

'So do we all, lad. Take no notice of the bravado in the Mess. We're all scared to death of the unknown. Once we've grappled with them we'll know what we're up against and be perfectly confident. A disciplined European enemy is one thing, fanatical tribesmen another. There are no rules of war so far as they're concerned.' Coming to a halt, he asked, 'Have you a good sergeant?'

'He has a very loud voice.'

'That'll do. Take my advice and stick close to him when the time comes. Before that we'll make the most of the amenities of this salubrious area. I'll expect you around ten.'

'I'm glad you're here,' Vere admitted, as Ross began to move off. 'The officers of my own regiment are still relative strangers.'

Ross glanced back at him. 'Get to know them. Any day now your life might depend on those men.'

The day came sooner than Vere expected. Kitchener tired of waiting and decided to shift the enemy blocking his path to Khartoum and glory, choosing the Christian festival of Easter on which to begin the attack. Spies reported that the Dervish force was still in relaxed mood behind the *zariba*, a high hedge of thorn bushes they had erected as protection. There were probably enemy spies, also, so a surprise attack was not even considered a possibility. The most Kitchener could achieve was to move his troops into position under cover of darkness ready to attack at dawn.

Vere prepared for an experience he had never dreamed of facing – one from which he shrank. He had shot birds and rabbits galore at Knights-hill . . . but to shoot a man! Private French seemed his normal self as he handed Vere his pith-helmet, water-bottle and revolver.

'So we're going to move them fuzzy-wuzzies along, sir. Saw something of them last time we was here. Look enormous fearful, they do, with all that black hair standing out around their heads, and they give out a terrible cry wot chills the blood. But they got no talent for soldiering. No talent at all. Done up like fighting-cocks, they are, and no better'n bleedin' hens . . . if you'll pardon the language, sir.' He grinned. 'Don't worry about a thing here, Mr Ashleigh. If we gets the order to move up, I'll pack your things real well and have it all safely at the new position when you gets there.'

'Thank you, French. I have every confidence in you.' As he left the tent Vere wished he could say the same of himself.

During that night he learned much about military tactics. It was curious how many of those after-dinner stories he had found so boring returned with fresh meaning. The old warhorses he had dismissed as figures of fun had known this dread, this tension, this pain deep in the stomach. They had moved through the dangerous darkness when only whispers were permitted. They had smelt the fear and excitement of those around them, heard the swishing of a hundred boots through spiky grass, felt the night breeze on their own stiff cheeks, known the awesomeness of the hours before the killing would begin. Sir Gilliard had experienced all these, so had the father he had scarcely known. So had Vorne. Whatever else he had been, he had faced this unafraid.

After the marching came the waiting, which proved even worse. Sitting on the ground, or walking restlessly up and down, the minutes seemed leaden. Vere discovered that being an officer was lonely. The men chatted in low voices to pass the time, but an officer was on his own. Sergeant Smithers had an anonymous personality so far as Vere was concerned, but a reputation for being unshakeable in battle. They shared a calm relationship in which Sergeant Smithers showed respect and Vere allowed him to run the platoon. Both felt this was the best arrangement for now.

As he walked back and forth beneath the stars Vere's thoughts turned fleetingly to Val, who could hardly wait to be part of this. No sergeant would command *his* men. He would be ranging along the ranks encouraging them with fine words and his own elated confidence. But had that ardent boy actually contemplated *killing*?

Vere jumped nervously when a figure loomed from the darkness. It was Smithers.

'Everything all right?' he asked the NCO automatically.

'The men are just fine, sir.' He stood beside Vere to gaze eastwards for a moment or two. 'Dawn'll be up any minute, by the look of that sky. Then we'll need our fingers in our ears. Always puts the fear of God in you when the guns start, but it's worse when they stop because that's when we go in.' He cleared his throat rather elaborately, then said in low tones, 'Excuse me, sir, but this is your first time, isn't it?'

Vere knew what he meant. 'That's right.'

'There's nothing to it once we get going. All this waiting is the worst. When we move off, we're all in it together. There's the regiment all around you, so you feel safe. When you see some black bastard coming towards you with a murderous look in his eye, you fire instinctively. If you don't get him, your mate will. It's a cosy sort of way to fight. Now, going it alone, that's different, sir. The man who earns my admiration is the one to go out and face the enemy with no one to give him a hand. Someone like your brother, Mr Ashleigh. He had real pluck.'

When Smithers moved off his words stuck in Vere's mind. He tried to imagine Vorne's thoughts and emotions as he had left Khartoum to face the desert containing the Mahdi's savage followers. Being one of a mass of several thousand did not seem so bad now. When the artillery began, he covered his ears with his hands. It made little difference to the volume of thunderous sound, however. Coinciding with the growing yellow light to the east, it suggested the splitting open of the world to reveal the burning core. It was the fanciful concept of an artist. Those around him showed no apparent awareness of the bizarre combination of sight and sound. Yet there was an undeniable splendour about this particular dawn over the desert, where the sand rose in tall funnels as shells tore into it, and where a distant scar across the landscape marked the massed enemy preparing to repulse their attack.

After an hour, the guns stopped to produce a silence more awesome than the bombardment. The regiments stood to. All conversation ceased and the tension grew almost unbearable. Vere had been instructed on the part he must play and stood with his platoon, waiting for the forward regiments to move off. When they did, it was to the sound of the pipes of Scottish regiments playing old tunes of glory. Incredibly, it seemed to Vere more like a military tattoo as the broad ranks advanced with slow pace and in perfect formation. But the deafening volleys of fire from their rifles as they drew within range put an end to that fancy. This was real and deadly. Return fire began to make gaps in the neat ranks. At that point, Colonel Winterton gave the order for his regiment to march. They were off in the same calm manner, marching out across that broad, barren area to the alien orchestra of screams, gunfire and regimental bands.

Vere walked as if in a dream. In the midst of such a mass it was impossible to see far ahead, so he simply followed where those in front led. Taking him by surprise, he felt his blood begin to warm with excitement and his chest fill with pride as the khaki mass moved steadily toward the Dervish force determined to keep them from Khartoum. The blood of bygone Ashleigh warriors was not entirely missing from the veins of this man of peace, apparently. The heat of battle burned his body, and rising gritty dust stirred by a million marching boots settled on his face to prick at his eyes. He narrowed them to minimise the torment, then wondered how he would ever see the enemy.

On they marched across arid land bathed in the yellow light of emerging sunshine, while the tumult grew to Doomsday proportions. Vere's head rang with the combination of martial music, human battle cries, explosions of rifle-fire and the deep roar of artillery. Then, in the momentary lulls, a new sound reached him. It was the fanatical cry of tens of thousands inviting them to die like the infidel dogs they were, beneath the blades of the faithful. The chilling sound rose up in crescendo as the gap between the two armies narrowed.

Even in the midst of all this Vere noticed Colin Steadman to his right, drawing his sword and taking his revolver from its leather holster. As he did the same, Vere realised his hands were shaking. Here was the ultimate test. Guns were familiar to him; a sword was reputedly the weapon of chivalry. He could not believe there would be much of that during the coming ordeal. Those around him were shouting encouragement to their men, and he knew they must be almost upon the enemy. His hands tightened around both weapons as he prayed that no man would die through his own inadequacy this morning.

It was the last of his coherent thoughts. The ground to his left rose up in a spout of fine particles taking Sergeant Smithers with it. The ranks behind Vere flowed onward, and shot began dropping all around them. Here and there, men fell; others staggered on with an arm hanging loosely or a leg oozing blood. Bullets whistled overhead, hoarse voices shouted obscenities, bugles relayed messages above the symphony of battle. The straight ranks ahead fragmented into groups as a high barrier of thorns became visible through the clouds of dust. The *zariba*. Behind it were men he must kill.

It was each man for himself. They scrambled through the gaps made by their own artillery and found a mêlée of desperate Dervishes slashing at troops who were better disciplined, better armed and filled with the fire of vengeance for General Gordon and all who had perished with him. Vere hardly noticed the thorns which tore his left sleeve as he crossed his personal rubicon and joined the mêlée. It was as if he became another man from then on, as if the shades of his ancestors commanded him.

Black eyes filled with hatred, others filled with fear; dark faces, white turbans, yellowed teeth bared in endeavour or pain; raised arms, sun on steel, screams, yells, pistol-shots; khaki figures grappling with robed defenders, tartan kilts swirling as troops twisted to left and to right fending off potential killers, soldiers shooting a Dervish about to take the life of a chum, only to be felled themselves by an unseen enemy to the rear.

When they came at him, Vere defended himself instinctively. Curious anger began to grow because they kept on coming. A fever to drive them away took control of him. From the stationary confusion he began to press forward. They all did. They continued to do so. The robed figures fell back, stumbling over the bodies of others like them strewn like a carpet of ebbing life for as far as the eye could see. A new sound was filling the air. Vere returned to sanity to recognise exultant cheering. The enemy was on the run; defeated.

Victory brought only momentary elation. With the enemy vanishing in disarray, the conquerors were left with an appalling spread of human suffering at their feet. When madness died it was then possible to see the outcome of it. Vere stood drained, mentally and physically, as he surveyed the blood and tatters of the erstwhile battlefield. His heart pounded, his lungs pumped air painfully, his right arm ached. There was blood on his sword; the chamber of his revolver was empty. Had he killed anyone? He could not say. All he knew for certain was that no one had killed him. His starched khaki was limp and stained dark in places, but he felt no pain so must be wearing the blood of others.

The comparative quietness after pandemonium was distressing because now the terrible cries of the wounded could be heard. It was then he realised that the sun was very little higher in the sky than when it had all begun. No more than an hour could have passed, yet he seemed to have lived twice his twenty-six years in that time.

'Are you all right, sir?'

He turned his head as if it were a great weight to see Sergeant Smithers looking anxiously at him. Vere frowned. 'I thought – I *saw* you go up in a great shower of sand,' he said, through lips so dry they stuck together painfully.

'Thrown off balance, that's all,' the man told him with a grin. 'Ancient weapons firing ammunition which failed most of the time, that's what they faced us with. They were very nifty with the blades, though, I'll give them that.' As Vere remained silent, he added, 'You did a real splendid job, sir. I've often come across members of one family, brothers in most cases, and seen the same qualities in each. I knew you'd be all right, Mr Ashleigh.'

Vere swallowed convulsively as he gazed once more at the carnage around him. 'This is . . . it's *unspeakable.*'

'The stretcher-bearers'll see to it, sir,' came the steady comment. 'If you're ready, I think we should fall the lads in and march them back now. They deserve a rest and their breakfast after the splendid effort they just made. I'm sure you're as proud of them as I am.'

'Of course,' murmured Vere wearily.

'Will you tell them that, sir, or shall I pass on your thanks?'

Vere began to walk slowly beside the man who seemed untouched by what had just occurred. He found he was trailing his sword, and sheathed it with a hand that was still shaking. His lowered gaze then fell on something which caused him to halt and take in his breath with shock. Colin Steadman's body sprawled grotesquely in a pool of his own blood, impaled by a spear driven into his flesh by a fuzzy-wuzzy lying across his victim's boots with a gaping wound in his back. Steadman's blue eyes stared sightlessly at Vere as if in accusation. The perfect warrior was no more; the counterfeit one miraculously lived.

'The men are waiting, sir,' prompted Smithers quietly.

Sorrow pierced Vere as sharply as the spear pinning Steadman to the sand. He had never liked the man. Why should he feel his loss so deeply? He glanced at the NCO walking calmly at his side.

'I'll tell the men personally how gratified we are by the steadiness and courage they displayed this morning.'

Smithers nodded. 'They'll like that, sir.'

The regiment re-formed with the inevitable gaps in ranks, then marched back to camp. Vere could not guess at the thoughts of the others, but his own were centred on Colin Steadman. How could that robust, bull-like, splendid soldier be dead? A foe filled with hatred, a spear and two seconds were all it took to end such vibrant life, such a promising future. Parents, brothers and sisters, a wife, perhaps, would all soon mourn that young officer. The news should reach them by the end of the week.

French had ready hot water for a wash, strong, sweet tea and a substantial breakfast. The man chatted throughout his attentive services without expecting answers. To his astonishment, Vere ate the breakfast with relish, but he was glad of the sound of his batman's cheery voice while he did so. Then he stretched out on his bed and closed his eyes. He was dog tired. After a good sleep he would write to his family to let them know he was all right.

Chapter 8

The new school year began very well. The results of a short written test were favourable enough to stave off the relegation Val had worked through his vacation to avoid. He was again captain of rugby, formed one of the rowing eight and the fencing team, and was still the fastest sprinter in senior school. Clive was nominated captain of Brooke House, to which Val belonged as a senior prefect.

He was not sorry to get away from Knightshill. The atmosphere was not the same since Vere left. He had not realised his brother possessed the kind of personality which made a profound effect on those around him. Charlotte had grown more intolerant, spending most of her time riding on the estate or in the hothouses with John Morgan. Margaret was withdrawn and rather touchy. Philip remained aloof from the family, obsessed with letters and pamphlets arriving in vast numbers from far-flung parts of the world. Even the children seemed quieter, almost sad. Sir Gilliard had appeared introspective, but he had his maps and charts, military relics and regimental histories, which were all he really needed. The subject of Val's future had not been broached. Grandfather had dealt with it ruthlessly then put it aside. Val had not. He thought of it all the time.

On a November afternoon he sat with Clive and other prefects of Brooke House in the parlour of rooms occupied by Herbert Grieves, their housemaster. Thin, balding and in his late fifties, he had returned from the summer break with a wife thirty years his junior. The senior school was agog. Brooke boys were envied their luck in having the opportunity to know her, and Clive was making the most of his captaincy by treating her to his smooth charm during the tea-party traditionally held for boys given responsible positions in the house for the coming year. Val thought she was an improvement on Grieves's first hearty wife, who had treated every boy with patronising superiority. This rather jolly young woman with nut-brown hair and overlarge eyes much the same colour had provided an excellent tea. Val did justice to it while the others talked enthusiastically, leaving their strawberry tarts half-eaten. He was just wondering if he could slide another one on to his plate without being noticed, when Mrs Grieves spoke his name rather loudly.

'Yes, ma'am,' he said, flushing at the sudden scrutiny of all eyes as he was about to reach for a tart.

'You've been very quiet over there in the corner,' she accused in friendly fashion. 'It's your turn to tell me something about yourself. As I said, I want you all to regard me as a friend, not a member of staff.' She smiled and offered Val the plate of tarts. 'What's your first name, Ashleigh?'

He told her but refused the cake he had wanted a few moments before.

'It's an abbreviation of Valentine,' Clive informed her slyly, knowing Val hated to be addressed thus.

'How very romantic. Were you born on February the fourteenth?'

Val nodded, furious with his friend.

Her smile broadened. 'I can see you haven't forgiven your mother for it, so I'll use the version you prefer. Are your parents at home, Val, or overseas like those of Clive and Roland?'

'My father died of wounds inflicted in Afghanistan. Mother married again and went to America.'

'So you have no one close?'

'A brother and two sisters. We live with our grandfather.'

Putting a hand to her brow in vexation, she said, 'How foolish of me. *Ashleigh*. Of course, you're the grandson of General Sir Gilliard Ashleigh. Herbert told me during our honeymoon that he had a boy from that renowned military family in his house. You're the brother of the hero of Khartoum.'

'That's right,' he agreed with less reserve.

'So you're following events in the Sudan very closely.'

Pleased that she should be so informed on a subject dear to his heart, Val found himself telling her he wished he could join Kitchener's army before it was all over.

'Of course,' she said with understanding. 'I'd feel the same in your place. There's no need to ask which profession you've chosen. The West Wiltshire Regiment, isn't it?'

Surprised by the extent of her knowledge about his family, Val hesitated.

'Am I wrong about the family regiment?'

'No-o,' he said awkwardly. 'It *is* the West Wilts.'

'But?' she probed.

'But he wants a commission in the cavalry and his family won't hear of it,' supplied Clive irrepressibly. 'He's going nearly crazy trying to think how to defy them. I suggested joining the Prussian army, but he thinks it a pretty senseless solution.'

'So it is,' Julia Grieves agreed, still studying Val. 'Going against family tradition is always a dangerous move, so you must feel very strongly about it. Why the cavalry?'

Clive had landed him well and truly in this predicament and Val could see no way of wriggling out of an explanation. All the boys present knew his reasons – heavens, he had aired them often enough – so he could not lie to this woman. They would tease him unmercifully if he did.

'The mounted arm is more my kind of thing. I like to be on the move . . . and I'm pretty good in the saddle,' he mumbled. Then, he found the cosy parlour with its bright fire and well-worn carpet, and the sympathetic woman who reminded him a little of Margaret, conducive to confession. Meeting her eyes, he added, 'I've studied every cavalry action in battles going back to Agincourt. I know about mounted tactics and how to move large groups of horse soldiers swiftly, to the greatest effect. I'd lead a charge without fear or hesitation. I know I would,' he told her fervently. 'But I'd be hopeless with static infantry. I'd be too impatient and order them forward before I should. Honestly, I'd be no use to the West Wilts.'

Her enormous eyes regarded him thoughtfully for a moment or two, and he began to regret having been so confiding. He was not normally at ease with women of her age. Girls and old ladies were all right. The former were full of giggles, which made him feel superior and therefore in command of the situation, and the latter mostly deaf or eccentric so one had no need to choose words with them. Young women with self-assurance and a sharp mind were a different prospect. If they treated him as an adolescent it annoyed him; if they approached him on equal terms he was embarrassed. Only with Margaret, and to a lesser extent Charlotte, did he feel relaxed. For a moment, he had seen Julia Grieves as Margaret. Now he realised she was a stranger, who had coaxed from him the details of something he wanted with passionate longing. He cursed Clive for raising the subject. He cursed himself for blurting out words which made him appear a fool who could never lead armed infantrymen.

'It takes a deal of courage to admit one's shortcomings, Val,' Julia said softly. 'While I wouldn't support Clive's proposal regarding the Prussian army, I do think a solution must be found. Have you explained all this to your family?'

Almost squirming with discomfiture now beneath the concerted gaze of his schoolfellows, Val said gruffly, 'They wouldn't listen.'

'Dear me, it's as bad as that.' She glanced around to include them all in her next words. 'Well, gentlemen, we shall have to put our heads together and come up with a solution to Val's problem.'

Hot under the collar, he mumbled, 'It doesn't matter.'

She rounded on him. 'Of course it matters! You're captain of practically every school team, aren't you? Would you put the ideal back three-quarter at scrum-half where he would be useless, or use a brilliant wicket-keeper as a spin bowler?'

His colour rose again. There was bemused delight on faces gilded by firelight as his friends watched the exchange.

'I can see by your mulish expression that you dislike the force of my argument,' she continued. 'Don't be angry with me, Val. I'm only trying to help.'

'Yes . . . thanks,' he muttered.

She rose at that point and suggested more tea. General agreement made Val curse inwardly, but Julia began chatting about her plans to arrange a Christmas ball for the senior pupils. His friends were so eager to discuss this exciting innovation, he was not obliged to take part, but as soon as they left the building and began to cross to their own quarters, the expected teasing began.

'Well, gentlemen,' announced Clive, walking with his hands linked professor-like behind his back and wearing an exaggerated frown. 'Let us put our heads together and come up with a solution to Valentine's problem.'

Various disgusting suggestions were put forward, then Roland Baines who hoped to be Prime Minister one day, assumed a high feminine voice. 'Please don't be angry, Val. I'm only trying to help.'

Normally well able to take ragging in his stride, Val found himself blushing, thus giving them further fuel for their fire. Furious over his idiotic behaviour in front of them and Julia Grieves, he could not retaliate in his usual fashion and suffered their high spirits until he reached the seclusion of his room. Although Val knew he would have done the same in their place, the incident left a curious ache inside him and intensified his yearning to follow his star. Vere had told him to do so, had spoken of a feeling that his young brother would be the greatest Ashleigh of them all.

A week passed during which Val so often recalled that heedless conversation with his housemaster's wife, he became miserably aware of his confession of inadequacy. He had vowed he would be of no use to the West Wilts. Deeply depressed, he found concentration elusive once more. Even the pleasure he found in sporting activities paled, because a voice in

138

his head kept asking if he would put a back three-quarter at scrum-half and he kept answering that it would be a disastrous mistake.

Clive noticed his silence on their weekly dawn run.

'I'm pretty certain you're not thinking about the pluperfect of some Latin verb, and I'm even more certain there's not a fast little piece behind your introspection lately. It's not still the old question of how you can get your arse on a saddle and gallop hell for leather at the dastardly enemy, is it?'

'You ceased to be funny years ago,' Val panted.

They ran on in silence through the November mist where berries were scarlet on the trees and leaves lay in a tawny mass over the mossy ground. Then Clive put forward a reasonable proposition.

'Why not forget it until June? Concentrate on your work – God knows you need to if you hope to scrape through the exams – and enjoy the masochistic pleasure you appear to find in sporting pursuits. When the moment of decision comes, adopt that headstrong defiance you employ so often and refuse to join the West bloody Wiltshires. Sir Gilliard can hardly make you drunk and force you to take the shilling with his precious regiment. Worrying *now* won't help anyone, least of all you, you idiot. Even if you came up with a brilliant solution, you couldn't implement it until next July.' They branched apart momentarily to pass a great oak growing in the middle of the track, then Clive resumed his appeal. 'You're captain of bloody everything, and a senior prefect. For heaven's sake enjoy your last year here. Life's short, Val, and may be even shorter for a determined soldier. Think of Vorne. Dead at twenty-four.'

Val continued his steady pace. He *had* enjoyed his time here. School life was much like that in a regiment, he supposed. Rules and regulations, echelons of command, companionship, endeavour and a common loyalty. He rarely kicked against regulations; he respected authority when it deserved respect. Popularity with his fellows had blessed him from his first year and no one was more keen than he on gaining laurels for the whole team and for this school. It *would* be foolish to spoil this final year, which promised to be the best of all. Knowing that his friend had been sincere, Val turned to acknowledge the fact. But Clive was never serious for long, and met his glance with a wicked smile.

'After you have disdainfully declined the West Wilts, you can sail the Atlantic to join your step-father on his plantation. I've heard cowboys look very dashing in the saddle.'

With a swift movement Val bent to scoop up a handful of mud-bound fallen leaves, which he threw at Clive's sleek, handsome features. His friend merely laughed and carolled in falsetto tones, 'Don't be angry with me, Val. I'm only trying to help.'

139

The incident did help. Val's depression lifted and he threw himself into the daily routine with his old gusto. Vorne had made a snap decision at Khartoum when faced with the alternatives. Vere had recently done the same. Why let something which lay in the future spoil the enjoyable present? A few days of rare late autumn sunshine also brought frosts to harden the ground. The Saturday afternoon rugby practice between the first and second teams accordingly resulted in more bruises and painful knocks than when the pitch was soft with mud. The boys were cleaner but walking gingerly when Geoffrey Manton blew his whistle to halt play for the afternoon. Val had a fast-swelling knee, a familiar throbbing in his stomach, and a badly grazed chin, but he was exhilarated as he walked toward the changing rooms with the sports master, discussing the match fixtures up to Christmas. Halting outside the building, Manton smiled. 'You'd better get a shower before those blighters use all the water. Your second try was one of the most audacious I've ever seen you pull off. Do it again next week against Cranbourne.' Two paces away, he half turned to halt Val again. 'I almost forgot. Mr Grieves wants to see you as soon as you've cleaned up.'

'Righto,' said Val, pleased Manton had singled out that second try for praise. It *had* been audacious, but it had also given him a painful knee and a bloody chin. He grinned as he stripped off and joined the others beneath the welcome wet cascade. The scars of battle! Towelling off, he dressed intermittently due to a heated discussion on whether the navy rather than the army was responsible for the successful capture of Abu Hamed. Several boys had relatives in the Royal Navy; others supported them. Val, and those others from a military background, claimed the gun-boats had been no more than valuable support to the troops in the attack.

One of Val's unsuccessful rivals for captaincy of the rugby team asked, 'What does your brother report on the situation, Ashleigh?'

He had to prevaricate. 'He hasn't had time to write. I expect he's in the thick of things . . . or on a solo mission to some inaccessible part of the desert.'

'Gosh,' marvelled a junior, who excelled in the scrum. 'It must take some pluck to do that. I've heard the Dervishes do the most terrible things to prisoners, like cutting off their tongues.'

'It's not the only thing they cut off,' his neighbour told him darkly. 'But you'd be quite safe, Blore. Yours isn't big enough to be of interest to anyone.'

Val left them still discussing Dervish atrocities and made his way across to Herbert Grieves's house. He was upset that Vere had not made contact since leaving so abruptly. With other boys getting first-hand news from their relatives, Val was driven to make far-fetched excuses for his own lack of information. His brother would almost certainly be given a staff position well away from any action. The intense heat or a fever would be Vere's killer. The thought saddened him anew. Would Knightshill settle permanently into gloom if Vere never returned?

On reaching the house he found the door open, so he rang the bell and announced himself in a loud voice.

Julia Greaves appeared at the top of the stairs. 'Come on up, Val. Herbert had to slip across to the library. He won't be very long.'

'I can come back later,' he offered.

'Don't be silly. Come up.'

He went reluctantly, smoothing a hand over his windblown hair as he would if about to confront Dr Keening. Blast old Grieves for going out right at this moment! She ushered him into the parlour in friendly fashion, and he told himself there was no need to feel awkward until her husband returned. She was really quite nice. The room looked welcoming with its bright fire, comfortably sagging chairs, and oil lamps which brightened the dusk. There was a tray on the circular table and several plates beside a silver muffin dish.

'I was about to have tea,' she said over her shoulder. 'Keep me company.'

He refused swiftly. 'I've promised to join Randall in his study. It's his birthday and he's been sent an astonishingly large cake by his godmother.'

She turned with an amused expression. 'So you're pledged to helping him eat it? Surely you could manage a cup of tea and a muffin while you're waiting. With that splendid physique you must have a good appetite.'

'Perhaps it would be best for me to come back later on,' he told her. 'This is an inconvenient time for you.'

Her smile was replaced by a look of concern as she came to where he stood on the rug in the centre of the room. 'Whatever have you done to yourself? Good gracious, that looks extremely sore.'

He had forgotten the cut on his chin. 'It's nothing.'

'Spoken like a true Ashleigh,' she said, as her lustrous eyes studied the small wound. 'Sit in that chair and I'll attend to it.'

'No – really – it doesn't matter,' he protested.

Taking his shoulders firmly she made him walk over to the chair. 'That's a favourite phrase of yours, isn't it? *It doesn't matter*. Do as I say while I fetch some water to cleanse that cut. It's quite deep.'

It was impossible to be rude and insist on leaving, so he sat beside a table bearing a lamp while she disappeared with a rustle of her long plum-coloured skirt into an adjoining room. Through the crack of the door, he glimpsed a bed with a white counterpane. Unbidden came the thought of dry old Herbert Grieves occupying that bed with this forthright young woman. It seemed almost obscene, for some reason.

She returned with a small bowl covered in pink roses, some gauze and a dark green bottle. Val felt more uncomfortable than ever after seeing that bed, so he vowed to let her deal with his cut and then leave.

'I'm quite deft at this kind of thing, I promise. I have three younger brothers who are forever coming home the worse for wear. Tip your head back so that I can see the place properly.'

Her resemblance to Margaret again struck him strongly. He relaxed and raised his chin obediently as she dipped the gauze into the water. She made rather a fuss over such a small wound, he thought, but the gentle warm caress of the damp gauze was so soothing he kept his head tilted back. Her perfume was distinctive – some flower or other but he could not think which – and much sweeter than Matron's antiseptic nearness. When the cleansing ceased, he was about to straighten when she said softly, 'Stay exactly as you are.'

Next minute, cold liquid touched his skin burning deep into it like a brand. He gave an involuntary cry of pain and jerked his head forward with the shock. Julia was sitting back on her heels, holding the green bottle in one hand and a small pad in the other. A frown creased her brow as he gasped at the prolonged burning which was making his eyes water.

'I'm *so* sorry,' she breathed. 'That cut must be deeper than I guessed. I had no idea it would hurt so much when I applied the antiseptic. I've never heard anyone yell like that over my ministrations, Val.'

Deeply embarrassed, he endured the considerable after effects of the antiseptic on raw flesh, muttering, 'It doesn't matter.'

Julia burst into laughter. 'You really must stop saying that. It's particularly inappropriate when your air of suffering shows that it certainly *does* matter. Poor thing!' Getting to her feet, she said kindly, 'Now you must have a cup of tea and a muffin while you recover.' Her eyes appealed to him. 'Can you forgive me?'

Unsure how to deal with that approach, and still feeling mortified over the incident, he said, 'It's all right, I'll get tea from Randall in a minute.'

She was already at the table, pouring from the silver teapot as if he had not spoken. 'I have something to tell you. I hope you'll be pleased because I believe I've solved your problem for you.' She came across with a cup of tea and a buttered muffin on a plate. Bending to put them on the table beside him, she glanced up with a conspiratorial smile. 'You do still want to join the cavalry?'

His heart lurched with faint excitement. 'Yes, of course.'

'Good.' She returned to fetch her own tea and took it to a chair in a shadowed corner. When she had settled and sipped several times from her cup, she glanced across at him. 'Eat up! What I have to say may take some time because there are complications to the granting of your great desire.'

Val bit into his muffin without being aware of its taste. 'I don't understand.'

'Of course not, because I haven't yet told you that one of my uncles is a brigadier in the Fifty-seventh Lancers.'

Val's heart lurched again and the hand holding the muffin stilled in mid-air. 'The Ghost Lancers?' he asked breathlessly, using the nickname of a regiment which wore an all-grey uniform.

'Clever boy! Do you know why they're so called?'

'In the Peninsular War they once emerged from thick mist to take the French by surprise, and frightened many of them into surrender believing they were apparitions. They've been dubbed the Ghost Lancers ever since.' He abandoned the muffin in his excitement. 'Your uncle really is one of their officers?'

She smiled. 'Too good to be true? If I wrote to him, I'm sure he'd do what he could to have you admitted to the regiment.'

Excitement faded and so did Val's short-lived hopes. 'It wouldn't be any use, I'm afraid. Grandfather would no sooner get wind of it than he'd carry out his threat to prevent anyone from taking me on.' He sighed. 'It's nice of you to think of it, but he wields the greatest influence in military circles. The plan wouldn't stand a chance.'

'It would, if Sir Gilliard knew nothing of it until after you'd taken your oath of allegiance and received the Queen's commission.'

Her calm words sounded infinitely persuasive in that room filled with soft light and shadows, where the embers glowed nearby to warm his cheeks. Gazing across at her he found it impossible to see her face clearly, but the sparkling green stones in a large brooch at the neck of her pale frilled blouse held his attention as he thought feverishly. Would it be possible to do as she suggested? The greatest point in his favour concerning anything military was the Ashleigh name and background. Any colonel asked to deceive Sir Gilliard must think little of a grandson who would be party to such behaviour, yet if he were kept in the dark about the old general's views he would be certain to speak freely about the acquisition of a young man who had shunned the family regiment in favour of his own. There would be the devil to pay then.

He shook his head. 'The colonel of the Fifty-seventh must be a man of honour who would never countenance such a plan.'

'Mm, I believe he is,' she said softly, 'but he retires in the spring and Uncle Max is to take over the regiment.' The brooch flashed green fire as she reached for the muffin dish and held it out. 'I'm not suggesting that he

143

is *not* a man of honour, Val, but I'm his favourite niece and he'd listen sympathetically to my request . . . especially if it concerned someone I was anxious to help.' Her hand waggled the dish. 'Have another muffin while you consider your answer.'

'My answer?'

'To whether or not you will allow me to help you fulfil your ambition.'

He went across to where she sat and took a muffin he did not really want. It seemed impolite not to when she had held them out for so long. Thoughts were tumbling around his brain, however, and he stared down without seeing her. Vere had told him to follow his star, however thorny the path. His brother was certainly doing so in the Sudan at this moment, and Vorne had not shied from daring the near-impossible, either. Only a fool or a faint heart would hesitate.

'It's beautiful, isn't it?' she said quietly. 'Herbert gave the brooch to me on our wedding night.'

Hot colour rushed into his face as he realised what he had been doing. 'I'm sorry. I didn't mean to stare at you. My thoughts were miles away.'

'That's not very complimentary.'

Val put the muffin back in the dish, feeling more gauche than ever. Her proposal had been so unexpected, her revelation so exciting he had lost all sight of the fact that she was practically a member of staff who must be treated as such. He struggled to rectify the situation.

'You must think me very rude and immature, which will hardly strengthen my case as a prospective officer of the Fifty-seventh Lancers. You've made an absolutely splendid offer of help and I've responded like an idiot. It's simply that it seems too good to believe.'

Her smile eased the fear that he had offended her. 'Would you like me to pinch you to prove you're not dreaming?'

Val smiled back in relief. 'I shall be doing that to myself for the rest of the day. The answer is, *yes, please*.'

When she stood, her eyes were level with his chin. 'I know Uncle Max will help, especially when I describe you. They like their officers tall and sturdy so they look impressive in uniform.' Taking his arm she led him to a bookcase and took from it a slim volume bound in grey leather tooled with silver. 'This is a copy of the Regimental History of the Fifty-seventh that my uncle gave me on coming of age. Would you like to borrow it?'

He was thrilled. 'I'll say! Trust me to take care of it.'

'I'd trust you with anything, Val,' she said, placing the book in his hands. 'Herbert speaks very highly of you.'

Suddenly intensely alive and happy, he said, 'You've been marvellous. I don't know how to thank you.'

'There's no need yet. Nothing has been resolved.' Walking to the door, she added, 'I'll write to my uncle and sound him out on the subject. When I receive a reply we can take it a step further, can't we?' When he nodded, she put her hand on his arm to say softly, 'I'm sorry my ministrations to your chin were so painful.'

'It doesn't matter.' He caught himself and grinned. 'There I go again.'

Her glance lengthened to a comprehensive study of his face. 'Yes, there you go again. We'll have to cure you of that habit before you join the Fifty-seventh. They expect their officers to be self-assured and assertive.'

'I will be,' he told her ardently. 'You can promise your uncle that.' He pulled open the door and stepped out to the dim landing. 'I'll read this thoroughly so that I'll be completely familiar with the regiment's battle honours and its customs.' Sighing to relieve his excitement, he added, 'I'm exceedingly grateful to you.'

'I know,' she responded in low, warm tones, 'and I'm sure you'll be particularly nice to me in return.'

'Well . . . thanks again.'

He clattered down the stairs and out into the frosty chill which increased his sense of exhilaration. Throughout the hour spent with Philip Randall, his thoughts continually wandered to conjure up images of himself as one of the celebrated Ghost Lancers. When they left Randall's study Val fought the desire to tell Clive his news, but when his friend came to his room later with a bottle of forbidden sherry the impulse to share his excitement triumphed. Indicating the grey leather-bound volume he was avidly reading, Val related the whole story. Clive listened attentively, sprawled in the easy chair, and his thoughtfulness continued when Val finished speaking.

Disappointed with his friend's reaction, he asked, 'Why the brooding calm?'

Clive regarded him with great seriousness. 'Watch your step, young Valentine.'

'Stow it, Clive! You've known all along that I'd have to take on Grandfather to secure my ambition. You encouraged me. When I'm on the brink of doing something positive to flout his ruling, you warn me of the consequences.'

'I wasn't thinking of Sir Gilliard.'

'What, then?'

'*Who* not *what*. Julia Grieves is devious.'

'That's rot! She reminds me of Margaret.'

'That's why you should watch your step. There are similarities, I agree, although Margaret is a real beauty compared with Julia, and a great deal more sincere. However, they both have unsuccessful marriages. Margaret is very unhappy but will do nothing to change her situation because she has Tim and Kate.'

'What do you know about all that?' demanded Val defensively.

'I used my eyes during my visit to Knightshill. You never see anything beyond a cricket or rugby pitch, and I sometimes wonder if you even possess libido, but those of us who understand sexual frustration can easily recognise it in others. It's almost criminal for a beautiful woman like Margaret to be tied to a man who no longer sees her; she's a captive because of her children. God only knows why our Mrs Grieves tied herself to dry old Herbert, but she has no children to consider and can therefore do something to relieve her obvious appetite for admiration and excitement.' Putting down his glass he fixed Val with a meaning look. 'If you liken the hungry Julia to another sister you're a greater fool than any Ashleigh should be. She has her eye on you, lad.'

'That's a pretty rotten remark,' he snapped with some heat. 'You may be obsessed by that side of life, but don't attribute the same base instincts to us all. She's a very nice person who sees a way of helping me. I heard she intervened to gain the Cowdrey twins permission to dine with their father, who sails for India at the end of the week. They're only twelve. I suppose you think she had some beastly ulterior motive for *that*.'

Clive got to his feet with languid grace. 'Think on my words, Val. Just ponder the wisdom I've offered,' he said, and departed.

Val did. The more he thought, the unhappier he grew. The way she had looked at him, changes in vocal tone now took on a significance he had not noticed at the time. She had certainly forced him to stay when he would have left; there had been unnecessary trouble taken over the cut on his chin. But she had three younger brothers and probably fussed over them the same way, as Margaret would. There was no doubt she had enjoyed teasing him. That was no different from sisterly treatment . . . except that she was not his sister but his housemaster's wife. More than once she had laid her hand on his arm. But he recalled that she had done the same with some of the others during that first tea party. The reason she had singled him out was because she was in the unique position of having an uncle in the cavalry. If her uncle Max had been a diplomat Clive would have been helped; if a politician, it would have been Roland Baines.

He prepared for bed, telling himself Clive's Italian blood made him see mischief where there was none. Once the lamp was out, doubts returned. He heard her soft voice saying, *'Once I receive a reply we can take it a step further, can't we?'* Then, when he expressed his gratitude, *'I'm sure you'll be particularly nice to me in return.'* He grew hot at the way his thoughts were travelling. She could not possibly have meant . . . She was married to old Grieves. The whole concept was ridiculous. Damn Clive for suggesting it!

Unable to settle, he struck a match and put it to the wick of the lamp once more. Then he tugged on a dressing-gown over his pyjama jacket and sat up to continue reading the fascinating history of the regiment he might join next year. When he eventually lost the battle against sleep he was elated and confident that Julia Grieves was simply a generous person who helped anyone she could. He maintained that belief, but found himself giving the grey leather book to Herbert Grieves after his lesson in European History.

'Your wife very kindly lent me this volume concerning her uncle's regiment, sir,' he explained as he stood at the tutor's desk. 'I found it deeply interesting. Please thank her for trusting a rare edition to my keeping. I have taken great care with it.'

Grieves smiled. 'I'm sure you have, Ashleigh. Any news of your brother yet?'

Val shook his head. 'I expect mail services in a country like the Sudan are fairly primitive.'

'No doubt, no doubt.' His attention returned to collecting up his books and papers, so Val left gratefully. He hated people enquiring for news of Vere. Something told him there would be none.

During the next few days he saw little of Clive. The match against Cranbourne was only a few days off so Val spent most of his spare time either in the gymnasium, running around the school perimeter or discussing tactics with Geoffrey Manton and the rest of the team. The problem of Julia Grieves was pushed to the back of his mind, although hardly an hour passed when he did not wonder if she had yet written to her uncle and when a reply could be expected. He tried to tell himself nothing would come of it, but hope bubbled eternally inside him.

On the afternoon of the match, she appeared at the touchline just after half-time and stood with other members of staff who had come to watch for a while. Val's spirits soared. Perhaps she had news for him, confirmation that the letter was on its way to her uncle. They were leading Cranbourne by just two points, but their opponents were tiring and only disaster on Chartfield's part could lose them the match. Knowing Julia was there gave Val an absurd desire to show her that he could be as self-assured and assertive as any officer of the 57th. With twenty minutes to go he began urging his team to step up their efforts to increase their lead, and then set a fine example by making a brilliant dash down the field, evading three opposing players with deceptive twists and turns, finally passing the ball to an unguarded team-mate who easily touched down right behind the posts. The try was successfully converted and the game took on fresh vigour as both teams caught the fever to win. The final fifteen minutes produced some sizzling play before the whistle made Cranbourne the losers by eleven points.

The teams shook hands, the captains exchanged thanks for a sporting game, then they all trooped from the field anxious to clean up and enjoy a hearty tea. Approaching Geoffrey Manton meant passing Julia, who stood with the thick fur collar of her coat turned up against the considerable cold. Val decided to stop and thank her for the loan of the book as an excuse to talk to her. She was looking his way – he had been conscious of her scrutiny during the match – and he felt his heart quicken with hope as he drew near her. When he was less than ten yards away, she turned her back and began a deep conversation with the dumpy, dapper man who taught French to the juniors. Val had no choice but to walk on feeling as if he had been doused with icy water. There was no doubt Julia had just deliberately snubbed him.

He hardly knew what he said to the delighted Manton, or how he got through the following hour as host to Cranbourne's team. He was desolate, knowing he had killed his chances of entering the 57th. Because of Clive he had suspected Julia Grieves capable of something quite unthinkable, and had consequently offended her deeply by returning the book via her husband. The expensively bound volume was of great personal and sentimental value to her. Small wonder she had been hurt by his casual return of it. He had not even enclosed a short note of thanks expressing his great interest. Dear God, how could he have been so stupid and rude? It was out of character for him to be suspicious of people, to see sinister ulterior motives for their actions. He must have been mad to allow the seeds Clive had sown in his mind to grow.

Misery became a physical pain in his stomach. He had actually half believed that a lively, warm-hearted bride of six months was making sexual overtures to an eighteen-year-old pupil at her new husband's school. It was bizarre, monstrous. It was also outrageously conceited. Damn Clive for his lewd suspicions! Damn his own inflated ego for believing them! His ill-mannered behaviour had put paid to his hopes. Julia had shown him where he now stood in her estimation. The zest for life vanished again. He was not only back where he had started concerning his future career, he might well have created an unpleasant relationship with Herbert Grieves. If Julia had confided her affront to her husband, this school year could easily become difficult. At that point Val realised that although he had been summoned to the house for the purpose of seeing his housemaster, Grieves had not been there, and had not returned during the considerable period Julia had entertained him. He had not mentioned the subject when Val had returned the book. Hot on the heels of that came the recollection that old Grieves was notoriously absent-minded. Disgust flooded Val once more.

Seven days of misery and recrimination followed. His work received poor marks; he was picked on several times for obvious inattention in class. He avoided Clive whenever he could, was brusque and off-hand when he could not. That his friend behaved as if everything were normal only heaped coals on the fire. That Saturday dawn run was the first Val had missed since its inception. He had no heart for it, and stayed in bed forgoing breakfast because his appetite had vanished. He forced himself to eat lunch because there was a team practice from two until three, which he could not dodge without pretending to be ill. Something he revelled in had now become an unwelcome chore.

Going to the prefects' study to collect Geoffrey Manton's notes on those aspects of play he felt should be improved, Val found a sealed envelope in his pigeon hole. The letter inside it brought the sun out to illuminate a world full of promise.

I shall be walking on Cartwheel Hill at three this afternoon. If you still want my help, come.

Julia Grieves

Thinking swiftly, he returned to his room, put on an extra pullover beneath his blazer before winding a woollen scarf about his neck and slipping from the building unseen. It would take half an hour to reach Cartwheel Hill so he could not attend rugby practice, nor had he a valid reason for asking Manton to let him skip it. Better to concoct a lie after the event.

When Julia eventually appeared on the path through the copse it was almost three-thirty. Val was chilled by then, convinced she had changed her mind about coming. She walked up to him unsmiling, giving no reason for being late. Having no idea how to greet her, he remained silent.

'I half expected my husband to pass me your excuse for not coming,' she said briskly, giving him comprehensive scrutiny.

He flushed at her tone. 'I'm sorry about the book.'

'Are you normally as arrogant as that with people who have loaned you valuable possessions?'

'No,' he protested, flushing more darkly still. 'I wasn't being arrogant. I just didn't think. I'm sorry.'

She walked on, so he fell in beside her feeling that they had started off badly. Had she asked him to meet her just for a telling off? She was warmly clad in boots, a dark red coat with a hood, a soft scarf and gloves with fur cuffs. Her cheeks were rosy from the growing chill of afternoon and her eyes were glowing with amber lights as they gazed straight ahead as if he were not there. Shivering from cold and nervousness, Val stuffed his icy hands in his pockets and wondered what he could do to appease her. She was plainly still upset over the way he had returned her book.

149

After a few more minutes of silent walking, he said tentatively, 'The Fifty-seventh have a very distinguished history. Any man would be proud to join such a regiment.'

'Would *you*?' she asked pointedly, still not looking his way.

'*Of course I would.*'

'I wondered. For someone who appeared to be prepared to do *anything* to gain the coveted prize, your subsequent behaviour suggested you had lost interest.' Her large eyes turned to accuse him. 'I almost believed you were telling me an Ashleigh did not consider my uncle's regiment good enough.'

It had never crossed his mind that such an interpretation could have been put upon his thoughtless act, yet now he saw quite clearly that it had seemed so to her. He was appalled.

'You must have gained a very low opinion of me,' he said, stopping and facing her unhappily. 'I now have a low opinion of myself. But please believe that exaggerated self-esteem isn't one of my failings. Quite the reverse. I wonder if I am good enough for your uncle's regiment.'

She looked him over consideringly for a moment or two. 'Can I believe that, Val?'

'Yes, but I don't know how I can prove it to you,' he said.

'By behaving yourself from now on and not treating me like one of your servants.' Before he could protest at that, she slipped her arm through his and began walking again. 'I've had a reply from Uncle Max.'

Warmth instantly suffused him. It was going to be all right. 'What did he say? Will he help?' he demanded eagerly.

She chuckled. 'Patience, boy, patience! He is very interested in you but insists that before he can consider inviting you to become one of his officers he must know a great deal more about you.'

'I see. What does he want to know?' Val was hardly able to believe the complete change of mood from a moment ago.

'Everything. Start at the beginning and tell me the story of your life. I'll write it all down in a letter to him.'

'I can't do that.'

'No one else can do it for you. You're the only person who knows all about Valentine Ashleigh. For instance, what names do the initials M. H. indicate?'

'Do I have to say?'

'Are they that dreadful? Yes, you have to tell me.'

He sighed. 'Martin Havelock.'

She turned to him. 'They're good, manly names. You shouldn't be shy of revealing them. Tell me about your childhood.'

'Is that really necessary?' he asked, feeling more relaxed now she sounded like Margaret again.

'*Yes*. Come on, offer up your secrets.'

Although he hardly did that, she managed to coax from him more than he had told anyone save Clive about his early days at Knightshill. He caught himself enjoying the reminiscences and laughing with her over some of his childish escapades. The winter darkness crept from the east behind them as he talked freely about his growing passion for the cavalry, culminating in a detailed account of the quarrel with Sir Gilliard on the night of the Khartoum Dinner when his cousins had forced him to reveal his hopes.

'Poor boy!' she said sympathetically. 'A stag surrounded by snapping hounds.'

'That's exactly what Margaret said . . . but my ageing cousins don't intimidate me,' he told her with energetic frankness. 'Neither does Grandfather. It's simply that he likes his own way and has the power to get it. One can't fight that.'

'Yet you are.'

'With your help,' he pointed out.

'You'd have done it anyway. I suspect you are very much like Sir Gilliard in wanting your own way, my dear. You have a very mutinous mouth.' She smiled up at him. 'There's pride there, too, so the comparison with a stag is extremely apt. Broad, powerful shoulders, graceful nobility in the way you move, blond splendour of form and an exciting latent arrogance which typifies the dominant male of a herd. Oh, yes, Val,' she continued softly, 'I suspect that when you want your own way you will do *anything* to get it. Am I right?'

In a flash, the suspicions Clive had aroused, which he had forced himself to dismiss as preposterous, returned. There was nothing of his sister Margaret in this young woman now. Her huge luminous eyes were studying him in a way that simultaneously excited and disturbed him while her words floated around in his head with seductive persistence which refused to be ignored. Intensely aware of his own height beside hers, his own broad build which emphasised her slender lines in the red fitted coat, a new eagerness suddenly invaded and silenced him.

Julia then appeared to notice how dark it had become, and suggested gaily that they quicken their pace. 'I have to meet Herbert in Tetherbury at five o'clock. You can escort me as far as the mill. It'll be safe enough for me to walk through the village alone from there. Come on.'

The way to the village lay down the far side of the hill, through a belt of wild blackberry and honeysuckle and thence to the path alongside water meadows which led to the mill driven by the flow of the river. They would be lucky to reach it by five. Once again Val experienced her bewildering change of mood as she chatted lightly about the village and its environs, revealing that her husband collected brass rubbings and found many opportunities to enjoy his hobby in the historical buildings around Tetherbury.

'Men tend to devote themselves to those things which fascinate them to the point of obsession,' she observed, as they reached the overgrown brambles through which there was only a narrow twisting track. 'They are excessively selfish creatures, in the main. You are the same, my dear. In your bid to join the cavalry you will happily sacrifice your family loyalty.' With hardly a pause, she said, 'Hold my arm more firmly through this bad patch. I can scarcely see you now and I'm afraid of the dark.'

Her proximity while they groped their way through the winding gap increased Val's sense of reluctant eagerness. Pressed close against her in the isolation of darkness he felt that, despite her accusation of selfishness, she somehow admired him for it. Clive's warning was forgotten; his own reservations were swamped by emerging awareness of the power of inbred desires. His mind knew only the inference of all that had happened this afternoon; his senses knew just the thrill of cold frosty darkness and a challenging young woman clinging to him because she was afraid of it. The chill which bit into his face and hands, the secret oncoming night which would bring stealthy creatures out in the confidence of being invisible to others, the scents of autumn dying and the nearby dark slither of the river, all combined to fill him with uncontainable exhilaration of a kind he had never before experienced. *He* was not afraid. Julia Grieves had put a match to the inflammable restlessness he had suffered since she had first mentioned her uncle Max, and the growing flames were so bright they illuminated something he had not seen before. Now, he could see nothing else because the fire was also within him.

When they reached level ground they walked faster. He held her steady along the dim riverside path with an arm about her shoulders. Their silence was natural enough against the sound of wind in the brittle branches, and the rush of water tumbling over the weir beside the dark silhouette of the flour mill. Val's throat was dry and his heart was thudding at the prospect of parting from her there. When they had met on Cartwheel Hill, he had been nervous and apologetic. Later, he had told her about himself with complete lack of restraint until she had likened him to a stag, 'the dominant male of a herd'. He was now a different person who was nervous for another reason. What would happen when they reached the mill? A dominant male should be just that, but she changed moods so swiftly he was consistently caught unprepared and put at a disadvantage. Twenty-five yards from the mill he found himself a victim again.

Stopping abruptly, she broke physical contact as she turned to face him. 'Whatever lie you've decided to tell Geoffrey Manton, as an excuse for missing rugby practice, won't hold water if you're seen in the village by any of the staff. You'd better return over Cartwheel Hill.'

Taken aback by this evidence that she had known he must forsake the practice session to meet her and would have to lie to Manton, his protest was consequently heated. 'It's *miles* by that route. I'd never find my way back at night.'

She shrugged in the faint light thrown by the mill lamp. 'I thought you had no fears of the dark.'

'I haven't but there's no moon tonight. Besides, it's twice the distance by road.'

'All right, but you'll have to wait here until Herbert and I have had tea at the Plough. If you start off along the road now old Maggs is certain to overtake you before we reach school. Herbert will tell him to stop the carriage when he sees your blazer. How will you explain what you are doing there?' Moving closer to him, she put a hand lightly against his chest. 'We can't possibly mention our meeting. Herbert would be furious with me for interfering with the school activities of his pupils. He made it quite clear that I must not do it under any circumstances.' So close now her body was almost against his, she added, 'See what I am prepared to risk in order to help you? I'll send all the information to my uncle tomorrow. There's no reason why he shouldn't then arrange a meeting so that he can formally invite you to join the Fifty-seventh as soon as you gain your commission.' Her other hand came to rest on his chest. 'That's what you want so desperately, isn't it?'

'Yes,' he said abruptly, thrown by her rapid change of approach and by the prospect of waiting until she and her ageing husband had eaten a good tea before starting his long, cold, lonely walk back to school.

'That sounds very ungracious,' she accused.

'I'm sorry,' he said through stiff lips. 'I didn't mean to give you that impression.'

'Mmm, the latent arrogance I mentioned is fast coming to the fore. Don't you say "thank you" when someone is good to you?'

He swallowed back a curious rising aggression. 'Of course. Thank you.'

There was a slight pause before her softly teasing voice said, 'Is that the best you can manage, Valentine Martin Havelock?'

Aggression triumphed. 'No. I can manage quite a lot more, except that I never know where I stand with you. One minute you remind me of my older sister, the next you're ticking me off like a member of staff, the next . . . well, just how do you expect me to treat you?'

Her soft laugh fanned the flames rising within. 'Cavalry officers should be prepared to take risks and face the consequences, but you appear to be a timid schoolboy.'

Hesitating only momentarily before bending to her upturned face, he tried a rather clumsy kiss. She immediately relaxed against him, pressing her lips harder and harder against his until they opened to allow her tongue to probe his mouth in a fashion which sent a shock of excitement through him. Rational thought flew on the wind and he began to respond instinctively. Pulling her against him with an arm around her waist, his frozen fingers pushed back the hood of her coat and began to fumble with the double fastening of its fur collar.

Next minute she pulled free of his hold, saying breathlessly, 'That's rather too much of a risk to take.' Then she walked away towards the mill without a backward glance leaving Val shivering convulsively, heart thudding, as he stared at her in the certain dread that he had misjudged the situation badly. She had provoked him into overstepping the mark. Had it cost him that coveted place in her uncle's regiment? He bit his lip hard as he fought the turmoil she had aroused in him. Oh God, what *did* she expect from him?

Chapter 9

Four days in the school infirmary with a feverish cold lent support to Val's story of finding a lost child on Cartwheel Hill, and spending most of the day trying to follow vague directions on how to find an isolated farmhouse home. Geoffrey Manton accepted the story. Matron told Val he possessed as few wits as the child for not asking Mr Maggs to drive him to the school from Tetherbury on such a bitterly cold night.

Val had time to reflect on Saturday's events. Time and again he recalled what a fool he had been to risk his greatest chance for the future by misjudging the relationship with Julia. How could he have been so stupid as to try to unbutton her coat? That she had wanted him to kiss her was indisputable, but her response had suggested to him that she had expected expertise and instinct had taken over. Had she reported him to her husband there would have been repercussions by now, but he could expect no further help from her. Why had he behaved so out of character and offended her again?

In truth, he had no notion how to behave with a young woman of such complex personality. There could be only one explanation for her asking if saying thank you was the best he could do. Yet why had she spent an entire winter afternoon in the countryside discussing his entry to her uncle's regiment only to walk away affronted when he did what she wanted? More confusing still was *why* she had wanted it. On Saturday afternoon he had believed Clive's claim that Julia 'had her eye' on him when she had compared him to a dominant stag. In the familiar surroundings of the school's sick quarters a week later he realised it was ridiculous. She was ten years his senior and married to one of his teachers. Even to have kissed her was playing with fire. When he had kissed Flossie Marchant at the bakery there had been a big enough hue and cry. Julia Grieves was no village flirt, and the Headmaster would act swiftly and irrevocably if any word reached him of what he would regard as indecent behaviour with her.

Each time Val's fevered thoughts formed that conclusion, an inner voice began the bewildering roundabout once more by telling him a housemaster's wife who merely wished to help a pupil in his ambitions would not have told him to meet her in an isolated spot far from the school and provoke him into kissing her out of gratitude. Additionally, she would never press herself against him in response and tease his mouth with her tongue. Yet she had walked away angrily when he had reacted to that provocation. It was as if she was playing a game. If so, it was one to which he was a complete novice. He remained feverish and disturbed. If he really wanted that place in the 57th he would have to see her and apologise. A sixth sense told him to beware but, in Julia's own words, he wanted it so much he was prepared to do anything.

At the weekend, winter set in with a vengeance. Temperatures dropped below freezing and the first snow of the season drifted down lazily in huge soft flakes. Local sages prophesied a hard few months ahead. Leaving Matron's care and returning to routine gave Val less time for introspection, although he was denied participation in the outdoor sports he loved due to the bitter weather which would aggravate his lingering chesty cough. Ill at ease with Herbert Grieves and off-hand with his friends, he spent his free time staring from his window at the snow-covered scene. It reminded him of last January when the family had been cut off at Knightshill. The Khartoum Dinner was painfully linked to the quarrel with Sir Gilliard. The memory revived a sensation of being swept in a direction he did not want to go, into the shoes of the brother they annually honoured. Val was not afraid of that obligation but knew he *must* wear his own shoes in order to fulfil it. Julia was his one hope of doing so. All the time this weather continued he had no chance of meeting her in the school grounds. That meant he must force the issue by seeking her out. As yet, the means of doing so had not presented itself. Torn between desperation and relief, he struggled to cope with the many hours of study required.

Two weeks after the fateful Saturday, he was gazing moodily from the window once more when Clive came to his room with two bottles of porter and a pork pie. 'I've brought you a little pick-me-up, lad. You've not been your warm, generous self since your incarceration with Matron.' His friend gave a wicked grin. 'Mother Fawcet didn't overstep her authority and handle your vitals, did she? Young Fuller claimed she let her hand wander beneath the sheet each time she tucked him in.'

Val flopped heavily into a chair and began to drink the forbidden alcohol, asking between gulps, 'Can you make any observation which isn't lewd?'

'A great many . . . in six languages. My skill is envied by many lesser men, but I'm pleased to reveal that even diplomats enjoy fornication, so lewd observation is a necessary qualification.'

'You're incorrigible,' declared Val with a faint smile.

They drank and ate before the fire in companionable silence as early darkness invaded the room. Then Clive said quietly, 'I've waited in vain for you to confide your troubles. I imagine the problem is serious because the light of life appears to have left you.'

Val sighed as he glanced around the small room lit by the flickering flames. It was cosy and comfortable, filled with treasured possessions and framed photographs of sports teams. This room was his substitute home during term and indicated privileged seniority. He had enjoyed his schooldays; he wanted to enjoy this final year here.

Turning back to his friend, he said diffidently, 'Julia Grieves *is* interested in me. I'm not quite sure why or for what she hopes in return.'

'Whatever it is, forget it,' Clive advised. 'The prospect is far too dangerous.'

'I can't forget it. She can get me into the cavalry.'

'She can get you into serious trouble. You're eighteen, she's the twenty-eight-year-old wife of a senior member of staff. Don't be a fool.'

'I'd be a fool to pass up this chance. Her uncle has already stated his willingness to consider my application.'

'How do you know she really has an uncle in the cavalry?'

Val was taken aback. 'She wrote and received a reply from him.'

'Did you see it?'

'No, I . . . Look, that's ridiculous,' he cried. 'Of course her uncle exists.'

'How can you be sure?'

'Because she has a history of his regiment. I showed it to you. Her uncle has written a dedication on the fly-leaf.'

Clive shrugged. 'That's not proof of his membership of the regiment she claims he will help you to enter.'

Val put the bottle on the table with a bang. 'You demanded to hear my troubles and now you're adding to them. She told me her uncle will arrange a meeting soon. The rest should be plain sailing.'

'Join the Prussians, Val.'

'Go to hell!'

'No, I've more sense than you seem to have.'

Silence hung between them as the fire crackled and spat bright sparks which they crushed with their shoes before the old rug was singed. Val felt more unhappy than ever because Clive's sharp questioning mind had considered something his never had. In his eagerness for the elusive career he had accepted all he had been told by her. Yet, why would she lie? What would she gain by such an elaborate hoax?

Getting to his feet restlessly, he said, 'You've ruined everything. I don't know truth from fiction now. I wish I'd never mentioned the damned cavalry that first day.'

'She wheedled it out of you. It was obvious even then that she was intrigued by your reticence and determined to make you the focus of attention because of it. That lady is extremely cunning.'

Val rounded on him. 'Why do you dislike her so much?'

'Because I have respect and admiration for her brilliant husband and she appears to have neither. They were married only a few months ago and already she's out to seduce one of his gullible prefects.'

'That's not amusing,' he said furiously.

'You really are in a lather about all this, aren't you? Face facts, Val. Ask yourself why you admitted a moment ago that the woman was interested in you. I'll wager your eyes weren't opened simply by discovering she had an overwhelming passion for your theories on cavalry tactics.'

Knowing very well what Clive meant, Val refused to answer. Instinct told him that kiss could have led further, and his friend's reference to seduction brought to the fore something he had been fighting for two weeks. Sexual longings, which had rarely plagued him in the past, were starting to disturb his nights. He was acutely conscious of being uninitiated. The words 'dominant male' constantly returned to him, disturbing his peace of mind and suggesting that he would be able to cope with Julia's volatile personality more easily if he was experienced with females.

'Am I to take your silence as an affirmative?'

'No, damn you,' he snapped. 'What do you take me for?'

Clive studied him with renewed seriousness. 'A lamb ripe for slaughter. You have that combination of physical beauty and apparent innocence which females of the species find irresistible. Outwardly, you're a six-foot powerfully built man with the envied Ashleigh good looks, but those clear blue eyes see everything from the viewpoint of a schoolboy who is honest,

trusting and committed to "playing the game" in every aspect of his life.'
Leaving his chair, he added, 'So far, you've been so keen on cricket, rugby,
fencing, rowing and sprinting, more adult pursuits have held no appeal for
you. When you're not indulging in playing games with other idiots like
yourself, you're galloping around the countryside imagining you're
leading a cavalry charge. It's time you grew up.'

Val said nothing. His self-confidence was taking a beating lately. Until
the Khartoum Dinner last January he had been supremely happy.
Knightshill was a house he loved in rather careless fashion; his family
received the same treatment, he supposed. He had never sought popularity; simply adopted that same free and easy affection towards those he
liked, and tolerated those he did not. His friends were numerous, enemies
few. It was envy rather than actual dislike of him which created them. The
things he had most wanted at school had come like a shower of blessings,
and the Ashleigh name would gain him the coveted military career. He now
knew Clive was right. He had seen the future as an extension of his
schooldays. A regiment would provide a purely masculine environment
much like the one he presently enjoyed. Women had never featured in his
hopes and dreams.

'You've got to take the plunge sooner or later,' Clive told him. 'There's a
winter carnival on in Tetherbury this evening, with skating on the pond
and a beano in one of the barns. Come with me. The girl I'm meeting there
is bringing a friend. You could keep her occupied while I slip off with
Jenny for a game I find more thrilling than your hearty team sports. What
do you say?'

He shook his head. 'Ask Randall. It's more his kind of thing. The friend
you want kept occupied wouldn't stay long with me. I haven't the first idea
how to amuse girls.'

Clive leered. 'She'll soon show you.'

'Not on a freezing night like this.'

'If I told you she had an uncle in the cavalry the temperature wouldn't
put you off.'

The barb went home as he thought how willing he had been to linger
with Julia two weeks ago. His resistance wavered. Clive managed to get
away with seduction, but his own first attempt would probably land him
with a father carrying a gun. Yet he could still hear that soft taunting voice
asking if saying thank you was the best he could do. Surely he would feel
more confident in her company if he discovered what *was* the best he could
do.

An hour later they slipped from the building and skirted the area lit by
lamps. Warmly clad in overcoats, woollen gloves and scarves, they stepped
out briskly on the snowy walk to the village. Clive assured Val his girlfriend

would arrange for her cousin to drive them back almost to the school on his cart, but Val recalled his previous return from Tetherbury shivering uncontrollably and fearful that he had thrown away the prize which had almost been in his hands.

Clusters of lights, and the sounds of music from a barrel-organ mingling with laughter greeted them when they reached the outskirts of the village. 'There they are, waiting on the corner!' exclaimed Clive. 'The friend doesn't look half bad, does she? When she sees you, she'll think Christmas has come early.'

As Val had no idea which of the girls was Clive's partner for the evening, he studied them both warily. In thick coats, with shawls covering their heads and wrapped crosswise over their chests to tie at the back, the pair looked uninteresting and rather dumpy. One began to wave, and Val guessed she must be Jenny. His mouth grew dry. He had no enthusiasm for this. How he would keep the girl occupied to oblige Clive he had no idea. She could not be expected to discuss rugby or cricket, and he certainly could not talk about Kitchener and the situation in the Sudan. This dumpy friend would probably know little about poetry or literature, the music of Brahms or Mozart, and her experience of horses would be limited. It occurred to him that Clive was right: it *was* time he emerged from the masculine world in which he was so successful. Regimental officers were frequently called upon to entertain ladies. Experience was essential.

The girls came to meet them and Val found himself being scrutinised by two pairs of glowing brown eyes.

'I told you so,' muttered Clive. 'A lamb to the slaughter.'

'Stow it,' he returned uneasily. 'Which is yours?'

'Neither, by the look of it. I'll have to use my wit and charm, as usual. Let me do the talking. Hello!' he greeted jovially. 'The prettiest pair in the district and we're lucky enough to spend the evening with them. Introduce your friend, Jenny. Val has been speculating on his good fortune all the way here.'

The taller of the two girls was still gazing at Val, but she was apparently the one with whom Clive had been amusing himself because she said in a strong country voice, 'This is Prue Davey from Wallerton. She came over for the weekend, and the carnival, in pertickler.'

'Hello,' said Val, then fell silent, uncertain on whom he should concentrate. Prue had turned very pink and appeared as uncomfortable as he, because Jenny was looking at him like a farmer studying a bull in the market.

'Right-o, let's head for the fun, shall we?' suggested Clive, taking Jenny's hand and commanding her attention. 'I suggest a warming drink first . . . and in case it's not stimulating enough I've brought along a little something to liven us all up.' He drew a brandy flask partway from his pocket and gave a knowing wink. 'Can't be sober during a carnival, can we?'

The girls giggled, and Val wondered yet again how his friend managed to get hold of alcohol so easily. Was it the secret of his success with the fair sex? With a regretful glance over her shoulder at Val, Jenny said, 'Come on, Prue, don't stand there gawping or he'll think you've sheep's wool for brains.' Then she went off clinging to Clive's hand leaving them to sort themselves out.

Feeling sorry for the blushing Prue, Val attempted to ease the awkwardness. 'Wallerton's a very nice village. Have you always lived there?'

Prue nodded, which caused her shawl to start slipping from her head to reveal very red hair. It contrasted badly with her pink cheeks, and Val sighed inwardly. It would take a lot of Clive's brandy to make this evening the fun he promised it would be.

'You got a funny name,' Prue said in a rush. 'It's a girl's.'

'No, it isn't,' he said. 'It's an abbreviation for something other than Valerie.'

'Oh.'

They walked on in silence. He wondered if she knew what 'abbreviation' meant. She really did appear to have sheep's wool for brains. So did he for allowing Clive to talk him into this. The pair ahead had turned into the main street which was filled with people bent on enjoying themselves.

Once among them Val's spirits began to brighten. The scene was full of colour and enchantment created by strings of lanterns each side of the street, which laid circles of reds, blues and greens upon the snowy surface so it seemed that they trod a mosaic pathway. Many of the little stone houses had decorations hanging over the door.

Children who had been allowed to stay out late for the occasion all carried balloons on long strings as they trudged beside their elders, or sat beneath rugs on small sledges being dragged to the pond. This year the surface had frozen hard enough to allow skating, otherwise fun was found with boats of all sizes. The sound of music grew as they neared the pond, and the air of carnival revelry descended on everyone. Val was taken by surprise when a hand grasped his. He had forgotten Prue and when he glanced down at her a surprising change appeared to have taken place. The blush had become a glow of excitement; her eyes were shining darkly to reflect the coloured lights from the many lanterns. Her mouth was slightly parted so that breath came from it as a frosted cloud, and it curved into a smile as she gripped his gloved hand tighter.

'You're ever so nice-looking,' she told him. 'It's going to be ever such fun tonight.'

He remembered what he was there for and some of the brightness dimmed. Jenny might be what Clive called a 'fast little piece' but Prue seemed too decent for that.

Introspection was short-lived because they arrived beside the pond at that point and were caught up in the excitement. The great barn beside the boathouse was bright with lamplight which illuminated tables set with food and sweets. Around the pond for several dozen yards in both directions was a selection of stalls, where revellers could buy cups of cocoa or tumblers of hot punch, hot chestnuts from the brazier, potatoes baked on red coals then split open and dotted with butter, fat, shiny brown sausages, warm gingerbread men, treacle tarts, muffins oozing with butter, meat pies, lardy cake and slabs of sticky toffee. Beside the narrow jetty where the boats were tied up in summer, the blacksmith dispensed ice-skates for sixpenny hire. Coloured lanterns had been strung along the curve of the pond to illuminate the skating area, but some bolder participants had ventured to the dim periphery to indulge in what was known in this part of rural England as 'dolly wobbing'. Clive was set upon it, and Val supposed he must also make the attempt to kiss and cuddle Prue.

That problem was delayed while all four sampled the food and drink on offer, the latter fortified with Clive's brandy. The girls threw themselves into the mood of the evening, and Val had first-hand evidence of his friend's charm and wit as Clive flattered, teased and coaxed them both into a state of willingness to agree to anything. Even so, the bright-eyed, voracious Jenny persisted in trying to engage Val's interest by asking pertinent and impertinent questions. He answered most of them with monosyllables and, as his dislike of her grew, so did his stubbornness. He was damned if he would allow a girl of her kind to cross-examine him. Julia had done the same a fortnight ago but she had had good reason for coaxing him to tell her intimate details about himself. Her uncle Max had wanted . . . He recalled Clive's doubts. Of course there was an uncle! *Yes, of course there was.*

'I was told you had to be brainy to go to Chartfield,' Jenny said, breaking into his thoughts. '*You* don't seem to have many. Talking to you is worse than talking to Toby Wells . . . and he's known as a right simpleton.'

'Then don't waste your time or so many wags of your tongue on me,' Val advised swiftly. 'Concentrate on Clive.'

His friend flashed him a long-suffering look then gripped Jenny's arm to lead her away. 'Come on, let's hire some skates before they're all gone.'

The girl looked over her shoulder at Prue. 'You're welcome to him. He might be a prime bit o' beef but *you'll* get none of it tonight. His pedigree's longer than anything else he might have, girl, take my word.'

At that point Val could very easily have walked away and returned to his warm cosy room. But Prue grabbed his arm quickly and said in tones which echoed her deep blush, 'Take no notice of her. She's always had a sharp tongue, has Jenny. She don't mean to be rude.'

He swallowed his anger and suggested skating to warm themselves up. At least he was experienced in that. The family went up to the pool in Leyden's Spinney whenever it froze during the Christmas vacation. Prue was also at home on ice, so he started to enjoy the evening as they glided and twirled together with other laughing couples. It was not long before she began to draw closer and closer until she was against his side, obliging him to put his arm round her waist to hold her steady.

She looked up into his face with a curious faraway expression. 'You don't talk much, do you? I thought it was because Jenny had so much to say that you was so quiet, but you've said hardly anything since they went off.'

'Sorry, I've been enjoying this so much I thought conversation was unnecessary,' he told her.

'You're ever so good at it.'

'Skating, or avoiding conversation?'

'Eh?' she asked, slow to follow his meaning.

'It doesn't matter.' Even as he said it he thought of Julia and her vow to cure him of that habit, because the 57th expected its officers to be self-assured and assertive. Should he now be self-assured and take this girl to some dim place for 'dolly wobbing', or assertive in his real desire not to?

Prue decided the matter by gazing up with undisguised longing in her expression. 'I like you ever so much. I've never met nobody before who treats me like I'm better than I am.' She rested her chin on his sleeve. 'I'm having ever such a lovely time. Jenny was rude because she's jealous. *She* wanted you.'

Thinking that he had better embark on what he had come for before the girl grew too embarrassing, Val guided her away from the bright area towards a small island beyond the centre of the pond. He had seen several couples make their way there, so it would not be so lonely that he would have no excuse for bringing the wretched business to an end fairly swiftly. Clive and Jenny had vanished a while ago, and Val's only fear was that he would have to wait endlessly beside a disgruntled Prue for them to reappear and organise the cart-ride home.

Away from the crowd it was so much quieter they could hear the slither of their skates on the ice, and the peculiar creak it made as they crossed the dark opaque surface past the clumps of trees on the island which loomed like a pale disc to their right. Resigned to the inevitable, Val brought them both to a halt in the lee of a snow-laden fir which glistened in the pale moonlight. It did not occur to him that there was hardly a more romantic setting for what Prue wanted. He was simply intent on getting the whole business over and forgotten. That being so, and because he had no idea what to say as an overture, he bent to kiss the eager, upturned mouth. Her lips were cold and chapped; her breath smelled faintly of onions. He groaned inwardly, once more regretting his decision to accompany Clive tonight. But her hands went up to fasten around the back of his neck so the kiss was prolonged against his will. Her body pressed tightly against his and there was no choice but to wrap his arms around it. She wore so many clothes Val felt no urge to explore further with his hands, as he had with Julia. How different it had been with her; how sweet the scent of her skin and hair, how warm her mouth, how persuasive her low cultured voice. The recollection served to renew his determination to gain sexual experience. Dragging his head up against the force of Prue's clasp, he re-orientated his mouth in relation to her parted lips and tried again. She wriggled with pleasure as he planted the kiss less clumsily and in the right place, but it gave him no more of a thrill than before as he sucked obediently at the rough, cracked skin and decided that there must be more to it than this or Clive would not be so keen on it.

His senses told him there *had* been much more to it when Julia had been his partner. Her tongue had probed his mouth, her hands had caressed his back, her pressing body had driven him to attempt to feel it beneath her thick coat. He had no desire to feel Prue Davey's dumpy shape, and the thought of this girl's onion-flavoured tongue entering his mouth repulsed him. He pulled away from the close embrace. Clinging to his coat, Prue was drawn along the ice on her skates as he stepped back.

'Ooh, you *are* strong,' she gasped delightedly, her breath clouding on the frosty night air. 'Wait till I tell Jenny how nice you kiss. None of the usual slobber and grope. Do it again!'

Telling himself he must persevere because she was willing to be a guinea pig for his experiment, Val had just embarked on his third attempt when he heard the faint sound of screams from the area ahead of the island. Lifting his head again, he listened intently so that he could identify the cries from those given by the excited crowd. He straightened when the sound came again. A girl was screaming in fear.

'Go for help,' he told Prue urgently, breaking into her dreamy capitulation. 'Skate as fast as you can and send some men out here.'

'Where you going?' she asked, bewildered by the sudden change in him. 'What's going on?'

Over his shoulder he told her what she had apparently not heard, then added, 'Go! *Go!*'

Bending low as he thrust his feet forward one after the other, he raced towards the area where he estimated the screams had been made. He could still hear them, but sound was deceptive in that clear air and the girl could be further away than it appeared. The quality of the screaming chilled his blood, although he told himself it could only signify a village girl who had taken exception to the advances of a drunken yokel. He believed he was well able to tackle the most aggressive man and hold him long enough for the girl to get away. But if he came upon something more serious than an over-amorous sweetheart urged on by too much punch, he would have to act instinctively and pray that Prue would inject sufficient urgency into her words to send help swiftly.

He wondered where the other 'dolly-wobbing' couples had gone and why he appeared to be the only person on that stretch of ice sheened by the faint moonlight. Next minute, there *was* another: a lone girl coming towards him. With a shock he realised she was Jenny. He stopped so abruptly the blades of his skates sent up a shower of ice as he drew alongside her. Shock deepened as her tear-wet face and hysteria told him that it had been she who had screamed. Because Clive had terrified her? Never!

Whether or not she knew who he was was uncertain as she moaned, 'He's in. He's fallen in,' before breaking into wild sobs which precluded further speech.

Val's blood chilled further as he left her and raced across the ice in search of the place where his friend must be in dire danger of drowning. In a heavy coat, Clive would be unable to move easily. The temperature of that water could be a swift killer. The pond became an eternity of sinister, desolate greyness stretching away from the warmth, gaiety and friendliness of the carnival as Val feared he might pass the spot without seeing it. However, the ice itself told him where to go. The creaking grew more pronounced as a tree-lined inlet loomed to his left. The ice was thinner in this place sheltered from the wind; thinner and starting to break up into slabs at least three feet thick. From there he thought he heard the sound of faint splashing.

The cracking ice gave out reports similar to the sound of pistol shots as he veered towards the inlet. The surface beneath his flying feet now seemed to be shifting as he moved across it, but personal caution was put aside in his fear for Clive. He practically sobbed with relief as he saw a vague dark blob floundering in the silvery surface.

'Hold on! Hold on!' he rasped. 'I'll soon reach you, and more help is on its way. Hold on!'

There was no more than a muffled cry in response before the ice opened up just ahead with a loud crack. Quick reflexes caused Val to swing away in time to skate back to the safety of thicker ice. Headlong progress would only endanger himself and be of no help to Clive. Breathing laboriously, he came to a halt and forced himself to concentrate on the hazards he faced. His chest heaved while he strained his eyes to judge how far the dark blob was from where he stood.

'Hold on! Hold on!' he called again, to reassure his friend that he had not given up. He strove against the debilitating power of fear to retain clarity of thought, and was soon removing his skates, then stripping down to his underclothes. The soles of his shoes found a firm grip on the surface, but he was acutely conscious of the severe frost in the air as he advanced with care. To run would be foolish. He must get as near as possible before taking the inevitable plunge when the ice gave beneath his considerable weight.

Stripped of his outer clothing, Val hoped to gain sufficient freedom of movement to allow him to help Clive to the bank by breaking a channel through the disintegrating surface. His friend would be a dead weight in a saturated coat and pullovers, to say nothing of thick trousers and yards of woollen scarf. Val knew he would need all the strength he could muster, even if that girl fetched help swiftly. He prayed Prue would rise to the occasion.

Only half aware of the convulsive shivering throughout his body, he took each step expecting to drop through to the dark water, hearing nothing but the groan of ice and the cry of a fox. There was no sound of an approaching rescue party or of the splashing he had heard earlier. Fear made him call out once more that he was on his way. He quickened his pace instinctively only to pay the penalty of haste. The sudden plunge into the pond was a greater shock than he had imagined. He gasped as icy coldness bit into his flesh before the water rose over his head, but he struck out bravely, impeded by floating sheets of ice which had razor-sharp edges. His lungs pumped faster to cope with the pressure on them as he thrust his way through, appalled by the numbing effect of the temperature on his arms and legs.

Gasping with effort, his heart hammering painfully, Val reached a large spread of water to find Clive hanging precariously to the bordering layer of ice. Almost immediately, there was another loud report. Like a scene from a nightmare, Clive slid beneath the water to vanish from sight. Horror set Val diving to recover the submerged body, but nightmare became reality as he found it almost impossible to support his friend's weight much less haul it to the surface. The years dedicated to gaining a superb physique now brought their reward. He threw every ounce of strength into the effort of lifting while his legs thrashed to keep himself afloat, and very slowly the thunderous pressure on his eardrums subsided as he broke through to gulp air again.

He believed his friend unconscious, until Clive gave a great gasp and his eyes opened to stare sluggishly at Val for a moment or two before closing again. Realising that he was unequal to bearing Clive's weight while making for the safety of the bank by breaking a passage through, Val gazed around for a large enough chunk of ice to support them both until help arrived. Still laboriously treading water while he held Clive clear of the surface, he spotted a likely buoy ten yards away. Fighting to keep them both from going under, he summoned superhuman energy in an effort to cross to it and drape his friend over the tiny raft. The feat proved impossible. There was not enough strength left in his arms to raise such a burden from the water, so he did the only other thing possible. Fastening his numbed fingers around Clive's wrists he hung, arms outstretched across the bobbing support, to counterbalance the body dangling on the far side of it. Their combined weights made the ice sink so that their arms were below water and their chins only inches above it. When dark anguished eyes opened once again briefly to meet his own across that frail lifebuoy, Val knew he must keep his friend from slipping into a stupor which would cause his head to drop forward into the water.

Time and sensation were both suspended as Val began to talk in loud convulsive tones. He spoke about anything and everything which came to mind, demanding responses every few minutes to reassure himself Clive was still conscious. He talked about school, sport, vacations, riding, his family, the army and then, inevitably, about Vorne. It seemed particularly appropriate to discuss his brother's heroic deeds at such a time. When he described the phenomenal courage, which had overcome the agony of his flesh until mortality defeated him, Val found extra strength of will by comparison.

Yet willpower of even the highest order could not match the power of the elements. Numbness began to invade Val's brain as well as his limbs. His voice grew weaker and more hoarse as he cast around for words, and he lost the sense of some phrases in the midst of expressing them. He was soon muttering incomprehensible strings of words which floated into his head willy-nilly. But he stubbornly refused to fall silent and, just as stubbornly, continued to demand responses from whoever it was he clung to.

He became a separate block of ice hanging vertically in the pond, no longer capable of movement. His hands were fused to the other's wrists as they waited together in that ghostly grey-white world inhabited by no one save foxes, and still he talked. Speech was halting and not much above a whisper, but it brought an occasional faint nod from the other block of ice hanging from his hands.

The hesitant voice began to echo in Val's head like the ramblings of a madman and he could not silence it. His body was now burning from the heat of the desert, and the torment from his open wounds was difficult to sustain. Each step brought torture, yet he knew he must reach the relief force if he was to save Gordon and Khartoum. Men swooped down on him from nowhere, tearing him limb from limb to find the communiqué he carried. He felt himself being dragged along the ground, then they began breaking his fingers one by one to persuade him to tell what message he carried. All he offered was a string of nonsense. They would never prise the truth from him.

Voices floated above his head . . . English voices, not Arabic. Heavy layers closed over him and he began floating up there with the voices. Something warm and spicy trickled down his throat; the darkness exploded into brilliance. More warm liquid slid down his throat and, soon afterwards, he descended into exquisite softness.

He tried to open his lids but they were so leaden all he managed to see was a blurred impression of a face. It seemed to belong to an ageing woman in a dark dress and frilly hat. The face told him he was quite safe and should try to sleep. Glad to comply, he closed his eyes, but her voice reached him again before he drifted away.

'You're something of a hero, young man.'

Those words stayed in his mind through an interminable period which suggested he was being roasted alive. Odd phrases reached him during periods of near clarity which suggested he was slowly dying of fever. It was inevitable, of course. He had been dogged by fever ever since childhood, which was why he could not join the West Wilts. He had known his chances of survival in the Sudan were minimal. Unsure now why he had left Knightshill and his family to embark on this madness, he tossed and turned in the wretched certainty that the gesture had gained him nothing but the early death Vere Ashleigh had been destined to meet. Yet they had told him he was a hero. Grandfather would be proud of that.

When Val emerged from his feverish state of shock they told him he had been in the cottage hospital at Tetherbury for three days. They also told him that, like Vorne Ashleigh, his heroic effort had been in vain. Clive had died two hours after rescuers reached them.

They discharged him from the hospital to attend the inquest before going to Knightshill a week before the official end of term. Dr Keening did not feel that it would be in Val's or the school's interest to oblige him to rejoin his fellows whilst he was still deeply shocked by the death of the friend he had valiantly tried to save. Despite that, the Headmaster considered it his duty to point out when he visited the cottage hospital that the tragedy had been the result of breaking bounds and rules laid down by the school. Headstrong behaviour, defiance of regulations to pursue personal indulgence of an unmistakable nature had cost Clive's life and almost his own, he told Val bleakly. The school's aim was to turn boys into men of stature, intellect and high moral tone, so he was saddened that irresponsibility had forced such a tragic lesson on someone whose family background should have imbued him with a greater sense of duty.

Val found it difficult to accept that Clive was dead, that he had gone from life so suddenly and senselessly. The horror of it lurked beneath his outward composure. Afraid that it would break through and seize him by the throat, he fought to keep it subdued. There were other signs of lingering shock. His voice was husky and lacked power, but as he spoke only in answer to direct questions that problem did not bother him much. Far worse was the condition of his hands. The doctor gave his opinion that the prolonged strain of holding Clive's weight in icy water had exhausted the muscles. They were now taking an indefinite rest. Unable to move or flex his fingers more than a fraction, Val could not grip with either hand or swing his arms without pain shooting through them when they rose past shoulder level. Although he was told in hearty manner that when he returned after the Christmas vacation he would probably find no difficulty with the sporting life he loved, he fretted over the prospect of hands permanently set in a cupped position like a pair of sculpted soap dishes. What use was a sportsman with paralysed hands? What use was a *soldier* with them? He had lost more than a close friend at that Saturday carnival. Depressed and uncertain, he found each day a long procession of empty hours and each night a dark reflection of his fears.

The inquest was an ordeal because his voice was barely audible to the coroner, who made him repeat answers to painful questions several times. Jenny and Prue gave tearful accounts of what had happened on that terrible evening. In their blunt phrases the escapade took on an unsavoury flavour, suggesting that Val and Clive had been bent on the satisfaction of lust and nothing else. The overriding emphasis on the fact that each had separately taken a girl to lonely spots on the pond pointed only to one thing in the minds of everyone present. Val refused to look at the girls. He held them responsible for Clive's death, and longed to reveal the truth about their provocative behaviour which had demanded a lonely spot to satisfy it. Being girls they received much sympathy, while he and Clive were seen as youths of privilege and arrogance who had sought to use them as playthings.

Herbert Grieves accompanied Val to the small courtroom to give evidence of the character of a boy who had been captain of his house, and of another who had been a senior prefect. He spoke well and sincerely, insisting that both were responsible, intelligent people who would not embark on a

168

dangerous escapade as a means of amusement and who were not in the habit of taking advantage of young females. He added that the concentrated study of their final year had led them to seek light diversion by attending the village carnival, and that breaking school rules was all of which they could be accused.

A verdict of accidental death by drowning was recorded and Val took the train to Tetherbury with Herbert Grieves, then the carriage driven by old Maggs, reliving the whole affair and feeling sick with rage that Clive had surrendered his life over a little whore like Jenny, who was now somehow seen as the real victim. His housemaster apparently recognised his mood and made no attempt to hold a conversation. When Maggs stopped the carriage outside his house he said his wife would have tea ready, and that it would be better for Val not to eat in school tonight.

It spoke volumes for Val's frame of mind that his only worry as he trudged up the stairs behind the tutor was how he would manage to hold a dainty cup. He had been sucking tea from a hospital mug like an oaf. Julia was wearing the brooch with dazzling green stones at the neck of a toffee-coloured silk dress, and her hair was dressed in a softer style with curls and a long looped swathe at one ear. Val noticed her appearance less keenly than her expression. He believed the intent, wide-eyed scrutiny she gave her husband meant that she was disconcerted, angry even, because he had been brought in for tea.

'It went well, my dear,' Herbert said quietly, as he took off his overcoat. 'No complications and no real unpleasantness. Young Ashleigh is free to go home on the morning train. The sad affair is over.'

It isn't, thought Val. There'll be memories of Clive wherever I go at Knightshill. Going home won't help me accept the stupid way he lost his life.

When the thin, grey-haired man began to unbutton his coat for him, Val found sudden tears of frustration stinging his eyes. He stared at the wall, hoping Julia would not notice them and wishing he had been allowed to return to his room. He was not hungry and would rather have been alone than in this curiously awkward situation.

'Sit down, Val,' said Julia gently. 'Today must have been an ordeal for you. Try to relax now it's over.'

Avoiding her eyes, he chose one of the saggily comfortable chairs arranged before the fire and discovered that he had been wrong. He *had* been expected because three places were set for tea. Why, then, had she cast that significant look at her husband? She would soon cast another when she saw the spectacle of this hopeful cavalry officer fumbling with a teacup like a half-witted yokel. He would make a bigger fool than ever of himself in front of her.

Julia poured tea and placed a cup on the low table in front of him. He managed a husky 'Thank you,' but made no attempt to pick it up. She offered a plate of dainty sandwiches to her husband, then to Val. He shook his head, mumbling that he was not hungry.

'Nonsense,' she said brightly. 'All boys are permanently hungry, I've discovered, particularly seniors who indulge in sport.'

'No, thanks,' he insisted, meeting her eyes at last and recognising in them that curious suggestion of challenge, which always made him uncertain of her.

'There's no need to feel self-conscious about your hands,' she stated with disconcerting frankness. 'Herbert told me you're having difficulty with grasping so for goodness' sake enjoy your tea as best you can. We both understand, you know.' Her smile was warm, generous and uncomfortably intimate. 'If you were alone you'd soon make short work of ham sandwiches, anchovy toast and several slices of this plum cake, wouldn't you?'

He thought of Clive's doubts about her and refused to answer as he stared back almost defiantly.

'You can't give up eating simply because it embarrasses you to do so in company,' she pointed out. 'Suppose the problem lasts a long time? Will you starve to death, or enter a monastery?'

His defiance increased as he continued to ignore the plate she held before him, the crackle of the fire in the long silence reminding him too vividly of the ice breaking beneath his careful advance on the terrible night.

Herbert Grieves spoke into the charged silence reminding Val of the presence of a third person in the room. 'My wife is exceptionally wise in matters of this kind, Ashleigh. Before we married she nursed an invalid mother *and* aunt. I think you should heed her advice.'

Turning away from Julia, Val mumbled, 'I'm really not hungry, sir.'

Herbert studied him gravely, said, 'Very well,' then gave a slight shake of his head in his wife's direction. He began to talk about his fascination with brass rubbing, which was intended to ease the atmosphere but did not so far as Val was concerned. He stared moodily at the fast-cooling tea, acutely aware of every dragging minute. The Grieves' munched their way through the generous spread and skilfully conducted the conversation so that he was included in it. Finally, he needed the drink so badly he reached out and took up the cup with as much care as he could manage. That neither Julia nor her kindly husband appeared to take the slightest notice of what he was doing made him feel ashamed. His behaviour had been ungracious. The longing to be alone deepened, yet the thought of his familiar room, where he and Clive had talked, laughed and planned their futures, filled him with a renewed sense of loss. That budding diplomat, fluent linguist, merry raconteur and seeker of the *dolce vita* had gone for ever. Grief bit into him again.

'. . . the school routine must continue, Ashleigh.'

Val grew aware that Herbert was on his feet and addressing him. He got up so hastily he jerked the table to set the china on it rattling.

'No, you stay for a while. It's still early, and my wife has something to tell you, I understand.' He smiled across at Julia, as he added, 'It concerns her uncle Max, who is shortly to gain command of his regiment.' He began to put on his overcoat. 'I'll see you before you go off to catch your train in the morning, Ashleigh. I hope my wife's news will cheer you a little.' At the door, he nodded a farewell. 'Supervision of junior prep awaits. I must go.'

Val's thoughts were a jumble as he stared at the pattern on the carpet running beneath the closed door. There *was* an Uncle Max who really would soon command the 57th! Herbert Grieves would not lie to him. Julia had told her husband all about it, so there was nothing in the least wrong with her offer to help a senior prefect gain a commission in the regiment.

'Aren't you anxious to hear my news?'

Val turned almost guiltily to find Julia right behind him. 'Yes . . . yes, of course,' he croaked.

'Then come over here while I tell you.'

She linked her arm through his and drew him across to the fire once more, her slight shiver adding credence to her complaint that the moment one moved far from the leaping flames the bitter cold seemed to creep in from outside. Val suddenly felt too hot as she sat gracefully on the floor beside her chair and urged him to join her.

'It's far more cosy down here,' she explained, gazing up at him with the light of feverish life in her eyes, 'and maybe you'll relax now that you have won your battle with me over the tea.'

It seemed he was still fighting for he perched on the edge of the chair and linked his cupped hands between his knees, leaving her alone on the floor several feet away. She ignored that to embark on a more important subject.

'My uncle was quite impressed by the small biography I sent him. He would like to meet you.'

About to respond, Val then fell silent beneath her intense scrutiny.

'You must surely be aware of the additional considerations in your case, my dear. The commanding officer of any regiment must fully approve each applicant to join it as an officer, but here he is also being asked knowingly to defy the wishes of a revered and very senior general, aside from virtually depriving the West Wiltshire Regiment of a man who should rightly serve with them. My pleas on your behalf resulted in Uncle Max declaring his willingness to consider you, but he must satisfy himself that your potential value to the Fifty-seventh *is* worth securing.'

As she made it clear that she wanted a comment from him, he took the plunge. 'I think it probably isn't.'

It took her by surprise and she let some moments pass before saying, 'I think you must explain that remark.'

'Surely it's obvious.'

The firelight burnished her hair as she shook her head, still fixing him with her challenging gaze. 'Not to me.'

He felt cornered, trapped by his own statement. The outer composure he had struggled to maintain all through the inquest had been stripped away by those words, leaving him dangerously exposed. The longer her unwavering gaze held his, the more vulnerable he felt. There was no escape from that room where the tick of an antique clock and the soft flutter of flames emphasised his sense of approaching the inevitable. When the suspended moment grew intolerable, he found himself blurting out something he had not intended to put into words.

'I failed, didn't I? I let him die.'

She rose up to lean forward and grip his knees, searching his face with an expression of faint anger. 'Is that what you have been telling yourself all this time?'

Completely thrown by his involuntary admission, he rasped, 'If I had thought more clearly I would have seen a better way to do it. If I were stronger, more courageous, I'd have got him to the shore somehow.' He thrust out his stiff hands. 'If these had greater power they would have saved him.'

Her soft warm fingers closed around his in a tight grip, and her eyes were strangely fiery as she said, 'They called you a *hero*.'

He looked away into the flames. 'Heroes win through.'

'No! Heroes are men who attempt something against all odds. *Val, look at me!*' she commanded, her voice containing such passion he obeyed. 'Stop behaving like a self-absorbed child and accept that being an Ashleigh doesn't mean you should have powers other men lack. No one could have saved Clive; there *was* no other way to attempt a rescue. No amount of human strength or courage could have overcome the difficulties of reaching the bank.' She raised his hands with her own and added in much softer tones, 'And these are so very powerful they held on to an incredible weight for far longer than anyone can believe possible.' Resting back on her heels, still holding his hands, she gave her slow teasing smile. 'Now apologise for being so idiotic, and admit to me that the Fifty-seventh is fortunate that Valentine Martin Havelock Ashleigh has chosen to join them rather than the West Wilts.'

As he gazed at the vivid face on a level with his own he sensed that he was more dangerously exposed than ever. How had he come to tell her something he had been unable to admit to himself before this? How could the situation here have changed so swiftly? One minute he had felt awkward and resentful, then Herbert had left and Julia had cajoled him into a personal confession before he knew what was happening. But what *was* happening? Voices had started whispering all manner of things to him, and he was beginning to listen. The winking emeralds at her throat mesmerised him, and the tick of the clock had taken on a curiously exciting rhythm which matched his thudding heart.

'Is it that you're not in the least aware of having behaved like a petulant boy, or that you're too proud to admit that you have?' she asked tauntingly.

He suddenly found his voice, but it again expressed something which took him unawares. 'You think every situation or problem can be solved by humiliating people into agreeing with you, or doing anything you say. You use words as weapons to get your own way, don't you?'

'Not always. I have other means.'

Before he knew it, she was on her knees and kissing his mouth with a fierce insistence which betrayed a wealth of experience. A shock of awareness raced through his veins like fire. It highlighted desires that had lain dormant until this woman first aroused him a month ago. Her fingers were suddenly in his hair, gripping it painfully as her tongue probed his mouth; then her hands were kneading the muscles of his back and shoulders with fevered urgency. Fired to the point of white heat he began to chase her roaming mouth with his own, while his arms attempted to hold her captive. Her love of teasing found physical expression as she lured him further and further forward until he left his chair to kneel on the floor in pursuit of something he could no longer ignore.

Rational thought deserted him when he realised he was being systematically stripped. The driving need to remove her clothes also set him fumbling with buttons and hooks, while her roaming hands made his urgency even greater. As if in a trance, he saw Julia's sensual smile as she studied the length of his naked body while expertly removing the confusing layers of her own garments. Stunned by the unbearable, unbelievable beauty of the breasts she slowly uncovered, he was afraid to reach for them. Giving a low sighing laugh, she took his hands, placed them firmly over her hard nipples and held them there until he could bear the agony in his loins no longer. Gasping with the need for relief he pushed her to the floor and covered her thighs with his own.

The gushing flood came almost immediately. He then lay against her breasts, blinking back tears of frustration that it had been so shatteringly brief. But Julia was practised in the art and swiftly returned him to the condition they both needed. Firelight gilded their entwined bodies as Val eagerly learned all she chose to teach him. He was so entirely captive he was unaware that the paralysis in his hands had vanished from the moment he had reached for the prize she had offered.

Chapter Ten

Christmas at Knightshill was traditionally a time of hospitality and goodwill. Friends, neighbours and employees were entertained in style, and the Ashleighs received a shower of reciprocal invitations. The festive season of 1897/98 was destined to be different. Gaiety did not come easily to the residents of that mansion without the presence of the laughing, good-natured man who had created the happy atmosphere when their home was hung with holly and mistletoe, and when one of the great firs from the estate stood at the foot of the stairs lit with several hundred candles. Vere had skilfully planned those social events at which the only military flavour was the uniforms of several revellers. Without him, Knightshill seemed rather solemn.

Val's journey home was extended by the hazards of a fresh fall of snow. In Maggs's ancient carriage, in the train to Dunstan St Mary, and in the sleigh Ned had brought down to fetch him from the station, Val tormented himself with his thoughts. When Herbert Grieves had wished him well this morning and expressed a hope that his pupil would return having been able to put the tragic affair behind him, culpability had settled like a sickening weight in the pit of his stomach. He could still hardly accept that it had happened. The overture was obliterated from his mind by the incredible excitement and delight of what had followed. She had set him alight and fanned the flames until desire had finally dwindled. Only as he had scrambled into the clothes she had removed with mesmerising skill had he realised the enormity of what he had done. Julia had led him into madness. What if Herbert had returned unexpectedly? For most of the night he had struggled with the conflicting feelings of guilt, elation and anger. How could he have allowed her to lure him into such a dangerous situation?

He was still struggling to come to terms with his erotic introduction to full manhood during Margaret's sympathetic welcome. Her condolences on the loss of his closest friend added to his burden of guilt, and she took his obvious wretchedness as a sign of grief so left him to eat tea in his room alone. The sober atmosphere at Knightshill did nothing to help his mood.

It emphasised the feeling that nothing would be the same again. He was confused and uncertain; laden with guilt yet bewitched. His senses still revelled in the power and pleasure of those riotous moments with Julia, yet he worried about having to return and face her again. How could they pretend it had not happened? How could he stop it from happening again?

It was in this complex state of mind that Val answered a summons from his grandfather, brought by Stoner when he had managed only one sandwich from the hearty tea sent from the kitchen. Sir Gilliard was studying a map when Val arrived, but the vivid blue eyes abandoned it to embark on a head-to-toe study of the boy.

'You grow ever more like your brother in looks,' the old man greeted. 'It's a great pity you can't strive to emulate his sterling qualities.'

Knowing he referred to Vorne, Val unwisely decided to reply. 'I did my best, sir. It was his example which sustained me during the ordeal.'

'Indeed?' The tall figure crossed to the fireplace and stood toasting his back while he repeated his scrutiny in a manner which bode ill for a junior who had had the temerity to venture a comment before being asked for it.

'This is the second occasion on which I have been informed by Dr Keening of your unsavoury involvement with a young female of the village of Tetherbury. The first instance was serious enough to warrant retribution from the girl's aunt, as I recall.'

'That was pure humbug, sir,' he protested. 'All I did was —'

'This time it heralded a tragedy in which a young life was lost,' the voice continued in growing anger. 'You have always possessed deplorable wilfulness which is swiftly roused into downright defiance. From an early age you have kicked against the traces at every turn. Your notion of duty is infamous; your respect for authority is low. You surrender to self-indulgence without a thought for your fellows. In short, you are a disgrace to this regiment, sir.'

Val was taken aback. Grandfather had always lived by the military rules he had known most of his life and treated anyone junior in age or standing as he had treated regimental subordinates, but he appeared to have lost touch with reality and wandered into another world. Was he succumbing to age, or was he ill? Moving across to him Val tried to put assurance into a voice still faint and croaky.

'Clive was my closest friend, sir. I held him until rescuers arrived, and it was the spirit of Vorne Ashleigh which gave me the will to do so. I failed to save his life, but I believe I did all that was humanly possible without regard to my own safety.'

The old warhorse squared his shoulders and fixed Val with a fierce glare. 'That is what I expect an Ashleigh to do in such circumstances. What I do *not* expect is that he loses sight of his duty to abandon his post, and comrades, while he goes in search of carnal adventure.'

175

Those last words revived the sick weight of guilt. Confronting this harsh, proud, unforgiving man, Val found the knowledge of having violated the mature wife of a respected and brilliant scholar overwhelmingly damning. Sir Gilliard condemned him for consorting with the likes of Prue Davey. What would be his judgement if he knew about Julia? Misery washed over Val as he realised again that his own weakness had been to blame. Ashleighs should never be weak.

Taking Val's silence as admission of guilt, the old general gave the severe reprimand such behaviour merited in military law. He added his opinion of any subordinate who allowed moral weakness to blind him to his sense of honour. Then he frowned at the culprit.

'You'll apologise to your brother officers after dinner tonight. That is all. You may return to your regiment.'

The fire crackled and spat, and the faint sound of children's laughter could be heard from the hall where the decorated tree stood, while Val tried to pull himself together and decide how to tackle this extraordinary situation. Finally, he said quietly, 'There *is* no regiment, sir. We're at Knightshill.'

Sir Gilliard seemed to look right through him as he spoke on an entirely different subject. 'Your brother abandoned his heritage when he went to the Sudan. He cannot survive, of course.'

Concerned by the sudden bowing of the white head and by the very faint tremble in a voice which had brought fear to many youthful offenders, Val drew nearer. His grandfather was now speaking of Vere.

'Why did he go?'

Sir Gilliard moved to sit at the desk as if lost in some distant vision. 'Eh?'

'What made Vere take such a sudden decision and face the inevitable consequences?'

'The weakness which rules us all,' the General mused sadly. 'No matter how splendid a man may be, he swiftly falls victim to the most gentle, scheming foe.' When he glanced up at Val there was a sparkle of moisture in eyes which had surely never held tears other than those of pride. 'You are all that is left. My son produced five boys. *Five*, you know,' he emphasised. 'Two were dead at birth. The most splendid one fell at Khartoum in the prime of his youth. The other outlived all expectations but still failed to do his duty in the only way open to him. That young woman went off, as such creatures do, and he was not strong enough to withstand her desertion. He surrendered his obligations, as he will surrender his life. A most foolish gesture.' Passing a shaking hand across his brow he then glanced at Val once more. 'You are the last of the Ashleighs. When I am gone, Knightshill and all that goes with it will belong to you. You must be worthy. The honour of this family and the

176

perpetuation of its distinguished line rests firmly upon those wide, youthful shoulders of yours. I want you to give me your word that you will do your bounden duty by upholding its traditions, and by giving loyal service to the regiment your forebears helped to make glorious.'

Taken unawares by this demand from someone who had never displayed the slightest hint of relinquishing the reins, or of emotional insecurity concerning the future after his death, Val began to feel trapped. 'Sir, all this is rather premature,' he ventured, keeping to himself the fact that Vere had verbally abdicated during that farewell visit to Chartfield. 'Unless you've been advised otherwise, there's every evidence of Vere's survival.'

Sir Gilliard continued as if he had not heard. 'You are my last hope, Valentine. My last hope. You must not take that from me. My life has been devoted to those things I now ask you to value as I have. Live Vorne Ashleigh's life for him. Take up that glorious allegiance he was forced to sacrifice. Swear to me that you will.'

Shaken to the core, Val heard himself say, 'I swear I'll not let you or the family down, sir, and I'll serve my country with my last breath . . . but I can't live my brother's life for him. I *must* live my own.'

New Year's Eve brought a swift thaw. Kate and Timothy were upset because rain kept them indoors and melted their snowman to a slushy pile. Val was also sorry to see the last of the snow. He had spent a lot of time with the children, tobogganing down the slope behind the shrubbery, building snow figures and castles, and allowing them to chase and pelt him with snowballs. They had proved better company than the rest of the family, even though they claimed Uncle Vere was better at making snowmen, reading stories, mending the toboggan and drawing pictures for them.

The shattering interview with his grandfather had ended in strained manner and governed the old man's attitude to Val throughout the Christmas holiday. Philip had muttered darkly about the sins of the flesh then addressed hardly another word to him. Margaret was preoccupied with the history of Knightshill and the Ashleighs she had begun to write about, dismaying Val with underlying evidence of bitterness over her husband's inflexibility with their children. Charlotte had grown sharper-tongued than ever since Vere's departure. When he had casually remarked that she appeared to be inseparable from John Morgan, she had rounded on him with advice not to believe all Ashleighs were tarred with the same brush. When she added that Vorne had waited until school was behind him before embarking on his deplorable pursuit of women, Val had smarted with fresh guilt. Even so, he felt it was unfair for her to make him the whipping-boy for Vere's desertion. Annabel Bourneville was apparently to blame for driving him away.

He decided to say nothing of Sir Gilliard's words on the future of Knightshill and the Ashleighs, just as he had never spoken of Vere's farewell statement. He had put his brother's words aside after their farewell meeting in the belief that Sir Gilliard would live well into the twentieth century. Now he was not so certain. It was yet another problem to add to those besetting him as the date of the Khartoum Dinner loomed. The entire family would gather yet again and, with Vere absent, emphasis on his own imminent final exams, followed by Oxford and entry to the West Wilts, would turn the event into an ordeal.

In this unsettled mood Val sat in the small parlour with his sisters, reading poetry to Timothy and Kate on the last morning of that momentous year in his life. Keeping his promise to Margaret that he would give the children tuition in subjects other than those taught by Philip, he was working his way through one of Vere's volumes of Romantic poetry. Kate was more attentive than Timothy and asked a stream of questions when she could not comprehend the lyricism of sentiments beyond her present experience. After one such cavalcade of interrogation on a point he also found baffling, Val closed the book in resignation and wagged his head at the sight of her perplexed expression.

'Sorry, Kate, that's the best I can do. Vere would explain it far better than I can,' he said ruefully. 'He's the only Ashleigh with the soul of an artist, not a warrior. He should have stayed here reading poetry to you.'

There was a flurry to his right and he glanced across to see Charlotte on her feet, eyes blazing. 'How much more insensitive can you get?' she cried with astonishing passion. 'He's out there slowly killing himself in an attempt to be what this selfish family demands of every male member, and you sit smugly deriding his sacrifice in front of the children.'

Val flushed. '*I've* never demanded it of him. I played no part in his decision to go to the Sudan. I wasn't even here when he made it. I'm not being insensitive. What I said is true. He *does* have the soul of an artist rather than a soldier.'

'Which makes what he is doing far more laudable than the so-called "glorious deeds" of those heroes whose portraits hang along our walls. The rest of the male Ashleighs – you included – can't wait to don a uniform and go a-killing. It's what you want more than anything else in life. Vere doesn't, so that makes him a greater warrior than any of you.'

'I don't agree,' he retaliated. 'If he's slowly killing himself to please this selfish family, there's little to admire in that. If he's doing it to impress Annabel Bourneville, it's even less admirable.' He gently put Kate aside and got to his feet still holding the book. '"Great warriors" die for their country, for their comrades or for a noble cause, never because they're foolish enough to embark on something they're not fitted for, Lottie.

178

"Glorious deeds" are not performed on the battlefield by disappointed artists,' he emphasised, tapping the volume in his hand. 'I always admired Vere for overcoming the penalties inflicted by his constitution and for holding his own in a family like ours. But abandoning his natural talents, *and* his self respect, by putting on a uniform and facing death merely to please those who don't approve of what he is was sheer lunacy.'

In a few swift steps, Charlotte crossed the room and administered a stinging slap to his left cheek before turning and heading for the door, her long swirling skirts unable to hide the irregular pace caused by the weighted boot on her left foot. Val stood motionless after the door slammed behind his sister, but the children were deeply upset by the scene. Kate moved to clutch his hand and ask tearfully why Aunt Lottie had smacked him so hard.

'You shouldn't have a smack when you've been good,' she wailed.

'Papa says no man should lift his hand against another,' declared Timothy fiercely.

'Aunt Lottie isn't a man, she's a lady,' Kate reminded him through her sobs, as she scrambled to be lifted up in the arms of someone she and Timothy had always regarded as an older brother rather than an uncle. When she was cradled against him, she put her small hand on the scarlet mark across his cheek claiming she would make it better. 'Poor Val! Does it hurt very much?'

'No,' he murmured, shaken by the incident.

'A smack from Aunt Lottie wouldn't hurt Val,' Timothy said derisively. 'He's going to be a soldier. They're extremely brave even when men put knives in them.'

Kate's sobs increased as she threw her arms around Val's neck. 'I don't want men to put knives in you. I don't. I don't.'

Margaret cast Val a significant look as she explained that no one would put knives in him. She then added that Aunt Lottie was worried about Vere and had not meant to hurt Val.

'*Is* Uncle Vere slowly killing himself?' asked Timothy. 'I thought no one knew where he was.'

'I wish he hadn't gone to see Sue Dan,' moaned Kate. 'It's horrid here without him.'

'It's not in the least horrid at Knightshill,' Margaret said firmly.

'Yes, it is. You've broken friends with Papa, Aunt Lottie is cross with everyone, and Great-grandfather is angry with poor Val, and — '

'Hush! You're becoming impertinent, Kate. Put her down, Val. She's growing too dramatic.'

'Is she?' he asked, retaining his hold on the girl as he sat down again. 'There's a lot of truth in what she said.' He cuddled Kate closer. 'Stop crying or we'll all be washed away by your tears like Noah in the flood.'

179

'*Is* Uncle Vere slowly killing himself?' repeated Timothy, standing defiantly before Val to force an answer from him.

'Perhaps, Tim. Anyone who succumbs to fever very quickly and is known to have a weak constitution is most unlikely to survive in an area like the Sudan. Although we have no idea where he is, Great-grandfather would have been informed if Vere were desperately ill. So we must conclude that he is holding his own.'

'His own what?'

Val gave a strained smile. 'His own counsel, at least.'

'Are you going to the Sudan, Val?'

'Perhaps . . . if the campaign is still being fought when I gain my commission.'

'I want to go. Do you think they'll be fighting it when *I* join the West Wilts.'

Casting Margaret a swift glance, Val then studied the determined face beneath a flop of hair as fair as his own. A natural warrior who would never be allowed to follow his star.

'I sincerely hope they'll have recaptured Khartoum by then, old chap.'

'Papa says the Dervishes should be controlled by teaching them the Word, not by meeting violence with more violence.'

'Does he?' It was the only response Val felt able to give.

But Timothy had more to say on the subject. 'What I feel is this. The Dervishes don't understand English so reading the scriptures to them will be useless. They'll stick knives in people just the same. Better for soldiers to frighten them away with swords.'

Val nodded. 'Very sound thinking.'

'Don't encourage him!' said Margaret sharply.

'He needs no encouragement,' he pointed out. 'He'll never knuckle down to anything else, you know he won't.'

'He's too much like you, that's why. *Must* you invite trouble?'

'Not you, as well, Aunt Meg,' he complained. 'No one seems very fond of me this morning.'

'*I'm* fond of you, Val,' Kate told him warmly, kissing the fading mark on his cheek. 'I want to marry you when I grow up.'

'You can't marry your uncle, Kate.'

'Why not?'

'Because the Bible says so,' her brother told him automatically. It was clear he had received that explanation for a great many things.

'Why does the Bible *always* stop us from doing all the nice things we want to do?' cried the voice of youthful wisdom. 'If God is good He should let us all be happy, not miserable like Papa.'

Margaret intervened at that point to direct the children to go up for their

180

mid-morning milk and biscuits. When she closed the door after them and came back to sit beside Val, neither spoke for a while. Eventually she told him to stop flickering the pages of the poetry book because it irritated her. Then, when he shut it with a snap, she apologised for Charlotte.

'She shouldn't have hit you, especially in front of the children. Things are difficult enough as it is. They don't understand and all these emotional undercurrents worry them. But it's your fault for saying what you did about Vere. You know how sensitive she is.'

'I only spoke my mind,' he said defensively. 'Is that no longer allowed in this house?'

'Not when it upsets people.'

'She airs her opinion of me enough and some of what she says is damned insulting. Lottie's never visited Tetherbury and certainly wasn't there on the night Clive drowned, yet she has concluded that we were both engaged in seducing a pair of helpless damsels and deserved the wrath of God who decided that Clive should pay for his wickedness with his life, while I should be taught a severe lesson by watching my closest friend die of cold.'

Margaret put her hand over his as it lay on the arm of the chair. 'Has she really suggested that?'

'More or less.' He sighed. 'I frequently wish to God I'd never gone to the carnival, but then I tell myself Clive would have gone through the ice anyway and I wouldn't have been there to drag him out. But I didn't, did I?' he reflected. 'I didn't save him.'

'You tried,' she said with compassion. 'Clive was very much aware that you were trying, Val. That's the important thing. What Lottie and Grandfather say shouldn't bother you.'

He looked at her frankly. 'It does, though.'

'Only because you are so vulnerable at the moment, my dear. And so are they. Grandfather is feeling the burden of age since Vere left, and Lottie is driving herself too hard over the running of the estate to keep anxiety at bay. Each time she sees Fred Barney coming up the hill with the mail she believes notification of Vere's death is in his bag.'

'He's survived for several months, which is longer than I thought possible,' Val admitted. 'I don't understand his drive to go when he must know he can't hope to return. He should send word now and again. Can't he realise how much he's upsetting you and Lottie?'

She shook her head. 'When someone has been hurt as deeply as he, there's no room for the pain of others. Poor Vere!'

'Just because Annabel turned him down?'

Margaret glanced away through the rain-splattered window. 'Maybe you'll discover one day that love for someone can be so all-consuming, life seems valueless when it comes to an end. Perhaps Vorne was wise to love a little and often.'

'He loved honour enough to give his life for it,' he pointed out.

She turned back with a sad smile. 'Perhaps Vere's doing the same thing.'

It made Val uneasily aware of Sir Gilliard's words on allowing moral weakness to blind a man to his sense of honour, something of which he was undeniably guilty. Adultery was worse than seducing a willing village girl behind the roller shed, as many of his friends had done. Had he lost all sight of honour in his attempt to gain what Julia had promised him? There had been no thought of her uncle's regiment in his mind that night, however. She had offered something irresistible, and he had wanted it without reservation. Part of his punishment was the torment of wanting it again now he had tasted the triumphant thrill of entering a woman. The other part was knowing she had triumphed more than he.

Briggs entered with their hot chocolate which Margaret poured into the cups as he left. Her next words suggested she knew Val's thoughts. Colour flooded his cheeks when she asked, 'Are you still unhappy about joining the West Wilts?' Noticing his reaction, she added, 'Good heavens, you're blushing like a young girl! I know that guilty look, my lad. Own up!'

Ignoring the cup she pushed towards him he got to his feet and walked to the window, furious with himself. 'If the rain stops I may take Merlin out this afternoon,' he said over his shoulder.

'Don't try to wriggle out of answering,' Margaret said firmly. 'You've never been a good liar and it's obvious you're up to something. If you're intent on defying Grandfather you'll need my support when the time comes.' When he said nothing, she came up behind him to touch his arm. 'Much has changed over this past year, but I hoped nothing was different between us.'

The flush had receded, so he turned to her with a few white lies. 'One of the fellows at school has an uncle in the cavalry. He's offered to speak to him about me.'

'Which regiment?'

'Oh . . . Lancers, I think.'

'You're playing with fire, Val,' she warned.

'I know,' he said heavily. 'There's nothing definite.'

She looked at him with great fondness. 'Does it mean that much to you?' He nodded.

'So much you'll risk everything to get it?'

Echoes of Julia. 'I . . . yes, I suppose so.'

'I thought as much.' She linked her arm through his. 'We Ashleighs are a headstrong breed, aren't we?'

'You're no longer an Ashleigh.'

'I'll always be one, no matter what happens . . . and I want my children to be Ashleighs in spirit, too.'

With a rush of affection he kissed her smooth cheek. 'I'll always support you, too, Aunt Meg. If you ever need help, call on me.'

She seemed surprisingly moved and attempted to laugh off their serious mood. 'All this talk of allies suggests a family at war.'

'There appear to be several small campaigns being waged at Knightshill,' he commented, 'but at the party tonight there'll be a truce to dupe everyone into believing we're united.'

'Speaking of the party, come upstairs and help me to choose which gown to wear.'

'Must I? Frocks aren't my strong point. You need Vere for that.'

'Vere isn't here and you are. You'll be nineteen in February so it's high time you began to show an interest in dresses . . . and in the creatures who wear them,' she added slyly. 'Unlike Lottie, I have faith in your virtue.'

Dear God, he thought with a fresh pang of guilt, if she only knew.

The party was given by a local retired judge whose numerous offspring gathered at the country house for New Year and invited shoals of lively friends to stay for several days. The Ashleighs usually enjoyed this annual event, but they set out in the carriage this year in quiet mood. Sir Gilliard was preoccupied; Charlotte had not apologised to Val for her unwarranted slap and remained aloof. Val sat beside Margaret lost in his own thoughts. A new year was about to begin. Eighteen ninety-eight could be a momentous milestone in his life, but to make it so he must pursue that place in the 57th Lancers whatever the risks. Was he prepared to do that?

The house was a blaze of lights, and the sound of an orchestra could be heard as they stepped from the carriage and approached the door beneath an awning erected to protect them from the downpour which had not ceased all day. They were greeted by their hosts, their cloaks were taken, and the ladies were directed to the room set aside for feminine titivating. Sir Gilliard, resplendent in uniform, and Val, dressed more soberly in tails, went through to the crowded salons and immediately parted company on meeting familiar contemporaries. But Val had exchanged no more than a few words with the judge's grandson, when the shifting groups of guests allowed him a view through to the adjoining room where he saw a dark, thickset man in a distinctive all-grey uniform. His pulse quickened and he excused himself to his companion before making his way through to the person whose presence had made the evening exciting in an instant.

Parties frequently foil serious intentions, and Val's were by the announcement that dancing would commence. His quarry moved off with a partner in pink silk and soon the only occupants of that room were the elderly, the arthritic or the garrulous. Dance followed dance while Val mooned about watching the Lancer captain partner a succession of eager young women. He did not care for dancing so made no attempt to approach the many youthful guests who glanced around that elegant room, panelled with lengths of Chinese silk, seeking fresh escorts. Finally, he was seized by one of his hosts' great-nieces who lectured him on his lack of participation and then dragged him into the throng of dancers for a schottische.

It was not until supper was announced that the grey-uniformed officer stopped still long enough for Val to approach him. Luckily the man was in a group containing people who knew Val and could effect the introduction he sought.

'Ashleigh? One of the West Wilts brigade before long, I imagine,' said John Fielding, shaking Val's hand and smiling. 'Doubtless, you'd like to be out there with Kitchener right now.'

'My brother is,' he said, ignoring the rest of Fielding's words. 'He's been there since autumn, but everything seems to be moving so slowly one wonders if they'll ever get up to Khartoum.'

'They'll get there,' his companion assured him, taking a hearty bite from a slice of cold pigeon pie and continuing to speak as he munched. 'Damned awful country. Almost impossible to conduct a normal campaign. Weather, terrain and the level of the river have to be overcome. The slightest unexpected delay in plans often causes troops to fall foul of one or the other.' He gave a slight frown as he popped several olives in his mouth. 'You say your brother's out there? I didn't know the West Wilts had been shipped to the Sudan.'

'He's not with the West Wilts,' Val explained, blessing the man for giving him the opening he wanted. 'We're breaking with tradition slightly.'

'Good lord! After thirteen generations?' he exclaimed as he attacked the pie again.

'Vere wanted to avenge Vorne so he joined a regiment already out there. The wrath of God hasn't descended on him because he hasn't followed in family footsteps,' he added defiantly.

John Fielding smiled again. 'Your fierceness clearly indicates that you also have no wish to.'

As the other members of the group around them were deep in various conversations, Val decided to confide in this man with a keen appetite. 'I hope to join the Ghost Lancers, sir.'

'Do you, by God! We're not in the Sudan, and seem unlikely to be sent there. We are, of course, the best cavalry regiment in the world,' he commented with typical military modesty, 'but is there any other reason why you have chosen the Fifty-seventh, young Ashleigh?'

'What other reason does anyone need?' Val replied swiftly. 'I was loaned a copy of your regimental history which I have memorised almost word for word. Your battle honours alone take my breath away. Are there a great number of distinguished officers in your present ranks? Someone told me of a brigadier who is shortly to take over command of the regiment.' He swallowed nervously. 'His first name is Max, I believe.'

Fielding nodded and began on a chicken leg. 'Max Beecham. Very good commander. Intelligent, experienced, knows how to handle men and can spot potential ability with uncanny success. We're very fortunate to have him.'

All this was music in Val's ears. This same man was interested in his own desire to join the 57th and had suggested a meeting after receiving a short written biography of Valentine Martin Havelock Ashleigh. The coveted commission was practically his. Then, piercing his euphoria like a dark lance came the thought of Julia. She called the tune. One word to her uncle could settle his hopes one way or the other. He had played into her hands on a night when he had been shocked and uncertain. There was no way of knowing how things would be when he returned for the new term.

'You're not eating anything,' his companion observed, nodding at the empty plate in Val's hand. 'A beefy young fellow like you must have a hearty appetite. Come on, make a few inroads on this magnificent spread or you'll never have the stamina to stay the course until morning.' Finishing the chicken and taking up a salmon puff, he added, 'We're all good trenchermen in the Fifty-seventh. Our unofficial motto is *Ride Hard, eat hearty and chase any petticoat which isn't on another man's wife.*'

His rich laugh took away any inclination Val may have had to eat, but he helped himself to several items from the laden table so that no one else would challenge his empty plate. His spirits were fluctuating so violently this evening his usual appetite was missing. He studied John Fielding morosely. A very masculine man with powerful lines to his features and muscular body. A man of assurance and action, probably, but not of wit. An uncomplicated person who took life at face value and enjoyed its pleasures to the full. Val envied him deeply. He also envied the well-cut dark grey uniform with paler facings and silver chain frogging on the epaulettes. He would do anything to acquire one himself. *Anything?* His spirits plunged once more.

Dancing began again. He avoided it by embarking on a discussion of rugby tactics with a youthful guest who played for Winchester. But only half his mind was on it, so he became aware of a slight disturbance a short while before he heard his name being spoken by those nearby. He turned towards them curiously to see his host's elder son making for him purposefully, while those around him fell silent.

'Ashleigh, I'm sorry to tell you your grandfather has collapsed,' said the judge's son swiftly. 'Will you come? Father has arranged for him to be taken to one of the guest rooms where Dr Grantley is presently examining him.'

Val turned cold as he set out with him between guests who were passing the news around the salon. 'Have my sisters been told?' he asked as they crossed the hall to the stairs.

'Mother is with them now. Once you've heard what Dr Grantley has to say, you can talk to them in one of the first-floor rooms.'

'How did it happen?'

'I have no details, but it seems Sir Gilliard was enjoying a cigar with Professor Gaunt when he suddenly folded and dropped to the ground.'

'I see,' said Val through a jaw grown stiff. Apprehension filled him as he mounted the stairs. Grandfather had seemed invincible, yet he had shown astonishing vulnerability two weeks ago during their interview. Surely he was not finished! His companion knocked at the door before they entered. The doctor, another guest, was watching the inert figure on the bed with deep concentration. However, he glanced up as they advanced and came across to meet them.

'It's serious, I'm afraid, Valentine,' he began as he removed his pince-nez. 'His heart is under great strain and recovery is doubtful.'

Having always been regarded as a junior by his sisters and Vere, Val suddenly found himself head of the family. It was he who was approached by doctors, their lawyer, and well-wishers. He struggled to rise to the occasion and mainly succeeded, but the dread of such responsibility becoming permanent dogged him. He had never sought it, never longed to inherit the estate, and he felt it was now being thrust upon him by a brother prepared to die over a heartless girl, and a grandfather determined to make him toe the family line. If Sir Gilliard and Vere died, he would be trapped with an obligation demanding the surrender of his freedom. Even when the old general rallied, Val was haunted by the thought that he could not live for ever.

The Khartoum Dinner caused much soul-searching. He was treated as an adult for the first time, but they all talked of his coming sojourn at Oxford before entry to the West Wilts. Val was forced to stay silent in deference to Sir Gilliard, who had defied Dr Alderton's advice to preside over an evening which meant so much to him. By so doing, he unwittingly restored Val's determination. Admiring Sir Gilliard's strength of character and his professional achievements, he told himself the old man defied anyone who stood in his way so he must be made to accept that others should be allowed to do the same.

The meeting with John Fielding seemed providential. It revived Val's longing to become one of the Ghost Lancers, and he thought long and hard about Julia's ability to make that possible. Once he had met Max Beecham and impressed the man with his ability, her part would be over. So would her curious game which had ended so dangerously. Burdened by the shadow of his grandfather's mortality and Vere's quixotic act, he returned to school vowing to press for the introduction to Julia's uncle. Then he would be free of her.

Val's resolution to work hard this term floundered immediately. Clive's ghost haunted his room and wherever he went in the school, adding to his deep sensation of loss of everything familiar. He saw no sign of Julia for two weeks – the longest he had known – and he could not contact her without arousing suspicion. When a third week reached Thursday, he found a note awaiting him in the prefects' study. He slit the envelope with a rush of nervousness.

Val

My uncle and aunt will be spending the weekend at Blandford Forum and have asked me to join them at the Bull Inn tomorrow. This is an ideal opportunity for you to meet Uncle Max and for him to size you up. I have obtained leave of absence for you on Saturday. Catch the 2.30 train which will get you to Blandford in plenty of time for tea. We'll wait for you in the lobby. He's a stickler for good manners, so don't come late and be on your best behaviour.

The note had no signature, ending with a typical example of Julia's delight in undermining his confidence, but his spirits soared. Only a day to wait! He knew he could persuade Brigadier Beecham to accept him in the regiment. John Fielding had described a highly professional soldier who could spot potential ability in his troops. Such a man would never dismiss someone whose entire life was bound up with military achievement and who could discuss cavalry participation in past wars as fully as any historian.

He walked to Tetherbury on that cold blustery Saturday fully an hour before he needed to, but he was taking no chances. Having missed lunch at school he had a cup of tea and a small meat pie at the station, but nervousness had affected his appetite and he swallowed the stale pie only so that his stomach would not gurgle with hunger during the coming interview. It was cold waiting on the station and he was glad when the train steamed in. During the forty-minute journey he ran over in his mind all the possible questions he would be asked, and only then did he realise he had completely forgotten Sir Gilliard's other threat to his plans at last year's

Khartoum Dinner. *Unless he followed family tradition he would receive no penny of Ashleigh money until a legacy was paid when he was twenty-five.* The meat pie threatened to return abruptly. It was useless to ignore that threat. Brigadier Beecham would have to be told that V. M. H. Ashleigh would be an impecunious subaltern relying on his salary for any expenses incurred.

For the rest of the journey he thought feverishly of solutions to the problem. Maybe he could borrow against the legacy; perhaps Margaret would lend him money until he was twenty-five. Such was his state of mind he even considered the substantial sum he would get under the terms of Vere's will – until he realised, with dismay, that he was mentally killing off his brother like the rest of the family. Gloom settled on him. The 57th would not want a penniless officer in their ranks. Perhaps he should emulate Vere and go abroad with no further word for his family. Was that what his brother had meant when advising him to follow his star however thorny the path?

It was raining hard when the train pulled in at Blandford Forum. Val turned up his collar and thrust his hands in his pockets as he stepped out along the main street with less than enthusiasm. What a fool he had been to lose sight of the financial hurdle in his eagerness to find someone who would defy Sir Gilliard by accepting his application. Max Beecham would be annoyed. Julia would be furious. She had been angry enough over his thoughtless return of her book. The prospect of what this might provoke in her did not bear consideration.

The Bull Inn was a substantial hotel with large stables outside which several carriages were drawn up, the horses well protected by waterproof coats as they waited. Inside the porch, Val stopped to turn his collar down again and to comb his wet, tousled hair with the aid of a dim reflection in the revolving doors. Then he took a deep breath and pushed them to enter the lobby. Heart thudding, he glanced swiftly around the dignified red plush interior. It was empty, but there were several deep alcoves where privacy could be found and he guessed they must be in one of those. An apprehensive inspection discovered only two elderly ladies, a young couple with two children, and a red-faced gentleman drinking port. Taking another deep breath to steady himself he approached the desk where an erect uniformed man with a dark moustache was studying him with a hovering smile.

'Mr Ashleigh?'

Val was taken aback. 'Yes, that's right.'

The smile broke out in full. 'I've been watching out for you, sir. Your sister gave me a very accurate description of you and said you would be arriving soon after three-thirty.'

'My *sister*?'

'She told me to direct you to her room. It's on the first floor, sir. Number fourteen.'

Val was confused. 'I'm here to meet Brigadier Beecham, Mrs Beecham and Mrs Grieves.'

'That's right, sir,' the man said encouragingly. 'Number fourteen. First door to your left at the top of the stairs.'

Val took off his overcoat as he went up. They must have decided to wait in a less public place. Well, their anger with him would be less public too. He knocked on the heavy oak door and Julia's voice invited him in. The room was decorated in elegant style with a desk, settee and chairs, and a low oak table. A fire provided warmth and a welcome from the dreariness outside. Through an archway was a four-poster bed with gold hangings. Julia was alone. She stood in the centre of the room beside the settee. The soft cream robe she wore was frilled at throat and waist, her brown hair hung loose almost to her waist, her eyes shone. She looked utterly sensual amid the sober trappings surrounding her.

Val found excitement shooting through him even as he realised that he had been tricked. Both reactions made him aggressive. 'Where's your uncle?'

'He had to cancel his plans. A pity, but military duty takes precedence over anything else. You should know that.'

'Military duty, be damned!' he cried. 'It was a pack of lies just to make me come here.'

She gave him a measured look. 'My word, you have a very high opinion of yourself.'

'Well, wasn't it?'

Taking a sheet of paper from the low table, she held it out. 'Here's his letter. Read it.'

To do so he had to cross to her. Her expression challenged him every step of the way. The letter apologised, expressed a hope that a meeting in Blandford would be possible later and was signed, *Affectionately, Max*. Val studied it far longer than he needed to give himself time to think. He lifted his gaze from the letter to look straight into Julia's amused eyes only to discover that he could think of just one thing. Fighting it with no more than token determination, he dropped the letter to the floor.

'You must have received that before you set out.'

Her lips twisted. 'Two hours before, to be exact.'

'I've had a wasted journey.'

'Stop looking so mutinous and take off your damp clothes so that they can dry before the fire.' As her fingers began to loosen his tie and unbutton his shirt the scent of her skin and hair teased him unbearably. Leaning forward he covered the softness of her neck with feverish kisses as he

189

struggled with the buttons on his trousers and then his underclothes. He was eager, impatient for her, and she laughed softly as she edged away making him pursue her beneath the arch to the vast softness of the bed. Beneath the robe she was naked, so he knew almost immediately the agonising triumph of possession. He had been an avid pupil last time, and the afternoon lengthened into evening before they lay back, temporarily exhausted, to hear the rain still thundering against the windows.

He caught the last train back to Tetherbury, then had to walk to school because old Maggs had taken an elderly couple in his carriage. The rain had finally stopped and a brilliant moon lit the road for him. Blissful lethargy ensured that he walked slowly; inner elation seemed as huge and bright as the moon. He would go anywhere at any time to be with her. She was the most wonderful element that had ever touched his life and he was insatiably greedy for it.

There followed a period Val would long remember. Julia dominated his days and nights to the extent of eliminating concentration and banishing sleep. Tutors noticed his inattention and reprimanded him. After a week, several took him aside believing that he was still deeply affected by Clive's death and gave him kindly advice to pull himself together. Geoffrey Manton did the same after Val put up a poor performance on the rugby pitch during the Saturday practice match.

He had seen Julia once that week, when she had walked past in deep conversation with the senior Latin master without acknowledging him in any way. Between lessons he had raced across to the prefects' study but his pigeon-hole was always empty of the envelope he sought. It was impossible for him to contact her so he waited almost desperately for a note. He began to hate the school routine he had formerly enjoyed, resented what he now saw as juvenile rules and restrictions. Sitting at a desk with schoolbooks seemed unacceptable when he recalled the sense of mastery he had known in that four-poster bed with Julia. He wanted her so much he was almost sick with yearning by the time he received her message to go to the house on the following evening, when her husband would again be supervising junior prep.

She took some time to tell him why she was obliged to ignore him whenever they met around the school premises, emphasising the need for secrecy each time he came to the house. Fending him off when he made to take her in his arms, she then told him of a small inn at a village served by a twice-weekly slow train from Tetherbury and suggested they might meet soon. Then she told him to leave. Wanting her as he did he seized and overpowered her long enough to kiss her quite comprehensively, but her body was encased in whalebone and layers of under-garments so his

190

roaming hands found no satisfaction for his desire. Telling him he must be patient, she disentangled herself from his hold and pushed him firmly to the door. That meeting left him even more restless and desperate.

Ten days later they went to the village inn she had named. There was a poor fire in the room, the bed was lumpy and seemed damp, and the landlord would only serve tea to them in the downstairs parlour. Julia was in a perverse mood, making Val work hard for what he wanted. In consequence, his performance was inhibited and she lost no time in telling him so. After dressing and going to the parlour for an indifferent tea, Julia revealed that she had decided to go on to Shaftesbury where Herbert was visiting a retired colleague and that she would return with her husband. She left Val with three hours to wait for his train. He returned upstairs, angry and deeply disappointed, to fall asleep on the bed where he had failed to please her or himself. He awoke after his train had passed through the village, so he had to beg a ride on a farmer's cart to within two miles of Tetherbury, and walked the rest of the way back to school with depression like a grey cloud above him. It remained there for three days until a note from her told him to call at the house that same evening. He arrived to find Herbert with her and had to cast around for a valid reason for his evening visit. It was not made easier by Julia's ability to appear friendly and natural. Val could not discover what had gone wrong. She sent no note of explanation and he was unable to approach her.

He spent most of his free time alone in his room, discouraging attempts by his friends to jolly him from what they believed was inordinate brooding over Clive. Neglecting his school work, he instead racked his brains to think of how and where he could meet Julia more often. She was like a drug. Being with her made him an Apollo. For the rest of the time he was lacklustre, bored, impatient and almost crazy for her provocative generosity once more.

At the beginning of March, something occurred to introduce Val to an emotion he had never known before: jealousy, deep and violent. After a week with no word from Julia despite a staff meeting which had been held on Wednesday evening, he was leaving the shower room after rugby practice when he ran into Roland Baines, Brook House captain. He looked well pleased with himself and his mellow mood encouraged him to fall in beside Val in friendly fashion, as if things were still the same between them.

'Hello, Ashleigh. Was it a good practice?'

'No. The pitch is a sea of mud and we all slithered around in it,' he responded heavily. 'What a damned silly pastime it is!'

'You've only just discovered that?' Roland commented laughingly. 'A host of muddy fools chasing a ball which isn't round so that they can fling

191

themselves headlong to the ground with it and do themselves no end of mischief.'

Val scowled. 'Very funny.'

'But very true.'

'What are you so bloody perky about?' Val demanded, as their feet crunched the gravel path leading round the playing field to the building which housed dormitories and the seniors' rooms.

'Julia Grieves, that's what . . . or should I say *who?*'

'Oh?' His throat grew suddenly tight. 'What about her?'

'She's a real corker,' Roland confided, little realising the effect of his words on Val. 'I happened to mention to her that I wanted to be a politician, although Father is determined that I'll follow him to the bar and take silk one day. But it's difficult to get started unless someone in the party takes one under his wing, you know. Our lovely Julia actually has a cousin in politics. I've just had tea with her and she's promised to speak to him about me – maybe even arrange a meeting.'

Something exploded in Val and he turned on his companion with a fury foreign to him. 'You *happened to mention* that you wanted to be a politician? You mean she dragged it out of you, and offered to help in any way she could! Did you have muffins for tea and did she lend you a book given to her by her cousin in politics?'

Roland looked astonished at the outburst. 'What's wrong with you? That affair last term must have hit you hard, but three months have passed since then and a fellow ought to be over it now. A fine officer you'll make if you go to pieces like this when a friend is killed! We're all getting sick of your histrionics.'

'Then stay away from me,' Val advised savagely, turning at a tangent to use the forbidden short cut across the grass.

Once inside his room he rode out the corrosive pain aroused by the thought of Julia with Roland Baines. Thumping the window-sill softly with his clenched fists, he fought back the mortifying threat of tears. She had tired of him, had been so full of disparagement over his comparative failure in that cold, lumpy bed that she was showing him she was looking elsewhere for the excitement she craved. Closing his eyes he put back his head in anguish. At Blandford he had triumphed several times over during those hours of naked, feverish wrestling. He had thrilled and satisfied her. He knew he had. In front of the fire on the final night of last term he had done the same. He could do it again if she would only let him. Everything had been wrong at their last meeting and her irritable, moody state had made him too anxious. How could she judge him on that?

He walked from the window, stomach churning, then took up a cushion to hurl it with unmitigated fury against the far wall. That fool Baines was in for a shock if he believed there would ever be a meeting with her influential cousin. *There was no cousin!* Yet there *was* an Uncle Max, and he had definitely intended to meet them in Blandford. He slumped into a chair and put his head in his hands. That opportunity had gone for ever. His one chance to achieve his goal had been sacrificed, because he had lost his senses over something Clive had taken in his stride. But Clive had lost his life in pursuit of it, he reminded himself soberly. All he, himself, had lost was someone who had promised him the moon, the stars and the whole solar system.

Three days later he found a note in his pigeon-hole and the firmament was again within his grasp.

The most providential news! This Saturday there is a lecture on brass-rubbing in Blandford – an evening lecture entailing an overnight stay. The hour of eight is most significant.

Waiting for Saturday was like being on a piston, spirits rising with excitement then plunging down into the fear of inadequacy. Val's sixth sense told him this meeting would be vitally important. He had to impress her with his virility, then persuade her to organise another interview with Max Beecham. The second was dependent on the first, he felt, but with a whole night in her company there was unlikely to be a repetition of his last attempt. A nagging doubt about occupying Herbert's bed gave him some bad moments, but he determined not to throw away this chance on scruples when it was probably his last. If he declined to occupy the bed, Baines would probably do so in pursuit of his political career.

Val avoided the Saturday dawn run and cried off from rugby practice by feigning a pulled tendon. He had to remember to limp throughout the hour he spent on the touchline with Geoffrey Manton watching his team play, and submit to a rigorous massage from the sports master at the end of practice. Eating supper was an ordeal because nervousness took away any desire for food. Then he paced his room as the clock slowly ticked its way towards eight and his throat grew drier and drier. The night was cold and clear as he crossed the grounds towards the house, keeping in the shadows whenever he could in case others were moving around the school. The door was slightly ajar so he slipped in and closed it behind him. Then sudden caution made him call out before climbing the stairs.

'Val Ashleigh here. May I come in?' Whatever reason would he give if *Herbert* gave him permission?

'Come up, Val,' called Julia softly. 'You're very punctual.'

193

He ran up the stairs in his eagerness and burst into the cosy room with sudden conviction that everything was going to turn out splendidly. She was waiting for him in a dark red gown of stiff silk which emphasised her slenderness. Around her neck was a band of flashing garnets. It was as if she were dressed for a gala evening and the familiar excitement coursed through his veins as he crossed to her.

'Impetuous boy,' she murmured against his mouth, after the ardour of his initial bout of kisses. 'Slow down a little.'

'I can't,' he breathed, already primed to prove himself. 'I've been waiting fifteen days for this.'

'So long? I've been incredibly busy.'

'With Roland Baines?' It was out and he could have bitten off his tongue. He had resolved to avoid any mention of the subject.

Arching back within his embrace, she laughed. 'The green-eyed monster! How enjoyable.'

'I don't think it enjoyable.'

'Of course you do, my dear,' she told him softly, as her brilliant eyes studied his face hungrily. 'Pain is the greatest joy of all. The most agonising rapture is when the whole being is aware and throbbing.' She laughed again softly. 'Can you deny that the last three months have been the most exciting you have ever known? Can you put your hand on your heart and tell me that you have *not* experienced the whole range of human emotions through my interest in you?'

His impetus was slowing. Conversation was not what he wanted at such a time. She appeared to be in her curious teasing mood, which always undermined his assurance and confronted him with the unexpected.

'*Answer me, Val!*' she commanded urgently.

'I . . . yes, I suppose so.'

Her fingers fluttered across his lips. 'Such a mutinous mouth, such delightfully innocent pride. I subdued the mutiny within you. I broke your pride slowly but easily. And you have revelled in every confusing, vital moment of capitulation. Haven't you?'

Releasing her in a sudden reversal of mood, he felt the anticipation that had built up since receiving her note drop away to be replaced by a sensation of being back where he had started with her.

'Look, what's this all about?' he asked uneasily.

'The stag at bay – my beautiful stag!' she breathed, running her hands over his torso beneath his jacket. 'You have a magnificent body. Strong, powerful, excitingly youthful . . . invincible.'

Pushing the coat from his shoulders and arms so that it dropped to the floor, she began to unbutton his shirt with swift, seeking fingers. Immediately, renewed excitement pounded through him when she

194

touched his skin. Passion flooded back as she caressed his chest with her mouth, bit softly at his nipples, and kneaded the muscles of his upper arms as the shirt fell to join the jacket at his feet. Within seconds, the rest of his clothes were there. Yet he was unsuccessfully attempting to unfasten an endless line of tiny covered buttons at the back of her dress, while she was free to indulge her own desire for his body. Then she was laughing softly once more as he gave a groaning plea for her to help with the dress.

'Not yet, not yet,' she whispered after she had stepped away from his hold and caught at his wrists. 'We have something more exciting to do first!'

He found himself being drawn towards the door which led to the bedroom, any compunction he might have felt over-ridden by his need for her, which was now so urgent he thought only of finding relief as they approached the foot of the large four-poster. From the corner of his eye he saw that the sheets were turned back in readiness, and he twisted his wrists to free himself from her surprisingly strong grip to make another assault on the buttons of her dress. But she pulled away so suddenly and violently the red silk parted to leave a long tear from the neck to left armhole. The sound of that material rending apart was so loud it broke through his concentration on the growing agony in his loins. It also signalled the start of a nightmare.

Oblivious to the torn dress Julia swung back to face him, eyes blazing and wearing an expression of curious ecstasy. In her hand she held an ornate cane with a thick leather thong attached.

'You can hold the bedposts while I do it, but I think it will be even more exciting if I tie your wrists, don't you?' she asked him in a tone charged with emotion. 'I put the bonds up there in readiness.'

Following her gaze Val saw loops of thick twine attached to the posts several feet up, and they suggested only one unacceptable thing. Horror, revulsion, deep shock manifested simultaneously to turn him icy cold. He began to back away from her instinctively.

'No – no,' he stammered, hardly aware of speaking as a cavalcade of sensations marched through his naked shivering frame.

'Yes,' she contradicted triumphantly, advancing as he retreated. 'Of course you must be secured. Soldiers are always tied by the wrists to a gun before flogging. That's what you want to be, isn't it? I'll punish you in fine military style. Twenty lashes, thirty lashes . . . How many do you deserve, do you think?'

He wanted to vomit, wanted to awaken from this nightmare. But those twine manacles hung from the bedpost obscenely, and this wrought-up creature in blood red silk who was pursuing him with a leather thong in her hands was all too real.

'So large, so powerful, so *arrogant*,' Julia said in a chillingly caressing manner. 'This will be the ultimate experience we shall share. Something we shall never forget.'

Back in the parlour by now Val acted automatically because reason had been suspended on first sight of the antique whip. He stopped to seize his trousers and step into them, an act which brought home to her the reality of his intentions. She began coaxing, cajoling, describing to him the pleasure they would both experience from his pain, and it was all the more chilling and terrible because she spoke as if describing consummate joy. Violent reaction to shock decreed that he should leave immediately. Snatching up the rest of his clothes he retreated towards the far door, certain that if he turned his bare back to her that whip would be brought down on it.

She tried a new tack. 'A cavalry officer has to know what suffering is, Val, and be able to withstand it.' When he was at the door, 'Think of Vorne Ashleigh. He would never run away.'

Val found his voice. 'You're mad. Quite mad!'

The hand holding the whip was raised. He ran. Outside the school library he was extremely sick, retching and shivering for some while as he struggled into his shirt and jacket. Then he made his way to his room in a state of continuing shock, and fell on his bed to ride out the aftermath of a relationship whose true nature was now all too clear. Pain, humiliation, ecstasy followed by rejection, promises, taunts, challenges, jealousy, physical endurance, flattery, mortification, sexual triumph – anything which gave her power over him; over any male, he now suspected. Herbert suffered in his own way, no doubt. Roland Baines was next on the list. Through his misery and pain and utter sense of humiliation, Val realised Clive had been right. He *had* been the perfect victim for a woman like Julia. A boy built like a mature man, who revelled in physical pastimes and was a virgin. Add to that, desperation to gain something she was in a unique position to dangle like a carrot before him, and Valentine Martin Havelock Ashleigh could be led through any convoluted hoops.

He lay face down plumbing the depths of self-denigration until the door of his room crashed open making him jump nervously. Rolling on to his back, he then clambered to his feet to face Dr Keening and Geoffrey Manton. The bottom dropped out of his world as instinct told him why they had come.

Chapter Eleven

Three events within one week changed the situation at Knightshill irrevocably. Sir Gilliard received notice from Dr Keening of his grandson's dismissal following an extremely grave offence against the wife of his housemaster, Herbert Grieves. The letter related how Mrs Grieves had offered to help Valentine with his wish to join the cavalry by approaching her uncle, Brigadier Beecham of the 57th Lancers. During the past few months she had several times asked the boy to her home to give him news, although she had sensed that his interest in the subject was waning.

On the evening of Saturday last, when Mr Grieves was in Blandford, Valentine had called at the house uninvited on the pretext of enquiring when he might have an interview with Brigadier Beecham. He had started paying Mrs Grieves impertinent compliments, but when told to leave he had grown aggressive and forced her to submit to an embrace during which her dress had been torn. At that point, Valentine had confessed desire for her which he was determined to demonstrate. Mrs Grieves had had the presence of mind to snatch an antique muleteer's whip which hung on the wall. Only when she had this weapon in her hand, and threatened to use it, had she felt safe from assault. When the boy left she ran to seek protection from another member of staff, not knowing if he might return later during the night. Mr Manton and Dr Keening had both gone to Valentine's room, where they had found the culprit in an overwrought state with his clothing in disarray. He had been taken to the sick bay, given a strong sedative, and locked in one of the rooms until morning.

The letter concluded with the information that the police had not been called because the lady refused to lay charges which would bring harmful press attention to the school and cause distress to her husband who must continue to command respect from his pupils. Dr Keening was assured Sir Gilliard would deal with his grandson in a manner commensurate to the severity of the offence. The pupils would be told Valentine had gone home on an urgent family matter. His possessions had been packed in his trunk. This would be sent by rail at the end of the week. Dr Keening was deeply saddened by an affair which cast a shadow over the long and distinguished association between Chartfield and the Ashleigh family.

Margaret was arranging flowers in the parlour when Winters brought her letters in. She glanced at each quickly in case there was one from Vere, even after his long silence. As there was not, she opened the envelope addressed in Val's handwriting. Coldness crept through her as she scanned the few lines.

Dear Aunt Meg,
You'll know by now what has happened. I won't be coming home. It's not that I'm too much of a coward to face you all, but I think Grandfather will take this better if I'm not there as a constant reminder. I pray he will. Please do something for me. Tell him I swear I'll redeem myself and bring honour to the Ashleigh name. With deepest affection,
Val

Running from the room in a state of deep apprehension, Margaret sought Sir Gilliard. He was in the library with a letter lying open in front of him, and seemed unaware of another presence as he stared into space. She picked up the letter with a shaking hand. It claimed something shocking, unbelievable. Gazing at the books lining the room Margaret tried to come to terms with what she had read. Where had the poor boy gone? How would he survive? The skating tragedy before Christmas had knocked him badly. This would surely break his spirit completely. She had warned him he was playing with fire when he had said another boy had an uncle in the cavalry who might help him. Had she known the truth she could have told of the hazards attached to asking favours of a married woman. Poor Val! How could she be his ally when she had no idea where he was?

Blinking back her tears she told herself weeping was of no help to him. Better to defend this ridiculous charge against him. She pulled herself together and concentrated on Sir Gilliard. He looked calm enough, but she thought it would be wise to call Clunes and suggest his master should rest for a while. Clunes had been the old man's batman in India, the Crimea, China and Ashanti and had continued as his personal servant when wounds brought an end to Sir Gilliard's active service. Devoted, stern, still a soldier at heart, Clunes was the best person to deal with the situation. Margaret rang the bell for him, then returned to the desk to fold the letter and put it out of sight in a drawer.

'Grandfather,' she began gently, 'Val would never behave as they claim he did. You know that as well as I do. He's very young and the obligation to match up to Vorne makes him burn to make us all proud of him. He's clearly tried too hard and come a cropper, through no fault of his own.'

The glazed eyes showed no sign of awareness as they continued to gaze at some point in the distance. She tried again. 'I've had a note from Val. He believes it will be less painful for you if he doesn't come home. He asks me to tell you he will redeem himself and bring honour to the name. I believe him. So must you.'

There was still no response from the figure in the chair. When Clunes arrived she told him Sir Gilliard was rather unwell and should rest. The voice of his batman brought the old warrior from introspection where his granddaughter's had failed. Frowning deeply he challenged the man.

'Why was the boy so set on the damned cavalry? To go to a *woman* in order to flout my wishes!'

'Unwise move, sir,' ruled the ex-soldier without understanding the comment. 'Petticoats have ruined many a promising youngster.'

Sir Gilliard shook his head. 'Headstrong, wilful, too much unbridled spirit . . . but the West Wilts would have made a man of him.'

'The West Wilts can make a man of even the worst ruffian, sir. Seen it happen many a time.' Glancing significantly at Margaret, he added, 'How about a short rest before tiffin, sir? You'll get to grips with the matter a lot better on the charpoy.' Clunes always used the language of those who have served in India and can never abandon the emotive terms.

The elderly man allowed himself to be assisted from the chair, and continued his theme as he walked to the door leaning heavily on Clunes. 'The *Ghost Lancers*, of all things. An Ashleigh in the Fifty-seventh? Unheard of. Good regiment, can't deny. Battle honours as long as my arm. But *cavalry*, Clunes. Couldn't allow my grandson to prance about in a fancy grey suit and spurs. Tried to make him see sense, y'know, but there's a mutinous streak in him. Saw it at an early age and attempted to crush it. Would have thought better of him if he had gone direct to Max Beecham. But to hide behind petticoats! Where's his pride, eh?' The white head shook again. 'First blooding, I suspect. Lost his head and let us all down unforgivably.'

The pair moved slowly, joined by a bond only other military men would understand, which made it possible for a general to ask of a corporal, 'So what's to do now, eh? One's gone off to war like a sacrificial lamb, the other occupies a hero's grave beneath the sands. The boy was our last hope, and he's disgraced himself in a bid to become a fancy horse-soldier.'

'Mr Valentine's a veritable eagle, sir, never you worry. He'll wear no grey suit. It'll be the scarlet of the West Wilts for him,' Clunes said soothingly. 'He's testing his wings like many wild young 'uns, that's all.'

'I'll clip 'em for him after this,' vowed Sir Gilliard as they passed through to the hall. 'Discipline, a tighter rein, that's what he needs. I'll give him continuous duties for a week or so; confine him to quarters for a few more.

Tamed many a rebellious subaltern that way. Send him to me the moment he gets back to barracks. I'll teach him a lesson he'll not soon forget. A *woman*, indeed!'

Margaret was left feeling more desolate than ever. Val was not coming back to 'barracks', and he had probably been taught a hard lesson by Mrs Grieves. Sir Gilliard's age was catching up with him: his thoughts wandered, he lived in the past, he was obsessed with the continuation of the line, and with the family regiment. All he had divined from Dr Keening's letter was that someone on the brink of manhood should have his bid for individuality crushed before he was sent out to imitate a long line of Ashleighs in all he did. He had missed the tragic depths of an affair in which burning desire for the one thing he wanted, above all else, had driven a desperate boy to gain it by any means possible. So there were now *two* dearly loved brothers seeking their doubtful destiny, having cut themselves off from home and a family which demanded from them something they had found impossible to give.

When Charlotte returned from the village just before lunchtime, Margaret sought her out in the set of rooms alongside those she shared with Philip in marital isolation. The weak sun had not yet left the eastern side of the house, so her sister's yellow and gold sitting room gave an impression of brightness to offset the gloom of Margaret's spirits. They had sat together in this room on so many occasions for heart to heart conversations in those first years following their mother's remarriage and banishment to America. Sir Gilliard had sent his daughter-in-law packing with her 'Southern gentleman', denying her any right of return. To leave her five children with such finality must have been heartbreaking, yet either love for Samuel Bruce had been so all-consuming or life for a gentle widow at Knightshill had been so unbearable that she had accepted the imposed conditions without a fight. Maybe she had felt that Ashleigh children should remain where they truly belonged; maybe she had been right. If she *had* managed to wrest his son's children from a proud, determined man, the boys might have returned to claim their birthright, one after the other. But what of herself and Charlotte? They had discussed the subject on many occasions in this room, imagining how different their lives would have been yet each time concluding that they were glad at the outcome.

Suddenly, Margaret realised that if they had all gone with their mother to a huge ranch she would never have married Philip, Vere could have been an artist with everyone's blessing, Val could have joined any regiment he wished and Charlotte would never have regarded herself as the spinster housekeeper for an ageing general whose own wife had run off with her Bohemian lover. Vorne would probably have returned to take up his inheritance and follow a predestined path to Khartoum. On the other

200

hand, he might have become too charmed with his adopted land to leave it, thereby surviving to enjoy life today. Remaining at Knightshill had brought none of them happiness.

Charlotte greeted her absently, wandering about the room in a fussy manner to put away gloves, scarf, purse and the small book in which she methodically detailed all financial outlay for herself and the house.

'I must find another haberdasher,' she commented, standing at the small chest where she kept her ribbons and threads. 'Dyke is becoming ridiculously expensive because he believes no one will bother to drive as far as Foxington for a yard of lace. He is wrong. I shall do so if he persists in adding three farthings to every item he stocks.'

'Lottie, I have something to tell you,' said Margaret.

Her tone suggested news the other had been expecting for long months. Turning sharply, she stared at Margaret with eyes darkened by pain.

'Grandfather has received news.'

'Not about Vere.'

'Not Vere? *Thank God!*' She limped to a chair and sank on to it with the weakness of relief. 'What then?'

'Val has been summarily sacked from Chartfield.'

Still in the euphoria of hearing her worst fears denied, her sister said irritably, 'Oh no! What has he done *now?*'

'Don't speak as if he were forever in trouble! Any boy who gains sporting trophies by the score, captains all the school teams and is made a senior prefect must be a credit to Chartfield . . . and to his family.'

'So why has he been forced to leave?'

The question was asked in acid tones, and Margaret hesitated. Her sister had never been fully in accord with Val. How would she view this affair?

'Well, why?' Charlotte demanded.

'We only have Dr Keening's version of what happened . . . or rather, that of the wife of Val's housemaster.'

'Which is?'

'That Mrs Grieves offered to help him apply for a commission in her uncle's cavalry regiment, and that while doing so he became . . .' she sought the right word, 'infatuated with her.'

'*What!* With the wife of a member of staff? He wouldn't. He *couldn't*. Someone old enough to be his mother! Even Val wouldn't do that.'

'What do you mean by even Val wouldn't do that?' she asked with considerable heat. 'It suggests that he's – he's — '

'He was chasing village girls at Christmas when that Jepson boy lost his life. The tragedy only happened because they had each taken a girl across the frozen pond to a dark, lonely spot.'

'*Taken*, yes. Not dragged, forced or lured. The girls went with them

201

willingly. Young people do that kind of thing, Lottie. It's perfectly natural.'

'Is it natural to do it with a mature woman who is married to your tutor? That *is* what Val did, I imagine. He would hardly be sacked for a secret infatuation.' Her mouth tightened. 'It's disgusting!'

'So is your acceptance of his guilt on no more than the word of this woman. You should know your brother would never do what he's accused of.'

'I know he has the same attitude towards females Vorne had, and has started a lot earlier. You can't have forgotten that sordid business over the baker's niece. The girl's aunt caught Val red-handed.'

'It wasn't sordid,' she cried. 'He simply tried to kiss the girl. She probably led him on. When a boy looks as attractive as Val he's fair game for bakers' nieces, and such like.'

Charlotte's mouth tightened further. 'Don't be crude.'

Wanting understanding and commiseration from the only person she could turn to for either, Margaret found her sister's attitude intolerable. 'Just because you decided long ago that your limp made any romantic exchange with a man impossible, you see evil in all such relationships. Val's handsome, healthy and very affectionate, that's all. He is *not* disgusting.' She took a deep breath. 'It's time you practised a little tolerance of those who haven't your narrow-minded attitude before you turn into a sour old maid.'

Charlotte flushed with anger. 'I think you'd better leave.'

'Not before I tell you one more thing,' Margaret said in accelerating distress over the events of the morning. 'I had intended to keep this to myself, but it might help you to better understanding of those around you. I have always been especially close to Val.'

'So much so it blinds you to his true character.'

'As you have shared a similar close bond with Vere,' she continued doggedly. 'He kept at least one secret from you, however. On an afternoon several weeks ago, when I was feeling particularly low, I had an urge to look at his canvases in the hope of somehow feeling close to him for a while. Among them, wrapped separately, I found a dozen or more very beautiful studies of female nudes.' Seeing her sister's visual denial, she added swiftly, 'His signature was on every one, Lottie. I didn't condemn him for wanting to gaze for hours at naked women so that he could reproduce each curve and plane of their bodies on canvases to hide away in his room. *Do you?*'

Flushing even darker, Charlotte cried, 'Artists are different.'

'They're *men*, who desire women as other men do. Vere didn't go off in a gesture of suicidal madness because he was an artist. It was because he wanted to possess Annabel and she had removed herself from his reach.'

'Stop it! You make him sound – '

'Disgusting?' she suggested tautly. 'But you know Vere could never be, and so do I. I also know the same of Val. *Why don't you?*' When there was no reply, she added, 'You see only what you wish to see. We all have a duty and sense of loyalty to the family, but we are still entitled to a life of our own. None of us should be forced onto a path we find unbearably thorny. It happened to Vere through overwhelming feelings for a girl who also demanded the impossible from him. In Val's case, Grandfather's selfish attempt to dominate drove him to seek any route to the path he is burning to follow. This woman promised all he longed for, so he went after it eagerly.' Feeling the threat of tears once more, she swallowed them back to add, 'I suspect Mrs Grieves might be younger than her husband and enjoys admiration from boys emerging as young men. It's a particularly vulnerable period in their lives, particularly for one trying to hold on to a dream his family is determined to crush.'

'He won't do it by getting himself sacked from school for unpardonable behaviour,' Charlotte countered coldly. 'Every regiment demands that its officers should be gentlemen. If he's so determined to have his way, he should conduct himself like one.'

'Lottie, you sound more like Grandfather with every word.'

Charlotte got to her feet swiftly, 'Dear heaven, I'd forgotten the worst aspect of all this. It will kill him!'

'It hasn't,' Margaret said acidly. 'He went off with Clunes vowing to teach the offender a sharp lesson when he returns to barracks. Like you, he sees only personal aspects of this sad business. *He* is acutely affronted by Val's bid to join the cavalry. *You* are affronted by the thought of your boy brother acting like a grown man. Neither of you has given any thought to the poor lad's predicament, or considered the misery *he* must be suffering now. It was you who dubbed the Ashleighs a selfish family, on the day you slapped Val's face in front of the children. He asked me then if I thought you were right. I now believe you were. Some members of it are very selfish indeed.'

'You're including Val himself in that statement, I hope,' her sister snapped. 'He clearly gave no thought to any of us when he courted disgrace. I shall tell him so when he gets home.'

'He's not coming home. I had a letter from him this morning.'

'Ha, a clear admission of guilt.'

'No, Lottie,' she said through a tightening throat. 'It's an admission of no faith in those who should stand by him in times of adversity. He prefers to face loneliness and hardship rather than a proud, unforgiving, intolerant family . . . and I can't say I blame him.' At the door she turned back to add, 'Grandfather wishes only to dominate those close to him. You see love as something disgusting which should be swept under the carpet and nailed firmly down. As for Philip, he – he — ' She swallowed in order to conclude and make her escape. 'I feel desperately sorry for you all.'

As she hurried along the corridor she realised, with immense regret, that they had just quarrelled seriously for the first time in their lives. Her one remaining ally had been alienated – But she would defend Val against anyone. Needing to escape the confines of a home which no longer offered the warmth and security of a united family, she descended the stairs and began to cross the hall for the privacy of the gardens. But the ring of her heels on the stone floor of the hall brought Winters from the small room known as the gold salon.

'Madam, we have a visitor,' he announced in his inimitable manner as head of a household containing a great many domestic staff. 'I understand Sir Gilliard is resting and Miss Ashleigh has only this minute returned from the village, so I have taken the liberty of informing Mr Nicolardi you will receive him.'

Longing for solitude, she said swiftly, 'I can't see anyone at present, Winters. It's extremely inconvenient.'

'In that case, I'll bid you good day and return when you tell me I may,' said a deep voice from the doorway of the salon.

Margaret looked beyond the butler to see a dark-haired man dressed in country clothes. He began to walk towards her as Winters retired. 'It is very irritating to receive a visit from someone who has not had the good manners to wait for an invitation. When the entire household is occupied, it's particularly so. Forgive me.' He halted, his warm brown eyes scrutinising her face intently. 'Yes, you are undoubtedly Margaret Daulton, but Clive's descriptive powers fell very short of the truth in your case.'

Ill-prepared for such an approach from this stranger whose striking, sun-browned features added to the impact of his frankness, Margaret could only ask, 'Who is Clive?'

'The boy you generously entertained here last summer. We shared a mother.' He took up her right hand and kissed it with old-fashioned elegance as he continued to study her face. 'Laurence Nicolardi, at your service.'

'You're his half-brother? I knew very little about his family.' Realising that her fingers still lay in his palm she withdrew them, thrown off balance by this encounter. 'My condolences on your loss. He was a charming boy and the tragic accident saddened us all.'

Laurence appeared moved as he said, 'When I arrived from South America three days ago, my priority was to express my gratitude to your young brother for his courage in trying to save him. I travelled to Dorset yesterday. Dr Keening told me Val had returned home, so I came to Knightshill straight away. The boys were such close friends. I hope Val will not be averse to describing exactly what happened that night.'

His words deepened the pain of this morning's news. How cruel of fate to send him on such a mission today. She cast around for a way out of the difficult situation. 'Val isn't here, I'm afraid.'

'*Not* here?'

'He's visiting friends. In Scotland.'

'Dr Keening mentioned a family matter.'

'They're friends of the family.'

'I see.' He watched her silently for a moment or two. 'Then I must save my message of gratitude until he returns home.'

'He won't. Not for a long while,' she amended, feeling more distraught with every sentence. 'His friend is ill.'

'I'm sorry to hear that.' His glance seemed to suggest that he knew she was lying. 'If you'll be kind enough to give me the address in Scotland so that I can write of my gratitude, I'll intrude upon your busy morning no longer.'

Out of her depth, Margaret stood deploring the twist of fate which had sent Clive Jepson's relative with a hero's laurels to bestow on a disgraced schoolboy. The silence lengthened, but she could think of no way to break it and relieve her of the lump gathering in her throat.

'There is no sick friend in Scotland, is there?' A hand slid beneath her elbow and Laurence guided her to the room he had just vacated. Margaret went without protest, aware of a personality used to taking command. Closing the door behind them he led her across to the fire, lit despite April sunshine outside. She was grateful for the comfort provided by the blazing logs because she had grown unnaturally cold. Holding her hands out to the fire she stared at the heart of it, supremely conscious of the man beside her waiting for an explanation. Yet she was loath to give one.

'Is your young brother in trouble?'

Unequal to telling more lies, yet reluctant to affirm something which must lead to revealing the truth, Margaret continued to gaze silently at the fire.

'While you decide whether or not to answer that, I must tell you something,' he said with welcome gentleness. 'Although my life as a diplomat prevented our seeing each other often over the past ten years, the blood of our mother's race ran in our veins to create a close bond between us. When I heard of Clive's death I was inconsolable for many days. It's natural to be deeply affected by the tragedies of those we love.'

She looked up with emotion misting her eyes, his frank admission making it possible for her to speak. 'Val blamed himself for failing to save Clive, even though he almost surrendered his own life in the attempt. It left him troubled and unsure of himself. I noticed how his self-confidence had been undermined during the Christmas vacation, although he struggled to cope with the demands made on him after Sir Gilliard's illness. He returned to school in a strangely restless mood.'

'And Julia Grieves took advantage of the fact.'

She was dumbfounded. 'I don't understand.'

'Clive and I exchanged weekly letters in which we passed on our observations of people and events surrounding us. He was extremely perceptive, able to bring alive situations and personalities from which I was distanced some thousands of miles. The devious wife of a tutor Clive greatly respected was described to me *most* precisely. It *is* she who is behind your reluctance to tell me the truth, isn't it?' he probed gently.

Margaret's hands smoothed the dark-blue cloth of her skirt so that it pressed against limbs chilled by reaction to the shocks of this morning. Laurence Nicolardi was adding to them.

'There is no reason why I should tell you anything. I have already indicated that you have come at the most inconvenient time, yet you refuse to leave,' she said.

'I've not been asked to leave, so far as I'm aware,' he returned. 'The lies you told me to explain Val's absence suggest that you need support in this distressing situation. From Clive's descriptions of your family I imagine Sir Gilliard is presently wallowing in selfish concern over the sullying of the Ashleigh name, and your sister is saying Val has met the fate he has wilfully been courting for some time. I'll wager neither is proving of any comfort to his worried favourite sister.'

This man was too dangerously perceptive for her peace of mind. With a curious sense of desperation, she said, 'I have a husband to support me, Mr Nicolardi.'

'Ah, yes. Clive wrote most intuitively on *that* subject, also.' Allowing time for the significance of his words to register, he added, more gently, 'I think you should confide in me. I can offer the sympathy others decline to give you.' Taking hold of her arms he coaxed her into a pale brocaded chair beside the fire, then sat on a matching sofa to her right. 'Am I correct in guessing your brother has been indulging his passion for Mrs Grieves?'

'He's a schoolboy,' she cried. 'How can you suggest — '

'*Has* he?'

'Of course not! Val would never do what he's been accused of.'

'Oh, I think we must accept that he did.'

She got to her feet again. 'This is really not your concern. You came to deliver a message of gratitude for Val's courage, that's all.'

'And found a household divided over something I probably understand better than any of you,' he said quietly, rising with a grave expression on a face she found difficult to confront with any composure. 'Please allow me to justify my statement that Val is probably guilty.'

'You know nothing of him,' she accused heatedly.

'I know a great deal about him. A boy on the brink of manhood will reveal more of himself to his close friend than he will to a sister who acts the substitute mother. Please . . . sit down again and allow me to tell you some facts you were not privileged to know. *Please.*'

Resistance crumbled. She sat, leaning back wearily against the cushion. Something potent was materialising here; Sir Gilliard and her sister would be responsible for the consequences, not she.

'Perhaps you did not know young Val was obsessed by determination to join the cavalry only because he feared his natural impetuosity would make him a bad infantry officer. Burdened by the obligation to live up to a family ideal – I wonder if women have any notion of that burden – he was forbidden the means of avoiding a course which might bring failure or ignominy. This cruel ruling by his grandfather increased the weight on his youthful shoulders and made him desperate enough to listen to promises of a solution offered by the attractive second wife of an ageing tutor.'

'So she *is* a younger woman!'

'About your own age. Clive wrote that Val initially regarded her as "sisterly and very much like Margaret". So Julia Grieves had three strong weapons: an uncle about to take command of a cavalry regiment, resemblance to a sister of whom her victim was deeply fond, and a unique position as the wife of his housemaster which made friendly relations acceptable. Add the lad's total inexperience of the fair sex and you have the perfect ingredients for easy seduction.'

Margaret said nothing. Here was an uncomfortable comparison with her own youthful folly: a sense of desperation after their mother's departure, an obligation somehow to replace her, fears of inadequacy and inexperience of powerful physical attraction. Philip had offered a way out and she had seized it. At eighteen, the flame of youth had burned with undeniable force. She would have surrendered to Philip before marriage if he had demanded it. Val possessed the passionate Ashleigh nature, too, it seemed.

Watching her closely, Laurence asked, 'Are you still resistant to the notion of his guilt?'

She shook her head lethargically against the pale brocade.

'Clive saw immediately that Julia Grieves was very taken with the one boy in the room who seemed immune to her charms – a dangerous challenge, had Val but realised it. When Clive warned him he was hotly indignant, and defended the woman who reminded him of you. Later, he appeared to grow uneasy over the relationship and held aloof for a while.' His expression saddened as he confessed, 'I heard no more of the affair because Clive's letters suddenly ceased. However, my vast experience of human nature tells me that the lure of a cavalry commission must have proved impossible to resist. The lady would have been determined to exercise the power such creatures enjoy, and Val would have recognised it too late.' He leaned forward with his arms along his knees. 'Where is he?'

'I don't know.' Overcome by the knowledge that her brother had walked into this disastrous situation because he had initially likened the woman to herself and had trusted her because of it, she found her throat thickening with emotion once more. Taking Val's note from the pocket of her skirt, she held it out. 'This came an hour before you did.'

After glancing at the contents, he looked up at her. 'Even at his lowest ebb he vows to bring honour to the name. Dear God, what an impossible family you are!'

'What a hopeless diplomat you must be if you always say exactly what you think, as you have this morning.'

'You still haven't ordered me to leave.'

'Perhaps because I have little hope of being heeded.'

He handed Val's letter back to her. 'He'll suffer a modicum of hardship and an overdose of mortification, that's all. Don't worry too much.'

'That's easy for you to say.'

'He's facing nothing so dangerous as the enemy . . . yet. That's the time to start being concerned for his safety.' After a short pause, he added, 'From my knowledge of young men bruised by experience I'd guess he'll make a move to defy his circumstances as soon as possible. Perhaps he'll join Vere in the Sudan.'

Her gaze swept over him from his smooth dark hair to his polished brown shoes, 'Is there anything about us you don't know, Mr Nicolardi?'

'Very little . . . and my name is Laurence.'

Struggling to hold down a sensation she should not be experiencing in his company, she said, 'It's surely only fair to enlighten me a little on your own family background.'

'Of course.' He gave a sudden smile which was as devastating as his personality. 'See how swiftly I've eased your anxiety over Val and turned your interest in my direction instead. How wise you were to take my advice to confide in me.'

'Your family background, if you please,' she prompted.

While he told her of his father's death and his mother's remarriage a year later when he was a child of six, Margaret absorbed every detail of this man who had walked in on her at a time of great isolation. Four or five years her senior, he was assured, elegant and full of a charm which was probably partly cultivated and partly due to natural warmth. His mobile features and acutely expressive eyes added emphasis to his words; his smile was irresistibly exciting. He wore expensive clothes with the nonchalance of those who always dress well. There was a gold pin in his tie, a gold watch-chain looped across his dark-green waistcoat, and a heavy gold ring on his right hand. He was a stranger who knew the Ashleighs as intimately as an old friend. Instinct told her every minute spent in his company was dangerous.

'Clive was born after Mother had been married to Arthur Jepson eight years, taking us all by surprise. By that time, I had been turned into a correct English schoolboy called Laurence, not Lorenzo.' He smiled at her ruefully. 'They tried hard to change the rest to Nicholson, but I drew the line at that. It hasn't the same melodic ring as Nicolardi.'

'So you're very proud of "the name", too?'

'And of my Italian relations. Clive and I spent many delightful vacations with them.'

'How long have you been in South America?'

'Three years. I'm now on six months' leave.'

Trying to sound casual, she asked, 'Is your wife here with you?'

'She died just before I sailed to take up the post.'

'Oh, how tragic.'

There was no longer a light in his eyes, a lilt in his voice as he said, 'She had not intended to sail with me. I imagine I do not have to describe to *you* how love slowly dies when one partner doesn't care to keep it alive.'

The danger increased dramatically, driving her to her feet. 'I think it's time for me to ask you to leave.'

He slowly stood to face her. 'I suppose it is . . . but I do hope you will not.'

As Margaret fought a battle with herself, Charlotte walked in without warning. Laurence recovered his composure swiftly, turning to greet her with a slight bow.

'Mr Nicolardi?' She advanced, straight-faced. 'Winters has only now informed me of your arrival, I regret to say.'

'Mrs Daulton was gracious enough to entertain me, Miss Ashleigh. May I repeat the apology I offered her? I am taking a short vacation in this area. After reading the history of Dunstan St Mary loaned to me from the vicarage library, I had such a desire to see the Great Window of Knightshill, which is mentioned in the book, I walked up from the village in the hope of catching a glimpse of it from the lane. When I found that to be impossible, I took my courage in both hands and ventured to ring your bell.'

Margaret marvelled at his self-possession after that moment of un-expected intimacy, which allowed him to lie with ease and conviction. Clive must have written details of the Great Window and its fame recorded in the book. The boy could well have borrowed it from the rector last summer. He had been the studious type. Had any detail of that vacation been omitted from the weekly letters to South America? Only when Charlotte melted slightly and began to discuss the window's antiquity with him did Margaret realise Laurence had no intention of revealing the true reason for his visit to someone whom he knew would be unsympathetic.

'As you so bravely took your courage in both hands, sir,' she was saying with a touch of acid in her voice, 'perhaps you would care to see the window at close quarters. I'll show you up to it.'

'That's extremely courteous of you, ma'am, but I understand this is an inconvenient time for a visit of any length. You see, I am not merely a curious passer-by. Professor Gwynne, whom Sir Gilliard has entertained here on several occasions, told me of the window some years ago and initially aroused my interest in it. I returned from South America on Tuesday with several determined missions to fulfil. Seeing the window was one of them.' His glance swept round to include Margaret. 'My father's family owns several workshops producing engraved and gold-inlaid glassware in Verona, in addition to their productive vineyards, so I am fascinated by examples of superb craftsmanship in that versatile medium. The Great Window of Knightshill is a work of art which requires lengthy study rather than a brief glance.'

Charlotte looked at him consideringly. 'Are you a historian or an artist, Mr Nicolardi?'

'I am a diplomat, ma'am. As such, I have been privileged to see many of the world's works of art and beautiful monuments from the past. One does not have to be anything other than a mortal to appreciate genius, Miss Ashleigh.' He glanced around the room as if seeking something in vain. 'You have an artist of considerable talent in your own family, have you not? Vere Ashleigh's water-colours are admired by the more discerning of London's gallery owners, especially those of the Wiltshire landscape. I appreciate their fine quality even more now I have seen the area. Your brother has a good eye for the minute detail other artists neglect.' He indicated the walls adorned by several huge gold-framed mirrors. 'You have none of his pictures in this room. A pity. The light is perfect.'

'Vere has never been encouraged to display his work in this house,' said Margaret, certain he already knew that. 'It has been inhabited by soldiers for many generations. There is little affinity here for men of more gentle disposition.'

His expressive eyes contained a message which she should ignore but could not as he glanced her way. 'I have always believed my own disposition to be reasonably gentle, Mrs Daulton, but I have no sensation of being rejected.'

'My brother is presently in the Sudan fighting for his country,' put in Charlotte sharply. 'He has unselfishly put aside his own inclinations to do his duty by his family.'

'And you applaud his sacrifice, Miss Ashleigh?' he asked.

Charlotte's mouth tightened. She ignored his question to say, 'I confess I am uncertain about what to do concerning your wish to *study* our window, sir. Perhaps it would be better for you to return on another day. Shall you be in the district long?'

'For some considerable time. I am occupying rooms at the Stag's Head, so it will be easy for me to walk up the hill at any hour you suggest. It's more than kind of you to be so obliging when you have a family crisis.'

'A crisis?' she repeated swiftly. 'Whatever can you mean?'

'Your man informed me Sir Gilliard has been obliged to retire due to an indisposition. After his recent illness any setback must constitute a crisis, I imagine.'

'My grandfather has been overtiring himself, that is all,' she said, as she pulled the bell-rope to summon Winters. 'If you are free next Tuesday morning you are welcome to spend all of it in studying the window, sir.'

Margaret stepped forward quickly. 'Perhaps Mr Nicolardi would care to have luncheon with us on Tuesday. If he is acquainted with Professor Gwynne, Grandfather will surely wish him to do so.'

Charlotte's mouth grew even more prim. 'I trust you will find yourself able to accept our invitation, Mr Nicolardi.'

'Your great hospitality bears out my earlier comment, Miss Ashleigh. My gentle soul senses no rejection from the warrior spirits occupying Knightshill, and I accept with pleasure.'

Winters entered to wait expressionless by the open door while farewells were made. Laurence turned to Margaret after kissing Charlotte's hand and causing her some confusion by so doing.

'I was told that you are engaged in writing a history of the Ashleigh family and the house which has been their home for some hundreds of years, Mrs Daulton. Perhaps you have some facts concerning your window for me. I sincerely hope you will spare me a little of your valuable time on Tuesday to discuss it.'

She tried to sound casual. 'My work is that of a novice, but if you think it might be of help to you I shall place it at your disposal.'

His lips were warm against her fingers, but she trembled as if chilled by his touch. Then he left with Winters, promising to be back within four days.

'I had little option but to suggest his return at another time, but there was absolutely no necessity to invite the man for the entire day,' said a cold voice bringing her back to reality.

Margaret studied her sister's angry expression. 'I didn't ask him to stay all day, just for the midday meal. It was a mere courtesy.'

'One which should have been extended by *me*.'

'Then why didn't you?'

'Who is he?'

'A friend of Professor Gwynne, apparently.'

'He knows a great deal about us.'

She turned to go. 'He admits to an enquiring nature.'

Leaving the gold salon she sought the fresh air outside, which had been denied her by Laurence's arrival. Walking swiftly in the clear sunshine, she crossed the terrace and began to climb the slope at the rear of the house. From half-way up she would have a clear view of the lane leading to the village. Reaching the spot, she saw his tall figure striding the downward track towards the curve which would take him from her sight. At the bend Laurence turned and looked back. Perhaps he saw the figure in a long blue skirt and an ivory figured-silk blouse watching him from her lonely hill; a woman of twenty-nine crushed by a failed marriage and the disintegration of the family which had been her protection from it. Perhaps he saw someone who had just glimpsed a rainbow after prolonged storms. Perhaps he saw someone who, like himself, had watched love slowly die because a partner did not care to keep it alive.

He made no sign of having seen anything but the grey stone house with the celebrated window he claimed to have come to study, for he continued to the village around the bend and out of her sight a few moments later. Sinking to the grass, she sat hugging her knees until the brisk breeze caused her to shiver. In getting to her feet something fell from the pocket of her skirt. It was Val's letter. She opened and read it again. A smile touched her mouth: he would be all right. He had learned a hard lesson at the hands of that woman, but he had too much determination to allow her to break his spirit permanently. A rainbow always appeared after storms.

On Tuesday morning Margaret put on a dress of plum-coloured grosgrain, with a necklet of pearls and garnets discreet enough for morning wear when entertaining guests to luncheon. Instructing her maid to put up her light brown hair in a soft, becoming style she had not worn for several years, Margaret then hastily made Louise change it to the more severe one the family had grown used to seeing. She must not arouse comment which would be difficult to counter without complicating matters. The coming meeting would be difficult enough to handle without unnecessarily betraying herself. But to whom, she asked silently. Philip acted as if she were a bundle of cloth with a face above it when he had no choice but to acknowledge her presence. Sir Gilliard treated everyone these days as if they were subordinates in a military barracks and appeared to forget that she was even female, much less his granddaughter. Charlotte had not forgiven her for the quarrel and avoided her whenever possible. The only person who might detect her true feelings today was Laurence himself, and he already knew. She was certain he knew.

On entering the small room with its walls decorated in rich silk, she found her husband at the breakfast table. Hesitating momentarily, she then walked to the sideboard for a spoonful of kedgeree and some toast. Why had he not left the house yet? Surely he had not decided to work at home today.

'Good morning,' he said tonelessly, as she sat at the table.

'Good morning,' she replied just as tonelessly. 'I thought you had an important meeting at Salisbury.'

He continued to eat and read. 'Dr Martineau was taken ill yesterday, so is unable to speak.'

'I see.' Her heart sank. If Philip decided to lunch with the family it would spoil everything. When he shut his book with a snap she realised he was looking at her intently. The necklet lying against her skin seemed to turn into a chain of flashing, gaudy jewels. *The baubles of Jezebel*. Fear of him rose unexpectedly, making her clutch the napkin on her lap as if it were a weapon to beat off his advance.

'I have been invited to participate in the annual convention in London by submitting a paper on the effects to the brain of drinking human blood.'

She could not bring herself to comment on a concept so hideous, particularly with breakfast on the table before her.

'I have studied reports by the most eminent medical missionaries and practitioners specialising in the behaviour of heathen tribes. I believe I have reached an important conclusion which will be of value to my brothers in the field.' He stood. 'I have accepted the invitation. The cancellation of Dr Martineau's talk gives me a full day in which to make a start on my paper.'

Margaret relaxed her grip on the napkin. The necklet resumed its true appearance.

'Tell Charlotte I shall be unable to partake of the midday meal. She has a guest, I believe.'

'A friend of Professor Gwynne . . . to study the window.'

He scowled. 'The poor have no windows whatever. Perhaps he should study that truth instead.' Crossing to the door, he stopped with his hand on the knob. 'I shall take Timothy to the convention.'

She twisted in her chair to protest. 'The boy is only nine.'

'Time he became more involved in the work he's been called to do.'

'He has *not* been called to do it. He yearns for the army.'

213

Philip's harsh expression hardened further. 'That old fool fills them all with notions of glory which disguise the basest sin of all – the slaying of our brothers for gain. The "hero of Khartoum" was no more than a man filled with vainglory, who paid the price of all such sinners. Vere has run away to kill unenlightened savages in the hope of pleasing the pampered temptress who threw his ring back in his face. His weakness is not only in his physique, that much is painfully clear. That young fornicator you guided like a mother engaged in *adultery* to gain the trappings this family considers so necessary.' His voice rose. 'Never say to me again that my son yearns for the army, for it is tantamount to blasphemy.'

Margaret rose. 'Timothy is my son, also.'

'A boy is the son of his father.'

'*No.*'

'Pray do not shout at me, Margaret. Your own brothers all remained at the paternal home when their mother departed for the land of the pagan Indian. They have each obeyed the will of their grand-patriarch, albeit with misguided loyalty. My son will bow to my will. He will come with me to London next week. The girl will play her destined role as soon as she is old enough.'

Her voice was unsteady as she said, 'They will not love you for forcing this on them.'

'They need only to love the Lord. Through Him they will find love for every human soul on earth.'

'Yet you have not yet found it,' she cried. 'You have just spoken of my brothers with patent disgust. Surely they are as deserving of your understanding as those distant black fellows who drink human blood.'

His scowl deepened. 'The heathens know not what they do. The lordly Ashleighs know it very well.'

His words hung in the room after he had gone. They were true enough. She still counted herself an Ashleigh, and she knew quite clearly what she was about to do this morning.

Laurence arrived in a pony and trap driven by one of the men from the Stag's Head Inn. When Winters ushered him into the conservatory, where morning chocolate had been served as usual, he greeted his two hostesses with a rueful smile.

'Your fresh country air seized hold of me, I'm afraid. I slept so late, I was obliged to ask Moorkin to send me up in one of his vehicles.'

Charlotte broke the silence she had maintained whilst waiting with Margaret for the visitor. 'It is well known that Wiltshire air is very enervating when one is not accustomed to it, Mr Nicolardi. Will you have some chocolate to revive you?'

'Thank you, Miss Ashleigh.' He looked at Margaret. 'Good day, Mrs

Daulton. I hope you have not forgotten your promise to give me the benefit of your researches into the history of the window.'

'Did I promise?' she murmured, thinking how striking he looked in his suit of light-brown fine tweed.

'Oh, I think so.'

'Then I must honour it.'

He had no sooner occupied one of the basket chairs and exclaimed on how pleasant it was in the large airy extension enclosed by glass, when the door opened to admit two small cannonballs who flung themselves at Margaret.

'Mama, say I need not go,' demanded Timothy fiercely, his hair ruffled and his eyes burning with indignation as he clung to her hand.

Shocked from her thoughts back to the reality of her life, Margaret looked at the faces of her children in dismay. 'Hush, the pair of you. Have you forgotten your manners? We have a guest with us.'

Timothy turned his pale face towards Laurence, but he was too wrought up to forget why he was there. 'I beg your pardon, sir, but I have to speak to my mother on a most important matter.'

'They're going to drink his blood,' wailed Kate in growing hysteria. 'Don't let them! Don't let them!' She ran to Charlotte. 'Aunt Lottie, don't let them drink Tim's blood.'

Charlotte held her close, looking over the child's head at Margaret. 'Whatever is this all about? Where's Nanny?'

Shaken, she said, 'I gave her permission to go to the village with Ned to fetch Val's trunk which is coming on the 10.45. She had a package to send to her sister. I left the children at their lessons not half an hour ago.'

'You must be Kate,' said a masculine voice above the child's continuing wails. 'I've heard all about you and your brother Tim. I promise you no one will drink his blood . . . or yours, for that matter.'

The girl twisted her tear-wet face towards this stranger who claimed to know all about her. The wails diminished into a succession of shuddering gasps as curiosity overcame fear. When she continued to scrutinise him from beneath Charlotte's encircling arm, Laurence smiled encouragingly.

'I imagine your father is not proposing to take Tim to South America.'

Still peering from beneath the arm, Kate asked thickly, 'Where is that?'

'A long way across the ocean. I live there sometimes. There are people who drink human blood, but they've never asked me for a single drop of mine.'

Kate straightened. 'Do they ask first?'

'It's only polite to do so, don't you think?'

She pondered that. 'So Tim can say no?'

'Is he going to South America?'

215

Margaret watched as Timothy took a few steps towards Laurence. 'Papa says I must go with him to London for the Mission Conference.'

'I see. No vampires there, old chap.'

The boy moved nearer. 'I don't want to go. You see, I'm going to be an officer in the West Wilts, not a missionary.'

Brown eyes regarded him sympathetically. 'It's not always possible to fulfil our hopes, unfortunately.'

'But I'm an Ashleigh. I *must* be a soldier.'

'Why does your sister think the missionaries will drink your blood?'

'She heard Papa say he's been invited to read a paper about heathens who do it.' Taking Kate's hand he led her right up to the visitor who had taken control of the situation. 'She's very imaginative, sir, and gets upset at any suggestion of violence.'

'But not over the suggestion of your becoming a soldier?'

'We're all soldiers in this family. She's used to that.'

'Uncle Vorne had knives put into him, but he still didn't give the horrid men the paper they wanted,' Kate announced, clutching her brother's hand tightly. 'Only the Queen could say that he should, you see.'

Laurence nodded. 'Of course.'

'Uncle Vere has gone to see Sue Dan and to be very, very brave. But I wish he hadn't. He used to read us lovely stories. Val tried his best, but he isn't as good at it as Uncle Vere. Val's at school and I'm going to marry him when I grow old enough.' She looked him over frankly. 'Can *you* read stories?'

The emergency appeared to be over, but Margaret made no attempt to intervene as Kate chattered on in her usual fashion and Timothy focused all his attention on someone showing interest and understanding. It was an indication of how much the children had missed Vere's presence in the house. They would not even have Val to substitute for him during vacations. She would have to think up an acceptable explanation for his failure to return to Knightshill. With growing sadness she watched the three who appeared to have forgotten herself and Charlotte. This was how they should be with their father: trusting, eager, and free to speak their youthful thoughts. At that point, Laurence met her gaze over the heads of her children, and she knew then that Clive Jepson had put him in possession of facts which gave him the fullest degree of detail on her life. The signal he was sending left her in no doubt of that.

Charlotte got to her feet, obliging him to do the same. 'I have promised to go through the orders for orchids which we grow in the hothouses you can see to your right, Mr Nicolardi. My sister will show you the window when the children have been persuaded to return to their lessons. We gather for sherry at twelve-thirty. My grandfather is looking forward to meeting you then.'

She left without glancing at Margaret. A short silence followed until Laurence crossed to sit in the chair beside the tray containing the silver pot, over which Margaret presided. He held out his empty cup so that she could refill it. As she poured the chocolate, the children came to stand before them.

'You have a very funny name,' observed Kate.

'Yes, haven't I?' He cast her a quizzical look. 'Would you like to sit on my knee?'

'Is it comfortable?' she asked with great seriousness.

'I really couldn't say, never having sat on it myself.'

Timothy grinned, but his sister was always thoughtful when holding conversations with adults. 'You *couldn't* sit on it, could you?'

'Who knows? A person with a very funny name might be able to do very funny things.'

Clearly full of doubts about sitting on his knee, she changed the subject. 'Are you a soldier?'

'No. I'm a diplomat.'

'What's that?'

He leaned toward her conspiratorially. 'A person who has to find out *everything* about *everybody* so that he can prevent them from upsetting each other.'

Her rather prim little face cleared. 'So that's why you've heard all about Tim and me. It seemed very funny that you had when we've never heard a *thing* about you.' Her thoughts progressed. 'Have you come to work here? Val upset Aunt Lottie so much she smacked him. Uncle Vere went away because Miss Bourneville had been very unkind to him, and Great-grandfather was so angry with dear Val because he wants to join the calver – cavler – the — '

'Cavalry,' supplied Timothy. 'We're all in the West Wilts really, but Val *is* a splendid rider and full of energy. I suppose he should be allowed to join any regiment he fancies.'

'That's a very reasonable attitude, Tim, but older people often believe that what *they* feel so very strongly about must be the best thing for others. That's why Sir Gilliard wants Val in the family regiment . . . and it's why your father wants you to be a missionary.'

They were now back to where it had all begun and the boy turned to Margaret, his face flushing with protest. '*Must* I go to London, Mama?'

'Your father thinks you will find it interesting,' she told him as calmly as she could. 'It will certainly give you a better idea of the work he wishes you to do.'

'But I don't wish it,' he cried with a defiance she had heard in Val's voice many times. 'All Ashleighs are soldiers.'

'You're not an Ashleigh, Tim,' she reminded him sadly.

'I am *inside*, Mama. I'll always be one inside. No one can stop that.'

Kate patted his arm consolingly. 'Papa says it's what we are inside which is really important. Our skins may be any colour and our faces may look very strange to others, but we are all the same inside. That means you *are* an Ashleigh, Tim. And so am I.' She turned to Laurence. 'Don't you think that's right, Mr Nick Lardy?'

He smiled. 'I think we are all entitled to be whatever we wish *inside*. Life might oblige us to do all manner of things but no one can take our inner selves from us.' He put a hand on Timothy's shoulder. 'Life has a way of changing things in the most unexpected way. It can happen through some momentous event, or a simple chance meeting. Your father has taught you to have faith. Why don't you heed that piece of his advice and sheath your sword until your moment comes?'

Timothy heaved a very deep sigh and sucked in his lips doubtfully. 'I still don't want to go to the convention.'

'Every experience, however unwelcome, makes a man a wiser one,' said Laurence quietly.

Sighing noisily once more, Timothy surrendered. 'All right.'

Kate moved round to gaze at the visitor in admiration. 'You are very good at being a diplomat. Tim isn't upset any more.'

Laurence laughed. 'And what about you, Miss?'

Her head shook vigorously. 'Now I know they have to *ask* before drinking his blood, it's all right. He'll say no, and that will be the end of the matter,' she declared in tones borrowed from Nanny. Turning on Margaret, she adopted a cajoling expression. 'Mama, may we have a tiny slice of Cook's apple-cake? *Please?*'

'If you promise to return to your lessons and work really hard until Nanny gets back from the village.'

They both promised. Then, rewarded with a slice of cake, they prepared to depart. Timothy had a last revelation, however.

'Papa took away the books you gave us and left some tracts to learn, instead. He said poems are fanciful nonsense . . . but they're much easier to memorise.'

After they left Margaret sat lethargically, her chocolate cooling in the cup. The day was proving more demanding than she had imagined. She eyed Laurence as he relaxed in the chair, studying her in turn as he drank from the Wedgwood cup.

'You were very good with them. Have you any of your own?' she asked.

218

'Marion claimed she was too delicate for childbirth. I gained my experience with the children of friends and colleagues. They're mostly the same the world over.' He placed the cup on the table between them. 'Yours have too much Ashleigh spirit for the confines put upon them.'

'How much did Clive write of the situation?' she asked frankly.

'More than enough to allow me to guess the whole story. I have had contact with mission people in various parts of the world. Many are compassionate men and women, who love those they try to convert. A few are driven by some kind of madness. They either achieve where their more human counterparts fail, or they destroy themselves and all those they touch with the fire which consumes them. I gather your husband is like that.'

Silence then fell, a silence during which they wordlessly confirmed a truth sensed at their first meeting. In that warm, palm-scented room which created the illusion of sitting in a sun-washed garden away from all eyes, Margaret found no embarrassment in holding his gaze for so long with her own. He had brought her alive again after long hibernation.

'Do you really know Professor Gwynne?' she asked softly.

'Being an admirer of Nicolardi glassware he spoke to me at length on the subject when I sat next to him at a dinner. The Knightshill window was mentioned then. My interest in it grew when Clive wrote of its splendour.'

'So you did come to see the window?'

'You know why I came!'

'What of Vere's pictures?'

'I am slightly acquainted with Gilbert Dessinger. He admires your brother's work and owns an enviable collection of his water-colours.'

'And Clive wrote to you of the work I have started on a history of the family and Knightshill?'

'Yes. The boy was full of admiration for you. I believe he even loved you a little, but he was very susceptible to feminine appeal and gave his affection too generously. I, on the other hand, give mine rarely.'

Avoiding that pitfall, she said, 'So everything you told Lottie last Friday was true?'

'You were the person telling lies last Friday, ma'am. *A friend in Scotland. Someone seriously ill.*' His smile slowly faded to be replaced by a look of great intensity. 'You realise what has happened between us?'

'Yes, and it's very wrong.'

'On the contrary, my dear, I've never known anything to be so completely right.'

Margaret was not the only resident of Knightshill on whom Laurence's personality wrought instant impact. Sir Gilliard responded to him to the extent of emerging from preoccupation with the past to resume his habitual domination of the conversation around the table during that luncheon. Although the guest lacked a uniform, he was conversant with world affairs and the politics behind military intervention presently underway in distant parts of the globe. He was also acquainted with influential people known to the elderly general, a fact he used to explain his knowledge of the Ashleigh family, and he possessed the brand of virile charm found in most Ashleigh men. It soon became obvious to Margaret that the only ailment afflicting the old warhorse had been the lack of a young man about the house. In his own proud way, Sir Gilliard had been as saddened by Vere's departure as she and Charlotte.

After the meal, Laurence was taken off by his host to the library spread with maps and furnished with military manuals. There, Sir Gilliard subjected him to his dogmatic theories on military expansion in all parts of the world. The civilian guest dared to disagree, offering political solutions or the interests of commerce as alternatives to the taking up of arms. Far from upsetting him, Laurence's arguments appeared to inject new life into a man who had had no one to browbeat for some months. Not that Laurence was browbeaten. Far from it. He was soon regarded with such respect, Sir Gilliard suggested that his room at the Stag's Head should be vacated in favour of one at Knightshill, an offer Laurence tactfully declined.

He spoke of his conversation with Sir Gilliard when Margaret walked with him as far as the bend in the lane on his return to the village. Dunstan St Mary lay, a dim, mist-covered hamlet, in the valley from which the rosy light of gradual sunset was shaded by the hill where they strolled, but it turned the grey stone of the house to coral and fired each window as if the place were ablaze from within.

'Your grandfather represents a dying breed. He can recall the moment his mother received news of the great victory at Waterloo when he was just five years old. He was a senior subaltern of twenty-eight when our queen first took the throne as a girl ten years his junior. Think of it, Margaret! His regiment went to the Crimea in a paddle-steamer, to India in a ship under sail. In his lifetime he has witnessed the passing of the stage-coach, the coming of railways, the telegraph, photography, all manner of commercial invention, the creation of the Suez canal, the discovery of gold and diamonds in Africa, and pioneering by explorers and settlers all over the world. In addition, he has had the great good fortune to be acquainted with some of the greatest men this country will ever produce.' He sighed. 'I wish I could believe my lifespan will be as eventful. I found his tales fascinating.'

'That was obvious,' she said lightly. 'You have been closeted with him for the entire afternoon.'

'Forgive me. It's the price I must pay for subterfuge,' he returned in similar light manner. 'But it has won me an invitation to visit Knightshill whenever I wish.'

The news pleased her, but she said nothing more as they slowly trod the dusty lane through fields containing sheep and their fat, frisky lambs, all tinted pink from the dying sun.

'I marvel that you drew from Grandfather any conversation on subjects other than soldiering. We never can.'

'That is certainly one aspect of the man I do *not* admire. His attitude toward women is deplorable. He will not concede that they can possess wit or intelligence, hence he dismisses you and your sister as he would children. I suspect he believes there is no other role for women than motherhood. Small wonder his spirited wife ran off with her warm-hearted Italian lover. We *are* very warm-hearted, you know,' he added with a smouldering glance.

Margaret stopped in surprise. 'He actually told you that Grandmama left him for another?'

'No. Clive related the story in one of his letters.'

'I begin to believe young Val must have chattered non-stop to him on the subject of the Ashleighs.' She sighed. 'I wonder where the poor boy is and what he's doing.'

'Considering his future . . . which is something my young brother cannot do.' When she put her hand on his arm in swift sympathy, he frowned. 'Does Sir Gilliard know Val has no intention of coming home?'

'I have told him several times, but he was too abstracted to absorb the news. Now he's regained his spirits perhaps I'll have better success.'

'Your sister doesn't appear to have regained hers. Have you two quarrelled?'

She nodded.

'Over the affair between Val and Julia Grieves?'

'Lottie said some cruel things about him, and I reciprocated. She hasn't been able to forgive me yet.'

'That's rather childish.'

'She's upset over Vere, worried about the danger he's facing.'

'So you are considerate of her feelings. Why doesn't she accord you equivalent sisterly compassion?'

'She has also taken on some responsibility for the estate since Vere left. It's quite a burden.'

'Don't make excuses for her,' he chided. 'Unless she's actually in love with her brother, her distress can't be compared with that which you are facing in this house.'

She began walking again. 'You shouldn't judge a person of whom you know nothing.'

'My dear Margaret, you should be aware by now that I'm in possession of enough facts about the residents of Knightshill to pass judgement on any of them.' He fell in step beside her again. 'Naturally, Val chattered non-stop on the subject to his close friend whose own relatives were scattered around the globe. All this was his world. He's now been forced from its narrow confines to explore the freedom beyond. That woman might well prove the making of him.'

She was silent for a while. 'All this has been my world, too, Laurence. I was tutored at home with Lottie and Vere, so I didn't have the wider experience of school which Val has had.' Gazing at the sky ahead which was darkening to mauve as evening advanced, she said, 'I wanted nothing more than this. I loved the old stone house, the acres surrounding it, the security of being one of a large family. Then Father succumbed to wounds inflicted in Afghanistan, and Vorne was murdered. My world turned black.'

In the pause which followed her words, the sweet sound of lambs bleating made nonsense of that possibility. Yet it had been true.

'So you married Philip Daulton in a fit of typical Ashleigh impetuosity, and the world grew lighter again?'

Continuing to study the pastel sky ahead she murmured, 'Why use that interrogative tone when you know it to be true? Lottie, Vere and Val still gave me the secure sensation of being one of a close, inseparable group with Grandfather at its head. Philip simply joined the group. My children were the joyous indication of another family beginning, so I still wanted nothing more.'

'And now?'

That was too probing a question. She avoided it by saying, 'Darkness is coming fast. You should hurry if you want to reach the village without having to stumble blindly for the last half mile, or so.'

He caught her arm to swing her to a halt. '*And now* your cosy, happy life as a parish rector's wife has ended. Philip has deserted you for the heathen. Vere has been driven away by a selfish girl to prove on the battlefield that he's an artist, not a soldier. Val has crawled off to lick his wounds. Charlotte has turned herself into a martyr and Grandfather is fighting his last battle against life itself. In addition, your children are being weaned from you on a diet of piety. My God, Margaret, you surely owe yourself some experience of a wider world than this one.'

Drawing free, she said, 'It's the male Ashleighs who do that.'

'Don't be naïve!' He gazed down at her for some time, but as her face was the one touched by the last light of day she could not see the expression on his. 'Sir Gilliard has given me an open invitation to Knightshill for the duration of my stay. He offered me a room here, but

I'm not so insensitive that I'd install myself beneath the same roof for twenty-four hours of every day.'

'I thought you capable of anything where this family is concerned.'

It was said in an attempt to lighten the situation, but she was surprised by the anger it evoked in him. 'Don't treat me the way Julia Grieves probably treated Val. I'm not an impressionable, inexperienced youth, but a man of thirty-three with a shattering marriage behind me,' he said savagely. 'What happened when we met was beyond my control. It's as deep as it's inevitable. I'm in England until November the fifth. Time enough to make our plans. However, if you see what has happened as no more than the opportunity for a little light relief from your misery, tell me. Sir Gilliard is expecting me for dinner tomorrow, and for a morning visit to see the window.' He began turning away. 'I shall be at the house by eleven. If you fail to put in an appearance I shall have your answer. Sir Gilliard will receive my apologies for the evening on the grounds of indefinite business in London.'

He was gone before she could react to his astonishing ultimatum.

Chapter Twelve

It was as if madness had seized her – the madness of youth and rediscovered identity. She was Margaret Ashleigh, a girl free to speak her thoughts, who responded eagerly to the vigorous man giving joy to her life when she had believed it had gone for ever. Laurence brought much more than joy into her life over the next weeks, however. He had travelled extensively and his experience of human nature was formidable. He spoke eight languages, which enabled him to explore and understand the cultures of those with whom he could converse in their own tongue. The circle of his acquaintance was large and multi-national, the result of ten years in the Diplomatic Service.

Once Margaret said to him, 'I'm so very unworldly, Laurence, so uninformed. Why are you still at Knightshill?'

His reply had been brief. 'Because you are the love of my life.'

Another time she asked about his marriage. He was always totally honest, demanding the same of her, so he answered without evasion. 'I married her within three weeks of our first meeting. Dear God, how foolish we are when afire with the fatal flame!'

'You could never be foolish.'

223

'Believe me, my dear, the immaculate diplomat can be as great a fool as a lovelorn shepherd.' He frowned. 'Marion could not bring herself to allow me to consummate the marriage, and my pride would not let me insist. I went elsewhere, believing that jealousy would solve the problem, but she never forgave me for giving other women what she did not want herself. My cold wife despised my passion . . . but she, of course, was unfamiliar with the gnawing pain which attacks during the lonely night hours.'

'Poor Laurence.'

'Poor Margaret. You have surely suffered it, too!'

'Not for a long time,' she murmured, remembering the night of last year's Waterloo Ball.

'And now?'

'You know the answer to that as well as you know everything else about me.'

At first, Philip's absence in London and Charlotte's continuing hostility made it easy for them to spend much time together at Knightshill. Laurence studied the window closely, the Nicolardi business interest in glass making him knowledgeable on the subject. His enthusiasm was infectious. Margaret found her own increasing as he explained the complexity of the craft, adding a wealth of information on the probable manufacture of work quite astonishing for the period of its installation. They also went through the first chapters of the family history she had compiled. Laurence devoured the facts eagerly. He had an insatiable thirst for knowledge and an enviable ability to store it in his mind, ready to recall when needed.

'This all throws illuminating light on what I know of the present Ashleighs,' he told her. 'Small wonder you claimed only the male members of the family went out to discover the world. For as far back as your records go the men have dominated the military scene in even the most inaccessible places, their deeds revealing a trait for fearlessness and daring which makes one almost gasp with admiration. Sir Gilliard is of that ilk. I imagine Val is so heavily endowed with those qualities they could work in reverse and destroy him. He has begun badly. If maturity fails to curb him there's a good chance he'll end the same way.'

'If we only knew where he was we could help him,' she reflected.

'No, my dear, he must do it himself.' His dark eyes challenged her. '*You* can expect no help from anyone in what *we* are set to do.'

She was silent as he reverted to the subject of Ashleigh women always having been expected to remain at home to bring up the next generation of military firebrands. As yet, he had done no more than refer to the future with an occasional remark like the one he had just dropped into the conversation. It was now May. November would come. Yet her present overwhelming joy made her loath to face the cost of holding on to it. She took each golden day and cherished it, refusing to look beyond the next.

When Philip returned from London a small crisis arose. Timothy was desperately unhappy. He had hated being away from home and family in company with those who talked only of a subject in which he had no interest. Defiance had made him reveal to a senior missionary that he intended to join the army as soon as he was old enough. Philip had been told of this and the boy had been severely chastised in public, before being confined to his room without supper as a punishment. Timothy's distress affected Kate so that both children behaved badly for several days, thus earning further punishments from their father. Margaret confronted her husband angrily, but Philip simply walked from the room without a word and left the house.

She confided this to Laurence as she walked with him as far as the bend in the lane. It had been a blustery day which had tossed branches bearing a mass of blooms which now lay as a spread of white over the grass leading to the gate. Wearing a light coat against the chilly gusts, Margaret longed for the freedom to hold his arm in loving proximity as they strolled slowly towards the moment of parting.

'Timothy has taken this business to heart and needs consolation.'

'Don't we all, at certain times?'

She glanced up at him. 'Philip insists he is obeying the Lord's dictates. He'll listen to no one.'

'What about Sir Gilliard?'

'Even Grandfather is no match for God. In any case, Timothy's a Daulton.'

'He's an Ashleigh at heart, as he keeps insisting.'

'So am I, Laurence. I'm also the boy's mother, but I'm allowed no influence over either of the children. There seems no hope of asserting it.'

'You do, however,' he said reassuringly. 'They sneak away to you whenever the chance presents itself.'

They reached the gate and he held it open for her to pass through. Once in the lane, where hedges rose on either side to give partial screening from the windows of the house, he took her hand in a close grip.

'I'm going to London for a few days to see a barrister I know. I wrote to him of a hypothetical case identical to our own, asking his opinion. His reply arrived this morning with an invitation to discuss the points he raised. He believes the mother might be granted custody of the children on the grounds that they are being denied a normal education and instead being indoctrinated with a creed which demands the surrender of all else for as long as they live. He writes that if there was evidence of cruelty on the part of the father, the case would be greatly strengthened.'

225

Margaret felt herself growing cold. Their love had filled her every waking thought. It was so immense it prevented her from considering anything other than the moment when Laurence would next be at Knightshill. He had just created clouds over her sunny horizon – large black clouds.

'Is there such evidence?' he asked. 'Does he ever beat them?'

Confused and suddenly afraid, she hit out. 'How dared you write to this man without consulting me?'

He forced her to stop and the swift anger she had known before was there in an instant. 'I can't believe you meant to run away with me, as did your mother and grandmother, leaving your children here. One can grant them slight mitigation, their children being true Ashleighs entitled to their birthright, but the future here for Daulton children would be bleak.'

Fighting the wind which buffeted her as his words did, she clutched the collar of her coat as anger also filled her. 'Don't preach to me! I have a husband who does that continuously. You really are the most arrogant man! You arrive unannounced and bully me into revealing private family affairs, then tell me four days later that I have eighteen hours in which to decide whether or not I'll pledge my future to you. Now you confront me with the fate of my children, warning me that their happiness lies in my hands.'

'You must have considered this. *Surely* you have considered it.'

'I've considered nothing save the joy of being with you.'

The Italian tendency for swift passion darkened his expression. 'Are you saying all you want is a flirtation to last for a summer? Are you telling me you have no intention of leaving that monster?'

'No . . . yes . . . how can I?' she cried. 'What we are contemplating is *madness*.'

'It is if you accept this as no more than a passing affaire.'

She turned away from the naked pain of his expression, shivering in the afternoon chill. He had shocked her by listing the cost of happiness, and she struggled to regain her composure.

'I wasn't ready for the cold facts. I'm sorry. You took me unawares.'

'We should walk on. We may be observed from the house.' His hand beneath her elbow coaxed her on down the lane towards the bend which would hide them from sight of all but sheep and skylarks. 'I am to blame. I deliberately allowed you unclouded happiness for a time before facing the problems. You were so distressed that first day, I hesitated to make you more so.' A moment later, he added, 'Margaret, I've seen two intelligent children in fear and desperation over what is happening to them. They don't understand what he forces them to learn, neither do they comprehend his obsession with people they have never seen who do frightening things. Young Kate was hysterical because she believed the missionaries would drink Tim's blood. She's a child of six, that's all. The boy is barely nine, yet he's being ruthlessly thrust into a brotherhood he hates, to face a future for which he's entirely unsuited. Any father who is party to all this is a *monster*.'

She had known it from the time Philip lost all sight of human love, and since the Waterloo Ball she had lived in fear of his violence.

'Well?' he prompted.

'Yes, they dislike and fear him more as time passes. He has taken their favourite things to destroy in front of them as punishment for inattention, and he has confined them for the same reason.'

'He has never struck them?'

She hesitated. 'Not so far as I know.'

'Then Frederick Lipton will have to consider our chances of obtaining legal consent to remove them from Philip's influence as soon as possible.'

'Sir Frederick? *He* is your friend?'

'We went to the same school.'

'But, he's — '

'Notorious? That's why he's more likely to win a case others might be reluctant to accept.'

Margaret grew even colder. She longed to spend the rest of her days with this man whose love matched her own, but the thought of dragging her private humiliation through a courtroom, to say nothing of what it would do to the children and her family, was appalling.

She appealed to him. 'Is there no other solution?'

'Certainly. We can say goodbye to each other here and now and resolve not to think of each other even once during the next fifty years,' he told her tight-lipped. 'Is that what you'd prefer?'

'That's cruel,' she countered with passion. 'You're free to do whatever you choose. Have you stopped to consider the cost to me?'

He looked haggard as he took her hand again. 'I never stop thinking of it and asking myself if I'm worthy of expecting such sacrifice from any woman.'

They turned the corner of the lane and were now hidden from view of the house. Margaret went into his arms with the wildness of her love for a man who had suffered even crueller rejection than she. He returned her desperate kisses with matching urgency. Knightshill was forgotten until they grew calmer.

Running a gentle finger across her mouth, Laurence said, 'We haven't an easy time ahead, but trust me to make it as swift and certain as possible for you. I'll be back on Monday.'

He left her and strode down towards the village. Margaret knew that four days without him would be an eternity. Fifty years would be a living death.

Sir Gilliard was in fine fettle during luncheon on the following day. It was difficult to believe he had been the vague, senile man the family had humoured since Christmas. He was back in form with a vengeance.

The quarrel still divided the sisters. Margaret had tried to mend matters, but Charlotte refused to relent and had been left to her martyrdom. Margaret suspected that the root of her sister's behaviour lay in her own disclosure of the nudes Vere had painted. The increasing primness of Charlotte's nature could not accept the notion of her beloved brother gazing at unclothed women even for the sake of art, and therefore she could not forgive the person who had revealed it to her. The lively expressions which had made her attractive seldom lit her face now. Her features had grown pinched and lifeless. Margaret pondered fleetingly on Laurence's belief that she must be in love with Vere. It was nonsense, of course, and yet her sister was withdrawing more and more into a world of isolation as time passed without news of him.

It was on the subject of communication that Sir Gilliard was complaining as he ate cold chicken and salads. 'In the days of the grand old mail coaches letters used to reach Knightshill without fail, y'know,' he announced energetically. 'Now these *steam engines* drag endless carriages behind them while attempting to carry mail, it rarely gets to its destination on time.'

'Yes, Grandfather,' murmured Charlotte dutifully.

'A derailment just outside Dunstan St Mary don't mean they can't bring the letters up today. Mount a trusty beast, ride along the track to reach the mail coach, then bring it up here! Confounded nuisance! Waiting for a reply from Lord Craven on that volume of his from Gordon's personal collection. Offered him a very generous sum. There's the latest edition of the *Military Times* due, to say nothing of the *Court Circular* and various other publications for which I pay a ridiculous sum for prompt delivery. They're all sitting down there while railwaymen run around in circles.'

'I'll send Ned down for the mail, if you wish,' Charlotte offered.

'Certainly not, Miss.' Sir Gilliard signalled the hovering servant to give him another slice of cold chicken. 'I have no intention of doing the business assigned to the railways and old Briggs in the postal office. They have undertaken to deliver letters and packets to the addresses written on them. Let them fulfil their undertaking.'

'But if you're anxious for Lord Craven's reply . . .'

'*No*, Charlotte.' He began on the additional slice of chicken with relish. 'Can't expect you to comprehend that it's a matter of principle. That young man would. Miss him. Very sensible fellow. Why's he gone off, eh?'

228

'Ask Margaret. She spents more time with him than I do.'

Sir Gilliard's vivid blue gaze shifted to the far side of the table. 'Still going through family history with him?'

'Yes, Grandfather,' she said as casually as she could manage. 'He's fascinated by our ancestors.'

'So he should be. Wonderful men, every single one.'

'He believes the women are quite as praiseworthy, if one takes into account the loneliness and anxiety they suffered during their husbands' many absences on active service. I had never considered that until Mr Nicolardi pointed it out to me.'

'When is he coming back?' demanded the man who had no time for the creatures who merely produced the succeeding generations of Ashleighs.

'Some time next week, I believe,' she said with deliberate vagueness.

'Ah, must get him up here. Need to ask his opinion on the best thing to do about the boy. Man of the world. Knows several cases where young cubs disgraced themselves then emerged as men of stature and great courage. No reason to suppose I can't lick the boy into shape with firm handling and strict discipline.'

'Val isn't coming home,' Charlotte reminded him acidly. 'He's too ashamed to face us all.'

'He is not,' put in Margaret swiftly. 'His note to me mentioned that most specifically. Out of consideration for your health, Grandfather, he thinks it's better that he stays away until he decides what to do. He is *not* ashamed to face us.'

'Then he should be,' said Sir Gilliard in harsh tones. 'Let us all down unforgivably. Sullied the name. First one who has.'

Silence fell while he finished his chicken. Then he signalled for the plates to be removed and the fruit bowl brought. Selecting a peach, he glanced from under his brows at Charlotte.

'Like the cut of young Nicolardi. Not a military man, but he's a sound thinker and moves in the right circles. You'll not find better, my girl, so do what's necessary to bring him up to scratch before he leaves the district.'

In the shocked hiatus that followed, Charlotte flushed crimson and Margaret's heart thudded with sudden apprehension. Sir Gilliard could create dreadful complications if he pursued this fancy to make Laurence his son-in-law. Determination to throw them together could put paid to the supposed collaboration on the family history, giving herself no hope of being alone with him to discuss their plans.

'No need to colour up, girl,' ruled the man used to expecting his own way. 'Time you found a partner. I'll not allow you to make your sister's mistake, so you'd best do my bidding before your chance is lost.' He turned to Margaret. 'When d'you say the fellow is coming back?'

'Early next week, I believe,' she managed to say.

'We'll have him here to dinner straight way,' he told Charlotte. 'Find out what he likes to eat – Moorkin of the Stag's Head will oblige with that – and look out something brighter to wear than that mourning gown we have seen so often lately. He won't look twice at a dowd. And try to smile more, girl. Since that young fool rushed off to the Sudan leaving no man around the place, all I've had from you are long faces and even longer silences. Young Nicolardi will brighten this place up, which is more than can be said of the dreary fellow you chose, Margaret. They'd never have him in an officers' mess, y'know. Bad for morale!' He leaned back with a slice of peach on his silver fork ready to reminisce. 'There was an outsider called Ridgeway, who was caught . . .'

The tale was interrupted by Winters with a tray bearing a pile of envelopes. 'Excuse me, sir, but I know you are anxious to receive the mail,' he said smoothly. 'I understand Mr Briggs sent his son along the line to collect the sack for Dunstan St Mary. Fred Barney has just delivered these with an apology for the delay.'

'Ah, splendid! Splendid! Put them down, man. If there's one from Lord Craven I'll read it now. You can take the rest to the library. I'll be there directly after tiffin.'

Winters set the tray on the corner of the table, then straightened to say, 'I have taken the liberty of setting aside two posted from the Sudanese town of Berber. One is addressed to you, sir, and the other to Miss Ashleigh. The handwriting is Mr Ashleigh's.'

'From Vere?' cried Charlotte, her blush receding to leave her very pale as she rose and went to the tray. 'Where is it?'

When Winters handed her the letter, she turned abruptly and took it to the far end of the room where pale sun shone through a set of windows. Margaret remained where she was, too many emotions flooding through her at once. But she had time to marvel at the pride which allowed Sir Gilliard to search for the letter he was expecting, leaving the one from his grandson lying unopened on the table. What had prompted Vere to contact his family after so long? Almost a year had passed since he had left without farewells. Her heartbeat quickened as it occurred to her that these might be his dying words forwarded by a fellow officer. She went to her sister, who was reading a letter of many pages' length.

'Is he all right?' she asked anxiously.

Charlotte's face was glowing as she glanced up. 'Yes, oh, yes! You'll never guess. He's been into battle at a place called Atbara. He came through it unscathed – but that's not all. He writes that his constitution appears to be a great deal stouter than we all thought. He caught the dread fever and recovered. Isn't that wonderful?' She held out several pages.

'Here, read these. There are several messages for you. He says he has written separately to Grandfather and Val, but that this is to both his dear sisters.'

Margaret took the sheets covered in Vere's precise handwriting and began to read an account of what had happened to her older brother since making his desperate decision. He wrote vividly of his adventures – his command of words had always been formidable – and places and people came to life beneath his pen so that she could visualise it all clearly. She chuckled at his account of various military *faux pas* he had made, but sobered at his description of the battle across desert wastes. He was presently at Atbara, where the army must remain for several months until the Nile was high enough to allow progress toward Khartoum. He was taking advantage of the break to create a series of pictures he believed were the best he had ever done.

Margaret read the final pages as Charlotte began again on the first. Her eyes misted at the final paragraph which asked forgiveness for his long silence, which must have caused them both anxiety.

I have learned much and am now able to distinguish more clearly between things of lasting value and those of transient pleasure. My home, my dear family I count among the former. Bless you both, and the children especially. Letters to the above address will follow the regiment to reach me eventually. I eagerly await news.

As she handed the last sheets back to Charlotte it occurred to her that Clive must have written thus to his half-brother. No wonder Laurence knew and understood the Ashleighs so well. Vere would find a kindred spirit in him, for they both admired beauty of a cultural nature. Her happiness faded slightly. By the time her brother returned to Knightshill, she would be gone. So would the children. She would never see Vere again . . . or Val, Charlotte and the grandfather whose stern rule had nevertheless supplied security. She would never again see Knightshill. For Laurence she must face an uncertain future, abandoning all she had known and loved. The thought was chilling when he was not there beside her.

'Whatever is the matter? We've just received such wonderful news yet you look as if it were the notification we have been dreading.'

Margaret looked up at her sister. 'I was thinking of poor Val, who'll not receive his letter and therefore won't know Vere is safe.'

Charlotte put her arm around Margaret's shoulders. 'If Vere can survive this, I am certain Val will be all right. He's always been the more assured of the two, hasn't he? You'll get a cheerful letter like this from him one day, and you'll then tell yourself how absurd it was to worry.' Her arm tightened. 'I've been behaving very foolishly lately. Can you forgive me?'

'Of course. I know the strain you've been under.'

'Perhaps I haven't shown you the same understanding. Vere's words are very telling, especially about things of lasting value.' She smiled. 'With both our brothers away we should cling together even more. After all, without each other we'd both be very lonely.'

When Laurence came to dinner Margaret had no chance at all to speak to him alone. They could not use the excuse of studying the window on this purely social occasion, and Sir Gilliard was so delighted to have his guest back that he monopolised him. He was seated next to Charlotte during the lengthy meal, and the elderly general clearly took her choice of a pretty yellow gown as an indication that she was obeying his advice to capture this eligible man. If the letter from Vere had not wrought such a change in her sister, Margaret might have shared this belief, for Charlotte was the happy, charming girl of old.

The presence of Philip put further restrictions on the evening, although he excused himself on a plea of work at the end of the meal. Laurence had been collected by Ned in the pony and trap, and would be returned to the Stag's Head in the same manner. No chance to walk with him in the lane. With Charlotte as a warmly generous hostess, and Sir Gilliard behaving as if Laurence were his son-in-law already, Margaret had little choice but to maintain the formal attitude her married status demanded.

The entire evening was difficult for them both, particularly as this was the first time Laurence had come face to face with Philip. Too sophisticated to show open antagonism, it was nevertheless in his eyes whenever there was direct contact between them. Between Margaret and her lover there could be no more than several speaking glances when they were unobserved, and a slight nod from him on arrival which suggested to her that his meeting with Sir Frederick Lipton had been successful. She longed to hear details. Throughout the evening she was tense and jumpy, contributing little to the conversation which centred on the letters from Vere, giving vivid accounts of life with Kitchener's army. The sisters had not been told what he had written to their grandfather, but the old man was certainly full of fresh vitality.

Sir Gilliard was again the dominant, energetic, sharp-witted soldier who could entertain for hours with military anecdotes both humorous and dramatic. When the guest was not an army man and he was in love with a lady of the house who was unhappily married, the evening was not particularly entertaining for either of them. Pleading tiredness after his business meetings, Laurence took his leave as soon as good manners allowed.

Margaret would have lingered downstairs rather than face a restless night, but Sir Gilliard immediately broached the subject of Charlotte's 'campaign to lay siege' to Laurence's affections, so she hastily bade them goodnight.

Although Louise prepared her for bed, Margaret knew sleep would not come swiftly. In an attempt to ease the frustration aroused by the lack of contact with Laurence at such a vital time, she took up one of Vere's books of poems and sat in a chair by the dying fire to seek solace in the verses. She was surprised when her maid returned an hour later, in wrap and sleeping-cap, to hand over an envelope brought by Ned on his return from the village.

'It's from Mr Nicolardi, ma'am. Some information for your family history, which he undertook to obtain in London. He apologises for neglecting to bring it with him earlier this evening.'

When the woman had gone Margaret tore open the envelope, only to be disappointed by the single sheet within it. His words told her nothing definite.

I need to talk to you at length where we cannot be disturbed. Can you come here? Seeing him with you was deeply painful. I shall never sleep.

Rain was falling relentlessly when daylight lit her room. It was impossible to set out for the village in a deluge without arousing curiosity in everyone from Sir Gilliard to the stable-boy. Knowing Laurence would be feeling equally frustrated made the empty morning worse. When the children sneaked down from their hated studies to beg a slice of cake as she drank her chocolate, their endless complaints caused her to snap at them. They departed sulking, then Margaret found herself pleading a headache in order to escape Charlotte's protests over Sir Gilliard's plan to play matchmaker.

'He has never before interested himself in my affairs,' she complained, as Margaret edged towards the door. 'Laurence Nicolardi is far too knowing not to realise what is happening. I thought he was off-hand last night, which suggests he already suspects.'

'I shouldn't worry, Lottie. He must so often be the target of hopeful mamas, he'll deal with Grandfather's clumsy efforts adroitly enough.'

Charlotte twisted in the chair to confront her. 'Do you like him?'

'I . . . admire his wide knowledge, his – his understanding of human nature.'

'But what of his personality?' As Margaret cast around for a suitable reply, her sister pursued the subject further. 'Don't you find him somewhat overpowering?'

'Not when we are studying the family history. I suppose he becomes more lively in Grandfather's company.'

233

'He didn't last night. Quite the reverse. I grew rather bored. From your expression, I imagine you did, too.'

'Oh dear, were my feelings so obvious?' she murmured in dismay. 'I really must lie down for a while. This headache.'

'How much longer is he going to come here on the pretext of interest in the Ashleigh family?'

She stiffened. 'What do you mean?'

'Why should a diplomat from South America be so fascinated by our ancestors? He has ingratiated himself with Grandfather, and flatters you by pretending interest in your study of Knightshill through the ages. It strikes me as questionable, and I begin to suspect a fall from professional or social grace which obliges him to rusticate for a while. Knightshill is a convenient escape from the Stag's Head, where the company must be less congenial and the fare too simple for his sophisticated tastes.'

'What utter nonsense, Lottie! I never suspected you of reading popular novels, but you must have obtained several melodramas of the most colourful nature. You'd do better to concentrate on the orchids Vere enquired about in his letter, and leave such rubbish to be read by those with less intellect.'

Regretting the outburst immediately, she escaped to pace her room while rain drummed against the windows. Had she given herself away? Why had Charlotte asked her opinion of Laurence now, after he had been coming to the house over a period of three weeks? What had she really been trying to say with her probing comments? The situation was growing impossible. It seemed both she and Laurence had been unable to hide their ennui last evening. What else had Charlotte deduced about them? Could she possibly suspect the truth?

Halting by the window, she watched the raindrops racing down the panes and asked herself why she was so concerned by a conversation with a sister who had always been loving and caring. When a married woman decided to run away with a forceful, charming widower, whom she had known for less than a month, deceit was inevitable and those close to her would be hurt. It was part of the price she must pay for happiness.

Too tense to eat, she did not go down for the midday meal. The supposed headache was excuse enough, and instructions to Louise for tea and buttered toast in her room would silence gossip below stairs. By two o'clock the clouds were breaking up to allow brief periods of weak sunshine, but lowering skies over the distant Dorset hills threatened further rain. Margaret seized her chance despite that purple gloom to the south. In a waterproof cloak and close hood, she ran lightly down the stairs only to meet Charlotte at the foot.

'Going out?' exclaimed her sister, in surprise. 'I thought you were in bed with a headache.'

'I need fresh air. It's so oppressive indoors.'

'Don't venture far,' Charlotte called to her retreating back. 'John Morgan says there's a storm in the offing.'

Margaret hardly heard the warning. She was too anxious to set out before further rain would make her outing seem suspicious. The pony was already harnessed to the trap, which had the hood erected as she had instructed in her message to the stables. Ned's perpetually gloomy expression matched his words as he watched her climb in.

'Tis a powerful bad day to venture out, ma'am. Get you back swift-like afore the storm reaches here. The lane's already very slippy, and liable to grow treacherous if we gets a prolonged torrent. I wish as you'd allow me to drive you.'

'I'm perfectly able to handle Maude in any conditions,' she returned, taking up the reins. 'We've only had one morning of rain, Ned, not a month.'

She drove off over the cobbled yard to the driveway crossing the bridge over what had once been a moat, then turned the vehicle towards the main gates. Her acerbic response to the man who had given her family warmly devoted service for many years must have caused him to ponder on her sudden need to reach the village. On a day like this Louise would have been dispatched on a trifling errand. A personal visit and her insistence on going alone suggested a vital private family matter. Would Ned connect her action with the note he had delivered from Laurence last night, and set servants' tongues wagging? Easing the mare into the turn which led to the lane, Margaret told herself heavily that tongues all over England would soon be wagging, so she must grow used to the idea of being the subject of scandal.

At the spot where she normally turned to look back at Knightshill standing solid and enduring on the hill above, she resisted the impulse. Her gaze remained on the village where her future awaited her at the Stag's Head. As the trap careered over the stone bridge spanning the stream where Vorne had given the Rundle girls a drenching, the first rumble of thunder came from the advancing purple mass in the sky. Praying that Laurence had not gone out in the belief that she would not come in such weather, she drove into the stable-yard, handed the trap over to Josiah Hind with a swift, absent smile, then entered the old coaching inn where she and Charlotte often took tea on market days.

Lionel Moorkin was a young man who now ran the inn for his disabled father, and ran it most successfully. He was bright, capable, and skilled in adjusting his approach to suit the quality of his guests. Members of the

Ashleigh family were accorded great respect, which in no way minimised the personal touch Moorkin used to great effect. He came forward now with genuine pleasure in his welcoming smile.

'Good afternoon, Mrs Daulton. A wretched afternoon to be out. Go you through to the parlour, where there's a nice fire, and I'll get Mrs Moorkin to make tea for you and Miss Ashleigh. How's the old gentleman, ma'am? I heard tell he's a great deal better, and aren't we all glad of it. And there's excellent news of Mr Ashleigh, so Ned Whitely was relating last night while waiting to transport Mr Nicolardi up to the house. Thanks be he's alive and well out there in that terrible place.' He threw open the parlour door for her. 'Shall you have your tea right away, ma'am, or wait for Miss Ashleigh?'

'My sister isn't with me today, Moorkin. She has a slight cold.' With her heartbeat racing, she asked, 'Is Mr Nicolardi here? He left a very valuable timepiece at Knightshill last evening. One of our maids found it at the side of his chair. I brought it down with me to return it to him and set his mind at rest over the loss.'

Moorkin's swarthy face lit with another smile. 'As far as I know, the gentleman is in his room. I'll send up to inform him of your arrival. He has been looking worried all day, ma'am. Reckon he'll be right glad at your news. A very clever gentleman, he is. Knows a powerful lot about parts of the world I'll not get to see in my lifetime. I never tire of listening to his tales. I'll be real sorry to see him go, when the time comes. Make yourself comfortable by the fire, ma'am, while I send a boy up to him and get Mrs Moorkin busy with some tea to warm you.'

As she passed through to the low-ceilinged room where ladies could be assured of refreshment and freedom from the undesirable elements found in inns, Margaret's heart sank. Two of Philip's former parishioners were taking tea at a table in the nook at the far end of the room. They saw her. There was no choice but to cross and enquire about their health, their grandchildren and the state of their gardens. Only too glad to supply the information in great detail, they were in full flood when the door opened and closed again. Afraid to turn, Margaret continued to feign interest in the women until Laurence's deep voice right behind her made her jump nervously.

'Mrs Daulton, Moorkin has just given me the glad tidings.'

Now able to face him, she succeeded in greeting him casually. But if the message in her own eyes matched the one in his it was pointless. These women had sharp wits and a number of inquisitive friends.

'Good afternoon, Mr Nicolardi. I'm afraid you must have been immensely worried since parting from my grandfather last night. One of the servants found your watch at the side of your chair where it must have slipped from your pocket.'

'It is certainly a great relief to know that it is safe, ma'am,' he returned in level tones. 'How kind of you to bring it.'

'I am here on a particular errand for Sir Gilliard, so it seemed a providential opportunity to hand over your property.'

He glanced over her shoulder at the two following their conversation avidly. 'Will you excuse me, ladies? The very least I can do is to offer Mrs Daulton some tea before she drives back to Knightshill.' Taking Margaret's arm he led her to a table in the opposite corner of the room. 'I cannot tell you how upset I was at misplacing Great-uncle Arturo's timepiece. It was given to him by a Neapolitan nobleman. A great honour.'

They reached the table and sat at it facing each other. 'Are you completely mad?' he demanded in soft anger. 'I did not expect you to venture out on such a day.'

Her anger flared in return. 'Am I not entitled to know my fate and that of my children? Your note told me nothing. *Can you come here?* you wrote. Now that I have, you accuse me of madness.'

Young Nellie Moorkin, six months' pregnant with her first child, entered with a tray to set on the table between them. Thin, fragilely pretty, but with a robust personality, her response to Margaret's obligatory query regarding her health was lengthy and cheerful. By the time she departed, the anger in them both had evaporated.

'Forgive me,' begged Laurence in the low tones they were forced to adopt. 'My concern is for your present safety, as well as for your future. There's a storm in the offing which will bring darkness early.'

'What did Sir Frederick say?' she asked, pouring tea to suggest that their conversation was of the inconsequential variety indulged in over cups and saucers.

'He's willing to take the case.'

Her hands stilled. 'Is he confident of success?'

'He wouldn't take it if not.'

'What will it mean?'

'You will have to file a divorce petition on the grounds of Philip's cruelty. No, don't look at me in horror. We're being closely watched. I told you it would not be easy.'

'How can I accuse him of cruelty?' she asked. 'I would be obliged to describe instances of it.'

'You cite his denial of your influence over your children, his neglect of you in favour of his obsessive work. Verbal cruelty cannot always be proved, but it sways a jury in a woman's favour to record any such instances.' He sipped his tea, but his expression was intense as he then asked, 'Does he still demand his rights as a husband?'

'No.'

237

'Since when?'

It took courage. 'Since June the eighteenth last year.'

'Why that specific date?'

'He . . . he forced himself on me.'

Lowering the cup and saucer slowly, he whispered explosively, 'By God, why didn't you tell me that before? A pompous, pious zealot who suppresses his children and uses violence against his wife! Norton can win over any jury on that.'

In that familiar cosy parlour the conversation had taken on an ugly flavour.

'No, Laurence, I won't have that experience made public,' she cried softly. 'There must be some other way, some solution which will be less painful.'

He leaned back against the dark velvet, his anger evident again. 'The alternative would lose you your good name and the respect of society. Your children would suffer from your actions even after we are in our graves. It will be equally painful.'

Her fingers played with the spoon in the saucer while she stared at the tea cooling in her cup. Then she looked up in distress. 'All this simply to be together!'

'That will be the reward. To be together always.'

The storm outside broke at that very moment, reflecting the one inside her. Moorkin came in with lanterns to brighten the sudden gloom. Rain thundered on the thatch making conversation difficult. Sitting there in silence, Margaret had time to think of what he had said. A divorce would attract full press attention. Her family would suffer humiliation and grief that she could expose them to it. She could even have Sir Gilliard's death on her conscience if it proved a fatal blow. The children were young enough to recover from the scandal but Philip's standing would suffer irreparable damage when his character was torn to shreds by the ruthless Sir Frederick. It would be the end of his work for the mission. That thought brought another. Laurence was watching her closely, as if waiting for further protests.

'What of your career?' she asked above the sound of the rain.

He edged closer, but the other pair in the room were speculating loudly on the prospects of their return home and appeared to have lost interest in all else.

'If we married as soon as you were free, I'd be finished as a diplomat. The connection would be too obvious to ignore. If we waited a considerable time before doing so, I would probably be allowed to continue in minor, uncongenial posts which would allow me no advancement. I'll leave the service and enter the family glass business in Verona. Living in Italy would also allow you and the children to escape the unpleasant aftermath of the divorce in this country.'

It was a while before she asked, 'You'd do all this for love of me?'

'I'm asking you to do much more.'

How much she was only just assessing. 'How long will it all take?'

'That depends on how soon we give Norton instructions to proceed and when he feels able to take the case to court. I would hope it will be over by the end of the year.'

The thought was daunting. She asked where she could go until then. 'I couldn't stay on at Knightshill, Laurence.'

'I suggest you take the children on holiday to an understanding friend or relative just before Norton serves notice on Daulton of your intentions.

She shook her head. 'He would never give me permission to take them on holiday.'

'Then you will have to do it without.'

A loud clap of thunder made her jump so much the spoon fell to the floor. The two ladies leaped to their feet with muffled cries as it was followed by more in swift succession. The storm appeared to be centred over Dunstan St Mary and, judging by the eerie rattling of doors and windows, was bringing a ferocious wind in its wake. Private conversation was no longer possible, and presently Moorkin came into the parlour to inform his patrons that the gale had increased to a strength which took people off their feet as they walked.

'Reckon you'd best make yourselves comfortable here, ladies,' he advised the pair in the corner. 'No use thinking of trying to get home yet. Mrs Moorkin'll being you more tea, with my compliments, and I'll get the lad to put more logs on the fire.' He crossed to Margaret. ''Tis a fearful storm, ma'am, much like the one we had back in 'ninety-four. I've seen to the stabling of your mare; the trap's all secure under the barn roof. You can't venture back up the hill alone, so I've told Nathaniel Dobbs to be ready to escort you. If it's very late when you go, I'd be obliged if he could snug up in your stables overnight.'

'Of course,' she said. 'Ned will see that Cook gives him something to eat. I'll be glad to have him with me, especially if it is late when I set out.'

She was unable to set out at all that day. The storm moved on, but the gale raged even fiercer as time passed. Mrs Moorkin served all the stranded customers with hot stew and dumplings followed by curd tarts and thick whipped cream at eight o'clock. Margaret ate little. Her brain was spinning with solutions to her problem, but each was out of the question. Trees were crashing down, fences were flying past the inn windows, bales of hay were dancing in the street outside as if they had come alive. Strong men were declining to venture out so a woman on a horse would never survive, nor a

239

woman on foot. For an hour or more she tormented herself with blame for ever having set out, and with frustration because she could think of no way to return.

Finally, Laurence said in calm, assured manner, 'My dearest girl, even if we should manage to conceive a plan which would result in your appearing before your husband and family covered in mud, drenched to the skin, and cut by flying branches, it would suggest to minds presently innocent of suspicion that to have remained where you were safe would constitute a sin. In short, you would arouse the very curiosity you dread.' He smiled. 'The two biddies beside the fire appear to be enjoying their adventure. *They* are making no desperate attempts to return to their spouses for fear of spending the night with the notorious Lorenzo Nicolardi.'

It brought a return smile from her, knowing he was right. 'Lottie would be afraid to do so. She suspects you of rusticating here until your social or professional misdemeanours are forgiven.'

He laughed. 'I sensed strong wariness in her manner last night. So that's what she thinks, is it?'

'Better that than the truth.'

'Why? She'll know the truth very shortly.'

She fell silent again. Every exchange between them led to the inescapable facts he had laid before her this afternoon. They had eaten dinner at a long table set for eleven, where Laurence had chatted easily with those around him. He had called her Mrs Daulton, and referred frequently to their mutual work on the history of Knightshill, which Sir Gilliard consistently interrupted by taking him off for hours at a time. The other diners had been friendly but respectful; certainly none gave signs of suspicion about their relationship. All but two, who were passing travellers, were well known to Margaret as doyens of the village.

After the general conviviality of the meal they had tended to form small groups, several of the men vanishing to the greater freedom of the tap-room. That Laurence remained with Margaret raised no eyebrows: he had confirmed his association with the Ashleigh family during the meal and it was natural for the two more cultured guests to seek each other's company during this emergency. They sat apart from the main section of the room in an alcove free from draughts. Perhaps the apprehension Margaret nevertheless suffered was caused by the sense of rightness being with this man aroused in her. She never wanted to part from him again. He told her how to make that a possibility and was confident that only time stood between this and permanent happiness. She must believe it, too.

Studying his dark face chequered by shifting firelight she fought the desire to move nearer, to touch him. Being so close in this intimate situation, yet being forced to adopt a pretence beneath the eyes of others was growing more and more unbearable.

'You're attracting attention by your prolonged silence. They will believe I have offended you with unwelcome advances,' teased Laurence.

'Grandfather has hit upon a plan to keep you at Knightshill. He has instructed my sister to "bring you up to scratch" before you leave.'

'She's in love with Vere.'

'Laurence!'

'Can you deny his letter has put joy back into her life? It should have been obvious to you all, but I suspect Vere's nature is so naturally affectionate that he would never have considered such a thing.'

'But her own brother!'

'You regarded Val as a son, yet he's your brother. Relationships are rarely straightforward, my dearest. Daulton is in love with sacrificial piety. Sir Gilliard is in love with the army. Val is in love with the cavalry. *And I'm in love with you*,' he added, in tones she could barely hear. 'So much so, I find this distant intimacy as painful as it is glorious.'

The hurricane was still thumping the sides of the old inn with ferocious gusts when Margaret bade everyone goodnight, and went off with lamp in hand to the room Mrs Moorkin had prepared for her. There was a bright fire and additional lamps to illuminate the low-ceilinged upstair chamber where a huge oak bedstead gleamed from devoted polishing. A plain nightgown lay across the counterpane; soap and tooth powder had been placed on the washstand. A girl came with a jug of hot water and a warm brick for her feet. Everything to make her comfortable for the night. Yet the water had grown cold by the time she left the chair by the fire, and resigned herself to occupying this strange bed on a night which was proving an ordeal.

Lying awake, listening to the creaks created by others as each decided to retire, Margaret stared at the beamed ceiling whilst growing increasingly tense. Could she repay her loving family with treachery? Could she put her children through months of bewilderment, take them from home and relatives to a confused, unpredictable future? Could she face the scorn and curiosity of those who read about her life with Philip in their daily newspaper? Most of all, could she survive all this pain without Laurence beside her – all the anguish of deserting Knightshill to leave behind a broken sister and a frail grandfather, which would come before she could be with the man for whom she was doing it all? Could she go through the stress of the courtroom scenes knowing that even one meeting, one letter between them would finish all hope of winning? Almost from this night on, she must not see or contact Laurence until the whole terrible business was over. Was she strong enough for that? She loved Laurence so deeply it almost frightened her, but had she the right to make others suffer in order to gain her own happiness?

Long into the night she asked these questions, finding no answer until she recalled Laurence's claim that Charlotte was in love with Vere. It then occurred to her that her brother had pursued a kind of personal happiness – peace of mind, at least – regardless of the effect his sudden departure would have on those close to him. He had gone without a spoken farewell, and remained silent for a year, for reasons of his own. And Val, whom she thought of more as a son, what of his pursuit of happiness? It lay in the form of a cavalry commission which he had gone after single-mindedly. Now he, also, had gone off without a spoken farewell and would probably remain silent for as long as he chose. Was there any reason why a female Ashleigh should not emulate them; any reason why she should feel guilt when they clearly had not?

She considered what lay ahead if she did not follow their example. Sir Gilliard would not live a great deal longer, and Philip would then leave Knightshill. She would be confined with him in a small house which would be used freely for mission business. There would be no companions save others like her husband, and she would watch her children being slowly cowed. There would be no love, no joy for her . . . yet the rest of her family would continue to seek their own shining stars. She had championed both her brothers, insisting that although they had a duty to the family, they also had a right to choice in leading their lives. Then, surely, so had she.

For another hour she lay coming to terms with the weeks and months immediately ahead. Then she rose and put on her cloak over the borrowed nightgown. Taking up a lamp which she had turned low, she left the room and went along the corridor which creaked at almost every step. The roaring hurricane outside put so many noises into the night, no one was likely to pay attention to a few protesting floorboards.

The door at the far end of the upper floor opened easily when she lifted the latch. It closed behind her with a soft click. For some moments they studied each other, she from just inside the door and he from the bed where he had obviously been lying awake. By the light of two lamps she could see the glow in his dark eyes. It told her what she was about to do was unquestionably her right of choice.

'I knew you would never come to me for fear of being rebuffed,' she told him softly. 'I have no such fear.' Shrugging the cloak from her shoulders she crossed to the bed. When she climbed in beside him and put her hand up to his face, her fingers felt the wetness of his tears.

Chapter Thirteen

Damage caused by the great hurricane, which raged for two days and nights, was extensive, taking three human lives as well as destroying animals and crops. The lane leading to Knightshill was impassable for a week due to a landslide. Margaret returned home when the gale subsided on the third day. She rode cross-country on a horse from the blacksmith's stable. Her slow progress owed little to the obstacles along her route.

The two nights she had spent in Laurence's arms had changed her irrevocably. Doubts and fears about the future had gone. The sexual neglect and humiliation she had suffered at Philip's hands had been wiped out by the intensity of her lover's passion. The sense of isolation in the midst of a disintegrating family circle had been banished by the knowledge that she no longer needed that uncertain bond of kinship. Consummation of a love which had overwhelmed her at her lowest ebb had made her strong enough to fight for her right to happiness, whatever it involved. The Ashleigh warrior spirit had emerged in her strongly.

Charlotte greeted her with immense relief, declaring that the entire household had been burdened with fear for her safety and that Ned had searched for her during the initial storm, only returning when the hurricane blew him and the horse half-way across a field in its ferocity. Having heard all the details from Ned himself only moments ago, Margaret cut her sister short.

'I had the good sense to head for the village when the storm began, rather than remain on exposed high ground. Moorkin served me with tea, but I little guessed I'd be under siege at the Stag's Head for two days. They rose to the occasion wonderfully well, providing rooms and essentials for eight unexpected guests.' She shivered deliberately. 'I must take off these damp clothes. There is still rain in the air this morning.' As Charlotte began walking with her towards the stairs, she continued in light tones, 'You'll never believe it, Lottie, but Mrs Clegg and Mrs Butterworth were taking tea when the storm broke. They were also obliged to put up at the inn, and they live but half a mile from it. Everyone said they had never known of such a hurricane in Wiltshire before.'

'You had the company of Mr Nicolardi, which must have been preferable to that of those two old chatterboxes,' laughed Charlotte. 'Did you manage to deduce why he is hiding out in Dunstan St Mary? You cannot have been discussing Ashleigh family history for two whole days.'

'We once spoke of Grandfather's attempt at matchmaking,' Margaret countered. 'He has no intention of wooing to order. As for why he is in the area, he made no confessions of embezzlement or intrigue. Perhaps the situation was not grave enough to suggest we were all about to meet our Maker.'

Charlotte looked at her sharply. 'No one would believe you have just been through an ordeal. I've seldom seen you look so full of life.'

'What a sad reflection on normality, then, if it takes a near disaster to make one look truly alive.'

Her sister then embarked on an account of the damage sustained at Knightshill. The hothouses had been flattened, destroying the orchids. Some ancient oaks had fallen. One had crushed the stable housing Val's favourite horse, Merlin, who Ned had had to shoot because of injuries. Chimney pots had been ripped from the roof and several panes in the Great Window had smashed beneath the elemental assault.

'John Morgan is unusually worried,' Charlotte confided as she trod up the stairs, her arm linked through Margaret's. 'We've lost the young wheat he planted in the twenty-acre field this year, and some lambs seem unlikely to survive the battering they received. Poor Vere! I wrote to tell him the orchids were doing well. Now they're all lost, he'll be dreadfully upset.'

'I imagine he has greater disasters all round him, Lottie. The loss of a few orchids will seem trivial, in comparison.'

Her sister glanced at her in surprise. 'You don't seem dismayed over the damage, or even over Merlin. Val loved that stallion. He'll be so distressed.'

'Who's going to tell him?' she asked calmly. 'In any case, he's another Ashleigh with greater problems to face than the loss of a beast he was unlikely to ride again.'

Charlotte stopped. 'Good heavens, I never thought to hear you so unconcerned for Val.'

Margaret freed her arm with a smile. 'I've finally realised he doesn't need a maternal sister's guidance. He's no longer a schoolboy, but a young man leading a life free of family obligations. So is Vere, Lottie. You should face up to that.' Turning to the door of her suite of rooms, she added, 'I really must take a bath and put on fresh clothes. What a luxury!'

Philip was at his desk in the sitting room and glanced up from his papers. 'So the Lord preserved you throughout the tumult. He is all-forgiving.'

She turned by the bedroom door. 'Not quite, Philip. He struck down three people of the village.'

'He moves in mysterious ways. It is not for us to question them.'

'Why not? If the Lord is so full of understanding He must surely expect us to question those of His actions which puzzle us. Why should one of the storm victims have been poor, witless Matthew Dyke, who cannot have sinned against anyone in his sixteen years?'

Her husband got to his feet. 'We each live our allotted span. The boy had served his purpose on earth.'

'Which was what? To cause distress and hardship to the parents who brought him into the world along with seven normal children they could hardly afford to clothe and feed?'

'The Lord gives no man a burden he cannot bear.'

She turned away, unwilling to remain in the company of this unrelenting man after the glorious freedom she had known for the past two days and nights. 'You have an answer for everything, Philip, but it hasn't stopped Kate from saying, *If God is good he should let us all be happy, not as miserable as Papa.* Even a child of six can question your creed of dumb acceptance.'

With the door open she was halted by his next words. 'Stay here! I have something to say to you.'

'I need a bath. You may tell me afterwards.'

'*Now*, Margaret! I have many things to do before we leave, so I can spare you very little time.'

She turned back warily. 'You're taking Timothy away again?'

'And the girl.'

'She's too young, *far* too young.' Apprehension began to overshadow happiness. Her own plan to take the children away was beset with enough difficulties without this setback.

He came forward, and her apprehension deepened when she saw the fire in his eyes. 'She is my child to fashion as I choose.'

'She is also my child, Philip. As her mother I dispute your right to take a small frightened girl to a missionary meeting she cannot possibly comprehend. I dispute it most forcefully.'

Reaching her, he said with ill-concealed elation. 'I am taking my young disciples to Africa at the end of next week. The mission accepted my application for field work without hesitation. I am to set up a new mission built in one of the most remote areas which has just been brought under British protection through the railway project. It is an indication of how much my work is valued by those at headquarters, who know how fervently I wish to bring the heathen to God.'

The blow was so great she could only stare at him. It could not be true. It could not! Yet the expression of almost orgasmic excitement on his face told her that he *had* done this unforgivable thing without consulting her.

Through stiff lips she said, 'You gave your word that we could remain at Knightshill while Grandfather lived. Your word as a man of God.'

245

'You are at liberty to remain here.'

She moved away to the centre of the room. *What must she do?* Her thoughts raced in time with her heartbeat. It was essential to make no rash move that would endanger her case for Sir Frederick Norton. Laurence had given her explicit instructions on that score. But neither of them had foreseen this.

'The children must stay with me,' she ruled emotionally. 'They are nine and six years old only. They cannot travel unchaperoned half across the world.'

'They will not be unchaperoned. A very worthy and capable woman will be travelling out as my assistant in this essential work. My children will be in excellent hands.'

She swung round in swift passion. 'They are *my* children! I carried them for nine long months and suffered the pain of bringing them into the world. They were created in love, and it was in that love I believed they would be raised. How wrong I was. They are not *your* children and never can be. You've suffered no pain of mind or body for them. You've never sat beside them at night when they are feverish or sick.' She moved toward him as her passion doubled. 'They are both afraid of you, afraid of someone they should respect and revere. You are their father, but you inspire terror rather than love.'

'The Lord is their father. I am merely His agent to teach them the greatest gift of all . . . as I shall teach it to the heathen.'

'I think you are insane,' she accused, losing her control in the face of his implacability. 'Some disturbance of the brain compels you to see yourself as another Messiah, a saviour of mankind. Why must you go to some distant dangerous land, force your creed on black people who despise and fear those who threaten them with a wrathful god they cannot see? They have their own gods. Aren't there enough sinners in England for you to convert?'

'The heathen is unaware that he is sinning. The Christian who lives in wickedness and depravity does so in the full knowledge of the wrong he is doing.'

'So you are turning to the wild tribes of Africa in the face of *failure* at home? They'll accept your dogmatic, oppressive ideas no more readily.'

'They are as children. An innocent mind is deeply receptive.'

'It is also full of questions. When the only answer is that this invisible saviour must never *be* questioned, barriers of resistance rise up. When Tim and Kate were much younger you used to explain your simpler beliefs to them in ways they were willing to accept. Since joining the mission you always say, *It is so, because it is so.* You have lost them, as you have lost sight of all humanity in the concept of the Christian God. You

246

have now simply turned Him into an instrument to wield your power over others.'

He stepped forward and struck her hard on the cheek in the full spate of his anger. She backed away, covering the stinging flesh with her hand. But the blow had strengthened not weakened her. She had the weapon she needed.

'Don't *ever* condemn Ashleighs again,' she told him with cold passion. 'They only strike at armed enemies, never at women. You claim to have universal love for mankind, yet you have twice assaulted me. No, don't come any nearer,' she warned as he stepped towards her. 'You will go to Africa alone. There is no court in England will take children from a loving mother and secure family home to give to a parent who means to steep them in a biased creed and take them to a country riddled with plagues and peopled by unpredictable tribes. The rights of a mother will always be upheld against a man given to acts of violence against her.'

'There is no court in England will take children from a man of God to give to a mother who is an adulteress.' He approached to within a few feet while she stood stunned. 'I imagine you shared his room at the Stag's Head Inn for the past two nights.' He let out his breath in a slow gust. 'Since that man came upon the scene you have defied everyone in this house. Not only did you raise your voice at me over the issue of my son attending the London convention, you have quarrelled with your sister and Sir Gilliard in defence of that amoral young brother you continue to support, and you have berated Nanny for obeying my orders concerning my children. When I eventually met this person who had ingratiated himself with your grandfather in order to be invited here, the truth was obvious enough without the covert glances you exchanged with him. When you dashed to the village the following day in the teeth of a storm, I deduced that the pair of you were making plans to abscond. Your grandmother ran off with a loose-living Italian, so history repeats itself. Will you write *that* in your family records, I wonder?' He turned away to the desk, where he sat and began to study some papers. 'As I have told you before, you are a selfish woman. You cannot act the devoted mother whilst indulging yourself as another man's mistress, Margaret.'

He glanced up at her again. 'The children will go with me to Africa to perform the work for which they have been chosen by the Almighty. There is nothing you can do to prevent that. If your love for them is as great as you claim, you will give up this sinful liaison in order to stay beside them. Your decision is of little interest to me, but let me hear no more about "acts of violence" against you. What I took from you last year was mine by right of divine union. What *he* takes is an offence and a sin against the Church. The whole of England would pass judgement in my favour.'

247

For several minutes Margaret stood in the centre of the room in a state of shock. Philip ignored her. It was as if the scene had never taken place. Icy, sick at heart, more isolated than ever in this old house, she told herself he was right. That she and Laurence had slept beneath the same roof would be enough, should he choose to pursue a charge of adultery.

Whirling round, she left the room with mounting desperation. Hardly aware of what she said or did in the stable, she was soon on one of Val's fast stallions. Using the whip, she had it galloping for the village across fields she had covered on her way up less than half an hour ago. The beast responded to her wild mood by taking all the obstacles in their path with courageous jumps. Choosing a short cut through the stream now swollen into a headlong slither of muddy water, horse and rider emerged drenched but unscathed to charge into the square and scatter those gathered there.

The villagers were out in force to view the aftermath of the hurricane, so many faces turned at the spectacular arrival. Laurence stepped from the crowd, his expression full of alarm and the kind of anger kindled by fear. Margaret slid from the saddle to his steadying arms and almost collapsed. She was slowly breaking apart inside: a volcano of emotion was rising and threatening to master her.

'What has happened?' he demanded with quiet urgency. 'Pull yourself together, for God's sake. You terrify me.'

She was unable to speak. Some force filled her lungs so that she had to fight even to breathe. Gazing into his face in a state of inexplicable dread, she began to shake from head to foot within his grasp. He was life; he was her only hope. Without him she would die. Her body might slowly age and decay, but Margaret Ashleigh would know sudden agonising death if he ever went from her. Laurence led her towards the inn and called for Moorkin to bring brandy. The tea room was empty save for an untidy girl clearing ashes from the hearth where the fire had warmed them both for the past two days. The wench watched them, mouth agape, as they made their slow progress to the seat, Laurence supporting Margaret with a strong arm around her waist.

'The lady is ill,' he told the girl sharply. 'Leave that until she recovers.'

Moorkin came with the brandy as Laurence settled Margaret on the velvet cushions. He looked concerned. 'How is she, sir? Came into the village in a manner I've never seen before. Shall I send for the doctor?'

Laurence took the glass containing spirits. 'Not yet. Mrs Daulton is more shocked than hurt, I believe.'

When the glass was held to her mouth, Margaret's chattering teeth made it difficult for her to drink.

'I'll fetch a blanket,' said Moorkin. 'Can't light a fire till the girl clears the ash.' He hesitated. 'Would Mrs Daulton be better lying down, d'you

248

think, sir? Her room's been cleaned, and Mrs Moorkin will be happy to sit with her until she recovers.'

'The blanket will suffice,' Laurence told him impatiently. 'If there is some kind of emergency at Knightshill, I'd best find out as soon as possible in order to decide what action must be taken. Thank you, Moorkin.'

When they were alone, Laurence asked her again what had happened. He was rubbing her icy hands with his own in between forcing sips of brandy down her throat. Now she was with him, the overwhelming sense of terror was beginning to recede. It had been replaced with the driving need to hold him and be held in return, like a child waking from a nightmare and seeking reassurance. Moorkin returned speedily with the blanket, told Laurence he would be in the yard if needed, then left them. The soft blanket, smelling of mothballs, was tucked around her tenderly despite Laurence's words as he did so.

'I sincerely hope there *is* an emergency at Knightshill to explain your arrival at breakneck speed, or you will have aroused the very interest we must avoid.'

'Philip knows,' she blurted out. 'He accused me of being . . . being another man's mistress.'

Laurence's hands stilled. 'You told me he took no interest in anything but his work, that he had divorced himself from life at Knightshill. How can he possibly know?'

'I . . . I have been too defiant of everyone since you came on the scene; he intercepted covert glances between us, he said.'

'No, that is impossible. He had excused himself on the plea of work before we allowed ourselves any optical messages.' His dark brows furrowed. 'He's guessing, hitting out at you because you were trapped here by the storm. Like my wife, he jealously guards what he does not want himself.'

Clutching the blanket tighter to her shaking body, she shook her head. 'It's not me he's guarding. I think he doesn't care what I do. It's the children he wants. His *disciples*. He said no court would take them from a man of God to leave in the hands of an . . . an adulteress.' She watched his expression closely. 'He's right, isn't he?'

He reached for her hands again, his fingers playing restlessly with her wedding-ring which fitted loosely enough to turn in both directions. 'A wife's adultery *is* a worse sin in the eyes of a jury than a husband's violence towards her. They might even feel he is justified to chastise a woman who betrays him.' His frown deepened. 'He has no proof, but it would take little more than his accusation for each person beneath this roof with us during the storm to recall sights they never saw, words they had never overheard. They would claim to have witnessed all manner of suspicious

249

behaviour in us, if prompted by counsel. But for those two nights here he would have no case against us.'

'You regret them? You wish I hadn't come to your bed?' she asked painfully.

'*No!* My dearest love, no! You gave me more than you will ever know with that brave gesture.' He moved closer to brush her temple with his lips. 'You don't regret it, do you?'

She shook her head, and then his gentle kiss was on her mouth. 'Those nights were worth half my life, I swear.' He straightened and sighed. 'Fate has weighted the scale against us. I had hoped to spare you as much distress as possible, but this does not mean we are defeated. Norton and I discussed the alternative. Although he strongly advised against it, he agreed to act for us in a divorce petition brought by your husband, if the need arose. The first essential is to book passage on a ship with limited accommodation which is heading somewhere off the normal shipping routes. Few people to remember us, less likelihood of being traced. I have money. We'll be able to live very well for several years until the dust has settled. You'll be distanced from the unpleasantness of the proceedings in court, and the children are young enough to survive scandal without lasting scars. As soon as we are able to marry, we'll go to my family in Verona.' His stormy expression lightened a little as he took her hands again. 'We shall be together in our secluded paradise until then. I'll arrange my affairs in London and book passages, then we'll be away before anyone is aware of our intention.'

Terror began to well up once more at his words, and she could manage no more than a husky whisper as she gripped his hands. 'No, Laurence. He's taking the children to Africa – at the end of next week. *That's* the crisis at Knightshill.'

He took the news badly. Getting to his feet he turned to stare from the window, his back rigid with anger. When he spoke in soft, swift Italian, Margaret needed no translator to tell her he was cursing.

'When did he arrange this?' he asked, without turning.

'The application must have been made some months ago. He said nothing to me of it.' In the face of his long silence, she added, 'He said his capable female assistant will care for Tim and Kate. I . . . I shall not be missed.'

Laurence swung round. 'The monster! He's attempting to make you choose between me and your children.'

'I can't go with him. I *can't*,' she cried.

'Is it possible for you to take the children from the house without arousing his suspicion, perhaps with the help of your sister?' Seeing her expression, he said bitterly, 'Of course not. No Ashleigh would aid another in a bid for happiness which would bring dishonour to the name. A girl like Charlotte would never understand all-consuming passion, anyway.'

'I won't give it up, whatever the cost,' she vowed wildly.

He came to sit beside her. 'Don't speak of giving up yet. We need time to think. I'll go to Norton as soon as the line to London is cleared of fallen trees. He's the man to give sound advice.' His smile was strained. 'I too will not relinquish a love which has arrived almost too late – but we can risk losing it by taking hasty action. Trust me to find a safe solution within the days we have left. Meanwhile, you must go back and endure the situation. Take my love to sustain you.'

The days were interminable. Avoiding Philip was not difficult because he was engrossed with preparations for the journey, but the truth had to be revealed to the family. Margaret suffered difficult scenes with Sir Gilliard and her sister without betraying her feelings. Her grandfather first declared his refusal to allow a pious nincompoop to take them all to a wilderness populated by the kind of savages he had fought in Ashanti, then told Margaret she had only herself to blame for defying tradition and marrying a churchman.

'If you had married a fine young officer, you'd not find yourself in this deplorable situation,' he raved several times a day. 'No gentleman worth his salt would countenance taking a lady to such a place. He would leave his wife and children in the security of the family home while he went off to perform his duty. I'll not allow it, I tell you.'

'The matter is out of your hands, Grandfather,' she told him at their first discussion. In successive ones she remained silent. The strain increased as time passed and still he would not accept that he was powerless.

Charlotte was deeply upset at the thought of losing another member of what had been so close a family. 'You're not a missionary, Margaret. Philip should go alone, like military men. Father didn't drag Mother all over the world to face danger with him. She stayed with us until he died. You must insist on the same treatment. You do not *want* to go, do you?'

'Philip intends to take the children with him and no one will prevent it.'

'It's cruel! They'll die out there. You all will.'

'Lottie, please stop,' she begged. 'I have enough to withstand as it is. A sister should offer support, not weep and wail.'

'If Vere were here he'd do something.'

'Apart from offering sympathy and understanding, there is nothing he could do. A father has the right to take his children wherever he pleases.'

'Why Africa?'

'The heathens are there.'

'There are heathens aplenty in England, if he cared to look.'

251

'They're not black. The mission believes its duty lies with them.'

'But not yours, Margaret,' Charlotte cried anew. 'A mother's duty is to protect her children from danger and sickness. *Insist* on their remaining here with you.'

Margaret saw an opportunity to broach her sister for help. 'I could only do that by taking them into hiding until Philip sailed. Would you be my accomplice in such a move?'

Charlotte looked faintly shocked. 'Surely such melodrama isn't necessary? Philip isn't threatening to kill them.'

'You just now claimed they would die in Africa.'

She coloured. 'If you *spoke* to him, explained the dangers to which he will expose the children, and pointed out the advantages they would have by staying at Knightshill, he would have to listen to reason.'

'He has not listened to reason since he heard Dr Benedict speak of his work in Africa. I marvel that you have lived beneath the same roof and failed to grasp that,' Margaret said in acid tones. 'You decline to help me protect my children by taking them away from his influence?'

'He is their father, as you have said quite forcefully.'

'Then please say no more, Lottie. You have never been a wife or you would know that the poor creatures have little influence over their husbands when duty calls.'

Timothy and Kate were distraught at the prospect of leaving Knightshill and all they loved to live with people whose skins were as black as coal. It was something they had never seen and could not imagine. The prospect frightened Kate, making her fractious and naughty. Timothy grew as defiant as Val at his most rebellious, claiming he *would not* go. He begged Sir Gilliard to intervene, which made the situation more distressing than ever. With her nerves stretched to breaking point, Margaret reacted as most mothers do when pestered during a time of immense stress. Her uncharacteristic anger shocked the children into a state of sullen withdrawal from everyone save Nanny, and they refused anything save milk and biscuits.

Margaret well understood now why both brothers had absented themselves from Knightshill when their world had darkened beyond bearing. Knowing that she, too, must soon leave, she spent much time walking or riding over the acres she knew and cherished. The peace of the Wiltshire scene deepened the ache in her breast so that she crossed the familiar countryside with tears on her cheeks. The pull of a beloved past added to her stress.

The date of Philip's departure drew nearer. Six days after their last meeting, Margaret felt so distraught she rode to the village in the hope that Laurence had returned on the late train the previous night. Moorkin told her the overnight express to Cornwall had not run due to a landslip further along the line.

'The milk train came in, Mrs Daulton, which means they must have cleared it now. Mr Nicolardi paid for the room up to the end of the week, so he'll be back by Friday or Saturday. Don't worry too much about that famous window of yours, ma'am. If Mr Nicolardi says he can arrange for someone to mend it good as new, he'll do it. Knows about glass, that gentleman does. The person he's gone to see in London used to work for his family in Italy, by all accounts.'

She rode back wondering how much longer she could prevent herself from taking the children in the dead of night and seeking out her lover with the help of Sir Frederick Norton. What was taking so long? Should she have bags packed ready to leave at short notice? With that in mind she went straight to her room when she reached Knightshill. Louise had made persistent enquiries about the clothes her mistress wished to take on her voyage. Margaret allowed her ageing maid to begin packing. The task would not only allay suspicion, it would facilitate her secret departure.

They were in the midst of selecting dresses from the vast oaken wardrobe, when a knock on the door sent Louise to open it. She returned with several letters brought up by one of the house-maids.

'Ned heard the express didn't go through last night because of trouble on the line,' she commented, handing Margaret the envelopes. 'Must be all right again now, and thank goodness for that, ma'am. Sir Gilliard likes the mail to be on time.'

Margaret heard none of her words. Seeing Laurence's handwriting on the top one, she dropped the green muslin dress and walked to the window. Her hands shook so badly it was difficult to hold the single page steady enough to read his message.

Norton will not act for us now Daulton has everything in his favour. To take the children would constitute a felony for which we could be imprisoned. He denied knowledge of our meeting and has destroyed all notes. I understand why he cannot endanger his reputation.

Two cabins have been reserved on a small steamer heading east; a single one on a liner bound for Italy. I am giving you as cruel a choice as he. If you can accept a future clouded by apprehension and remorse, the loss of a beloved family, and a union society will not recognise, come to the Bird Inn at Southampton on Thursday evening. The steamer sails at midnight. If you decide to hold on to your birthright and fight for your children's futures within the protection of social and legal approbation, I shall go to Italy that same night and torment you no further.

253

I longed to give you all a man can offer the woman he loves. All I can now do is pledge eternal devotion and accept your decision. It may be one of the most difficult things I have been asked to do.

The sunlight falling on the page darkened as she read the stark message which conveyed Laurence's anguish more clearly than an impassioned one.

'Madam, are you all right?'

Margaret turned to her maid and saw a stranger. 'I need some air,' she murmured in trancelike tones. She pushed past the woman and a mountain of clothes in her urgency to reach the corridor, where she walked faster and faster until she was running. On the staircase a figure loomed and spoke, but she thought only of the need to be alone. Her feet flew over the floor until they were crossing the gravel drive, then the grassy slope behind the house.

At the crest she found she was sobbing, racked by emotions so deep they were frightening. A cruel choice, he claimed. She *had* no choice. She would as soon sign her death warrant as let Laurence go from her life. Yet others must inevitably suffer. The children would have freedom and an undemanding love, but they would be deprived of their heritage, and a mother's sin would be held against them all their lives. There would also be the dread of discovery and forced return to their father.

Tipping back her head in an effort to control herself, Margaret gradually quietened. The chill of reaction overtook her. Hugging herself tightly she walked back and forth while she assessed the cost of her future happiness. Laurence had chosen a steamer due to sail on the night before Philip left for Africa, correctly guessing that *nothing* would prevent him from going to those he burned to convert. By the time their absence was noticed, they would be on that steamer with Laurence. Would Philip lay charges before he left and set in motion a police search for the children, or would he surrender his disciples in the greater fervour to enlighten the multitude? The apprehension Laurence knew would cloud their days.

What of herself? Her past with loving brothers and a sister must be sacrificed. Would that cause the remorse Laurence mentioned? On certain anniversaries, and when she grew old. Being Laurence's mistress would deny her social acceptance and leave her open to snubs by those who would embrace his wife. He would lose his present standing, but still be welcomed by lower echelons of society providing he did not have his paramour with him. Their children would be bastards, treated with scorn and abuse. That was the highest price they would pay for what she was about to do.

For many minutes she paced the slope down which they had tobogganed

254

as children. Then, when she was quite calm, she sat on the grass hugging her knees while she relived the Ashleigh world which had once been brighter than gold, and gazed at the old house to imprint its image on her mind for the years to come.

Wiltshire produced a perfect summer's day when Margaret and her children left their home. It was as if Knightshill was seducing her into staying. The roses were a blaze of pink, red and creamy yellow, and the formal gardens were scented by syringa, jasmine, lilac and sweet-smelling broom to add a further lure to remain. Yet it was not the brilliant blue of a sky which made the house and its surroundings stand out in relief that caused Margaret such pain. Nor was it the call of sheep and the aching song of skylarks high above. It was the fact that no one knew she was not returning.

Sir Gilliard had talked throughout luncheon, as usual, then retired to the library and his maps and military documents. Charlotte had gone to the hothouses where John Morgan was supervising the replacement of glass. Winters had lowered the ballroom chandeliers for cleaning before the Waterloo Ball. Benson and the twins hoed and dug the borders. Ned was chivvying his stable-boys into putting more effort into the polishing of leathers. Margaret walked from the house with her children, climbed into the dog-cart Ned had ready, and simply drove away. No one waved goodbye; there were no farewells. They were being saved for tomorrow.

As she turned the cart into the lane, her throat ached with the sadness of everyone's normality on such a momentous day. Yet that was how it must be. She was supposed to be taking the children to collect new shoes in the village. On two earlier trips she had taken parcels of clothing on the pretext of giving to the poor those things she would not take to Africa. She had instead put them on a train for Southampton to await the arrival of V. Ashleigh. Those two parcels and the one at her feet contained all she and the children would have for the voyage to an unknown destination. In her leather bag were her jewels wrapped in a velvet cloth, a family photograph, one of Vere's small watercolours of field mice among cornstalks, a handkerchief sachet embroidered by Charlotte at the age of eight, and a tiny painted horse from Val's room.

Only by simulating resignation to the new life in Africa had it been possible to dupe Philip into allowing her to perform a mother's tasks for the pair who now sat listlessly on each side of her. She would not tell them the truth until they reached Winklesham station. In six hours' time they would be leaving the land of their birth to discover what lay beyond, as countless Ashleighs had done. Laurence would be the father they deserved; they would have their mother's guidance. They would be *loved*. That was surely worth any sacrifice.

They reached the bend in the lane which gave a fine view of Knightshill. Margaret looked over her shoulder, as she always did, and wondered if her thoughts echoed those of her mother and grandmother on saying goodbye to it all.

'Forgive me,' she whispered silently, then turned away to urge the mare to go faster.

Chapter Fourteen

The letters from his sisters reached Vere in early June. He read the long, descriptive one from Charlotte with great eagerness, delighting in her account of John Morgan's efficiency in running the estate, and of her own management of the orchids and formal gardens. Everything appeared to be prospering in his absence, he realised ruefully. Sir Gilliard had been right to claim it would. Charlotte's words took his thoughts back to the verdant county he loved. Had it, like Annabel, seemed so enchanting due to his restricted life? Did his home still suggest a peaceful haven because his present situation was nearer to a semblance of hell than he had ever known?

Margaret's letter was entirely different, typical of the maternal role she had attempted to play towards them all. It mentioned Sir Gilliard's heart attack – news Charlotte had withheld – and Val's courageous action during the tragedy at Tetherbury Pond. He then read with deep dismay of the boy's dismissal from Chartfield and his subsequent decision not to return home. The description of 'an unscrupulous woman who had led Val a cruel dance with the promise of persuading her uncle to take him into the 57th Lancers' disturbed Vere. Surely his brother had not become scandalously involved in his eagerness for a cavalry place? It sounded totally out of character, yet expulsion of a senior prefect who had brought great sporting honours to the school suggested a grave offence.

Sitting in his tent in the summer camp at Atbara, Vere gazed out across the haze hanging several feet above the harsh, unrelenting landscape and saw Val in his cricketing clothes standing in Dr Keening's sitting room. He had been dumbfounded, but aggressively firm in his view that to go to the Sudan was a suicidal decision. It now occurred to Vere that his own action might have put too great a burden on a young brother at a vulnerable time in his life. The obligation to match up to Vorne had always rested heavily on Val, rightly or wrongly, and by handing him the added responsibility of inheritance Vere might have contributed to this sad affair.

He remained lost in thought for some time. A lot had happened in his absence. There was no reply from Sir Gilliard, but he had not expected any response to the few pages he had sent outlining details of the battle, the subsequent wait for the Nile to rise, and the general estimate of September being the most likely month for the retaking of Khartoum. The only personal touch had been his hope that his grandfather was in good health. Apart from that, the letter had resembled a military communiqué rather than a message from a devoted grandson.

The news from home unsettled Vere. Contact with his family revived feelings he had put aside in his complex new life, reminded him of responsibilities he could not ignore as easily as he had imagined. All might be well with the estate, but not with the residents of the grey stone house. Guilt touched him for the first time since leaving it. Misery had swamped all other emotions then and, although it now sounded melodramatic, he had come out here to die. Now he faced the unexpected possibility of surviving the final battle for Khartoum. Could he go back to his life as a Wiltshire landowner after running away as he had?

He had been so certain of Val's success where he had failed. What would become of the boy? Sir Gilliard would never forgive him. Poor lad! He had risked everything in a bid to live up to what everyone expected of him, little knowing the shining example held before him from birth was more than a little tarnished.

For several days Vere wandered moodily about the camp, or lay on his bed for long periods tormented by heat and restlessness. Most officers had gone on leave, some even returning to England and their families. He had been one of a few who had had no wish to go anywhere. Despite the plagues of the new camp, he had found some contentment working on a series of paintings and pen drawings which depicted things he would never before have considered subjects for his own talents. Battle had so impressed him with its overriding horrific splendour, he had been impelled to depict it in the only manner open to him. Against his natural instincts, he had returned to the terrible scene to make swift sketches. From these, he had painted stark reality with the eye of a man who yearned to see beauty in everything. The resulting pictures had surprised him into accepting them as the best work he had ever done. The famous artist's impression of the last moments of Vorne Ashleigh's heroic crawl across the desert vastness was not more impressive than Vere's scenes of that pastel sunrise shattered by the dark puffs of exploding shells, above sands rising in a myriad whirlwinds around the mass of fearful, aggressive ranks. Without vanity,

257

Vere knew his sepia paintings of the aftermath of battle were as splendid as they were shocking: yellow sky, dun-coloured sand, khaki uniforms, blood-stained robes turned brown by light from an ochre sun. A far cry from field-mice or butterflies on buddleia!

Excited by this evidence of a wider talent, he had embarked on a series of pen-pictures featuring the things which surrounded him. Every aspect of the local scene, from the crumbling archaic panorama of Berber to the alien charm of a small Sudanese girl with her pet three-legged dog, came alive beneath his moving hand. Then he turned to military life with its absurdities and overtones of nobility. There was no shortage of willing models for his pictures. These men he repaid with a swift likeness in crayon, which they invariably sent home in letters taken up to Cairo on the steamers.

This work had kept him engrossed and slightly less afflicted by the ever-increasing temperatures, the scorpions, flies, gigantic poisonous spiders and the dragging hours than most of his companions. The advent of letters from home made him aware of these things. He began to grow irritable in the soaring temperatures, and the persistent biting flies drove him to take savage measures against them. When Private French disturbed a nest of scorpions behind Vere's tent it seemed the last straw. But it was not. A sandstorm hit the camp that same night, felling tents and covering everything left exposed by layers of grit which were impossible to remove.

At first light, Vere made his way through the scattered lines to the tent of his first and most stalwart military friend. Ross Majors was humped beneath a blanket on a bed which was now supported by a stone at each corner, the legs having been ripped from it during the ferocity of the storm. Vere shook the sleeping man vigorously, setting sand flying. Ross turned over slowly to reveal curls which looked to have turned blond overnight.

Squinting up at Vere belligerently, he growled, 'What do you want?'

'The steamer leaves for Cairo at eleven this morning and I intend to be on it.'

'Good for you!' The curly head disappeared beneath the blanket once more.

Vere said loudly. 'This place has grown unbearable. We need a break from it.' When there was no response, he added, 'Are you awake and listening to me?'

'No,' came the muffled reply from the young officer who had heard, just before the battle, that the girl he had loved since adolescence had married a naval officer she had known for only a brief time.

Ross had taken the news badly. It had reached him at the worst possible time, and he had not recovered his natural ebullience or even a semblance of it. Vere sympathised; he knew that anguish well. He also knew that it

258

faded more quickly when mind and body were actively engaged. Ross had been wallowing in self-pity, drowning his sorrows too liberally and too often. Vere determined to provide the antidote by taking him north to Cairo, where they would both benefit from its exotic attractions. It would have to be a short visit, however. Vere's funds had been all but exhausted by the settlement of his brother's debts, both financial and moral, but he could manage a month in the city with the aid of his subaltern's salary.

Gazing down at his lacklustre friend, Vere decided drastic measures were necessary. Bending swiftly to take up the end of the camp bed, he tipped the occupant to the sandy floor. Smiling down at the furious face confronting him, he said mildly, 'You've ordered me around enough in the past. I'm turning the tables now. Get up and start behaving like an officer and gentleman!'

By way of reply, Ross hooked his foot around Vere's ankle and pulled. Rolling into a sitting position after the heavy fall, Vere poked the blanketed figure with the toe of his boot. 'With my delicate constitution that could have finished me off.'

'*Nothing* will finish you off, Ashleigh. That was another damned hoax you played on us all. I have every expectation of seeing you outdo your famous brother with some flamboyant piece of gallantry outside the gates of Khartoum, just to show us how utterly deceived we have been.'

Vere got to his feet, brushing sand from his uniform. 'Before I amaze you with my bravery, my friend, I'm going to march you up to Cairo for four weeks. Get up, get dressed, eat a hearty breakfast and be ready to ride into Berber by nine.'

They had been in Cairo for almost a week when Vere received a note from Floria Pallini. Berating him for not visiting her immediately on arrival, she explained that the influx of so many officers presently on leave had delayed her learning of his presence in Cairo for longer than usual.

My dear, I am overjoyed at the prospect of seeing you again. I have thought of you many times and you must know that it is true when I confess that I have asked everyone for news of you. They all said you had chosen to stay at Atbara. I am holding a reception this evening. Come, I beg you.

Having decided not to contact Vorne's former mistress, Vere then found himself writing a formal note of acceptance which expressed the hope that his friend, Lieutenant Majors, would also be welcome. She was unlikely to expect him to compete with his brother this evening, Vere guessed, and began to look forward to it. Ross had brightened somewhat, but was still a shadow of his former self as he climbed into the carriage. Resplendent in scarlet and blue they were unconscious of presenting a picture of contrasts: Ross dark, sturdy, morose and Vere slender, graceful, fair-skinned and more assured than on his first visit to this intriguing woman. Telling Ross only that Floria had known his brother, he related the story of how Pallini had gone off with a European companion and a team of native porters, never to be seen again.

'Killed by nomadic tribesmen,' concluded Ross. 'It's a fool who wanders the desert without an army to protect him.'

'Poor old Steadman couldn't believe I'd done it, and survived to tell the tale,' Vere remarked, as they were conveyed through streets still teeming with people. 'As I was doing it in response to orders, does that make me less of a fool?'

'It certainly came as a surprise to many, especially Colonel Meers and Reggie Forrester.'

Vere decided to settle a suspicion he had had for some time. 'Did Meers really want those sketches, or was I sent on a useless mission merely to get me from under his feet?'

The heavenward roll of Ross's eyes told him the truth more succinctly than words. Yet he caught himself laughing. 'The old bastard! He'd get on well with my grandfather and ageing second cousins. They'd fully approve such a scheme.'

'So would I, normally, but I'd taken a fancy to you and thought it a rotten trick.' Shifting in his seat, Ross then asked, 'So the lady is a widow?'

'Rather a grateful one, between you and me. Pallini was much older and she prefers . . . well . . .'

'Young officers on leave? Brief, bittersweet, with no lasting commitment?'

Vere offered no reply. He still felt uncomfortable over the matter of Vorne's pearls, which he had left here in the bank to be returned to Floria on his own death. If he should survive this campaign, what then? There was no question of his obeying her command to give them to the girl who had driven him to Egypt. He no more loved Annabel now than she had loved him on comparing him with his brother. He sighed. One day, he might find true devotion.

'Is that sigh indicative of unrequited love for our Italian patroness, or over-indulgence in the rather rich meal served to us this evening?'

Vere turned to smile at Ross. 'You're beginning to sound more like the military martinet I first met at Abu Hamed.'

'Martinet, be damned! You needed licking into shape, young Ashleigh, but your charm appears to have worked a greater miracle than my exhaustive drilling. Doubtless, it is the Contessa who is fighting unrequited love.'

'Then you should find much in common with her.'

Ross merely scowled and remained silent until the carriage arrived at the foot of the long flight of steps.

The house looked very different tonight. The elegant rooms were ablaze with lights, noisy with the talk and laughter of those crowding them. The army was there in force, it seemed, for uniforms were predominant among the evening dress of Floria's multiracial guests. As they stood in the arched entrance to the main salon decorated in pale green, pink and gold, waiting to be ushered in, Ross murmured, 'I was expecting a high-class bawd house, not the kind of place even my mother would admire.'

A young, white-robed servant came for them at that point and led the way through a series of connecting rooms to where their hostess was talking to an elderly couple of evident high station. The tall, gaunt man wore the broad sash and jewelled star of a foreign order over his evening dress; the lady had a fine tiara on her greying hair. Yet Floria left them with a respectful curtsey when she spotted her new guests, and came quickly to where they stood. She had eyes only for Vere, studying him with disconcerting intensity for a moment or two before taking both his hands.

'You have changed so much, my dear. Men are never the same after communing with the desert.' Kissing him lightly on the cheek, she then gazed into his eyes. 'You are stronger, I can tell.'

'More like him?' he asked, without knowing why.

'Even less so than before.' Clasping his hands tightly, she said, 'I prayed for you every day.'

Shaken by this emotional greeting from an exceptionally beautiful woman he had met just once before, he hastily introduced Ross. His friend was evidently overwhelmed by the opulent vision she presented in a long gown of shimmery apricot satin trimmed with tiny silver and gold beads, which bared her shoulders in breathtaking fashion and clung to her generous curves. His dark eyes glowed with more life than Vere had seen in them since losing his childhood sweetheart.

'Because you are Vere's friend, I shall call you Ross from this first evening,' she declared, as he stood bemused. 'Are you appreciative of the arts, also?'

Ross shook his head. 'I'm not in Vere's class, ma'am. I'm a plain soldier.'

She laughed lightly. 'You shall call me Floria, and I shall discover in you more than a plain soldier. Come, I shall introduce you to some very interesting companions while I walk with Vere on the terrace.

'Won't your guests expect you to be with them?' Vere asked swiftly.

'Oh, yes, but I cannot always please them . . . and you will be in Cairo for so short a time. If you are to capture Khartoum by September, you will have to leave Atbara at the start of August. That leaves you just a few weeks in Cairo, my dear.'

This was said as she walked with her arms linked through theirs, until they reached the main salon once more. Vere and Ross exchanged astonished glances above the fluttering feathers of her hair ornament. Then Vere asked, 'How do you know this when we have not yet received official orders?'

She gave her light laugh. 'Military officers commit all manner of indiscretions to impress ladies, you should know. From exaggerated boasting to hesitant, bashful confessions, the whole of Cairo has now deduced that your Kitchener will advance by river and desert by the first day of August. The decisive battle against the Khalifa will almost certainly be fought on the plain of Omdurman, across the river from Khartoum.' Glancing mischievously from one to the other, she added, 'So you may speak to me of *anything* without fear of betraying military secrets, gentlemen.'

'Good lord!' exclaimed Ross.

Vere was still speechless with surprise when she stopped by a small group comprising several officers from Scottish regiments, in conversation with two young girls of mixed blood. While she presented Ross to them, Vere received another surprise as he recognised two of the men. They glanced at him in the manner of those who faintly recall a face but cannot remember a name or occasion to put with it. Vere would never forget the meeting. What he had said to them had led to Annabel declaring him a pygmy among giants. John and Frank Reeder could not match the smart officer before them with the man who had declined their offer to avenge the death of his brother. Even when Floria made a careless general introduction on the excuse that she must have a private conversation with Mr Ashleigh, the Reeders were still less than half-way to recognising the truth.

When they were on the terrace, Floria said gently, 'Those two very large creatures disturbed you in some way.'

He halted to study her appreciatively and at some length. 'You are remarkably astute.'

'I am.' Her amber eyes glistened with tears. 'You came out here to die. Now you are glad to be alive. I see that in every aspect of you, my dear.'

'I believed I would never return to Cairo,' he admitted.

'I am so glad you did. To lose you to the desert as I lost him would be too much.'

Vere guessed she was not speaking of Pallini. Knowing it was really why he had come this evening, he asked, 'Why was Vorne so different from the others, so unforgettable?'

He thought she chose not to answer when she walked away along the paved terrace mellowed by light from decorative lanterns hidden among creepers rioting up the pillars. He followed, until she stopped at the far wall, gazing into the starry distance.

'Why, Floria?'

Still gazing at the stars, she gave a sigh. 'I have asked myself that so often. When he was close, he made even the slightest thing exciting. Those dreams one has from childhood, he turned into reality. Vorne banished sadness, dismissed troubles with the exuberance of his careless spirits. Those whom he touched, as a butterfly alights briefly on all the most colourful flowers in a garden, were caught up in the joyousness of his own way of living.' She turned with a sad shrug. 'He was handsome, with a smile which could soften even one's bones, and he knew that. Yet his passion was joyful, too. Never selfish, cruel or too intense. I always felt deliriously happy in his arms.' Her eyes again grew too bright in the lamplight. 'He understood but never loved me. It was the same with everyone. Only when he had gone did one realise the dreams were still only dreams. The sadness and troubles lay waiting where he had cast them away with a wave of his hand. And I knew he would never come back. That is why he is so unforgettable.'

'What if he *had* come back?'

'The magic would have been destroyed.'

'Now it is still intact?'

She put her hand on his sleeve to ask softly, 'Why this questioning?'

It was his turn to sigh. 'Following in his footsteps has made me very aware of someone I never really knew. I had no expectation of reaching Khartoum. It seems that I might well do so. I'm almost apprehensive at the prospect of visiting his grave. Foolish, isn't it?'

She took her time before saying, 'What is it you fear?'

Regretting his impulsive confession, he changed the subject. 'I think I must see the pyramids while I'm in Cairo. I had no time to do so before.'

'You have seen the desert. Is that not enough? I have heard men claim that all else is forgotten when the sands stretch in every direction and only the sun and moon mark the passing of time. Is that so? Has the desert allowed you to forget her?'

Where this woman was concerned pretence was pointless. 'Not forget. Cease to worship.'

Before he guessed her intention she moved into his startled embrace to kiss him with lingering pleasure, regardless of others on the terrace. Drawing away, she said softly, 'So you no longer have cause to refuse my invitation to stay when the others all leave.'

He shook his head slowly, although her kiss had aroused a sleeping hunger. '*I* could never make your childhood dreams assume reality, even for one night.'

'Ah,' she murmured with enlightenment. 'Now I know what it is you fear.'

Furious with himself for those revealing words, he said, 'Perhaps we should go in. I've monopolised you for too long.'

She caught his sleeve as he turned. 'Is it your hope to die on the sands outside Khartoum, as he did?'

'Of course not.'

'Then why hope to emulate him in anything else?'

'Why else would you choose me?' he demanded heatedly. 'There are many dozens of men presently in Cairo, only too willing to accept your offer to stay the night.'

She stiffened. 'That is something he would *never* have said to me.'

Shaken by his own uncharacteristic behaviour, he made to leave. 'I beg your pardon. It was unforgivable.'

'*Vere!*'

Two paces on he stopped but could not face her.

'The cry is still in your heart. Perhaps not as loud as it was, but still there. Please let me quieten it a little more by driving him further away.'

Vere stayed with Floria on many nights during his leave. Only occasionally did the thought of his enigmatic brother restrict his response to her sensuous generosity. The pleasure of something he had denied himself since meeting Annabel contributed to the relaxation of those weeks in Cairo. With Ross similarly entertained by a girl he had met at Floria's reception, the time flew for them both. It was not all physical passion, however. Vere gained as much delight from Floria's personality, for they shared a love of music, art and poetry. Besides having an admirable collection of *objets d'art* herself, she had many acquaintances whose homes contained priceless possessions which Vere was invited to view in her company.

He eventually persuaded her to pose for him, both nude and dressed for a ball. During these sessions he spoke of the pictures he had done at Atbara, which he intended to send to Knightshill before leaving Cairo. She asked to see them and was strangely silent when he took them to the villa and displayed them. That the desert disturbed her he knew very well, but his sepia paintings made a deeper impression on her than he had expected. Her reaction was almost one of shock.

'Is this *really* battle?' she breathed.

'Without the tumult.'

Her amber gaze turned on him. 'I wish I had not seen them.'

'You asked me to show you.'

'I did not realise they would be so . . . so *awesome*. You are very talented, my dear, but these pictures are unbearably real. They frighten me.'

He kissed her gently. 'I had no wish to do that. But battle *is* real, Floria.'

'Why have you decided to send them to your family, who will put them away in embarrassment because they do not understand that each man has his own means of glory?'

He shrugged, wishing he had not been charmed into revealing so much. 'If I ever go back, they will remind me of this episode in my life. I certainly can't take them all the way to Khartoum with me.'

He had reckoned without Floria's many acquaintances. Two days later, she took him to meet Armand Lisère, a dealer in fine arts who had a gallery in Cairo and another in Alexandria. The monocled Frenchman liked the set of four sepia paintings depicting battle at Atbara enough to offer to frame and display them.

'There is great interest in the war, Mr Ashleigh, but only for as long as it lasts, you understand. I can possibly sell them for you now, but not when the campaign is over. People forget very swiftly.' He stroked his chin speculatively. 'If you should turn to more commercial subjects, I would be more than happy to act as your agent. You have an eye for detail which I find refreshing amid so many impressionistic pictures.'

Quoting the percentage he would take, plus the cost of framing, he went on to put a price on the pictures individually and as a set. In his present financial situation, Vere found the prospect of additional funds attractive and accepted the man's terms.

Floria had not finished, however. Before the week was out, Vere was showing a journalist his pen pictures of Berber and its inhabitants, as well as those he had made in and around a military camp. The man was employed by an English illustrated magazine, and had been following the campaign from its commencement almost two years earlier. Jaded, overweight and too fond of whisky, Ted Bovis initially studied the pictures with lack of enthusiasm. When Floria casually mentioned that the artist was the brother of the hero of Khartoum, the change in the man was dynamic. This was hot, this was an exclusive, he declared. There were photographs galore in every publication including his own, but artistic impressions of life with Kitchener's army made by the hand of Vorne Ashleigh's younger brother, who was on his way to avenge the dastardly murder, were vastly more appealing to readers with relatives suffering in the Sudan. With Floria's prompting, his offer reached a surprising sum plus an advance for more pictures along the same lines as the army got under way again. Vere would send these down on steamers.

They left the building with Bovis's money in Vere's pocket, and he took Floria to Cairo's most exclusive restaurant for a celebration lunch. During the meal, however, she was forced to comment on a strange abstraction in a man cherishing success.

'Have I offended you, Vere?' she asked, touching his hand across the table. 'Perhaps your work was too much a part of you to let it go. Some artists suffer wounds when separated from the canvas which reveals so much of their inner selves. Perhaps I was too clumsy in what I did . . . but I could not bear to think of them being dismissed by a family who condemns you for having such sensitivity.'

Once again he wished he had not allowed her to seduce him into speaking of why Vorne had always dominated life at Knightshill. After passion, a man was helpless in the face of sweet persuasion. He had been on many nights with her. Looking at her now, he understood those moments of honesty. In a dress of palest green chiffon with a large, deep cream shady hat, she was irresistibly beautiful.

'I think I am in danger of falling in love with you,' he said quietly.

'I know, my dear.' She smiled into his eyes. 'That is another great difference between you.'

'He was a fool.'

'No, Vere.' You are the one who is foolish to think of love where I am concerned. As Armand said, it is for only as long as the conflict lasts. There is a poignancy about relationships forged in times of danger. No one is as endearing as a uniformed hero about to go to war, or the lady he leaves behind thinking never to see again.'

Her words were almost exactly those of Colin Steadman on Vere's arrival in the Middle East. They reminded him of that perfect warrior transfixed by a spear on the sands of Atbara, staring slightlessly at the last morning he ever knew. It caught at his senses, bringing Vorne closer as he pictured that corpse but with the face in a portrait an entire family honoured each year. His brother had sat at a table with this woman; he had caressed her, entered her body in passion. Why was he following this particular path trodden by a merry, careless lover who would never be forgotten?

'Ross and I are travelling back on Thursday's steamer,' he said, signalling for the bill.

She leaned back to study him with softness in her splendid eyes. 'Is that a sudden decision?'

'I didn't mention it before because it might have overshadowed our enjoyment of this last week together. Everyone's returning from leave, and Ross is growing far too fond of Yasmin Fernol. He came to Cairo believing himself heartbroken, so was ripe for a new unattainable creature to dream about on the march. From what he says, just dreaming about Yasmin won't be enough for him, so the sooner I get him back to Atbara the better. As you said, there's none so endearing as the girl you leave behind.'

'So his broken heart has mended?'

He nodded.

'And yours?'

Putting a handful of notes on the silver tray left at his elbow, he rose to leave. 'The girl I first left behind was in love with a ghost . . . as you are, Floria. The sooner *I* get back to Atbara the better.'

She accepted his decision not to spend another night with her, although they dined together on the terrace of her villa in painfully romantic manner on his last evening in Cairo. Vere then experienced another emotion well known to military men, which he had never considered when deriding them from his static life at Knightshill. The shadow of what lay ahead hung over the evening to make each moment vibrant. In that starry darkness softly lit by candles, with Floria in a blush-pink boudoir gown, he came close to understanding why Vorne had never allowed himself to grow close to those who had loved him. Parting from Floria was going to be more difficult than he had considered.

With that in mind, he prepared to leave soon after the brandy which they drank with their coffee. The evening was too seductive, Floria too desirable. Taking a box from his pocket, he held it out to her. When she opened it, she gazed at the contents wordlessly.

'Those are *my* pearls,' he told her. 'You won't be approached for payment if I join him at Khartoum.'

Tears hung on her lashes when she finally looked up at him. 'Foolish boy! I have failed to silence that cry in your heart, after all.'

'Think of me whenever you choose to wear them.' He left quickly, making no attempt to touch her or look back from the doorway.

They arrived back at Atbara to find the camp vastly enlarged. During their absence, reinforcements had been arriving from England and moving up by rail and barge. There was the usual initial clash between the swaggering healthy troops fresh from home and those who had suffered the plagues of the country for months whilst fighting their way to the present position. Fights broke out, but many a fresh-faced braggart straight from his gentle homeland keeled over from heatstroke, dysentery, spider or scorpion stings, the ever-present Nile fever, or snakebite. Others suffered the misery of persistent boils, infected throats or coughs created by constant flying dust. There was also the insupportable heat. No man could escape that.

Vere once again found Atbara little short of hell. A violent attack of dysentery was followed by swollen glands in his throat, which made speaking painful and arduous. He cursed the inactivity in an overcrowded camp as August drew nearer. Not only was he growing as dispirited as everyone else, he could not stop thinking of Floria. He was certain no other man had stayed with her during his own leave. He would surely have known. Who would take his place now? Her past lovers did not trouble him: her future ones gave him no peace of mind. Yet he knew there was only one of whom he need feel jealous, and that man would stand between her and anyone who enjoyed her company in the days and years to come.

With Ross suffering similarly over his Yasmin, Vere escaped from his thoughts by the only means open to him. Finally persuading Reggie Forrester to pose for him – not in the nude, of course – he then gained no pleasure from drawing him. Forrester was delighted with the portrait, however, and claimed he would send it home to his wife and five children on the first available steamer. No longer excited by the man's god-like looks, Vere further punished himself by brooding on the fact that while Forrester could produce five – all boys, no doubt – he could not hold a woman's affection long enough to produce one child. This invariably led to brooding on the fate of Vorne's bastard son in Berber. How many more had his brother fathered? How many women, in all, were cherishing memories of his merry, unforgettable philandering?

Vere was only one of thousands in that huge force who greeted the news of an advance with heartfelt relief. The prospect of a fierce battle against the Khalifa's combined armies was infinitely more attractive than that of staying put. The general enthusiasm paled somewhat when regiments began to embark on twin-decked barges, only to discover that the vessels were taking double the number they were intended to hold in order to meet Kitchener's orders. Horses and troops were packed into every available foot of deck for the voyage to Wad Hamed, the tiny hamlet chosen for the final assembly of the army of retribution before it marched to claim Khartoum. As soon as each craft was jammed to capacity, the steamers which were each to tow four of them up the swollen river got underway. The Royal Navy captains and crews obeyed their orders with tight jaws for they knew the hazards ahead for any vessel, much less those lying well below the Plimsoll line on the end of a tow-rope.

Ross departed with Colonel Meers, Reggie Forrester and those men Vere still felt closer to than the officers of his own regiment. With the camp emptying fast – the cavalry had set out on hoof for Wad Hamed several days earlier – he made a determined effort to find a companion as likeable as Ross among his colleagues. As his friend was fond of saying, he might rely on them for his life soon. They all regarded him with greater respect since the battle, but there was not one who offered the rapport he felt with Ross. So Vere continued to wander moodily along the banks to watch the frenetic business of embarkation, feeling more and more restless with each passing day.

They were among the last to be called, which meant they had been regaled with horror stories of earlier voyages by the crews of the returning ships. Unsure whether or not this was another example of mariners' contempt for men who knew nothing of seafaring, the troops nevertheless believed tales of heat-maddened horses jumping overboard, of soldiers fainting or slipping on the vomit of their companions, and of barges being dashed to pieces on the rocks of the infamous sixth cataract. Sergeant Smithers came to Vere on the morning of their departure to say that the men were unhappy about what they had heard and hoped Mr Ashleigh would intercede to ensure that such disaster would not occur on their vessel due to overcrowding.

In the middle of shaving, Vere spoke disjointedly as he grimaced to tauten his skin. 'Sergeant, tell them they would have seen a steamer towing only *three* barges if one had really been dashed to pieces at the cataract. As for the fainting and vomiting, it's no more than the men have been doing here for the past few months. The one difference will be that we shall be making the final advance towards our objective. That's surely better than kicking their heels here.' He turned to grin at his sergeant. 'Tell them a voyage will do them good and put some colour in their cheeks. Besides, what we do know for certain is that Wad Hamed is very green and shady. A paradise compared with Atbara. I am quite prepared to suffer the worst our nautical friends can invent in order to reach it.'

'Very well, Mr Ashleigh,' said Smithers with a return grin. 'I'll tell them they may have every confidence in you.'

Even so, Vere had misgivings when they began to embark later that morning. The men were grim-faced as they marched aboard fully accoutred and sweating freely. With orders to take the entire detail for the day, with no exceptions, even the NCOs, used to bullying men into doing the impossible, were appalled when they spied another regiment arriving in readiness to board vessels already too low in the water. Leaving them to their muttered imprecations, Vere moved away to check the loading of his horses with those of other officers. They were restricted to two each. The remainder could be brought up to Wad Hamed once all the troops had been conveyed. The beasts did not take kindly to their cramped floating quarters, either, several showing temperament by kicking holes in the bulkhead the minute they boarded. Vere's animals were good, steady geldings that were strong rather than showy. They rolled their eyes in apprehension but were otherwise quite manageable.

The whole business created pandemonium: voices shouting in stentorian tones to the troops, sailors moving expertly about the vessels in a way which looked suicidal to those unused to these bobbing homes, horses screaming in fright, boots thudding on wooden decks, hooves clattering along gangways, winches squealing, smoke descending over all as steam built up, those aboard cupping hands around mouths to shout final messages to others who must wait for the vessels to return, and the inevitable, indomitable pedlars and urchins who had haunted the camp for the past few months. Finally, funnels belching black clouds, the steamer began to move out to midstream with its impossible burden in tow.

Allocated a tiny area on the upper deck of the vessel with nine other subalterns, Vere stood by the rail looking back at the bank as the band of water between them widened. He was leaving behind his first experience of battle, his awareness of a constitution as strong as those around him. He was leaving behind his painful lesson in learning that companions would not accept him as a pseudo-hero. He was leaving behind a beautiful older woman who knew more about himself than he did. He was also leaving behind a boy who, by right of birth, had greater claim to Knightshill than he. He turned away from the dejected figures on the bank with a sigh. Ahead lay Khartoum . . . and the final confrontation with someone who still dominated others despite a lonely, agonising death in the desert.

Not all the horror stories had been invented. Some men did collapse from the heat and overcrowding; there was a very tense period when one of the barges seemed in danger of breaking away. Vere sympathised with the naval crewmen trying to perform a complex job while hampered by lack of space which restricted movement considerably. Arguments broke out between soldiers and sailors. It was inevitable under such conditions. They were all feeling the strain. Every so often they would see one of the cavalry regiments plodding wearily onward, their plight beneath the merciless sun seeming little better than their own. They exchanged waves of commiseration as well as offers to change places for a while.

Then they were nearing Metemma, where the Relief Force had halted to prepare for the march into beleaguered Khartoum, but where they had instead received news of its fall and subsequent sacking. A few of the officers aboard Vere's steamer had been with the earlier force; some were relatives of those who had. When they reached the river station these men were permitted a short visit of homage ashore. A captain named Gough Philips, who had been there in 1885, offered to show Vere the grave of his famous brother.

'I didn't actually see the body brought in by the Sudanese scouts, but we all attended the funeral, Ashleigh. The West Wilts put up a decent headstone – as decent as they could under the circumstances. We had to leave in something of a hurry,' he concluded, with lingering bitterness over that hurried withdrawal.

His offer forced the issue. Vere had considered staying aboard, due to an incomprehensible reluctance to visit the spot where the remains of his enigmatic brother lay. He had come to the Sudan on a wave of false pride, never considering that he would survive to reach this place. Family duty demanded that he make this pilgrimage, yet personal apprehension at the prospect of treading the sands above the bones of a man who had influenced his life so dramatically warned him of danger.

He went ashore with the small group, still suffering from that sensation. Colin Steadman had suggested in Cairo that it must be an emotive moment to step ashore where his brother had trodden. Absorbed in his own misery on that occasion, Vere had felt nothing. Today was different. This place was more emotive than any he had yet visited. He felt it in his bones and in all his senses, especially his sixth. Indeed, the sensation of dread was so strong he would have turned back if he had been alone.

They walked from the jetty following directions from those who recalled the place from '85, but their steps slowed as they grew aware of an overwhelming stench and a sound which, although unrecognisable, was deeply unnerving. On turning a corner, they received the first hint of what was to come. The narrow way led through ruins stained dark with ancient blood, but the blood was more recent on several bodies lying there.

'Good God,' said Philips slowly, 'they're not part of the carnage left by the Mahdi's men. It could only have happened a few weeks ago.'

They moved on, still disturbed by the noise which was getting louder as they progressed. Vere felt the hair start to rise on the back of his neck, and the desire to return to the steamer redoubled. More corpses lay in the tiny streets between empty stone buildings. If anyone was alive in Metemma he must surely be in hiding. Then they came across bodies in greater numbers, interspersed with ancient skulls and bones from which the flesh had long ago been picked by scavengers. A sense of foreboding touched them all at that point. A very young subaltern, whose father had died here of fever during the abortive mission, suggested that it might be better to leave well alone. Yet there was a fearful fascination about the place which led the others to ignore him.

Around the next corner the alley widened into a square. There, they pulled up suddenly and unanimously as they discovered the source of that awesome noise. It was now almost deafening. Millions of flies buzzed above and amid the human debris of wholesale slaughter. The stench was

271

such that they had to press handkerchiefs over their mouths as they stared in shock at the skeletons of the first poor wretches murdered by the Mahdi's troops, mingling with the sun-stiffened corpses of those who must have been cut down by the army defeated and driven back at Atbara in April. Innocent people slain out of pique, for control of a ruined city named Khartoum.

Philips touched Vere's elbow, taking his horrified gaze from a scene he would never forget. 'Ashleigh's grave is over there,' he mumbled through his handkerchief. 'There are four altogether. The others died of fever. Let's make it quick and get out of this hell-hole.'

Similarly gagged against the sickening stench, Vere followed him while the rest turned back. Picking their way through the ghastly carpet, sending up clouds of black flies with every step, they headed towards a corner shaded by palms. The cold sensation at the back of Vere's neck intensified to spread down his spine as their approach disturbed a nest of snakes, which slithered into hiding in the coarse grass surrounding the roots of the trees. He could see nothing which resembled the description the family had been given of the grave by men of the West Wilts, who had buried their hero before departing ahead of the blood-crazed Mahdists. There were no crosses or mounds of earth marking burial places. Philips must have mistaken the spot, for this was an area of stony desolation.

His companion pulled up, lowering the handkerchief to reveal his expression as he breathed emotionally, 'My God, they must have dug the poor devils up again as soon as we left!'

Iciness gradually invaded Vere's veins as he realised the larger stones lying there were the remnants of shattered monuments reverently erected by a departing army. The smaller ones were not stones at all, but the bleached fragments of human skeletons. For thirteen and a half years a family had believed in this hero's grave, had taken comfort in the knowledge of its existence. But Vorne Ashleigh had no such resting place; his body had been further mutilated after death and left to moulder in the sands by his enemies.

Philips turned away without another word, and began the hideous walk back to the river bank. Vere fell in beside him, but he saw nothing of the carnage at his feet. His eyes were blinded by hot tears.

Chapter Fifteen

Wad Hamed was as attractive as reports had indicated. The Nile was broad and comparatively smooth there, with verdant islands scattered between its banks. These, together with the grove of palms along the stretch chosen for the encampment, gave the tiny hamlet the appearance of being set in a different land from the one the weary troops had known for too long. Morale rose immediately. The poisonous creatures of Atbara were not in Wad Hamed; the eternal empty sands had been replaced by a pleasant river scene reminiscent of home.

A holiday feeling touched the vast army settling for a few days' rest while final plans were drawn up by Kitchener and his staff officers. Aiding them was an Austrian known as Slatin Pasha, who had been a prisoner first of the Mahdi, then the Khalifa for many years. He had escaped from the prison in Omdurman, leaving behind other Europeans shackled and ill-fed, never sure whether each day would be their last. Slatin had written an account of his experiences, and of the Khalifa's cruelties to his own people in his bid to become a second Mahdi, and it had been this volume published in Britain which had greatly contributed to the decision to send out a force to bring the Sudan and its people under Anglo-Egyptian control. Slatin was eager to push on, eager for vengeance against his former captor, eager to free those who possibly remained his prisoners even after fourteen years. Kitchener shared his fervour, but added military caution when laying his plans. Another few days of captivity would not matter to those who had endured years of it.

The final march to Omdurman, where the Khalifa's army was known to await them on the great plain before the city, would be made in battle order. Tents would have to be left behind, along with all creature comforts. Rations would be basic; beds would be the desert floor. Both men and officers luxuriated in the pleasant environs of Wad Hamed while they could, and tried to think more about losing their tents than their lives in the days ahead.

Vere was still haunted by what he had seen at Metemma, which overrode any other feelings on reaching this tiny settlement over a thousand miles from Cairo. From Metemma to Wad Hamed he had been uncommunicative and abstracted. Guessing the cause, his companions had respected his solitude. Even during the dramatic shooting of the sixth cataract, when swirling white-crested brown water had raced their flotilla in crazy fashion through the rocky section known to have claimed the lives of many who tried to navigate it, Vere had been untouched by the sense of danger. It was now clear why he had survived fever, the sudden excessive intake of alcohol, the killing heat and the poisonous creatures of the desert. He understood why he had managed to travel from Abu Hamed to Berber across sands frequented by enemy marauders, without being attacked. What he had seen at Metemma told him he would find the answer to why a man slain at only twenty-four could so dominate the lives of all those he had touched along his carefree path to death. He would find it when he reached Khartoum. Fate decreed that he should. The coming battle would therefore not claim him as a victim . . . at least, not until he had visited the ruins of that fabled city.

Shunning even Ross's company, Vere walked for hours along the riverbank during the cooler periods of the days. His constant companion was a spectral young man in a scarlet jacket, who had once taken him aside and instructed him to grow stronger because he was the next in line. After three days, that vision became so dominant it began to merge with his own ego in the most disturbing fashion. Recollections he had successfully subdued returned to plague him. The woman constantly in his thoughts now was Annabel Bourneville. The face he had thought forgotten was again clear to him in every detail of its pure perfection; the words which had wounded him so deeply cut into him once more and he knew a return of the misery which had driven him to this place.

He took to riding several miles from the huge spread of tents to a high place overlooking the desolation stretching towards Khartoum, and staring across the lone and level sands in silent contemplation. He could envisage the three robed horsemen, and the sudden attack of two upon a helpless third. He saw the sun glinting on blades which entered the felled body time and again before the treacherous pair rode off. Then the familiar iciness invaded him as he watched the bloody figure discard his alien robes to reveal the uniform beneath, before starting out on his agonising bid to deliver the vital communiqué still strapped to his body.

Vere returned to his tent each time as drained and exhausted as he used to be after bouts of fever. Other words he had put behind him then rang in his ears with dreadful clarity: words his grandfather had used when disparaging his failure to perform the one duty to his family open to a weakling. He tossed and turned on his bed while struggling with the roaming spirit which was slowly subduing his own in an attempt to enter this Ashleigh body. For several days Vere experienced the bizarre sensation of being commanded by impulses foreign to him. When the entire force of twenty-six thousand troops formed up in the desert for final inspection by General Kitchener, the officer who stood to attention and snapped a smart salute at the man known as the Sirdar hardly resembled the graceful Pre-Raphaelite with a sword who found no affinity with things military.

The inspection was the prelude to the final offensive. Early on the morning of 24 August, the tents stretching several miles along the riverbank were vacated in sections as the Anglo-Egyptian army went forward to meet the Dervishes reputed to be awaiting them with eagerness and the assurance of victory against the infidel. If the Khalifa's men were truly on the plain before Omdurman, as spies had indicated, there were sixty miles to cover before the enemies would come face to face. The distance was not daunting to men used by now to marching in the Sudanese heat, but Vere Ashleigh had not been sent this time on a useless mission to get rid of him, so details of the terrain were unrecorded. High spirits soon plunged when the flat ground gave way to undulating ridges culminating in heights impossible to scale. It was necessary to make a long detour, exceedingly arduous for infantry laden with full packs, rifles and ammunition in temperatures well over a hundred in the shade.

Whether riding or leading his horse over the steepest shale-covered slopes, Vere never flagged. Men of his platoon were dropping with sunstroke or sheer exhaustion; others, who had ignored the rule of taking water in small amounts and had emptied their bottles before the march was half completed, suffered the torment of thirst and swollen tongues. Riding back and forth along the ranks to give encouragement to those who were flagging, Vere had the sensation of being under an irresistible influence. His voice sounded more clipped, louder than usual. His energy seemed boundless.

They bivouacked beneath the stars, but few save the outlying cavalry piquets saw them. The bulk of the force fell asleep as soon as supper had been eaten. Vere lay for a long time on his folded cloak, his hands behind his head, gazing at the vast, compelling sky. Vorne had lain like this. His bright blue eyes had seen this magnificent star-scattered darkness; his restless spirit had known the quietness of a desert night which would surely humble the greatest of men. Had his thoughts been of a woman? Had he dwelt in recollections of his family and the beautiful grey stone house he would inherit on Sir Gilliard's death? Had he contemplated military glory and fame to come? Had he sensed coming brutal death out here where one man's life was insignificant?

One day nearer to Khartoum. A week might yet pass before Vere trod the dust of a place whose name was one of his first conscious recollections of childhood. He had known of this main city of the Sudan before learning the name of England's capital, and it had been inextricably bound to every year of his life since then. Khartoum! The very sound of it was daunting when spoken by men in red coats at Knightshill. It rhymed with *doom*. The tone of their voices echoed the fact. Lying beneath the sky less than fifty miles from that ruined place, Vere knew in his heart he had been following a predestined path. When he reached Khartoum he would either surrender to Vorne Ashleigh, or walk away from his influence for ever.

For four more days Kitchener led his army forward without a sign of the enemy. Villages were deserted and mostly in ruins. The troops began to grow uneasy, and believed the gods were against them when it actually *rained*. It was not the short, sharp shower known to occur at times in the Sudan, but a deluge which continued for half the night. With no protection against this unforeseen enemy, the troops had no choice but to endure it until the morning sun came to dry their saturated uniforms on their chilled, cramped bodies.

On 1 September things at last began to happen. The gun-boats, which had advanced along the Nile, came in sight of the city of Omdurman where the great white dome of the Mahdi's tomb stood out against the skyline. The Royal Navy began a bombardment of the Khalifa's capital, with the tomb as the prime target. To destroy this symbol of a fanatic who had begun the rape of the Sudan would demoralise the Dervishes. It certainly spurred them into action. Enemy riders were seen reconnoitring on all sectors of the chosen battlefield. Small engagements between cavalry patrols or advance guards and these roaming groups took place but they were merely preliminary skirmishes to size up the cut of the enemy. No one doubted the next day's sun would shine on a million flashing blades, and every British soldier on the field would heed the command *Remember Gordon!* as he faced the dark multitude.

Vere was awoken by Private French at 3 a.m. The batman had everything ready for a shave and quick wash, as well as a cup of tea and two biscuits. He was a good man. Vere told him so, adding that he appreciated his loyalty throughout the last trying months leading up to this moment.

French frowned. 'You don't need to make no such speech, Mr Ashleigh. You'll come through all right.'

'They weren't the words of a doomed man,' he responded lightly. 'Merely a grateful one. I know I'll survive, French.'

After a brief silence while Vere continued to shave, French ventured a personal comment. 'It may not be my place to say so, sir, but you've changed from the gentleman you was at Atbara. Anyone would think you was an old campaigner with a dozen battles behind you.'

'Yes.'

That affirmative appeared to confound the other man. After an audible sigh, he said, 'Well, the best of luck, sir. I hope as how you gets at least a dozen of them fuzzy-wuzzies for your brother.'

The razor stilled momentarily. 'Thank you, French. I'll do my best.'

The wind was still cold as Vere and Sergeant Smithers made their way to where the regiment was taking up its allocated position behind the deep *zariba* of thorn bushes. With dawn still to come it was only faintly possible to see the great darker block of men assembling in a massive front of infantry, supported by artillery and mounted troops on the flanks and in the centre. This battle would be the reverse of the one at Atbara, for Kitchener planned to wait for the Dervishes to come to him instead. No one knew what would happen if they failed to comply with this plan. Would they sit behind this protective barrier all day in the searing sun staring at an empty skyline? Hearing this theme murmured by many as he wandered back and forth behind his men, Vere thought suddenly of Val. *'I want to ride out and challenge the enemy, not wait for them to come to me.'* The boy was probably right. This approach to battle was unnerving.

Dawn provided another spectacular display. The eternity of sky gradually turned a fiery yellow as the blinding disc rose above the horizon, showing Vere the impressive assembly surrounding him. Twenty-six thousand armed men. Behind this forward line were the reserves ready to fill the gaps left by dead and wounded. Away to his left was a regiment of Lancers in neat mounted ranks. He thought once more of the young hothead who had lost his chance to become one of their officers, and sudden gladness swept through him. He would not want his schoolboy brother to be facing what he was presently facing. There would be no guarantee of Val's survival as there was of his own. One handsome, merry Ashleigh hacked to death out here was enough.

Full daylight arrived. Still they waited, gazing out across the undulating plain with eyes that ached. Then they grew aware of a sound rather than a vision. It was the ferocious war-chant of warriors who refused mercy to their enemies. It froze the blood of those men who could not yet see them, or estimate their numbers. There could be as many as several millions. As the minutes passed and that awesome sound grew in magnitude, many a waiting soldier licked his lips nervously and gripped the rifle so tightly his knuckles turned white. What use was a gun against a tide of glittering, murderous blades?

All at once, that demoralising, echoing cry took shape as a distant mass of white-robed men cheering themselves on with the sound designed to strike fear in any adversary.

'They're coming then, sir,' murmured Sergeant Smithers studying the horizon.

'Yes, they're coming,' agreed Vere, aghast at the onward flow which appeared to have no end. 'Is the platoon all set?'

'All set, and full of confidence. They'll back you to a man, sir, and be proud to do so.'

Vere glanced at the NCO thoughtfully. 'Because my name is Ashleigh?'

'Because they know a good officer when they come across one. And that goes for me too, sir.'

Vere turned back to the enemy approaching, confident that their lord was on their side. Good officers were a secondary consideration for *them*.

As the Dervish force advanced, the sound of their drums and horns could be heard accompanying their vocal threats. A swift glance along the ranks showed Vere that the deafening approach was taking effect on those forced to wait and go on waiting. Were they all lambs for the slaughter?

'My God, sir, they're coming all the way in a frontal assault,' Smithers exclaimed, staring in disbelief at the horde which was no more than a mile off by now. 'They should be splitting up for a three-pronged attack, by all rules in the book. Unless they've a million more in reserve, we'll make mincemeat of them when they come within range.'

Vere glanced quickly to where Alex Johnson, the company commander, was watching through field glasses in the manner of a man who did not credit what he saw. His counterpart in charge of the adjacent platoon caught Vere's eye and signalled his excitement at this suicidal move by the Khalifa. It was known through spies, and through their experience at Atbara, that the Dervishes had ineffective guns and ancient rifles. Courage and unshakeable belief in the Prophet was not enough to combat what these men of Omdurman were racing towards with hysterical fervour. Evan a man as inexperienced as Vere could see what must happen before long. He felt sick at the thought.

The Dervish cry so filled the air across the plain it seemed no other sound would ever be heard. The thunder of their stamping feet shook the earth like a subterranean tremor. It could have been another man's voice, when Vere heard himself give the command to present arms as Alex Johnson sent the signal. From then on, he hardly knew what he did as the white tide flowed nearer and nearer like a great, low, racing cloud which darkened the earth beneath it. Vere's throat felt raw; his brow was beaded with perspiration. He knew fear, despite that inner knowledge which guaranteed his life until he had set foot in Khartoum. Perhaps it was instead fear of man's immense depths of inhumanity when driven by the force of evil.

His nerves jumped when the ear-splitting roar of their own artillery suddenly deadened the sound of the war-chant. Next minute, he was shouting the orders which regulated fusillades of rifle-fire from those under

278

his command, and the morning turned into the hell he had known at Atbara. As then, he was possessed by motivation other than his own. He continued to shout orders while his horrified gaze watched the Dervish ranks blown apart as each succeeded the other, only to join the growing bloody pile several hundred feet from the *zariba*. Smoke billowed across that gap, but bullets still found their mark and yet more fell. There was the acrid smell of cordite; the air was filled with the screams of men and horses, the whine of shells, the staccato rattle of rifles, the hoarse command '*Fire!*'

Running back and forth to encourage his men, signal stretcher-bearers for his wounded, and exchange brief words with Alex Johnson, Vere found his Ashleigh blood stirring as it had at Atbara. Depression was certain to follow in the appalling aftermath of today, but there was an undeniable savage excitement inspired by the symphony of war. It was that which dulled his awareness of what had happened when he felt a burning sensation just below his left ear. Almost immediately, there was a thud against his pith-helmet and another on the revolver case at his hip. Only then did he realise that he had become the target of a Dervish who had miraculously survived the volley of death which greeted each rank. The man in a blood-stained robe was valiantly coming on for as long as he could remain upright. That robe, and the display of immense courage in the face of agony lit a fire in Vere which he had never expected to burn. Raising his revolver, he took aim and fired. The man dropped to the ground, rolled a short distance, then lay still.

'In the name of my grandfather, your life for Vorne Ashleigh's,' Vere murmured unsteadily, staring at the stranger on the sands which had once covered a hero. In that moment, Vere had realised what Sir Gilliard had wanted from him all along. His debt to the old warhorse was now settled.

'Mr Ashleigh, you've been hit,' said a voice beside him.

He turned to see a lad wearing an armband bearing a cross. 'Eh?'

'You're bleeding heavily, sir. Better get a dressing on your neck.'

Putting up his hand, Vere encountered the warm stickiness of blood. The left shoulder of his jacket was covered with it. He then grew aware of a warm trickle running down inside the high collar. He smiled at the medical orderly.

'An inch to the right and I'd have been dead, wouldn't I?'

'Yessir.'

'The devil looks after his own.'

'Better let the MO look after you now,' advised the wary boy, who was used to officers showing unconcern for their wounds.

'Perhaps I should,' he murmured.

The doctor in command of the nearest casualty station was the same who had watched him struggle against fever and survive at Atbara. His first words to Vere were, 'The devil looks after his own.'

'That's what I told the lad just now,' laughed Vere. 'Are you claiming the honour?'

'Sir down, you young fool,' the man growled. 'The third time you might not be so lucky.'

By the time the wound had been cleaned and dressed, the battle was virtually over. Vere's third brush with death would not come today. Twenty-three months had passed since the start of the campaign to regain Khartoum and avenge Gordon. No more than a few hours had been needed to defeat the Khalifa's army and put it to flight.

The battle aftermath at Atbara was as nothing when compared with that on the plain before Omdurman when the guns stopped firing. A few dozen casualties in Kitchener's army were in the field hospitals behind the *zariba*. Many thousands lay dead or wounded beneath the blistering sun, all Dervishes. It was impossible to tend the enemy wounded. The corpses not only lay in great piles impossible to move, the few humane attempts to seek those left alive had been met with bullets from men who preferred to die with honour. Although several thousand prisoners had been taken and as many had fled for their lives, the victors all agreed that the Dervishes had lost the day through inferior weapons and lack of skilled command. Their courage had been breathtaking. With modern guns and good officers they might well have turned Omdurman into one of the greatest battles of all time.

Elsewhere in the region, fighting continued between bands of resistant Dervish horsemen and outlying contingents of the Anglo-Egyptian army. These were not as one-sided as the main conflict had been. Stories began to filter back to the victorious infantry that their comrades were encountering stronger opposition, giving them the chance to make their mark in this curious extended war. The gun-boats were also doing sterling work against the fleeing enemy being hotly pursued by the cavalry. Those who had seen the morning's fighting began to feel they had missed out on the real essence of the bid to take Omdurman. This was strengthened on hearing that the 21st Lancers – a regiment keen to gain its first battle honours – had captured the most gilded laurels of the day with a full-blooded charge. This had turned into near-disaster when, a hundred yards from the several hundred visible fuzzy-wuzzies, they realised several thousand more were crouched in a deep gully invisible from a distance. Unable and unwilling to halt, they had plunged into the mass of men and rifles, losing a great many troopers and officers before scrambling up the far side to re-form. The enemy had retreated in the face of this threat to charge again from the opposite direction, and the 21st had gained their coveted battle honour with several regimental heroes to laud.

The cavalry and the Camel Corps were still under orders to round up any remaining Dervishes in a large area around the capital and, in particular, to ensure that the Khalifa did not get away. The remainder of Kitchener's army was fed and refreshed before advancing on the distant city, where the enemy leader was believed to be praying for guidance at the Mahdi's tomb. Until the Khalifa was Kitchener's prisoner the reign of terror in the Sudan would not be over.

Vere's regiment was well to the rear of the general advance on the walled city, much to the disgruntlement of his men. If Omdurman itself was fortified there was little evidence of it. Spasmodic firing could be heard when the leading Sudanese regiments disappeared within it, but that soon ceased. With the bands of various regiments rendering favourite march tunes, rank after rank flowed into the Khalifa's capital to see the wonders it contained. There were none. Omdurman was like all other settlements along the Sudanese Nile, only larger. Cramped hovels, narrow, stinking alleyways, deprived, lacklustre people.

A mile or two of this scene beneath the dying heat of late afternoon was as much as most troops wanted of this disappointing city, but a great thick wall reared up at that point in their advance, signifying that the inner stronghold had now been reached. Were there temples inlaid with gold behind the walls? Was the glory they had hoped to see amassed beyond this massive stone barrier? Did the Khalifa await them within, surrounded by a picked army? Sharp exchanges of gunfire suggested that the last was true. Rumours circulated that the Sudanese were engaged in battle with the last defenders. Then all firing ceased. A message was passed to say the remaining enemies had now surrendered because the Khalifa had left the city in disguise thirty minutes earlier. Without their leader's inspiration resistance had crumbled.

'That's a real nasty bit of news, sir,' Sergeant Smithers commented to Vere, as they stood around aimlessly in one of the narrow alleys outside the inner wall. 'The lads'll be right downhearted when they hear it.'

'The cavalry are certain to catch him,' said Vere dully. In truth, he was feeling giddy and rather sick. He had been on his feet for more than twelve hours, three of them actually fighting the Dervish onslaught, and the last few marching up from the plain. He had lost a great deal of blood from the deep gash which was now giving him more pain than it had at the start. In addition, the stench within these cramped lanes reminded him too strongly of what he had seen at Metemma. Right now he did not give a damn where the Kahlifa was and he would give his kingdom for a bath and a bed with clean, scented sheets.

'Are you all right, sir?' asked Smithers in concern.

Vere forced a faint smile. 'Compared with those poor devils out on the plain whose screams we can hear too clearly, I'm absolutely fine, Sergeant.'

Day deteriorated into fitful night without any significant development save the news that cavalry had been sent in search of the Khalifa, with Slatin Pasha driving them on in his desire to get his hands on his former cruel captor. When orders were issued for troops to bivouac in the western sector of the city, the lingering remnants of elation vanished. The open desert provided a better bed than the vile, stinking streets of Omdurman, where the sullen populace could not be trusted enough to enable anyone to sleep peacefully. But orders were orders, and the officers complied with them.

After seeing his men appropriately settled, Vere went with the other officers to seek a more salubrious resting place beyond the wall of the inner citadel. Darkness hid any splendours it might have contained, but reliable reports claimed there were none save the Mahdi's shattered tomb and the Khalifa's tawdry palace. Almost dropping with fatigue, Vere settled on his blanket in a larger than usual house which Colonel Winterton had proclaimed his regimental Officers' Mess. Something which Vere Ashleigh of Knightshill days would have considered ludicrous was now easily acceptable as he ate potted meat from the jar and dry biscuit, which he washed down with lukewarm brackish water. One of the officers had a bottle of wine – God knew from where – but it was proclaimed quite foul and abandoned. Drawing up his cloak, Vere settled for sleep on the dried mud floor. Flickering light from several lamps was almost hypnotic as he lay half listening to the conversation around him.

'They found the prisoners who had been incarcerated for years. Kitchener greeted Charles Neufeld personally, I hear.'

'Who's Neufeld?'

'The former German attaché to Khartoum. The poor devil was in chains and weighted with a great iron bar and cannon balls.'

'Slatin Pasha was similarly treated. Did you read his account?'

'Never read books, old chap. Stimulates the mind too much.'

'Our Austrian friend has always been slightly mad, in my opinion.'

'Wouldn't you be mad, Douglas, if you'd been chained up here since before Khartoum fell?'

'I heard a rumour there's at least one woman among the captives.'

'She was fortunate not to have been treated in the usual manner.'

'She's a nun.'

'That's never stopped men from doing what they habitually do to female prisoners.'

The low voices continued as Vere gradually slipped into the sleep of painful exhaustion, only to be plagued by hideous dreams of all he had witnessed that day. He was awoken by a hand on his shoulder and an urgent voice in his ear. In the pale light of dawn Ross was crouching beside him. Vere closed his eyes again.

'Go away and leave me in my peaceful purgatory.'

'You've already heard the astonishing news, then?'

'What astonishing news?' he enquired, squinting up through one eye.

'You haven't,' concluded Ross. 'Roberto Pallini is one of the prisoners discovered here last night.'

Vere struggled painfully into a sitting position to study his friend's face at close quarters. *'Floria's husband?'*

'He's been ill recently and broke down completely when our staff officers appeared. Neufeld said only that he was an Italian explorer, but the man himself seemed totally unable to understand what was happening. After fourteen years in chains, under the constant threat of death, it's hardly surprising.'

'Why should they imagine the man is Pallini?'

'He's just recovered enough to tell them how he was taken prisoner by one of the Mahdi's chieftains, and thrown in the jail. He's been there ever since. Just imagine it, Vere.'

Vere could imagine nothing but Floria's future. 'Are you certain it isn't one of the wild rumours which circulate at times like this?'

Ross sat back on his heels. 'James Ellison told me the news. He's one of the staff officers responsible for doing what they can for the poor devils . . . and he knows Floria quite as well as you do,' he added significantly. 'It's true, believe me.'

'Well, thank you for telling me,' Vere said heavily.

'How's that wound in your neck?'

'Not nearly so painful as the news you brought.'

'You were certain to hear it before the day is out.' He made a rueful face. 'There'll be others feeling the way you do.'

When Ross departed, and French brought shaving water and a cup of tea, Vere smartened himself up along with his fellows. Most chatted to each other, but he was silent. Ross was right. There would be others in this British contingent facing the daunting truth that, while a man had been suffering pain and humiliation in captivity, they had been making free with his wife in Cairo. It did not help that he had been believed long dead. Pallini was here among them, bearing his scars, and Floria's many lovers would have to come to terms with their sense of guilt in various ways. Vere Ashleigh, who had allowed himself to love her, bore the culpability of two men – one of whom would posthumously possess Floria for the rest of her days.

Colonel Winterton outlined the orders for the day, which promised to be an arduous one. Their own dead must be decently buried. The wounded were to be taken aboard steamers fitted out as hospital craft. The enemy dead and wounded were piled so deep out on the plain they must be left there in the greater demands of rounding up those still at large, in securing the city and bringing up the commissariat supplies left behind in the advance. After detailing their sergeants to put the men to clearing several compounds of the carcasses of animals slaughtered when the city seemed certain to fall, many regimental officers went off to hunt for souvenirs which would be displayed in country mansions all over England.

Vere did not join his fellows. Knightshill had more than enough tokens of victory, and he had no heart for the treasure hunt. Kitchener had ordered the Mahdi's tomb to be blown up, the remains within it to be thrown into the Nile. Scandalous though some thought the order, none could deny the demoralising effect of such action on those who believed he would return from paradise to lead them again. With that area sealed off, and the rest of the city a blend of corpses, sewage and other filth being cleared by the long-suffering troops, Vere soon surrendered to the impulse which had plagued him since Ross's visit. The erstwhile captives were to be taken aboard one of the steamers as soon as the wounded had been loaded on to the hospital vessels. They had been fed and made as comfortable as possible while their shackles were struck off by the farrier. It would be rubbing salt in the wound, but Vere had to see the man who would return to Cairo to find his 'widow' was a courtesan of the highest order.

He found the group in a shady area near the river, and the sight of them halted him. Emaciated and burned almost black by the sun, it was only possible to recognise the woman among them by the absence of the long grey beard worn by the rest. To an artist it was a scene of overwhelming poignancy, which he was driven to capture on paper. Sitting some yards from them, his pencil moved in deft strokes as he concentrated on the moving contrast between these silent, bemused people and the lively, voluble men aboard the boats alongside the banks. Since Metemma, his sketches had been a collection of haunted impressions of the desert. This would start a new series featuring Omdurman and, of course, the ruins of Khartoum.

Engrossed in what he was doing, Vere temporarily forgot why he was there. He recalled it when a loud blast from one of the steamers about to move off made him jump nervously. Realising that he might lose his chance if the captives were taken aboard quickly, he got to his feet, pocketing the pad and crayons he had carried everywhere since signing the contract with Ted Bovis in Cairo. He approached the seated group diffidently, wondering how best to discover which was Roberto Pallini without then being obliged to speak to a man who had last seen Floria sixteen years ago. It was too late to turn back. One greybeard had risen and made to approach.

'Is it time, sir?' asked a frail cracked voice. 'Are we to board now?'

Humbled by this man who had endured so much, Vere shook his head. 'I am not in charge of embarkation, sir. Have you been waiting long?'

'Thirteen years.' He sank back into a resigned squat, losing all interest in someone unable to help him.

Vere then knew he could not question these poor souls on the identity of a man he had merely hoped to view from afar, so he walked resolutely past the group of around twenty people and stopped to talk to the medical officer who had claimed the devil looked after his own.

'You look decidedly sickly, young Ashleigh,' the doctor proclaimed in his forthright manner. 'What are you doing walking around in this damned heat when I gave you orders to rest whenever you could?'

'You look rather sickly yourself,' Vere responded, gazing beyond to the crammed decks of a vessel with a red cross painted on the side. 'That looks even more overladen than when we came up.'

The man grimaced. 'These passengers are all lying down, so they're being piled on top of each other. Get more on that way.' He sighed. 'I've never seen anything like this in my entire career . . . and it'll take the rest of my life to forget how I left that carnage on the plain without doing anything to help ease the pain of those dying for want of attention.'

'My grandfather said much the same about the Crimea,' said Vere. 'He's eighty-eight and still remembers the suffering all around him. Soldiering doesn't change much, it seems.'

'But you have, young man. In Abu Hamed I treated a fever patient who was a total military misfit. Yesterday I patched up a man who had found what he was seeking, and had stopped acting a part. You've proved us all wrong, but I suspect you're even more surprised than we are.'

He gave a faint smile. 'Perhaps.'

'Goodbye, Ashleigh. I shall be accompanying the serious cases to England.' They shook hands, ignoring rank. 'I hear Kitchener is planning a memorial service in Khartoum tomorrow. I hope you'll finally lay the ghost you've been chasing when you set foot in the ruined city.'

He turned to board another vessel ready to cast off, leaving Vere unsettled by that last remark. Would Vorne Ashleigh's ghost ever be laid?

It was hot in the full sunlight, so he took off his pith-helmet to mop his brow as he turned to retrace his steps. He walked letting the slight breeze lift his damp hair, but he had not progressed far when a faint cry drew his attention back to the cluster of former captives beneath the trees. One man was struggling to his feet as he stared at Vere with curious intensity; then he stumbled toward him with arms outstretched, moving in the manner of someone who has not done so for a long time. Halted by compassion, Vere was further disturbed to see the wrinkled features working with emotion and the dark eyes shining with tears. Another who mistook him for the Embarkation Officer.

But there was some other reason for his approach. He seized Vere's hands in a fierce bony clasp, and gazed into a face he appeared to recognise. Immensely moved, Vere tried to calm the trembling which prevented the man from speaking.

'Is there some service I can perform for you?' he asked quietly.

Continuing to grip his hands with astonishing force, a cracked voice whispered with great urgency, *'Does he have it?'*

'Who, sir?'

'Does he have it? Is it safe?'

Vere attempted to disengage himself, but the old fellow seemed desperate for an answer and clung to him, crying, 'You have come to tell me it is safe?'

'Please, don't distress yourself,' Vere begged. 'You have mistaken me for someone else. We all look alike in khaki.'

'There, there, good sir, come back with me and rest in the shade,' said a deep soothing voice in French. 'All is well. Yes, all is well.'

Another of the captives had approached. He laid his arm around the old man's shoulders to turn him away and lead his faltering steps back to the group he had left. Vere watched with wonder the one comfort the other, for the second man was as weak and emaciated as the first. In such situations there were always those who remained spiritually strong despite physical wasting. Could the second be one of the missionaries known to be among these poor victims? To Vere's surprise, the man returned with an explanation. That surprise grew when he saw that the man's blue eyes were vitally alive in a body sadly decimated by brutal treatment.

'The poor fellow did not do well in captivity, sir. You must excuse him.'

It touched Vere deeply to hear this supreme understatement from a man whose courage must be equal to that of any soldier here. 'Who is he? What is it that bothers him so greatly?' he asked in the other's chosen language.

'We cannot be certain, of course, but he claims to be an Egyptian who served in a minor capacity under General Gordon during the siege of Khartoum. He is certainly Egyptian, and says he owes his survival of the Mahdist massacre to hiding in a cellar. How long he remained in hiding we do not know, but the sight which greeted him on emerging apparently so shocked him he was regarded as mad by those who eventually discovered him. Instead of killing him they brought him here for their own sport. I regret, sir, he was cruelly baited by our captors throughout and has now genuinely lost his reason.'

'You mean he *wasn't* mad in the beginning?'

The grey head shook. 'Sister Grigolini nursed him until the shock of what he had seen in Khartoum receded. Then he had to play the fool in order to escape the prison gallows. Almost daily hangings of the Khalifa's more unfortunate followers forced him to maintain the deception for almost fourteen years.' The blue eyes narrowed slightly. 'We are not certain when pretence moved into reality, poor fellow.'

Vere looked beyond his companion to where the Egyptian still watched him with a wild gaze. 'A tragic story!' Meeting the blue eyes once more, he added, 'He is one of few men who could tell exactly what happened in Khartoum on that January day, yet he cannot.'

'Those of us who have lived with these people can guess at the Devil's work performed there. We need no eye-witness to confirm it.'

Vere nodded. 'Who are you, sir?'

'Father Brunn. A man of God sent to teach His word.'

'And you have seen failure,' he said in gentle sympathy.

'Not at all. I shall take only a short rest before returning to show the way to these poor wretches left with no one to guide their steps. Now evil has been driven away the Lord can enter in with joy.'

Vere smiled. 'My sister's husband has begun mission work, but I have to say he needs some small fraction of your experience to make him a little less of a holy firebrand.'

Father Brunn smiled back. 'We are all holy firebrands at the start, sir. *We shall change the world!* In reality, the world changes us.' He indicated his skeletal figure with his hand. 'As you see.'

They began strolling slowly back to the shady trees, but Vere was still conscious of being watched by other eyes. The Egyptian intrigued him. If he had truly served Gordon during the siege he might have seen Vorne, spoken to him. If his brain had not deteriorated so badly he might have spanned the emotive years with memories of those final tragic days.

'What will happen to him now?' he asked, as they stopped beneath the dappled shadows created by the palms. 'Has he relatives?'

'A son in Cairo, at least. Let us hope he will be kind to a father who has lost his reason.'

'I wonder that any of you still has control of it,' said Vere with warmth. 'You all have my deepest admiration for your courage.'

Father Brunn turned towards the old man who continued to watch them with unwavering intensity. 'He had courage enough to risk becoming what he is now by submitting to their brutal tormenting in order to stay alive. Give your admiration to that man, sir.'

They fell silent for a moment or two. Then Vere said, 'He was so overcome by emotion when he approached me it's difficult to believe he is not aware of his actions. It was as if he knew me as an old friend.'

'Ah, it is many years since he has seen a khaki uniform. He has been very agitated since several of your officers appeared like visions of our eternal longings yesterday. We can all scarcely believe you are real.'

'He asked the same thing several times: *Does he have it? Is it safe? Do you know what it means?*'

'Yes. He tends to return to the subject whenever he is particularly distressed. It appears there was a scarab, rather a fine one if he is to be believed, which was greatly important to his family. These emblems are passed to the eldest son of each generation, much as we pass titles and property to ours. Fearful that Khartoum would fall before help reached the garrison, he sent the piece out with a British officer who promised to get it safely to Cairo. He has tormented himself with anxiety over whether or not his son enjoys the protection of this sacred ornament. He believes each of you is that same officer, and has asked the same questions of as many as will stop and listen.'

The hair on the back of Vere's neck began to rise as the chill he had known at Metemma returned. Did more than one British officer leave Khartoum during the siege?

'Do you know the name of the man who took the scarab, Father?'

He shook his head. 'We do not even know if the story is true or just another of his imaginings. The officer in question seems a great deal less than honourable, which makes us doubt his veracity.'

With icy apprehension settling in his every fibre, Vere asked, 'Will you tell me the story?'

Father Brunn frowned. 'You asked if I knew the name of the British officer. Why?'

He was as frank as he could be. 'Someone I once knew was killed after escaping from Khartoum. If you know any details of this incident, true or imagined, will you please relate them to me?'

The missionary drew in his breath consideringly. 'Was he a friend?'

'He was much older than I so that was not really possible. I . . . knew and admired him.'

'Then you may not like what the Egyptian claims.'

'I nevertheless ask you to tell me,' he said quietly. 'Like you, I also once wanted to change the world, but the world changed me instead. If you leave Omdurman without doing as I ask, the change in me will remain for ever incomplete.'

For several moments the man thought over Vere's request. Then he said, 'Sit down with me, my son. The tale will take a little time to tell and I am not as strong as you.'

So Vere sat beneath the shade of some palms beside the Nile at Omdurman while he heard what the Egyptian had once confessed in his early sane days. A British officer with a Sudanese guide arrived in Khartoum with a message from the Relief Force then at Metemma. He was dismayed to find the garrison in worse straits than the British guessed and immediately realised that the starving, dispirited populace would never hold out until reinforcements reached them. The Mahdi's army had already begun to gather on the opposite bank of the river. He knew Khartoum was doomed. He said as much to Gordon and his staff, telling them they should leave at once if they wanted to save their skins. With bravado induced by alcohol he subsequently told the Egyptian officers that *he* had no intention of staying with a white madman determined to be a martyr, only to be killed by a black madman determined to be a god. On the following morning he persuaded Gordon that he could reach the advance guard of the relieving force, tell them of the critical situation, and be back with a gun-boat within three days.

On hearing of this, an Egyptian from an important family saw his chance to send a jewelled amulet to his eldest son in Cairo. He asked the Englishman to take the package. The officer agreed to do so only if he were given money which was of no use to a doomed man. Accordingly, the Egyptian handed over all he had to persuade the man to undertake the mission. Dressed in native robes and accompanied by two Sudanese who knew the desert, the British officer rode out under cover of darkness with the scarab, a large sum of money, and a communiqué he knew would arrive far too late. Within four days Khartoum fell, the entire garrison was massacred, the civilian population suffered rape and mutilation. Many were carried off as slaves to undergo all manner of degradation. General Gordon became a martyr. The Mahdi died six months later to be succeeded by the Khalifa. Neither became a god. The prisoners did not know whether or not the Englishman had got through and saved his skin. As for the Egyptian, he had no way of discovering if his son ever received the scarab. The uncertainty had further increased his ordeal in Omdurman during the subsequent thirteen years and nine months.

On the following day, 4 September 1898, General Kitchener, his staff, and selected officers from every regiment in the Anglo-Egyptian force crossed the river to hold a service of homage for Charles Gordon and all who had perished with him. They had finally been avenged. Many men present had personal reasons for taking part in that deeply significant ceremony, but Vere Ashleigh was not among them. No one had been able to find him to deliver Kitchener's personal invitation.

Chapter Sixteen

It was unusually hot even for June. The temperature in the stables of A Troop of the 57th Lancers was excessive as the men carried out their morning duty of mucking out, grooming the glossy beasts which were the pride of the regiment, then feeding and watering them. Stripped to the waist, the troopers shouted to each other above the sound of clattering pails as they brushed the coats of their mounts. Each man had an attachment to his horse which bordered on deep affection. A lancer's bond with his equine partner was often stronger than that he shared with his fellows. A Troop were confident they and their mounts were the best in the entire regiment. They defended that belief with their fists.

The friendly banter faded away thirty seconds before the time for inspection. If Second Lieutenant Pickering had a virtue at all it was punctuality: his men all hated him and fell silent whenever he came near. Troop Sergeant Grouse called them to attention when the subaltern entered. Pickering was tall and thin with greasy brown hair and a greasy brown moustache. He sported a monocle and drawled in foppish fashion when he spoke. He had never been known to address a trooper personally. His instructions were always given through an NCO. He was a hesitant rider, a mediocre swordsman and an abysmal dunce on the subject of military tactics. He was reputed to shine in the ballroom and distinguish himself in tenor ballads at soirées. He was distantly related to royalty. The rank and file of the 57th Lancers thought he should be shot at dawn – the sooner the better.

Pickering and Sergeant Grouse made the slow inspection while the men stood beside their horses, looking at the point where the sloping roof met the far wall of the building.

'No, no, oh, *really*!' exclaimed the officer. 'Mudd cannot *surely* believe this harness is *clean*. Tell him it is a total disgrace. If he cannot manage a simple matter of polishing, how can we *possibly* rely on him to kill the enemy? No, no, it is clear he has done no work on his leathers today. He will stay behind during the recreation period and rectify the matter.'

Sergeant Grouse repeated his every word to the unfortunate Trooper Mudd, starting with, 'Mr Pickering says . . .' The men marvelled that a volatile character like their sergeant controlled himself well enough during this ridiculous business every other day. But Grouse was no fool and had his heart set on promotion.

The pair moved down one side of the stables then crossed to the other side. Half-way along, Pickering stopped for a long while to study first the spotless floor covered with clean straw, then the gleaming harness and glossy coat of A29 known to his rider as Samson. His pale gaze then slowly wandered over the trooper's shining blond hair, good-looking face and strong, muscular torso. Pickering's thin mouth tightened as he turned to Sergeant Grouse.

'There are *cobwebs* on the ceiling of this stall. I suggest that Havelock begins his stabling duty again and attempts to *clean* the place properly. He needs to learn that there is more to being a cavalryman than giving showy displays of horsemanship whenever the Colonel is passing. Bending one's back and soiling one's hands are the *essence* of soldiering. You had better remind him of *that*, Sergeant.'

In stepping away after Grouse had repeated the comments word for word to a young man whose blazing blue eyes betrayed the anger his carefully schooled features hid, Pickering collided with the buckets which had contained the water to fill the drinking-troughs. They fell over and rolled across the cobbled floor between stalls.

The subaltern turned on Sergeant Grouse furiously. 'That's a damned dangerous place to leave buckets! I could have broken a *leg*. That man is totally useless! He will carry water for the entire troop at "stables" this evening. Perhaps that will teach him a lesson.'

As soon as inspection was over the expletives began.

'Bluddy fop! Why don't 'is 'orse throw 'im and break 'is bluddy neck?'

'There's nowt wrong with your leathers, Jim. He picked on you a'cause you splashed his boots with mud in passing, accidental like. Don't you do them agin.'

'I'd like to put horse-piss in his ale, I would.'

Sergeant Grouse returned at that point. 'Orl right, that's enough grumbling fer this morning. Tidy up quick. There's a game o' cricket being got up. Soon as you finish you can go and watch.' He began walking between the stalls until he reached Jim Mudd. 'Give them leathers a polish fer about fifteen minutes, then you can watch the game until dinner-time,' he said quietly, before continuing until he drew level with the man known to them all as Trooper Havelock. There, he frowned. 'You'll have ter learn ter mask your thoughts better'n you do or you'll find yourself deep in trouble, lad. Insubordination won't help you one bit.'

'That was all he could find to complain of – *one cobweb!*' he said explosively.

'It's there, you can't deny.'

291

'So are dozens of others in this stable. There's nothing in regulations which states that troopers are responsible for the state of the *ceiling*.'

'Watch it, Havelock! You're speaking to an NCO, remember.'

'Mr Pickering knocked them pails over deliberate,' said the man in the neighbouring stall. ''E's got it in fer 'Avelock.'

'I didn't hear that, Daniels, didn't hear one word of it,' ruled Grouse in mild tones. Then he beckoned to a massive man named Deadman. 'You're strong enough to support Havelock on your shoulders while he disposes of that cobweb, aren't you? Good.' Frowning at the blond trooper once more, he added, 'Better take it easy after that if you've ter fetch all the water on yer own ternight. Still, you're a big strong fellow well able ter do that without much trouble. In the old days, I see a man flogged fer as much.' He went out into the sunshine, his boots ringing on the cobbles as he marched away.

Left to their own devices the men rallied round the pair who had been this morning's victims. Within minutes, the cobweb had been brushed away and the buckets collected to stack neatly in place. Trooper Mudd's supposed dirty leathers were given a token rub before they all donned their grey tunics and headed for the cricket field to find out what was happening there. Only one bothered to sluice himself down to wash away the sweat of his hard toil in the stables. This penchant for cleanliness had made life very hard for him on first enlisting in the regiment two months earlier, under the name of Martin Havelock.

Dressing again in the smart all-grey uniform of the Ghost Lancers, Val sat on a bale of hay in the shade, while the anger Pickering had aroused slowly died. It was foolish to let that idiot spoil things now the worst was over. However, rank, social position, could break another man's career very easily. Val knew that, yet pride would not allow him to hide his own excellence at military skills which Pickering so evidently lacked, and which was the root cause of the man's victimisation of the most recent addition to A Troop.

Lying back against the sweet-smelling hay, Val let his mind drift back over the last three months. Twelve sobering weeks, but he was only just starting to recover from the disaster he had courted by playing into Julia's hands. In retrospect, he saw himself as a gullible fool, the perfect pawn for the Black Queen. How he could have behaved so stupidly he could not now think. But he had, and had reaped the harvest of his folly. Dr Keening had forced him to drink a strong sedative before locking him in a room of the sick-bay like a criminal. The potion had mercifully knocked him out all night, but fear and despair had rushed in in the morning. He had expected to be arrested on a charge of assault – even attempted rape – but he had instead been handed the amount credited to him in the school bank before

292

being driven to Tetherbury station under the escort of a silent, grim-faced Geoffrey Manton.

Obliged to purchase a ticket to Dunstan St Mary, Val had then been watched onto the train by the sports master who had once been so full of friendly praise, as if he could no longer be trusted. He could not, he supposed, because between Tetherbury and Nodford stations he had realised he could not go back to Knightshill under a cloud of these proportions. Leaving the train at Nodford on the side away from the platform, he had walked back along the track to Tetherbury and exchanged his ticket for one which would take him as far in the opposite direction. He had slept in a barn somewhere in Surrey for the next three nights, wandering the fields during the chilly daylight hours, feeling miserable, despairing, full of self-contempt for what he had done at Julia's bidding. What a pitiful, gormless fool he had been! He had abandoned Ashleigh honour for a place in the Ghost Lancers.

It was that recurring thought which had eventually pulled him out of the well of humiliation. His appetite suddenly returned. Armed with a crusty loaf, a cheese, some ham and a pound of apples, with a quart of milk to wash it all down, he had sat in the barn while rain danced on the roof, persuading himself there was no reason why he should not have what he had paid for so dearly. Well, almost. Discarding his school coat and cap, he had then spent the last of his funds on a rough wool jacket from a market stall and become Martin Havelock.

The 57th Lancers were quartered near Oxford. Walking, begging rides on carts taking produce to market, seeking labouring work where he could in order to eat, he had eventually approached a recruiting sergeant to offer his services as a trooper in the regiment commanded by Julia's uncle. After signing away his allegiance, he had felt some return of self-esteem. He was a Ghost Lancer, albeit the lowliest kind, and he would make his regiment as well as his family proud of him one day. He might never be another Vorne Ashleigh, but he would come as near to the *beau idéal* as possible.

Full of enthusiasm and good intent, Trooper Havelock had donned the smart uniform and lance-cap in two shades of grey only to find that he did not meet with the approval of his barrack-room colleagues. His voice was 'too posh', his hands were too well manicured, his fondness for washing and brushing his teeth was too effeminate, they declared unanimously. When they then discovered he was a first-rate horseman who knew every minute detail about cavalry drill manoeuvres, besides outdoing everyone in the entire squadron with his command of the nine-foot lance, he stood no chance of being accepted by his fellows.

Having always been popular with those around him, Val was dismayed by the animosity he aroused in men he had approached with his usual friendly assurance. Items of his equipment vanished when needed, then were discovered in the latrines. He was frequently 'accidentally' elbowed into barrows of manure, or tripped so that he fell headlong into the channel taking filthy water from the stalls to the drains. Buttons were pulled from his tunic, burrs were placed beneath his saddle prior to parade so that Samson sidled and reared up during inspections. The point of his lance was filed so that it no longer picked up the wooden markers during lance training.

Having suffered and also inflicted indignities at school, Val had known he could only ride the business out until they had had enough. Grimly determined not to retaliate or restrict his prowess in a profession he had been born to enter, simply to put an end to his persecution, he had endured all they dealt out. There were the inevitable bullies in A Troop, led by a huge brute named Deadman. With a certain shady past himself, the beefy trooper declared the gentlemanly Havelock was 'a nob wot disgraced 'isself and got frew aht o' 'is own set' and the troop objected to having an upper-class criminal thrust amidst them. Deadman told Val that they were all good honest men who would make mincemeat of him if he continued to act like a commissioned bastard. They wanted no fancy airs and graces from someone who put on a proud uniform to avoid proper punishment for what he had done.

Cornered by Deadman and his few henchmen after 'stables' one evening, Val had been told to confess his crime or take his punishment. Sticking to the story he had invented concerning Martin Havelock, he had subsequently been seized and virtually tortured by having his face held for long periods in a bucket containing horse urine, allowed to emerge for air only briefly between each ducking. When he began to vomit and almost passed out they let him go, promising they had not finished with him yet. Deeply worried about his best course of action in this new, more dangerous, situation, Val had gained salvation in the form of Audley Pickering returning from leave. But it had been a frying-pan-to-fire form of salvation.

In the manner of many bullies when a detested rival picks on the same victim, Deadman's persecution changed to protective championship the moment Pickering turned on Trooper Havelock. When the subaltern and the new member of A Troop came face to face, deep aversion was mutual and instantaneous. Using his rank in lieu of strength to wield power over others, Pickering had no sooner begun to take his revenge on someone who outshone him in every aspect of his profession than Deadman rallied the whole troop to Val's aid.

But this was a more complex enmity than the one between a group of simple men and one who so obviously did not belong with them. Pickering's persecution was based on resentment and jealousy. Val delighted in provoking it by demonstrating his professional superiority at every opportunity, knowing exactly how he would deflate the fellow if things were as they should be. On that score, Val was resentful and jealous. Audley Pickering was a military failure, yet he wore the uniform and sword Val Ashleigh still yearned for in the command which should have been his. The effeminate subaltern delighted in demonstrating *his* superiority at every opportunity, with rank on his side. Knowing he could not possibly win against the man and even stood to lose what he presently had, Val took no heed. His nature would not allow an Ashleigh to be bested by a military nincompoop.

Lying back in the hay this hot June morning he thought sadly of Clive, who had suggested joining the Prussian army under a false name. Being Trooper Martin Havelock gave him none of the élan Valentin von Aschenheim would have had, yet he felt Clive would approve of what he had done. One thing his friend would condemn was his pig-headedness over Pickering. Clive had never understood the drive to measure up to the family hero which demanded that he should maintain his pride even in adversity. He turned away thoughts of Julia. His pride had slipped disastrously at her hands, but she had used the unfair weapon of her sexuality to take him by storm. He would steer clear of all women from now on.

As if to mock that resolution, he was astonished to see through the open stable doors a figure riding side-saddle on a huge roan. Whatever was a woman doing in the troop lines without an escort? A visitor would not be allowed to wander through the barracks as she pleased, and a trooper's wife would not be mounted. He shot to his feet as the mare gave a shrill shriek and stumbled badly, sending the rider headlong. Running to their aid, Val was more concerned for the animal than a rider who would have hurt little more than her vanity in the fall. Catching at the bridle, he steadied the mare with soothing words whilst stooping sideways to assist the woman to her feet with his left hand.

'Are you all right?'

'Perfectly, thank you,' she mumbled, brushing straw from her long blue skirt. Then she glanced up at him. Her hands stilled as faint colour crept into her thin freckled face, and her eyes widened in a startled study of him.

Val was annoyed to see she was a girl of little more than seventeen, too slight to manage a beast of such size. He said crisply, 'You shouldn't be riding this mare. She needs veterinary attention immediately.'

Her flush deepened dramatically. 'Haven't you been told to be more polite when speaking to a lady?'

Her superior manner made him bristle. 'A *lady* wouldn't be in the troop lines when the men are off duty. Females aren't allowed in this part of barracks.'

A quick temper suggested by her red hair flared. 'Don't be insolent!'

'Isn't that a case of pot and kettle?'

'What's your name, my man?' she demanded in tones more suited to an outraged duchess in a play by Oscar Wilde.

'What's yours, my girl?' he retaliated.

'Vivienne Beecham.'

It was a blow. No one had told him Max Beecham had a daughter. Certainly not Julia. The rank and file would have little interest in the fact, but the officers would be well aware of this excellent means of furthering an ambitious man's career. As Val Ashleigh was not one of their number he was supposed to toe the line where she was concerned.

'I've been with the regiment only two months, which is why I didn't know you.'

'I shall know *you* from now on,' she told him with relish. 'What's your name?'

'Havelock.'

'*Trooper* Havelock?'

That surprised emphasis was salt in his wound. 'That's right. Does your father know you ride in forbidden areas?'

'I don't have to ask his permission for what I do. I'm not a member of the regiment.'

'You'll lose the respect of those who are if you make a habit of touring their quarters when they're relaxing.'

His shaft went home. 'You apparently have no respect for anyone at all, Havelock. One word from me to Father about your rudeness would bring you serious trouble.'

'I'm simply trying to help you to avoid the same thing,' he told her with matching crispness. 'Colonel's daughter or not, you shouldn't intrude upon that small part of the troopers' difficult lives they can call their own. They might be rough diamonds, but they also have a rough sort of pride. Your father understands that. Maybe you should have a word with him on that subject, instead.' Before she could take the ridiculous business any further he added, 'I'll take a look at your mare. I'm pretty certain I know what happened just now.'

So saying, he squatted to take the fetlock in his large, careful hands to seek for telltale signs. 'This swelling suggests an abscess of some kind. Merlin had the same trouble last year. I told Ned to summon our vet right away, although he had his doubts on my opinion because these things tend to fluctuate. They fill up, then the pus somehow disperses to suggest that the trouble was really muscular. Then they fill again.' He stood up. 'You must get Captain Keene to her right away.'

She managed an expression of superiority even when glancing up from a height at least twelve inches shorter than his. 'I was trying to find Michael Keene when I mistook the way. *That's* why I'm in the troop lines, Havelock.'

He reversed the intended reprimand. 'The Veterinary Officer expects to wait on anyone named Beecham. You shouldn't have to chase after him. But he's presently operating on A thirty-two. That's one of the troop horses.'

'I know it's one of the troop horses. I've lived with the regiment all my life,' she said coolly. 'But they have names as well as numbers. What do you call yours?'

'Samson.'

'So who is Merlin?'

Realising he had slipped up by mentioning his favourite stallion, he said swiftly, 'One of the horses in the stables where I used to work.'

'And Ned?'

'The head groom.'

'Yet *you* told *him* to summon the vet.'

'I *urged* him to do so,' he amended, disliking this thin haughty girl more by the minute.

'Not very experienced for a head groom, was he?'

Val had had enough. He offered her the mare's bridle. 'It'll take you a while to walk her back.'

There was a hint of malice in her voice as she declined to take the bridle from him. 'After reading me a rather impudent lecture on propriety, you have no choice but to escort me back to the house. I cannot possibly progress through a military barracks *alone*, Havelock.'

Hoist with his own petard, he put on the jaunty cap in two tones of grey and set off leading the limping mare back through A Troop lines towards the barrack perimeter. The Commanding Officer's house was situated on the far limits at the head of a long avenue running through the officers' quarters. Val had never been in that part of Halvidar Barracks, but he had seen Julia's uncle from a distance on many occasions. He thanked Providence the meeting at Blandford had never taken place or his imposture would have been out of the question. Everyone he had come across admired and respected their colonel. Mrs Beecham was also well liked for her ability to combine an easy, friendly manner with her social status. Their precocious daughter had not inherited their combined virtues. As it seemed likely she had arrived from school for the summer vacation, Val hoped she would be fully occupied for the rest of it.

Passing the sports field he saw the game of cricket under way. He longed to be taking part in it instead of accompanying this objectionable girl to her home. Her tendency to get her own way by using her father's rank, and her habit of calling him Havelock rankled deeply. Val Ashleigh would soon have taken her down a peg or two.

'You're not very talkative, are you?' she commented pertly.

'I don't think anything I have to say would interest you, Miss Beecham.'

She coloured. 'Were you so arrogant as a stable-boy?'

He refused to rise to that and silence fell until they turned the corner of the avenue leading to her home, when she suddenly asked, 'What made you become a trooper in the Fifty-seventh, Havelock?'

Struggling against the urge to tell her it was no concern of hers, he said stiffly, 'It was something I always wanted.'

'So, until you were old enough, you worked as a stable-boy?'

'That's right.'

'Where?'

'South of here.'

Her lips twitched. 'Where is your family?'

'My parents are dead.'

'What about brothers and sisters?'

His mouth tightened and he walked on in silence.

'Well, have you any or not?' she demanded imperiously.

He rounded on her. 'Being Max Beecham's daughter might entitle you to force me to escort you through barracks, but I don't have to answer your cross-examination.'

She stopped, grasping the mare's bridle and making Val stop, too. Her greenish eyes studied him speculatively once more, which angered him further.

'You're the rudest person I've come across for a long time. If you were a mere stable-boy, why did you speak with such authority about Dinah's leg? And if you've always wanted to be a trooper in the Fifty-seventh, why do you behave as if you're an officer? I'm afraid I don't believe half the things you have said, Havelock.'

The awkward moment was saved when a vigorous voice greeted the girl. Val's Troop Captain, a pleasant man in his mid-thirties called Felix Wheeler, drew alongside on a black gelding. He smiled at Vivienne as he returned Val's salute.

'It's very evident Dinah is lame,' he continued. 'Is there some problem about getting her home?'

Val waited stiffly for the girl to complain about him, but she merely said, 'Not at all. Now you're here to see me safely to my door, poor Havelock can be relieved of the tedious task. I've deprived him of his off-duty period which goes some way towards easing a trooper's difficult life. Isn't that too bad of me?'

Wheeler was still smiling. 'I'm sure Havelock was perfectly willing to forgo that in order to be of assistance to you.' He gave Val a nod. 'You can return to your quarters now.'

As he saluted before turning smartly and marching away, Val told himself Vivienne Beecham might be precocious and fond of using her father's rank as if it were her own, but she was no fool. Although she had let him off just now with no more than a sly reminder of his reprimand concerning being in the troopers' lines, he might yet have cause to regret the encounter.

All such fears were banished after the hearty meal he had finally grown used to calling dinner rather than luncheon, when the afternoon riding session began. He revelled in this aspect of his new life. His heart sang, his spirits rose above the lingering sense of failure and guilt, his enjoyment of matching senses with actions was fully satisfied. Whilst performing the precise cavalry movements as one of a troop or a squadron, and when riding solo at the hurdles, lancing imaginary enemies or picking up the flat discs on the point of his lance, Trooper Havelock was temporarily eclipsed by the glorious images which had lived with him for as long as he could recall.

This afternoon, they were practising for a display which was to be given during a tattoo next month. The regiment was to be 'at home' to the public. The war in the Sudan was moving very slowly, and the British people were liable to lose faith in their army unless reminded of its superiority in dashing fashion. After the victory at Atbara, the entire campaign appeared to have come to a standstill. Explaining that the Nile water was too low during the summer months to enable troop barges to progress was not enough for the majority, whose only knowledge of rivers was of those near their homes in green, peaceful country areas. General orders to home-based regiments required them to 'intensify communications between the garrison and local populace by every available means'. Max Beecham had planned a programme of military displays, band concerts, sporting events and a grand ball to which dignitaries for some miles around had been invited. On the last night there was to be a spectacular tattoo containing a re-enactment of the incident during the Peninsular War which had led to their nickname, the Ghost Lancers.

The troops were happy to present themselves as the cream of British manhood to men and women who longed to hear that Khartoum had been taken and Gordon avenged. For the disgruntled regiments still at home maintaining the thankless routine of peacetime soldiering, the week of events gave an opportunity for shades of glory. It also gave a welcome boost to morale by seeing new faces, meeting and talking to townspeople who did not always welcome troops in their midst, and breaking the year-round routine for a while.

Val cared little for all that. He had not been with the regiment long enough to become bored by routine. His great delight in being part of something which was in his blood had but one shadow over it. Because of it, he deliberately showed off before Audley Pickering, two other subalterns and Captain Wheeler, who were watching the troop go through its paces this afternoon. Samson was a good strong stallion. With Merlin beneath him Val could have done even better, but the beast he had been given understood his commands and responded with great courage. The men of A Troop had reversed their resentment into admiration for their champion now, so Val was flushed with elation when a halt was called and they rode back to stables. During the break for cups of strong tea and doorstep sandwiches, they discussed the proposed cricket match between officers and other ranks to be played during the week of public events.

'Goodman of B Troop says they've a coupla good steady players ready to knock spots off the orficers,' said a youth called Ready, who had habitually scored for matches in his home village. 'Then there's Sergeant Binns, Lance-Corporal Dunnaway and an orderly from the 'orspital. Put them with Corporal Chase, Sergeant Major Canning and them two spin bowlers in D Troop and we've the start of a right good team.'

'*Right good team?*' sneered Trooper Dobson, who decried everything by force of habit. 'The officers'll make mincemeat of any team we puts up against them. Mr Larkins played for Cambridge and got a blue. So did Major Grovely. All the rest learned at some fancy school or other. We'll look to be right daft when they gets to the wicket.'

'Shut yer gob!' ruled Deadman in his normal blunt manner. 'Them piss-pants won't make us look daft. If they gets a chance ter practise, our lot'll show any civilians 'oo's the real men in this regiment. It's us, not nobs wiv a "blue", whatever that means.'

Val finished off his sandwich, then said casually, 'I've played a bit of cricket.'

'Any good, are you?' asked Trooper Mudd.

'Not too bad. It sounds as though all our team needs is a get-together as soon as possible and some concentrated practice at the nets.'

'There's a list up on the notice-board,' Ready told him. 'Better put your name on it. There's only four, so far.'

'That's no good,' he said. 'You've just mentioned a lot more who can play. We need as many volunteers as we can get so that we can try them all out and choose the best. They're often too modest to come forward.'

'That's not one of your virtues, Havelock,' sneered Dobson once more. 'We all saw you showing off in front of Pickering s'afternoon.'

'Pickering's a stupid bugger 'oo don't know an 'orse's arse from 'is nose. Nor 'is own, shouldn't wonder,' claimed Deadman. 'Showin' 'im 'ow, that's wot 'Avelock was doin'. Wasn't yer?' he demanded of Val.

He made no reply to that, instead declaring that as he had to carry all the water for evening stables he had better make a start. While he carried buckets back and forth he thought about the cricket match. Village players were often very good. They lacked the finesse of those taught at public schools, but possessed a boldness and flair which could be very effective if captained properly. He was certain he could coach a good team for the match. An inner voice suggested that all he wanted was another opportunity to show his true worth to those he could not join, but he resolutely silenced it by saying under his breath, '*Shut yer gob!*' His dawning smile broadened. How he would enjoy saying that to Audley Pickering when the day of revenge dawned.

On the following morning Val was told by Sergeant Grouse to report to the Troop Captain in his office. He was deeply apprehensive. Vivienne Beecham must have complained about him, after all. Why else would his captain want an interview? That girl could make trouble for him. He cursed the chance which had sent her past the stables when he was there alone.

He entered the small office with as much self-possession as he could muster and saluted. Felix Wheeler studied him shrewdly for a while.

'Good morning, Havelock.'

'Good morning, sir.'

'Please stand at ease.'

He did so, mystified by the reasonably friendly manner of his officer.

'I was watching you yesterday afternoon during riding practice, and agreed with various reports I have been given concerning your progress with A Troop. After a somewhat erratic first few weeks, you appear to have settled down and made remarkable strides.'

Val was delighted. Praise instead of reprimand!

'Sergeant Grouse says your regimental ability is exemplary, and your appearance is first-class now you have recovered from the tendency to lose buttons and fall over during mucking out in the stables.' Wheeler's lips twitched in amusement revealing that he had a good notion of the reason for all that. 'He and the other NCOs report that you are popular with your barrack-room fellows and with the troop as a whole. The Riding Master tells me that it is a long time since he came across such a skilled natural horseman. That was apparent to me when I watched you very closely yesterday.'

Almost bursting with pride by now, Val schooled himself not to show his feelings. What was behind all this?

'In short, Havelock, you have all the potential of a perfect cavalryman . . . but you're not content with that, are you?'

'Sir?' he asked in confusion.

Captain Wheeler pursed his lips. 'Despite the truly excellent reports on your professional ability, Mr Pickering says you are lazy and insolent.'

Delight darkened into anger. 'No one else thinks so.'

'I didn't ask for an opinion, Havelock,' Wheeler said crisply. 'I was stating a fact. Several others have noticed this tendency in you, myself included. We do not say you are exactly insubordinate, but you seize every opportunity to act as an individual rather than as one of a troop of men under orders. If you fancy yourself as a leader, Havelock, your chance will come in the fullness of time. We are always eager to promote men of ability, and there is little doubt of the extent of yours. But until you are given minor rank you must accept that you are just one of a highly trained group. In times of war, any man who cannot control his impulse to act on his own is not only a liability, he's a real danger to the remainder of the troop.'

The last vestige of Val's pleasure vanished. After praising him to the skies this man had told him to curb his natural ability and become little more than an automaton. This was all Pickering's doing, he felt certain.

Studying Val's expression, Captain Wheeler said quietly, 'I'm not reprimanding you, Havelock, just offering a piece of advice.'

'Yes, sir,' he said, unable to keep the anger from his voice.

'You must also learn to take such advice without adopting that mutinous expression. It could easily be translated as insubordination by some people.'

Val said nothing. Pride in the earlier praise for his horsemanship had well and truly evaporated. He resented being made to stand there by a man who appeared to have said all he wanted on the subject of Trooper Havelock. None of it would be applicable to Second Lieutenant V. M. H. Ashleigh. When he was about to risk a further charge of insolence by asking if he could go, Wheeler leaned back on two legs of his chair to smile at him in friendly fashion.

'Where did you learn to ride so superbly, Havelock?'

He answered without thinking. 'On my grandfather's estate.'

'Your grandfather's estate?'

He recovered swiftly. 'He worked there, sir.'

'Where was this?'

'In Dorset. A small place near Tetherbury.'

'But large enough to provide good riding country.'

He said nothing.

'You lived there with your grandfather?'

'I stayed with him when my parents died.'

'I see.' Wheeler glanced from the window to his left as a body of lancers trotted smartly past the office. Then he turned back to Val. 'Where did you obtain your schooling, Havelock?'

Val grew instantly wary. This questioning had been prompted by the Beecham girl, he was certain, yet he had no choice but to give some kind of answer.

'The son of the owner of the estate was an invalid unable to attend school. I was fortunate enough to be invited to the classes given by a private tutor in order to provide company for the boy.'

'So you spent a great deal of time with the son of the house?'

'Yes, sir.'

'Mmm. Having very generously armed you with an education befitting his own son, the man then employed you as no more than a stable-boy?'

Val stared at him nonplussed.

'Small wonder you decided to leave. What made you choose us?'

'The regiment has an enviable history.'

'Which you knew all about before you joined us, I gather. How was that?'

Growing very hot under the collar, Val realised lying was not one of his strong points. Each successive one landed him deeper in the mire of deception.

'There was a copy of the regimental history in the library of the house. I read it with total fascination.'

'No record of military service in your family at all?'

That was a facer he met the only way he could. 'Havelocks have always been concerned with the land, sir.'

'Farmers, eh? That would account for your physique.' He let the chair drop back onto all four legs. 'Well, I'm glad you decided to break with tradition. You'll be a credit to the regiment once you come to terms with what is required of you.' He rose with a smile. 'I asked you to see me this morning to say you have been unanimously selected as one of the squadron team which will compete in a tent-pegging contest during our public week. Colonel Beecham believes in giving equal opportunities to all men in the regiment when it comes to these events. Skill comes before rank, in his opinion. It's a very good maxim. That's why he's one of the best commanders in the army today. You and Corporal Manx will join Captain Edgar, Captain Burril, Lieutenant Wright and Mr Leggatt to form our team. Report to Captain Edgar at noon to receive your instructions of practice times, and so on.'

'Thank you, sir,' mumbled Val, hardly in command of his thoughts by now. His spirits were emulating a see-saw during this interview.

'You have also been chosen to give a solo display of precision riding, involving jumps through flaming hoops and other difficult equestrian feats, for the tattoo which will end the week of events. The Riding Master has details of the programme you'll be expected to perform, ending with a full charge with dipped lance to collect a series of very small rings dangling from an overhead pole. He assures me your horse Samson is equal to the challenge.' He perched on the corner of his desk to add drily, 'This morning you have persuaded me *you* are equal to *any* challenge, Havelock.'

Val was so high in the clouds he hardly registered the import of that last comment. He was to represent the regiment in a dangerously skilled ride; he had been selected for the squadron tent-pegging team, a sport unique to lancers. If only he could do it as an Ashleigh. If only he could do it before the eyes of Sir Gilliard!

Hardly knowing what he said or did as he thanked Wheeler and saluted, he was brought to a halt at the door by the entry of a tall, thickset man wearing captain's insignia. Val stepped back into the office with a sense of shock as he recognised John Fielding, the officer he had approached at the New Year party. They had conversed for some minutes while Fielding had consumed a vast amount of food from the buffet. Val hoped to God the other's interest had been more in eating than in a schoolboy called Ashleigh, who had talked of nothing but the 57th Lancers.

Fielding returned Val's salute while studying him closely. 'What's your name, Trooper?'

'Havelock, sir,' he croaked through a dry throat.

'Havelock? It rings no chords, yet you look remarkably familiar. Have we met before?'

'I couldn't say, sir.'

As he made to leave, Wheeler said laughingly, 'Take a good look at him, John. Havelock is Napier Squadron's latest acquisition. With him in our team, the tent-pegging trophy will be wrested from you chaps at long last.'

'I rarely forget a face,' mused the unworried rival from Lockheart Squadron. 'I've seen you somewhere, I know I have.'

'He once worked in the stables of an estate in Dorset. Perhaps it was there.' Wheeler turned to Val. 'Who was the owner?'

'Sir Clive Jepson,' he supplied wildly, longing to get away.

'Only Jepson I know is Sir Arthur, of the diplomatic service. Never mind, it'll come to me.'

'Cut along, Havelock, or you'll miss your cocoa,' said Wheeler, turning his full attention on his visitor. 'What can I do for you, John?'

Val closed the door behind him thankfully. On the point of silently asking his friend's forgiveness in using him to aid his deception, he realised Clive would revel in the situation and think it a wonderful jest. Clive would carry off such an imposture with aplomb and faultless acting. He, himself, was so deeply and totally an Ashleigh it was almost impossible to believe in Trooper Martin Havelock. But he must. If his deception should be discovered he would have to go before Max Beecham. The schoolboy who

304

had been sacked for the supposed attempted rape of his niece would be shown no mercy by the man who would see the imposture for what it truly was – a defiant and unrepentant act against the woman who had brought about his disgrace.

The men of A Troop were more than ever convinced of their leading place in the regiment when they heard that one of their number had been selected for such distinctive roles during Public Week. Val was thumped on the back and taken off to the canteen to celebrate. Two hours later, he was carried back a great deal worse for the ale his comrades had insisted on buying him. He had a headache fit for a horse in the morning, which was not the best condition to be in to receive a summons to report at Colonel Beecham's residence at eleven a.m. It was a terrible blow. John Fielding had clearly recalled their meeting. Val had been a Ghost Lancer for a mere three months.

He went through his stable duties in a state of silent misery, then made his way to the large pillared house. He hoped no one would guess from the bold manner he adopted that his head was throbbing and his legs were like rubber. What would they do with him? The only military charge they could lay against him was that of enlisting under a false name. He supposed there would be a court-martial before dismissal from the regiment. The facts were sure to leak out – Pickering would see to that, if no one else – and the Press would make the most of it. It would finish Sir Gilliard. So much for his words to Margaret that he would make them all proud of him one day! Dear God, Julia had a lot to answer for.

He was admitted and told to wait in a sunny sitting room with a view of the spires of Oxford. Vorne had studied there and gained his degree. Turning from a sight which hardly cheered him, his gaze rested on a low table containing glossy magazines. Words leapt at him from the cover of one and he took it up eagerly, forgetting all else.

HERO'S BROTHER ON HIS WAY TO KHARTOUM. Exclusive impressions of the Sudanese campaign from the pen and brush of Vere Ashleigh.

Turning the pages swiftly, Val found the central detachable booklet containing a series of pen drawings depicting the environs of Berber and others of tent life beside the Nile. They were stark and arresting, undoubtedly the work of a gifted artist. He read, with growing emotion, the columns bordering the pictures. The fierce yearning which had lived with Val for as long as he could remember gathered strength, bringing tears to hang on his lashes. Vere was alive. He had been into battle at the head of his men. How absolutely tremendous! What an achievement by a man who had always been an invalid! Yet there was deep envy mixed with the pride and excitement. Vere had survived armed combat against

305

fanatical warriors, and had been singled out to fulfil a dangerous solo mission for which his artistic talent had fitted him. He had triumphed in his individual manner, yet he had triumphed as an Ashleigh.

'Good morning, Havelock.'

Val looked up guiltily to find his commanding officer had entered. The erect sandy-haired man frowned slightly as he studied his trooper.

'Is something wrong, man?'

'No, sir,' he said through the thickness in his throat.

Max Beecham came forward. 'Interesting aspects of the Sudanese campaign, aren't they? The artist has an eye for detail which is uncanny.' His frown deepened as he looked closely at Val's face. 'Know someone out there?'

'Yes, sir.'

'Someone close, I take it.'

'Yes, sir.'

'Would you like to keep the magazine? I have several copies and you're welcome to that one if it interests you.'

Val had no answer for that. Generosity and tones of understanding did not equate with a charge of false identity and the attempted rape of a niece.

'Sit down, Havelock. I have a few questions to ask you.'

Val did as he was told, still clutching the magazine containing Vere's brilliant pictures, which had knocked him for six. All he could think was that Beecham had decided to be discreet for the sake of family honour. However, his colonel proceeded to ask a series of questions along the lines of those put to him by Felix Wheeler yesterday. He answered automatically, sticking to his story but waiting for a sudden accusation of telling a pack of lies. It did not come. Instead, there was a friendly smile from Julia's uncle as he reached the reason for the interview.

'You came to the assistance of my daughter several days ago, Havelock. She was very grateful and most impressed by your knowledge of what ailed her mare.'

'Thank you, sir,' he murmured, still in a daze.

'I am after a new groom for my personal stables, and I believe you will be eminently suitable. The appointment carries with it a supplement in pay, and you will occupy quarters above the stables. You will answer directly to me or the Adjutant for your orders, and you will have your meals in the kitchen here. It's exacting work, with irregular hours, but you will find a degree of independence not enjoyed by a troop member.'

Val got to his feet in relief, and asked with much greater assurance, 'Is it an order, sir?'

Beecham appeared bemused. 'An order? I don't understand.'

'Have I a choice in the matter, sir, because I would much rather remain with my troop.'

The senior man rose. 'I see. How extraordinary.'

'I'm aware of your generosity in selecting me, sir,' Val said hastily. 'It's just that I want to gain as much experience as I can of regimental training. I also want to understand the men, the way they think and the way they react to things. If I came here, I'd be cut off from all that.'

'And you'd not gain quick promotion, is that it?'

'Partially,' he admitted. 'I want to be an active member of the regiment rather than take on special duties.'

'And if they carried with them the rank of corporal?'

'I'd still not be part of a fighting force. That's what I want most.'

Julia's uncle studied him for so long Val grew afraid again. Had he gone too far?

'Very well, Havelock. You may continue with your troop.'

'Thank you sir,' he said, with such great relief the other man raised his eyebrows quizzically.

'I had no idea the prospect of being my personal groom was so daunting. Dear me! Well, you can go, man.'

Outside in the sunshine, Val realised Vivienne Beecham was in for a sobering surprise. But it was not the prospect of further encounters with the girl which had governed his refusal to work here. After reading of Vere's exploits against all odds, it had seemed particularly humbling to be offered the non-combatant role of colonel's personal groom. It seemed Vere had had to become a soldier in order to be recognised as an artist. Perhaps he, himself, must become a hero in order to be recognised as an Ashleigh. He would never achieve that in Max Beecham's stables.

Chapter Seventeen

The weather at the start of the 57th Lancers' Public Week could not have been better for the events which Max Beecham had planned. Sunny and warm, with enough breeze to prevent the air in marquees from being stifling, the grounds around the red-brick barracks seemed the ideal place to spend an afternoon in the open air. People flocked in as soon as the gates were opened at two o'clock. An air of gaiety entered with them. The sight of women in pale, pretty dresses and shady hats gladdened the soldiers' eyes, and those with families were just as delighted by the children who stared at them and the animals with wide eyes and begged rides on the troop horses. That was forbidden, of course, but some docile mules ready to emulate seaside donkeys were on hand led by responsible troopers who were fathers and understood children.

The regimental musicians were busy. There was a marching band which performed immaculate drill in the regiment's most elaborate uniform whilst playing favourite march tunes, and the orchestral section gave concerts in the octagonal bandstand. There were side-shows, coconut-shies, machines to test the strength of the more brash male visitors, wrestling matches, grinning through horse-collars and all the other delights beloved by the British on fête days. Teas were provided at trestle tables in the sunshine, the proceeds going to the fund for soldiers' widows and orphans. There was also ale and cider obtainable from a marquee, where a team of beefy troopers stood ready to escort from the barracks any man who could not hold his liquor and became a nuisance.

The main attraction was the huge exercise field, where displays and competitions took place at regular times throughout the day. The tug of war between soldiers and volunteers from the spectators always drew a good crowd, and so did the horseshoe-throwing contest. But it was the mounted displays the people had really come to see. These were all vastly entertaining in a variety of ways. Aside from precision drill by entire squadrons in the dashing grey uniforms trimmed with silver and the tall square-topped helmets still worn for ceremonial occasions, there were individual items. Six officers with particular equestrian skill dressed as knights to give jousting displays. Six troopers followed them with a clowning version which brought shrieks of laughter at their antics. The tent-pegging always brought noisy encouragement from rival supporters, but the teams were so evenly matched the winners would not be known until the final day. A corporal who had once worked in a circus thrilled everyone with his trick riding; another who had trained a barrack dog to ride caused laughter by putting the little animal through his paces.

It was not all clowning and entertainment, however. The prime purpose was to demonstrate the might of the nation's army, so there were mock battles, grand marches, and displays of aggressive lance drill. No one went home believing the 57th Lancers to be anything but a splendid body of men.

That week was a halcyon period for Val, despite Pickering's intensified campaign against him. His fears over John Fielding had died; the man would surely not recall their meeting now. His fears over the Beecham girl had also faded. A month had passed since their encounter. He had seen her in the distance several times, but she had never ridden through the lines again.

Practising for the tent-pegging or for the risky solo display he was to give matured him swiftly. He no longer felt like a schoolboy who should have been taking his final examinations at this time. The periods spent with the officers in his squadron team were exhilarating. At ease with them, he soon established a relationship which was as friendly as rank would allow. So, by the time Public Week began, he was thinking like a man rather than a boy.

It was inevitable that he had been elected captain of the cricket team to play the officers. Awkward questions had been asked about his prowess at what was primarily a 'gentleman's game', his claim to have played in a village team being met with some scepticism. Once he was on the field he unconsciously slipped into a role he knew well, and to many watching it was obvious the young trooper was in the wrong team. For two and a half hours he could not deny Val Ashleigh total control over Martin Havelock. That joyous sportsman led his team to a mere two-run defeat, contributing seventy-three towards their commendable score with an innings as polished and dashing as that of the Cambridge blue, Lieutenant the Honourable Peregrine Larkins.

Shaking hands with Major Grovely, who captained the officers, Val Ashleigh was congratulated on a first-class team who had given them a jolly good match. It was Val Ashleigh who left the field surrounded by men clapping him on the back in appreciation and fellowship, Val Ashleigh who pulled on his sweater and combed his tousled hair prior to joining the men of both teams in liquid refreshment on offer in the neighbouring marquee. Leaving the dressing room of the small pavilion with several of his team, Val Ashleigh was instantly banished when a feminine voice called from the stand above.

'Havelock! I want to talk to you for a moment.'

He looked up, startled. Vivienne Beecham was gazing down at him in determined fashion. In a dress of soft, floaty material and a white hat trimmed with cornflowers she looked almost attractive, but that did nothing to ease his annoyance over her peremptory manner.

'I'm expected to take a drink with the teams,' he said, slowing but not stopping. 'It would be awfully bad form not to.'

'*Awfully bad form*,' she mimicked. 'Surely not as bad as if I came to the marquee to fetch you. I'll be driven to such a course unless you come up here.'

Aware of the interest of those around him, he stopped. 'That's entirely up to you, but I imagine your parents would be deeply embarrassed by such behaviour.'

She smiled with the hint of malice he had glimpsed in her before. 'Father is up here chatting to Major Cornwall. I can get him to *order* you to come, you know.'

'That would be childish.'

The smile vanished, and it was she who appeared deeply embarrassed. 'I *do* want to speak to you. It's important.'

'And it's important that I should be in the marquee.'

'They'll understand when they know who's detaining you. Come up here. *Please*,' she added, much to his surprise.

Strongly against his inclination he turned back into the flow of men leaving the dressing rooms and began clattering noisily up the wooden steps at the front of the pavilion in his studded boots. When he reached her he felt distinctly wary. It was quiet there, almost intimate, despite her mother and father being no more than twenty-five yards away. The sun was almost completely below the horizon, leaving a luminous lemon-coloured glow in the darkening sky against which the silhouettes of late-roosting birds flitted like bats. The hush of a July evening, which was still warm on his skin, lent sudden enchantment to the moment. Her face was softened by the gentle light of dying day so that her freckles were not so apparent. The pale, fragile dress and elegant hat suggested a maturity beyond her years. It caused him to remember who she was, and who he was supposed to be.

'What did you want to say, Miss Beecham?'

'You played a magnificent innings this evening. We all agreed you are an exceptionally good cricketer.'

'Thank you.' He waited while she did no more than gaze up at him in speculative study for too long. 'May I go now?'

'No, you may not,' she told him in tones which left no doubt that she was enjoying this. 'Havelock, why are you always so arrogant?'

Shades of Julia Grieves! He grew even more wary. 'You had stopped speaking, and I'm supposed to be elsewhere.'

'Where did you learn to play?'

'In the village team.'

Her eyes gleamed in the deepening dusk. 'Father said your strokes are too classic for a mere stable-boy.'

He tried to side-step that. 'I don't consider a stable-boy to be "mere". He works jolly hard and for long hours.'

'Which doesn't leave him enough time to learn to play cricket like a public-schoolboy, does it?'

'I used to practise with the son of the house.'

'You told Father he was an invalid.'

'Not so much that he couldn't indulge in a little gentle sport.'

'Gentle sport . . . against *you*?' Another comprehensive glance at his physique preceded a light laugh. 'You're far too aggressive for that.'

Growing angry, Val asked, 'What is this all about?'

She took her time. 'Who are you, Havelock?'

'You know who I am.'

'I know who you claim to be.'

Unwilling to get deeper into the mire, he looked pointedly at the marquee. 'I'll have to go.'

'Because it's *awfully bad form* not to be with your team? I've never known a stable-boy who speaks in upper-class manner.'

'As you consider them so lowly, perhaps you've never bothered to get to know one well enough,' he retaliated.

'How will I, now you've turned down Father's offer? I asked him to give you the advantage of joining his personal staff. Your ill-mannered refusal made me look very foolish.'

'It wasn't in the least ill-mannered. I thanked him for considering me for the post, then gave sound reasons for my decision.'

'Which were?'

'Your father knows them,' he said firmly.

'No one has ever done that to him before.'

He refused to rise to that, but she stepped nearer to look searchingly into his eyes. 'Was it because of me?'

'Good Lord, no.' It was definitely time he departed for the safer company of his fellows. 'You'll have to excuse me. If I don't join the others Major Grovely will think me extremely rude. Good evening, Miss Beecham.'

As he turned away, she halted him with an urgent whisper. *'Havelock!'*

He sighed and looked over his shoulder as she approached to the edge of the steps where he waited. 'Yes?'

'I just wanted to say that whatever it is that has driven you to do this, I'm sure it's not as bad as they claim. It *couldn't* be.'

He descended the steps at inadvisable speed, almost pitching headlong half-way down. The danger was nowhere near over, as he had thought. That girl 'had her eye on him', as Clive would have put it. The parallels with Julia were too worrying to dismiss. Vivienne Beecham appeared to delight in using her position to oblige him to speak to her and, whether consciously or not, was very definitely fascinated by his physical strength. She had none of Julia's sophisticated tactics, of course, and was far more interested in him than in herself, but therein lay the real danger. She would not stop probing now. Max Beecham had apparently not accepted the story he had been told concerning a trooper whose 'strokes were too classic for a mere stable-boy', and his daughter would fuel the fire of his suspicions. The celebration drink with the two teams was not the happy business it should have been.

On the following evening the ball was held in the Officers' Mess. Each troop commander had been told to provide a man for duty, either mounting guard outside or waiting on the carriages of guests. It went without saying that those selected should be virile, with the kind of features which were enhanced by the full-dress uniforms they would wear. The men of the 57th had to be seen as the pick of England's manhood. No one wanted the 'honour'. It was a thankless business standing around for hours on a hot evening, showing a hundred or more privileged people into a building they themselves were forbidden to enter. It was not possible to relax much, even when the officers and their guests danced, ate and drank champagne, for the heat would bring many out to the terraces and gardens from where the attendant lancers could be seen. The affair would not end until the early hours, then the tricky business of directing carriages all departing at much the same time would begin. Those given this duty were told they would have the following morning off to catch up on their sleep.

Val groaned inwardly when Felix Wheeler told him to report to the Officers' Mess an hour before the commencement of the ball. Firstly, he had missed his off-duty period last night through playing cricket. Secondly, he had hoped to have a final rehearsal of his solo display. Thirdly, it was far too hot for the discomfort of full-dress uniform. Fourthly, it would be particularly irksome to stand like a dummy outside the building an Ashleigh had every right to enter. Lastly, he just plain did not want to do it. Yet Second Lieutenant V. M. H. Ashleigh would probably never have spared a thought for the men performing this onerous duty. Life as a trooper was as much an education as the lessons he had detested at school.

When they assembled outside the tall red-brick building, they were given instructions by a sergeant major. Val took up his position by the left-hand pillar at the top of the flight of steps, where a broad terrace gave access to the main entrance and ran around the building on all sides. Although the married officers would arrive with their wives before the official start of the ball, no one expected civilian guests until at least half an hour after the time stated on invitations. Colonel and Mrs Beecham were entertaining to dinner several senior officers from Horse Guards, and some distinguished men of Oxford. These would arrive from the CO's house in carriages early enough for the hosts to be ready for early guests.

Val had a few qualms about the senior officers from Horse Guards. He did not know their names so had no idea whether or not he might have met them at Knightshill. All he could do was hope they would arrive in a group and have no interest in the grey-clad living statues lining the steps.

The evening was close and sultry, hinting at a storm in the offing. He prayed it would not cause cancellation of the tattoo tomorrow. His solo display would be the highlight of his week, the proudest moment in Trooper Havelock's short career as a lancer. But he knew it would be Val Ashleigh in the saddle as he completed the spectacular jumps and manoeuvres which tested a rider to the limit.

Longing for a breeze, he chatted spasmodically with another six-footer named Moyles who was beside the right pillar. It was unbearably hot in the close-fitting serge uniform and leather gauntlets. The lance-helmet felt too tight around Val's head; the high collar of his tunic too tight around his throat. The laughing guests who trod the red carpet to the entrance cared nothing for the human embellishments ranging the steps. Growing indignation made Val grow hotter still. Then the men below signalled that the Commanding Officer and his guests were coming. Everyone straightened instinctively. Val said a fervent prayer that none of the military men was a friend of Sir Gilliard.

Max Beecham managed to escort his VIP guests with the attention they commanded, yet still glance at the men of his regiment who were doing this uncongenial duty on a stifling evening. He was proud of his human statues and smiled to make certain they knew it. Val was less concerned with his approbation than with the faces of those accompanying his colonel. With great relief, he recognised none of them. Various groups left the carriages following the main party, and made their way up the steps to the Mess where music was playing for the dancing. The final vehicle in the CO's party contained Vivienne Beecham in a dress of white satin and pearls. With her was a thin, grey-haired man and a younger brown-haired woman in an emerald-green gown which bared her shapely shoulders.

Val was so intent on the Beecham girl, it was not until the man had alighted and turned to assist the other woman that he saw a face he would never forget for as long as he lived. Herbert Grieves handed his wife from the carriage, then turned to help her cousin. Staring down at Julia in a state of shock, Val felt the skin on his back begin to crawl. The sense of humiliation instantly revived. He saw those bonds attached to the bed-posts, saw the whip in her hand and the sadistic lust in her eyes. He relived that moment when the truth had hit him, the degradation of being sedated and locked up for the night like a dangerous animal.

When the three started up the steps he reacted instinctively. Stepping swiftly behind the pillar, he then took the only direction open to him. Heading along the terrace as fast as he could without attracting attention by the speed of his progress, he thankfully rounded the corner of the Mess to lean against the wall while fighting nausea. The heat of the evening combined with shock to set everything around him tilting crazily. He closed his eyes while his heart continued to pound. In his determination to gain what she had promised, why had he not taken account of the possibility of encountering Beecham's favourite niece at some time?

'What the devil do you think you're doing here?' demanded a voice Val knew all too well. It was very close and, for once, was addressing him directly.

He opened his eyes and straightened. Audley Pickering, in immaculate military evening-dress, was regarding him with malicious outrage from the midst of a group of four junior subalterns.

'I felt ill, sir,' Val managed, a distinct increase in the desire to find a convenient patch of bushes supporting his claim.

'*Felt ill?*' repeated the foppish whine. 'You're on *duty*, Havelock. Get back to your post immediately.'

'I daren't,' he said, to the amusement of the other officers.

'You'll damn well do as I say.'

'I'll throw up over the red carpet.'

Pickering turned red. 'You insubordinate bastard! Get back there before I call out the guard to take you in charge.'

'I've explained that I feel ill,' Val insisted, his consummate dislike of this man who did not deserve his rank beginning to rule him.

'Are you refusing to obey me? *Are you?*' Pickering almost squeaked in his fury, causing his companions to smile with delight at this unexpected entertainment.

Their smiles drove Val to further defiance. 'Surely you can see that it's better to have a man missing than to post a vomiting lancer at the Mess entrance. A fine impression the guests would gain of the regiment!'

Pickering was prepared to take no more, and stepped forward with an expression of vicious dislike. 'I've been waiting for you to overstep the mark with me. I knew you would. Pride goes before a fall, and you're so puffed up with it I'll ensure your fall is hard enough to break you apart.'

Val's Ashleigh blood began to boil. Nausea was banished by anger. Julia had humiliated him to the deepest degree. He would not let this pompous fool do so. 'Breaking me wouldn't build you up, Pickering. It would take someone of considerably more stature than you even to attempt it . . . and he'd still not find it easy.'

Felix Wheeler surveyed the accused gravely when he was marched in. It had been a hot, exhausting week for the regiment, and he had not had much sleep after escorting his fiancée home after the ball. He was now faced with this tiresome business over a trooper who made little effort to conform. Why had A Troop been unlucky enough to get Martin Havelock, who was an enigma? His voice, his bearing, his command of English, his horsemanship, his cricketing style all pointed to an upper class background. His natural tendency to lead dictated commissioned rank in the regiment. Only a scandal or, worse, a felony, which had been settled privately to save family honour, could have forced him into the ranks.

There was no Havelock bloodline in Debrett which helped to solve the mystery, so the majority of the officers had concluded that he came from a line of minor landowners or high-class importers who had acquired wealth fairly recently in business ventures or stock-market investments. They also unanimously agreed that the reason for his disgrace more likely concerned a member of the fair sex than finance, although the two often went together. An infatuated youngster often threw integrity to the winds to obtain the funds to impress the object of his passion. John Fielding was convinced he had seen young Havelock before, but he was a notorious socialiser and met so many people he could never recall names or where the encounters had taken place.

Felix knew partial sympathy with his troublesome trooper this morning. Females were the very devil and played havoc with a man's life and career. He knew Havelock had been subjected to cruelty by his fellows on first joining them, and admired his courage in withstanding their vicious hostility without complaint. It had eventually won him their united championship. But if the boy had taken the shilling in order to lie low after social misdeeds, he was going the wrong way about it. Everything he did drew attention to himself. A natural extrovert, he had a great deal of pride to offset his exceptional ability. Max Beecham was watching his progress thoughtfully. So was young Vivienne, much to Audley Pickering's annoyance. On the brink of coming out, the Colonel's daughter was a prize catch for an ambitious subaltern. Pickering's ancestry might interest any doting father, but that girl had a mind of her own and it was presently on Martin Havelock.

It was not surprising, Felix supposed, as he studied the accused. Add to his physical appeal a mystery, a hint of black-sheep identity, and any seventeen-year-old girl would find him overwhelmingly irresistible. Audley Pickering stood no chance against such a rival. Therein lay the partial cause of the astonishing affair last evening. Several subalterns had witnessed Havelock's heated insubordination, but they had also heard Pickering state that he had been waiting for a chance to break the other's pride. That a state of war between the pair had existed was known to all the officers of Napier Squadron. Felix resented having to add his heavy artillery to Pickering's light guns in a case which no officer worth his salt would have allowed to get out of hand. Young Havelock looked hollow-eyed and rather strained, but not in the least cowed.

'You are charged with abandoning your post without permission and responding in gravely insubordinate manner when instructed by Mr Pickering to return to your duty,' he said heavily. 'Do you understand those charges?'

'Yes, sir.'

'Do you wish to say anything in your defence, Havelock?'

'Sir, I found it extremely hot and suddenly realised I was in danger of passing out or throwing up. Rather than risk either, I slipped along the terrace as unobtrusively as possible while the Colonel's guests were alighting from a carriage. I encountered Mr Pickering at the side of the Officers' Mess.'

Felix waited for him to continue. When he did not, he asked, 'Is that all you wish to say?'

'Yes, sir.'

'That is the reason for leaving your post at the top of the steps?'

'Yes, sir.'

'Did you explain why you had done so to Mr Pickering?'

'Yes, sir.'

'I see. Did you refuse to return when he ordered you to?'

'Yes, sir.'

Felix longed to shake him. Agreeing with everything was no self-defence. The young idiot would break himself at this rate. Yet he had no option but to continue his questioning.

'In refusing, did you use abusive and threatening words to an officer in the hearing of several others?'

'Yes, sir.'

Damn him! If he made no plea for possible justification to put on his record, he would delay his hopes of promotion for many months. Felix stared at the charge sheet while he tried to see a means of minimising the penalty he would have to award. Then he glanced up at the youthful rebel.

'When the Medical Officer examined you last night he found your temperature to be rather higher than normal, but no other signs of illness. On the contrary, his report states that you are in excellent physical condition.'

'Yes, sir.'

In mounting irritation Felix asked, 'Is there anything you wish to add before I sum up?'

Silence.

'Very well,' he declared, determined to teach Havelock a lesson he would do well to remember. 'In view of the fact that it was an exceptionally hot evening, that you had been engaged in more than the usual number of activities during the Public Week, and that you had a high temperature, I will accept your explanation for leaving your post. I will also accept that you could only use the side terrace of the Officers' Mess to avoid the guests alighting from carriages. However, I find you guilty of gross insubordination towards Mr Pickering, and of using abusive and threatening language in so doing. You will spend twenty-eight days in detention.'

Havelock came suddenly alive to cry an anguished protest. 'But I'm giving the solo display in the tattoo tonight!'

316

'There'll be an additional charge of insubordination if you're not careful, Havelock,' Felix snapped. 'You had every opportunity to speak before I gave my ruling. It is final.' He nodded to the sergeant major. 'March the prisoner out.'

Val was too active a person to accept being locked in a small cell. He paced and prowled in confinement, adding to his resistance by fretting over the solo ride he would not now perform. During that first evening behind bars he listened to the sounds of the tattoo and cursed Julia for his further punishment. When it was over and the barracks slept, he sat on the hard bed and owned that she had not been fully responsible. If he had not allowed himself to forget the imposture which was giving him the place in the 57th she had almost denied him, he would not be locked away like a common criminal. Head in hands, he realised he must be the first Ashleigh ever to be imprisoned in a military guardroom. So much for making his family proud of him!

The men of A Troop were livid over the charge which had put their champion in 'the clink' for a month and denied him the glory of a solo display which would have reflected the excellence of the troop. They made no secret of their anger to Sergeant Grouse, who in turn made the troop officers aware of discontent over something the soldiers felt had been deliberate persecution of Havelock. Felix Wheeler heard it all and wished once more the young hothead had been assigned to someone else. He knew of the enmity between a trooper who should be an officer and an officer who should not, so it was prudent to follow a course which would be a relief to them all.

When Havelock emerged from detention, Felix summoned him to the office and suggested the advisability of transferring to another troop. The response irritated yet impressed him.

'I'd prefer to stay with A Troop, sir.'

He frowned at a young man who looked considerably chastened. 'Isn't that a somewhat short-sighted attitude, Havelock?'

'Quite the reverse, sir. I had some trouble with the men, at first, but we all understand each other and work as a team now. With time, I hope any other problem can be overcome.'

'Not unless you knuckle down to taking orders.'

'There's no difficulty with that if they're unbiased, sir.'

'I think it will be best if I ignore the implication of that comment, or you might find yourself marching straight back to the guardroom.' He tried once more. 'As captain of this troop I'm responsible for maintaining good order, discipline and high morale. You are making all three difficult.'

317

'I appreciate that, Captain Wheeler, but I really would prefer to stay with my troop. My grandfather has always said it's essential for men to learn to tolerate each other, that separating incompatible personalities often worsens the situation and endangers lives in time of war, when each man may rely on any other for survival.'

'For someone who had always worked on the land, your grandparent was a remarkably astute military sage, Havelock.'

With faintly heightened colour, he replied, 'I think it was something he once read.'

Felix sighed. 'Very well, I'll keep you for a while longer as you're so keen to stay. But I shall expect clear signs that you're adhering to that piece of wisdom your forebear once read. If they are not forthcoming . . .'

'I'll do my very best, sir.'

It was as well Captain Wheeler was not aware that it was really due to a desire to deny Audley Pickering the erroneous impression that he had broken the spirits of his rival that Val pleaded to stay with A Troop. To move would suggest he could not take what Pickering was in a position to deal him. He could and would, until the other admitted defeat. So intent on this concept was Val, he did not recognise that he was also loath to leave the company of men he had come to know and respect by sharing their daily lives in a profession he loved.

The 57th Lancers departed for summer manoeuvres in Wales at the start of August. The following six weeks were the most exciting and enjoyable of Val's life. Living under canvas in a valley comprising some of the most lovely vistas to be found in the area suited his nature and his love of outdoor activities, but it was the military action which sent his spirits soaring. He revelled in every moment of exercises designed to simulate a state of hostilities against an unnamed enemy, and by so doing deepened the convictions of officers watching through field-glasses that they had a highly skilled leader who was wasted where he was. The pure delight of something he did supremely well caused Trooper Havelock to become one with Val Ashleigh during that period. The one blight to his happiness was removed when Audley Pickering was thrown by a temperamental stallion he failed to hold steady when guns began firing. A broken arm put the hated man in hospital and thence to the baronial home for recuperative leave. The men managed, with the greatest difficulty, to refrain from cheering when told the news. But they all celebrated around the camp fire that evening, none more so than someone who had suffered a month's detention because of him.

Val had always been quick to put things behind him. He swiftly forgot his imprisonment and the shock of seeing Julia again. Something else contributed to his high spirits in Wales. News of Kitchener's victory a

318

Omdurman set the regiment cheering. The newspapers were full of details of the battle, and it was in a spirit of cavalry brotherhood that the 57th rejoiced over accounts of the dashing charge by the 21st Lancers reported by Second Lieutenant Winston Churchill, an attached officer who had taken part in it.

Although Val obtained copies of the illustrated magazine holding exclusive rights to Vere's pictures, it was not until the third issue after the victory that he was rewarded. The series of pen drawings in and around Omdurman, of the troops relaxing after weary months progressing toward their goal and of the unique Camel Corps returning from pursuit of the fleeing enemy with a group of the Khalifa's many wives, were as impressive as his brother's earlier ones. Yet it was one single evocative study of the European captives, released after as many as fifteen years in chains, waiting in dazed resignation on the banks of the Nile where a gun-boat loomed over them in warlike contrast, which brought tears of pride and emotion to Val's eyes. That picture said everything about the reasons why. It was unforgettable.

He read the columns alongside the pictures. Vere had fought in the battle for Omdurman. Val wondered how he had felt as the waves of shouting men bore down on his position. He also wondered how he had felt on seeing Vorne's grave at Metemma, and on first sighting Khartoum around a bend in the river. He would surely never be the same man again after treading in a hero's footsteps. But Vere had become something of a hero himself. Not only had he faced death by fever and battle, and survived, he had become a notable figure of the second Sudanese campaign in the artistic guise for which he was best fitted. Good old Vere!

One thing puzzled Val. There was no mention in the columns of his brother's presence at the memorial service held by Kitchener to honour those who had been killed in the first campaign of 1885. Surely the kinsman of a glorious hero should have been given pride of place alongside the victorious general. And why was there no pen-picture of the ruined city for which a brave man had sacrificed his life in an attempt to bring help? It was a mystery.

Not until several days had passed did Val consider that the family at Knightshill must have seen Vere's drawings and read of his exploits. Charlotte would be thrilled; Margaret, too. How would Sir Gilliard react? The quarrel which had estranged them would now surely be set aside and Grandfather would finally be proud of his heir. How ironical that Vere should have attempted to abdicate in favour of a schoolboy he believed more worthy of his inheritance, only to distinguish himself in the most unexpected manner while the schoolboy was trying to recover from a shameful episode by adopting a false name! However, his youth, a mutinous spirit, and the energetic enjoyment of that spell in Wales soon had Val feeling optimistic once more. He *would* make them all proud of him one day. It was a case of being patient, something which had never come easily to him.

The regiment returned to Oxford and settled back to the old routine. Now that the Sudan had been taken under Anglo-Egyptian control and the regiments were returning home, those who had missed the campaign began looking for alternative prospects of action abroad. There was always India and the Frontier. The men of the 57th believed they deserved a foreign posting. The regimental wives prayed they would not get one, particularly India. They had no wish to live in sweltering quarters while their husbands fought in frontier wars miles away from the station. The climate was bad for children, and no one had forgotten what had happened at Cawnpore forty years ago. No, the women wanted no other home than Oxford. It was pleasant, temperate and very pretty down by the river. It was *England*.

Val also liked Oxford, although he naturally hoped for a foreign posting soon. When he was off-duty at weekends, he headed for the city with his fellows. They invariably parted company there. Most sought a girl and an ale-house. A few had less basic interests such as collecting stamps, or fishing. One who was particularly fond of dogs helped out at the hunt kennels when he was given the chance. Val went either to the river or the rugby ground where undergraduates indulged in the sports he loved. If there was no match to watch he made his way to the boathouses where various eights turned out for early preliminaries to select a crew for the inter-varsity race next spring.

It was on such afternoons that he knew sudden loneliness. The young men he watched were like him: they were his kind. Yet his trooper's uniform barred him from their company. He had once wandered too near the boathouse and slipway, only to be told very smartly that he was trespassing. If he had been dressed as an officer, he would probably have been welcomed. Same man, different clothes. It had been a sobering experience, but it had not stopped him from watching the crews with a knowledgeable eye and much enjoyment.

On an afternoon in early November, he was enjoying a brief burst of sunshine beside the river after several days of grey mistiness. The crews were out on a river still enough to reflect the vivid colours of autumn leaves on trees lining the banks. How poignant that they should look so beautiful just before they fell. Dying in their full glory . . . like Vorne Ashleigh, he thought. Handsome, virile, irresistibly merry, only twenty-four, he had departed from life in heroic splendour. Lucky Vere to have trodden those same sands! Fresh yearning washed over him. To have *two* brothers who had distinguished themselves heightened his eagerness to emulate them. He would not do that in barracks at Oxford. If the regiment were given a posting to India there would be a far greater chance of action . . . even for a trooper. He sighed and stamped his feet in their highly polished boots to warm them up. It was cold by the water, despite the invigorating sunshine and aqua skies. It would be a lot hotter in India, in more ways than one.

The autumn scene faded as he visualised himself in khaki and a pith-helmet, riding across a great scorched plain scarred by dried-up water-ways, searching for the flash of a heliograph in the hills or the giveaway glint of sun on a tribesman's rifle as he lay in wait for them.

'Hello, Havelock.'

Second Lieutenant V. M. H. Ashleigh left India with startled speed, and Trooper Havelock discovered beside him a freckled girl in a rich blue coat with a matching hat sporting a dark plume.

'What are you doing here all by yourself?' she asked.

'I'm off-duty,' he told her, annoyed by her destruction of images which had eased his yearning for a while.

'Where are your friends?'

'I have no idea.' Then, to punish her for spoiling his reverie, he added, 'Your father wouldn't approve your walking here without an escort.'

She merely smiled. 'How you worry about my reputation! Actually, I'm with my friend Mary Macmillan. Her brother coxes one of the crews. He's taking us both to tea when the practice is over. I told her to wait for me at the boathouse.'

He glanced in the direction of her nod to see a girl in a plum-coloured costume trimmed with fur. She was looking curiously at him as she strolled slowly on along the tow-path.

'She doesn't appear very happy about the arrangement. Perhaps you should catch her up.'

'I want to talk to you.'

'I was on the point of leaving.'

'No, you weren't,' she declared pertly. 'When we spotted you, you appeared so lost in thought there was no question of your going anywhere.'

He decided not to respond. She then disconcerted him completely with her next words. 'You looked rather lonely, even a little sad, standing and gazing into space as if you had forgotten where you were.'

'I was watching the crews,' he said in defence.

'Why are you alone?'

'The others aren't all that interested in rowing.'

'You are?'

He nodded.

'Were the stables near a river?'

'Stables?'

'Where you worked as an employee who was not in the least "mere".'

'If you're going to cross-question me again, I *will* go.'

She sighed. 'I'm just trying to be friendly. How can one talk without asking questions?' Her greenish eyes looked appealingly at him. 'Is it me you hate or girls generally?'

'For heaven's sake!' he cried. 'You're the daughter of my colonel. You can't ask me things like that.'

'I just have.'

'I refuse to answer.'

'All right. Let me ask you something else. Do you ever smile?'

It was so absurd he felt his tension fading. 'If people are nice enough.'

'I'll truly try to be.'

Unsure of how to handle that, he said, 'You'll get cold standing still. We'd better walk towards the boathouse.'

'You'll have to begin a conversation or I shall be accused of starting a cross-examination again.'

They strolled slowly side by side. 'Which eight is your friend's brother in?'

'You see,' she exclaimed triumphantly, 'it *is* impossible to converse without asking questions.'

'I've been watching the boats for some weeks and picked a likely crew to represent Oxford. It'll be interesting to see whether or not I'm right,' he said with dogged determination to prove her wrong.

'I suppose you know a fair bit about rowing and have even done some yourself.'

That was artful, because he could not claim it as a direct question. He ignored it, and said instead, 'You'll be taken to tea in the Riverside Hotel, no doubt.'

'No doubt.'

'I expect your friend is upset because you left her in order to speak to me.'

'Envious, I should think. You do look tremendously dashing, and she's never met a trooper.'

'You shouldn't be walking with one in a public place.'

'Nonsense! I told you before I'm not a member of the regiment. What I do is my own affair.'

'What you do reflects on your father's standing.'

'I think that concept is quite ridiculous,' she declared, stopping to face him. 'Each person is responsible for his or her consequence alone. No child should be obliged to live a life governed by what a parent has become. If my father happened to be a notorious thief, would angelic behaviour from me

322

improve his standing? Of course not. Why, then, should anything I do worsen it because he happens to be the colonel of a prestigious regiment?' When he said nothing, she demanded, 'Are you going to refuse an answer to that, too?'

'Yes . . . for the simple reason that I can't think of one.'

She smiled. 'You're awfully nice when you stop being arrogant.'

'Your friend is waiting for you,' he pointed out swiftly.

They set off again. 'Father said *you* have a friend in the Sudan. A close friend. Do you know if he's come through the campaign safely?'

What had Beecham *not* passed on about that conversation a few months ago? 'Yes, he's all right.'

'I'm glad.' She took three more slow paces, then said, 'Tell me how you met your friend and what he writes to you of his experiences in the desert.' Halting once more, she hastened to add, 'That's not cross-questioning as you define it. I'm being inquisitive about your friend, not you.'

He stopped, too. 'You're incorrigible!'

'You *do* smile. It makes you look so much more friendly. This is such a beautiful afternoon, you're lonely, and I'm very keen to talk to you. Can't you forget who I am for a while?'

'Of course not . . . and if all you want to do is pry, I shall stop being friendly.'

'Why are you so prickly?' she challenged.

'Why are you so determinedly inquisitive?'

'Because you *are* so prickly. It's as if you have something to hide.'

'Just because I don't choose to tell you all you want to know?'

'You don't tell me *anything* I want to know.'

'Why should I?'

'Because I rather like you.' She blushed then at her impulsive admission, and Val was again struck by the contrast of precociousness and adolescent gaucherie in this unusual girl.

Realising the danger created by her words, he said, 'I think it would be best if you were to join your friend, don't you?'

'You've grown arrogant again,' she accused in frustration. 'Can't you see that I'm on your side? I've made it plain enough on more than one occasion.' As he turned away angrily, she said, 'Don't walk off. I want to help you.'

He looked back at her. 'This conversation is getting us nowhere, Miss Beecham.'

'Father calls you a mystery man.'

'That's ridiculous!' he declared uneasily.

'They all do . . . and Audley hates you without really knowing why.'

'There are over four hundred troopers in the regiment. Why should you all be so concerned about one?'

'Because you stand out from the rest; because you are the only one who says he comes from farming stock yet knows as much about military life as Father, and who enlisted in the ranks when he should so clearly have gone to Sandhurst for a commission. In addition, you never receive any letters – I asked Felix to check that – and you've never applied for short leave. It suggests that you have no friends or relatives, yet you've just admitted that you have a close friendship with someone in the Sudan. Why hasn't he written to you? Why have you no further contact with the invalid son of the man you say employed you? After sharing his tuition and playing cricket with him it seems very strange that someone who must be around your age has no time for the companion of his youth.'

Shaken by all this, Val said, 'Take as much interest in any of the troopers and you'll find he's also a "mystery man". When we pledge ourselves to the regiment, that is for the future. Our pasts are our own. We pledge our bodies and our loyalty, not our souls. The Fifty-seventh Lancers don't *own* me, Miss Beecham. Who I am is their only concern, not who I was.'

'So you *were* a different person from the one you are now?'

Trapped, he said, 'This childish nonsense has gone on long enough. I'll escort you to the boathouse and hand you over to your unfortunate friend.'

Seizing her arm he set off at a good pace, but she resisted so obviously that he had to stop to appease the curiosity of passing couples. She gazed up at him, pale and determined.

'Don't be angry, Havelock. I know there's a forgivable explanation for the mystery, as surely as I know you don't deserve Audley's vindictiveness. Father is an awfully good judge of people. He was very impressed by your refusal of the post in our stables. Most men would have welcomed the chance to escape the dreary routine in a troop. I share his intuition. Whatever you've done, it surely can't warrant forcing you to live as you are. It must be extremely lonely for you. Please let me make it less so by being your friend.'

It was worse than Val guessed. Max Beecham's intuition was wildly wrong. His judgement would undergo swift reversal if he knew the identity of the mystery man. This girl had instigated all the interest in him. He must put a stop to it in the most brutal manner he could devise.

'You don't want to befriend me, you merely want something to occupy your empty, pampered life. A melodrama to give it some spice. Find some other poor devil to investigate and offer *him* your patronising friendship. I can do much better without it.'

He left her on the tow-path and began the long walk back to barracks. As he trudged along in the fast-gathering dusk his mood grew bleaker. Females created nothing but trouble. Vere had been driven to the Sudan by one; Clive surrendered his very life over another. The flighty niece of

Tetherbury's baker had brought trouble quite disproportionate to what she had encouraged him to do. Julia had . . . well, he would not dwell on that. Now this girl was endangering his attempt to defy Julia and build his future. Could none of them be fair, open and genuinely affectionate? Was it impossible to make a true friend of a girl? Was Margaret the only one of her sex to be trusted?

As he recalled that evening before the fire in Herbert Grieves's parlour, he owned that sexual hunger had been building up for several months. His companions spoke frankly of their adventures with local whores, but Julia had turned the act into something shameful for him. His body paid no heed to his mind, however, and the problem was growing. In a curious way, Vivienne Beecham had heightened it this afternoon. Damn the girl!

Walking through the Saturday evening quietness of the barracks, Val suddenly felt acutely homesick. At Knightshill there would be lights everywhere, huge fires, family conversation. Grandfather would be telling repetitive tales at the table set with silver and winking crystal, Margaret smiling across at him. The children would have begged a story from him before going to bed, and Kate would have smothered him with sticky kisses, vowing to marry him one day. Charlotte would discuss the orchids, the lower meadows, the forthcoming plans for Christmas.

He paused outside the door of the two-storey building, unwilling to enter. What a fool he had been to sacrifice everything to a burning desire for the cavalry. But for that he could now be here in Oxford as an undergraduate; could be a crew member of the rowing eights he watched so enviously. He could have friends who shared his interests and background, and he could still indulge his passion for rugby, cross-country running and cricket. Evenings like this could be spent in cosy companionship, discussing world affairs, personal theories, one's hopes and ambitions, with fellows like Clive. There would still be lewd talk of women – nothing would ever stop that between men – but there would be good food, wine and easy laughter to accompany it. Then there would be Sandhurst to look forward to, keen competition, proud traditions handed down through generations. There would only be Cadet V. M. H. Ashleigh. Trooper Havelock would never have existed. He swallowed the lump in his throat. What a fool he had been! All that could have been his if he had only agreed to follow tradition and enter the West Wilts, as Grandfather demanded.

Sleep would not come that night. He lay wide-eyed listening to the rain which now thundered against the windows. The men came in noisily as they returned from Oxford in groups, drenched and chilled. Swearing, most of them the worse for drink, they staggered around preparing for bed whilst exchanging accounts of the anatomy of various females they had met. Even when the last had settled and the lamps had been doused, there was a noisy chorus of snores, belches and other unpleasant human sounds, which was eventually drowned by distant rumbles of thunder. The autumn beauty of the afternoon had given way to a November storm.

Val shivered beneath the coarse blankets. He always slept naked rather than in the thick underwear provided by the army, but he guessed he would have to emulate the others now winter was coming. Slipping from his bed he reached for the vest and long underpants, appreciating their scratchy warmth. To hell with hygiene! Still he lay heavy-hearted, filled with the fire of his own foolishness which had been fuelled by Vivienne Beecham's interference in his affairs. He had been quite happy until she had suggested that he was a lonely misfit who needed a friend. Damn all females! If they did not exist he would not presently have this tormenting urge to feel and caress rounded softness, part white thighs and enter deeply into the rhythmic triumph of subduing weakness with strength.

Half an hour later, the storm broke directly overhead with violent force. Still awake and troubled by his longings, Val felt at one with the elements. The thunderclaps aroused several men, but only enough to set them cursing before drifting back to sleep oblivious of the blinding, fizzing light which alternated with darkness.

It could have been no more than minutes later that a different flickering light nearby took on a frightening reality, when Val heard against the roar of thunder the faint echo of bugles sounding 'stables'. He scrambled up on the bed to peer from the high window. Flames were shooting from the roof of the stables housing his own troop's horses.

'Christ!' he breathed. 'It's been struck.'

Propelled by fear for the animals trapped inside, he leapt to the floor and began to yell at his sleeping comrades, shaking each one violently as he ran from bed to bed before racing down the stone steps to the lower floor of the building. Men were spilling from doorways all around him, half asleep, still a little drunk, responding automatically to a call which years of discipline had taught them to obey. They were soon soaked to the skin by pelting rain. How could a fire blaze in this, Val wondered as he raced along on bare feet.

It was an awesome sight: an inferno fanned by storm winds which sent rain beating into the faces of those who pulled up in shock. Some had already reached the spot and were bringing out the terrified horses with the greatest difficulty. The animals had lost all sense of confidence in their human partners in this frightening situation, and fought their attempts to lead them to safety. The screams of those still trapped added to the beasts' fear. They reared and kicked, rolling their eyes as they spewed foam from mouths drawn back in terror. In the short moment Val halted to take in the overall picture, one great black stallion stopped resisting and rushed

326

forward instead. The man leading him was felled and trampled, letting go the rope so the panic-stricken horse charged through the gathering crowd into the night. Two burly men ran to pull their injured comrade from the path of another animal being dragged along by three troopers.

Val ran forward, calling to those beside him to enter the blazing building. Ten yards from the entrance they were halted by the collapse of the roof, which cut off hopes of reaching those animals inside. Samson was among them. Equine screams filled Val's ears to the exclusion of all other sounds as he started forward again. His path was immediately barred by a man in a blackened dress shirt and dark trousers, whose hair was tumbled and whose face was working with great distress. It was the duty officer.

'Get back!' he shouted hoarsely. 'The fire engine will be along soon. It's hopeless.'

Val swerved past him and made for the small access door half-way down the stables. As he ran, he shouted to some men nearby to follow him. Tugging at the door, he then realised it was bolted inside. Together with those who had followed him he flung himself at it several times, but even their combined weight could not shift the door. The roar of the flames was so loud he could hardly make himself heard. Smoke roughened his voice as he added gestures to his instructions that one man should stand on another's shoulders so that he could climb up them to one of the skylights in the tin roof.

'It'll be no use,' cried one, backing away. 'The rest'll go up any minute.'

'*Do it!*' Val bellowed. 'There's not much time.'

''ere, let me.' The giant Deadman was there beside him. 'Get up there quick, boy. I'll come in soon's yer opens the door. So will these buggers, I promise yer.'

Deadman had two men stacked on his broad shoulders in no time. Val began to scramble up the wavering human ladder, his feet slipping on their sodden garments. If only he had stopped to put his boots on! Rain almost blinded him, but the glare of the flames showed the skylight as a fiery pool in the darkness. Reaching the guttering, he then found the slippery roof even more difficult for keeping a foothold. He prayed for help, something he had done only once before, at Tetherbury Pond. As then, very little came in response to his desperate plea. It appeared to be all up to him as he clung precariously to the surface where rain slid down the corrugated tin in an unbroken sheet. Even so, he inched towards his goal while flames raced over the ridged roof to turn it into a glowing skeleton liable to disintegrate, section by section.

The skylight was made of thicker glass than Val had anticipated. Thumping it with one fist was useless, and he had to risk his handhold in order to use them both. Three mighty blows jerked him from his slender foothold, but the glass shattered as he began to slide. Flinging up his arms he grabbed desperately at the shattered window. The jagged edge cut deeply into his palms, making him gasp with the pain. For a long moment he hung there spreadeagled. Then he gritted his teeth and pulled himself up, driving the glass deeper into his flesh. Once he was sitting securely on the framework of the skylight, he gave himself a few moments to gather his strength and fight the pain in his bleeding hands before attacking the glass again to make a gap big enough to squeeze through. For once, he cursed the physique he had so determinedly built up.

One downward glance at the scene inside took away all thought but the need for action. Abandoning caution he kicked viciously with his left heel to shatter the remaining corner of glass. His entry was almost suicidal, for he tumbled twenty feet to the floor. Only the covering of straw saved him from further injury, but he was momentarily winded before struggling to his feet and running for the door. He groaned with dismay when his bleeding hands slipped on the heavy bolts he tried to pull back. Snatching up some straw, he used it for purchase as he dragged each one along and flung open the door.

He did not wait to see who entered. The fire had claimed four beasts and was licking at the stalls of the next two in line. They were mad with fear, dancing around and jerking at the ropes tethering them. Val ran to one, risking injury as he sidled towards the animal's head. It was beyond listening, or seeing anything but the flames. The heat here was overwhelming; smoke billows threatened breathing. The vivid core of the fire almost blinded Val as he tugged at the knots of the tether. Even as he released the stallion he told himself it would be almost impossible to persuade it through the door only just high and wide enough. The horse was too fearful to heed commands.

Pulling off his saturated vest, Val wrapped it around the animal's head then loosed the tether completely and pushed on the black shoulders. Cut off from the fearsome sights, if not the sounds, the stallion then became manageable enough to push and drag from the stall into the aisle running between them. Only vaguely aware that others were in the stable, Val used his formidable strength to force the beast in the required direction, his concentration on the task such that noise, heat, smoke and a sense of danger retreated to the background.

That curious oblivion to all else continued after he had sent the one out through the small aperture and approached another – Samson. In this detached world he was only half aware of shouting to those around him, directing them, rushing to their aid, taking over when they became too exhausted. There was then only one other in that growing hell: a giant of a man even stronger than he. The hell then expanded to become a flaming

328

purgatory. In it, there was the Devil's mount: a rearing, red-eyed monster, a killer stallion running free and intent on death for them all. Against a background of flames and the black night, the beast charged time and again to prevent ropes being thrown around its neck. Val seemed to be living a nightmare of the darkest kind as the great head with flaring nostrils and glowing eyes came at him yet again. He twisted away, slipped and fell on the wet stone floor. But hands seized his ankles and he was dragged free of hooves which stamped at him in fury.

The nightmare reached its climax then. With a roar which penetrated his half-awareness, the world collapsed in a mass of flame all around Val. His whole body began to burn with it, but a voice within him spoke of another man in the fiery hell of the desert who had kept going in his agony. *He must keep going now.* The giant who had dragged him free of the murderous hooves now resembled a grotesque gargoyle rolling in fire. Seizing hold of him, Val told him to stay awake and not go under. But he was tired and confused himself. How would they reach the bank through the ice on the pond with that wall of fire ahead? Clive was so heavy to keep afloat in his saturated overcoat. How could there be such burning agony in icy waters? Ice burned, of course. He had been taught that at school. Voices told him he must get the message from Gordon to the Relief Force. The knife wounds in his chest were slowly killing him, but he must continue somehow. Had he enough courage – or would he fail in this, too?

He summoned the courage, and perhaps the message was delivered. Or was it the bank of Tetherbury Pond that he reached? And was it Clive he had saved, or a man of the desert, as black as coal? All he knew was that he finally reached friends. He could lie down and sleep. They told him he must do so.

It was mid-December before Val was allowed to leave the military hospital. Even then, he was put on light duties for a month. The anguish of the burns to his arms and torso had dulled. The puckered flesh was no longer bright red, although movement was still painful. The scars on his palms might never vanish completely. Thankfully, the deep cuts had not damaged the tendons, so he could use them without restriction. They had trimmed the singed ends from his hair so, when fully dressed, no one would guess at the marks of his suffering which remained as a penalty of that night.

Six men had been injured badly enough to warrant treatment in the nearest army hospital. Deadman was still critically ill in isolation. Six others had been detained in the barracks infirmary. Those in the hospital had received a letter from Max Beecham, and a parcel from his wife. Only one had been sent additional tokens accompanied by an anonymous message. Several books, including a volume of poems, hothouse peaches, and bunches of winter roses delivered to Trooper Havelock had earned him merciless teasing from other men in the ward. He thanked Vivienne Beecham for having the sense not to put her name on the gifts.

The worst burning was on his back, forcing him to lie prone most of the time. Reluctant though he was to admit it, Val had enjoyed her letters. She wrote as she spoke, with great enthusiasm and a mixture of confidence with immaturity. He had read each one avidly, disappointed when they came to an end. Through these communications, he had learned the full toll taken by the fire, of the rebuilding of the stables, and of Pickering's discomfiture over stories of a certain person's courage and daring. When Val had despaired of learning what he most wanted to know from her first letter, he found a reassuring postscript. *A26 misses you and waits for your return . . . as others do.*

Vivienne's letters helped him through the worst days. He had not answered them, of course, but he had reread them whenever pain prevented sleep. They spoke with a familiar voice of things he understood and loved. He had strongly disagreed with some of her declarations; others had made him smile. She could have been Kate, ten years older, writing such things to him. He had thought of his family during the weary days of recovery. On his enlistment paper the word *none* had been written in the space for the name of next of kin, with a note to inform the rector of Dunstan St Mary in the event of his death. If he had perished in the fire, Margaret would have been deeply stricken, Charlotte too, he supposed. What of his grandfather? He now had an heir of exactly the right calibre. A disgraced schoolboy who had died under a false name, wearing the wrong uniform with no insignia of rank, would possibly be considered better out of the way.

On his return to barracks, Val was soon faced with a problem. He was told to report to the CO's house at eleven one morning, and he began to worry. An official matter would be dealt with in Beecham's office so it must be a personal interview. His heart sank as he wondered if the trend was going to continue, with an accusation of offensive behaviour towards Vivienne Beecham. He had done nothing worse than talk to her along the tow-path, although the Macmillan girl had probably seen him pulling her by the arm and arguing. Females seemed to delight in beckoning to him then pleading outraged innocence. He wished he had not destroyed all the girl's letters on leaving hospital. They were evidence of her part in the affair. But *gentlemen* did not resort to such tactics. Instead they stoically bore the blame for the misdeeds of the fair sex. Val thought it totally unjust.

He was told to wait in a library very similar to the one at Knightshill, but on a smaller scale. There was a desk, and a number of maps on a rotating frame for easy reference. The atmosphere reminded him of his last interview with Sir Gilliard, when he had been told he must live Vorne's curtailed life for him. His reply had been that he must live his own. A fine mess he was making of it, he thought dismally.

The door opened to admit a small figure moving with furtive speed. She wore a woollen dress of green and black plaid with a satin collar and long ribbons at the waist. Her eyes were glowing as she crossed to him in the same swift, furtive manner.

'I saw you arrive.' Before he knew it, she gripped his upper arms and stood on tiptoe to kiss him full on the mouth. '*Darling* Havelock. I knew you couldn't possibly be a villain.'

He stepped back very smartly, expecting the hand of a vengeful parent to fall on his shoulder. But they were still the only people in the room.

'If your father finds you here, there'll be the very devil to pay,' he protested, completely thrown by her behaviour.

She was deaf to his words. 'I knew you were too ill to answer my letters, but just sending them helped. You did read them, didn't you?'

'Of course,' he said, with his eye on the door.

'Poor Havelock! Were you in *terrible* pain?' she asked, stepping nearer.

'No . . . well, yes. Sometimes. Look,' he continued, fearing she was about to do something else impulsive, 'I'm here for an interview with your father. Please go before he walks in.'

Her tender smile defied him. 'It's absolutely lovely to see you. I was so afraid you'd be dreadfully scarred.'

'No, just dreadfully afraid of Colonel Beecham.'

'You're not afraid of *anything*. You proved that beyond all doubt. I'm so proud of you . . . and so is Father.'

'Please go,' he begged.

'Only if you promise we'll be friends.'

'How can I?'

'*Promise!*'

Feeling trapped again by the unfair weapons these creatures used so cleverly, he said what she wanted to hear in the hope that she would stick to her bargain. At the door she gave him a dazzling, delighted smile.

'I've practically won the battle. Before, you would have put on that arrogant air and set me in my place. You've now stopped resisting. I'll soon have you eating out of my hand.'

As the door closed behind her, he muttered, 'Oh, no, you won't. None of you will ever make me do that again.'

He was left for a further ten minutes to develop that thought. Then Max Beecham came to greet him in a brisk fashion which gave Val no clue to his mood. Sitting behind the desk, the senior man told him to take the chair on the other side of it. Val did so with apprehension.

'Feeling all right now?' Beecham asked, studying him keenly.

'Yes, thank you, sir.'

'Good. That was a fine display of courage you gave. I've seen to it that mention of your action goes on your record.' He frowned. 'There's no question of an official commendation, of course. You ignored a direct order from Captain Richards, risking not only your own life but that of a dozen others. This is not the first time you have seen fit to overrule the commands of your superiors, Havelock.'

He remained silent.

'Do you believe such behaviour is justified?'

'In the second instance, yes,' he said frankly. 'The situation was extremely difficult to assess due to the storm and the unpredictable reactions of the horses. Captain Richards was attempting to control everything at once. No single man could be expected to make order from such chaos under those impossible conditions. It was my troop's stable afire, sir. I knew the layout intimately and I reckoned there was more than a good chance of saving some of the trapped animals through that side door. There was no time to explain it all to Captain Richards. He had more than enough to cope with, and the stables were in danger of collapsing at any moment.'

'But that knowledge didn't deter you from climbing in?'

He shook his head slowly. 'Apparently not. I heard the horses screaming. It's a most terrible sound, sir.'

'I know, Havelock. It chills one's blood.' He frowned again. 'Have you ever heard the screams of burning *men*?'

'No, sir, but my grandfather once described the —' He stopped abruptly, aware of the danger into which he was heading.

'Yes?'

'Nothing, sir.'

'I see.' He studied Val assessingly for an uncomfortably long period. Then he said with a return to briskness, 'I am extremely proud of this regiment. It has a fine history, and I intend to maintain its reputation during my command of it. I want men like you, Havelock. You're a credit to the Fifty-seventh.'

'Thank you, sir,' he breathed with relief.

'*But* . . . if you are going to take it upon yourself to act on your own initiative and lead your fellows into dangerously courageous situations, I want you wearing the insignia of rank which entitles you to do so. I cannot have my troopers taking command whenever they see fit.' He leaned back in the leather chair. 'In case you have failed to grasp my message, I'll put it in plainer terms. I asked you to come here rather than to my office because I wished this conversation to be utterly confidential. You've been with the

Fifty-seventh for nine months, and for most of that time it has been apparent to your troop commanders that you have a great deal of daring and personal pride. The latter has frequently led you into trouble.' He pursed his lips thoughtfully. 'We all have pride of some kind or other, young man. Mine takes the form of believing my judgement of character is infallible. It tells me you would serve my regiment better as one of its officers.'

Val's expression must have betrayed his feelings, for Max Beecham gave a faint smile. 'As I thought. You share my opinion. That brings us to the question of why you enlisted in the ranks instead of applying to enter Sandhurst and take up a commission. No, don't answer yet,' he warned, holding up his hand. 'I want first to tell you I would be very gratified to have you as one of my officers . . . and I don't say that to every man who applies to me for the honour. But I expect young men to be worthy in every respect. Havelock, I am going to ask you if there is any reason why you could not accept the role of officer and gentleman. Whatever you say in reply will go no further than this room. It will also be put aside by me at the end of this conversation. A man's past is his own affair and should not be held against his future. But I demand honesty from you . . . and I am conceited enough to believe that I shall get it.'

The silence that followed was so intense Val believed his racing heartbeat must be heard by the man who had just offered him the world on a plate. All he yearned for was his for the taking. Here was that golden opportunity to prove himself, regain self-respect, fulfil his vow to make his family proud of him. Here was the chance to honour the memory of Vorne Ashleigh. Here was the world on a plate, yet he must dash it to the ground. This man had just made it impossible for the lies to continue.

Getting to his feet, he looked back at Julia's uncle feeling sick to his stomach. 'Martin Havelock are my middle names, sir. I'm Val Ashleigh.'

He waited for the expression of deep disgust, the condemnation, the outrage. But the moment went on and on until he believed his legs would no longer bear his weight.

'You can't be one of General Ashleigh's grandsons. They serve in the West Wilts.'

'Not this one, sir.'

'Good God,' came the slow, astonished exclamation. 'But why . . . ?' He got up with a frown. 'I can't make any sense of this. Why this damned ridiculous masquerade, Ashleigh? Why not apply to me straightway for a commission?'

Val stared at him in a state of complete turmoil. 'I thought . . . I was certain you'd . . . I was sure you'd turn down an application from *me*.'

'Nonsense, you young fool. You must have known very well you'd not be turned down by *any* commanding officer. One of Sir Gilliard's boys? It's the wildest explanation for the mystery that I can imagine, and I won't accept the feeble excuse that you thought I'd not have you in the Fifty-seventh. There must be more to it than you've said.'

As he tried to grapple with this incomprehensible conversation, Val heard himself say, 'My grandfather vowed to block any attempt by me to join the cavalry. He – he insisted on my following family tradition.'

Max Beecham expelled his breath in a gust as he looked Val over from head to tow. 'An *Ashleigh*, eh? That makes so many things clear. My judgement of men never lets me down. I knew you possessed all the qualities I look for but, unfortunately, your determined old grandparent will have his way in one respect. There'll be no Ashleigh from Knightshill in the cavalry. You enlisted as Martin Havelock and that's who you must continue to be, whatever rank you attain.' He held out his hand. 'When you leave this room I shall forget your true identity, but I shall put you where you have every right to be as soon as opportunity permits.'

As Val shook hands with this warmly genuine man he had to accept the staggering truth. Julia had never written or spoken to her uncle about a boy desperate to join the Ghost Lancers. She had never tried to arrange a meeting between them at Blandford. Until now, Max Beecham had not heard the name Val Ashleigh.

Chapter Eighteen

Vere returned to Knightshill a week before Christmas. He did not advise his family of his impending arrival, so he crossed to the Stag's Head Inn from the station to hire one of Moorkin's carriages. It was half an hour before he set out, so great was the enthusiasm of the landlord and his customers on seeing him safely home. They welcomed him as a hero, but he now knew that heroes were soon created by those needing reflected glory.

He told the driver to stop at the bend in the lane, saying he would walk from there, leaving his baggage to be delivered at the front entrance. When the carriage rolled on, he turned towards the house with its great window dominating the central façade. It looked almost formidable in the cold December light. Turning up his overcoat collar, he studied the home and prosperous surrounding acres which he had left in a state of frozen misery eighteen months before, not expecting to return. The house had once been filled by a large, loving family. One by one, they had departed in less than glorious circumstances. Only Charlotte remained with a grand old man who alone bore Ashleigh pride on his shoulders. The rest had done little to preserve it.

The news of Margaret's flight with the children had shocked and saddened him. She had apparently known Nicolardi only a few weeks, and no one save Philip had guessed the truth. Charlotte believed dread of going to Africa had driven their sister to such madness, and feared for her future with a man she had suspected from the start of hiding from the consequences of an earlier disgrace. Philip had damned all Ashleighs to hell and wiped his family from his life on leaving Knightshill, but discreet enquiries instigated by Sir Gilliard suggested the lovers had gone abroad. Nicolardi had resigned his post, and his banker had only the address of the family in Verona who could forward correspondence. The four had effectively vanished. There was no hint of scandal because friends believed the Daulton family to be in Africa, but the affair had devastated those left at Knightshill.

Not yet acclimatised, Vere's teeth began chattering when he turned into the icy wind and walked upward through the gate leading to formal gardens. He noted with pleasure that John Morgan had worked hard and devotedly on land which was deeply productive. As the bailiff could never own it, this was true labour of love. His attention was then caught by an excited cry, and he stopped to watch a girl in a dark red coat running towards him so fast she seemed in danger of falling headlong. Charlotte flung herself against him, and he enclosed her in a bear hug as they laughed and cried their mutual delight.

'Why didn't you let me know you were coming?' she demanded, as they walked with their arms entwined. 'There's no fire in your rooms, the bed is unaired. And is that baggage really all yours?' She stopped again to study him with concern. 'How are you feeling, Vere?'

He grinned. 'Somewhat bewildered.'

'But you're strong – *really* strong?'

'I think I must be, don't you?' He urged her forward. 'How's Grandfather?'

'Better than he was. First Val, then Margaret.' She sighed. 'The news of Omdurman restored some of his spirits. He's very proud of you.'

'Is he?'

She did not notice the doubt in his tone. 'We saw your pictures in the magazines. They're not in the least like your usual work, but they're *so* impressive. Everyone's full of admiration.'

'Is *he*?'

335

She glanced up as they crossed the terrace. 'Grandfather? Of course! They're his kind of world, aren't they? You can command high prices for your work. I've had many written enquiries about your earlier canvases. You can answer them yourself now.' She squeezed his arm. 'It's *so* good to have you back, Vere.'

The baggage was piled in the hall beside Winters, whose warm smile softened his austere features. 'It's a very great pleasure to welcome you home, sir.'

'How are you, Winters?' he asked, shaking the man's hand.

'In good health, thank you. It was a fine victory at Omdurman, Mr Ashleigh.'

Omdurman. The name was burnt into his breast for ever more. It now echoed around this vaulted hall, as if seeking out some sleeping ghost to awaken and drive away to the place where it truly belonged. It chilled Vere more than the winter outside.

'Is my grandfather expecting me?'

'He's waiting in the library, sir. I have been instructed to bring tea to the sitting room in about half an hour. Will that be convenient?'

'Perfectly.' He shrugged off his coat. 'We'll join you there, Lottie.'

'*Do* hurry,' she begged. 'I have so much to ask you.'

Sir Gilliard was standing by the fireplace, as erect as ever and showing few signs of age other than his white hair and slightly gnarled hands. His eyes were as vividly blue as Vere remembered, his face as full of character. How curious that in gaining greater respect for this proud man he had grown less in awe of him. It was now possible to understand how life had moulded him into the person he was. Those eyes had gazed across plain, desert or jungle-clad hills seeking the enemy; that mind had controlled an entire army; that body had triumphed over pain, sickness, incredible hardship. During all that, the woman he loved had slipped away in the cruellest fashion leaving behind an embryo warrior, whom he had also lost. There had been three further hopes for consolation. One was a soldier who had triumphed as an artist; another was a rebel who had courted disgrace. Surely this man deserved his hero.

Vere stopped a few feet from Sir Gilliard. 'Hello, sir.'

'You resemble a damned Dervish.'

'Yes. This brown face looks out of place in the middle of Wiltshire.'

They studied each other for a while, then the older man slowly put out his hand. 'Welcome home, my boy.'

Vere gripped it hard. 'It's good to be back.'

'Did you travel with your regiment?'

'They're awaiting a ship at Alexandria. Those of us who didn't take long leave after Atbara came on ahead.'

'You saw action, I believe?' Sir Gilliard said with feigned casualness.

'The Dervish is very courageous, sir. He's badly trained and his weapons are antique, otherwise we'd have had a much harder time of it.'

'Mmm. Heard it was a rather one-sided affair. Made me wonder why we didn't go after 'em long before this. What of Kitchener? Is he a general?'

'You must know the details of how he regained Khartoum in a land nature has cursed. A general yourself, you're better qualified to judge him than is a mere second lieutenant.'

The bright eyes studied him shrewdly from beneath a furrowed brow. 'You've become a man.'

'I was already a man,' he replied firmly. 'I've simply become an Ashleigh.'

'Ha! Typical subaltern! Plenty to say for yourself.'

This attitude of gruff approval typified their changed relationship. The old general was in a province he knew and loved; a junior officer was a different creature from a nature-loving artist. Vere accepted this. The soldier understood his grandfather better than the painter had.

'Heard about the boy, I suppose,' Sir Gilliard said then. 'Disgraced himself and let us all down badly. Wasn't man enough to come and apologise, then accept his punishment. Slunk off somewhere. Haven't heard of him since. Good thing, eh?'

'No, sir, it's a very *bad* thing,' Vere told him gravely. 'If you hadn't forbidden him to join the cavalry, none of it would have happened. With your backing he could now have been at Sandhurst ready for an honourable career. Instead, the poor lad is probably living rough, mistakenly bearing a burden of guilt and shame. He's not yet twenty, and the golden life which should have been his has been irreparably tarnished. Do you really consider that a good thing?'

Sir Gilliard seemed dumbfounded, but he soon recovered. 'How dare you speak to me in that manner?'

'Because I'm your heir. You had grave doubts on whether I could replace you, even whether I could outlive you. I believe I can do both. As I shall become head of the family when you go, I must be allowed to express my opinion on anything which will be my future concern. Val is one of them. Any truly responsible commander consults his subordinate and listens to what he says, knowing he could be called upon to take over. Your justifiable pride in this family should have led you to recognise that Ashleighs through the ages have been men of individuality, like yourself. Their success was due to each one using the talents he was given. You must not attempt to force us to be copies of you . . . or of any other Ashleigh. You might have ruined a boy who has the capacity to be the greatest of all.'

'The greatest of all lies beneath the sands outside Khartoum.'

337

The painful decision to allow an old man his dream kept Vere silent.

'Did you . . . did you find his resting-place?'

'Yes.'

'You saw the stone, the moving inscription?'

'The regiment had honoured him in the best possible style.'

'Good. Good.' The bright eyes misted with tears. 'You paid homage on behalf of us all?'

'A group of us went ashore for the purpose. Others were buried there.' A vision of that horrific scene made him add, 'The Sudan is a land of bones, sir. Thousands will lie buried beneath the sands for ever and few will be honoured as he has been.'

'Few were heroes.'

'They were good, honest men. Each one who perished in that God-forsaken land could be called a hero, in my opinion.'

There was a short silence. 'You appear to have formed a number of opinions since we last met.'

'I've always had opinions. I now voice them because I've been with men prepared to listen.'

'As I was not?'

He hesitated. 'I was a man of peace. I still am, but have learned that it's not always gained by remaining silent. Sometimes it's necessary to use a loud voice so the enemy understands what's being said.'

'You regard *me* as the enemy?'

'I hope to find you my ally in the days to come.'

Sir Gilliard considered that as he studied Vere with a frown. He then moved slowly to a small table containing decanters and poured brandy, saying over his shoulder, 'I suppose you are robust enough to take spirits?'

Vere crossed to him and took one of the goblets. 'At Abu Hamed I was actually warned about my excessive drinking.'

They crossed to sit in chairs flanking the fireplace, warming the brandy in the glow from the blazing logs. Sir Gilliard spoke thoughtfully. 'So Alderton has been in error all these years.'

'For the past few, certainly.'

'One of your future concerns is the question of producing sons of your own. You'll be looking out for a bride. I hear the Bourneville girl is still unwed.'

'And likely to remain so,' Vere said with a spark of anger. 'The man she looks for doesn't exist.'

'So who will you go after, eh?'

The anger burst into flame. 'You now have an heir who is healthy and commissioned in the service of the Queen. With that you will have to be content. The question of when and whom, even *if* I marry is my own

338

concern. I'll tolerate no interference in my personal life. Now, sir, unless you're prepared to slacken the reins and recognise me as your second-in-command, I cannot remain here.'

They faced each other by the light of a fire which brightened the late-afternoon gloom: a general with no army and a man who had silenced the cry in his heart. Finally, Sir Gilliard said gruffly, 'If you were one of *my* officers, I'd give you a very sharp set-down then mark you as extremely promising.'

Vere realised it was the only response he was going to get, but he smiled and raised his glass. 'Your health, Grandfather.'

'And yours, Vere.'

Christmas came and went. Vere tried to enjoy something he had anticipated with pleasure. They brought in a fir, as usual, but dressing it with candles and sweetmeats was an empty task without Kate and Timothy. The carol-singers came up from the village; he ate roast goose and plum pudding in company with local friends. Yet he felt totally isolated from traditions he had always enjoyed. Without Margaret and the children, without Val's youthful exuberance, everything fell curiously flat. The house contained too many ghosts. Charlotte's clinging solicitude grew increasingly irritating. They had been so close; he had found pleasure in her undemanding company. Now, he caught himself sneaking from the house in a bid to be alone. The tranquillity she had once radiated had been replaced by an almost desperate desire to share his every moment, even his every thought. He guessed she had been very lonely after Margaret left, but resistance to being the alleviator of it was building up.

His future as an artist had never been so promising. Vere Ashleigh was the man of the moment in the world of those who bought a name rather than a picture they admired. Armand Lisère in Cairo had sold the set of sepia paintings and wrote inviting him to send other canvases. But the muse had left Vere for the moment. He was trying to come to terms with his future.

His leave was almost over. His regiment was due for a quiet period in barracks in Lincolnshire. He had intended to resign his commission and follow his desire to run the estate, grow flowers on a commercial scale, and paint. For the first few days he had spent much time with John Morgan, impressed by the way he had managed everything, but his thoughts had wandered to the remembered sight of a camel caravan on the horizon when discussing cattle, and to the beauty of Floria Pallini on being shown gardenias which had replaced the orchids. He compared the bucolic earnestness of the bailiff with the unconscious philosophy of Private Perkins, or the cheery respect of Corporal French all the way to Omdurman.

339

Memories of Cairo intruded when Vere surveyed the vista around Knightshill. The winter moon shining into his room set him yearning for the cold clarity of its beams reflecting in the Nile, as seen through the open flap of his tent. He missed Ross, and others like him. He often thought of Steadman, the perfect warrior who lay beneath the sands for ever, and even of the man whose name he could not recall who had stood on the jetty at Berber, joking that only a bally fool would wait with no more than a sergeant for a boatload of Dervishes. Time and again his mind strayed to those with whom he had marched, thirsted and joked beneath the blistering sun. Curiously, it was not the suffering, the enormous inhumanity of battle he could not forget, it was the friendship and unassuming stoicism of those on whom he had depended for his life. There was nothing at Knightshill to match it.

On the morning of the last day of 1898 Vere received a letter from the magazine which had printed his pictures. It offered him a contract for exclusive rights to any future sketches he might do during campaigns anywhere in the world. On the point of writing a letter of resignation to Colonel Winterton, Vere again reviewed his future. A minimum of two years in barracks did not suggest the answer to his restlessness. Was it time to part from the men who had crossed the desert with him, or would Lincolnshire in winter still his yearnings? Perhaps he could go to theatres of war as a civilian artist. Would the magazine accept that idea? Could *he* accept it?

Unable to get to grips with the problem, he took up the newspaper and began to read. The first column dealt with the situation at Fashoda, where the French had attempted to gain some influence along the Nile by raising the tricolour over the unimportant settlement. Kitchener had taken a small force from Omdurman to raise the British flag instead. Among that force were Ross, Reggie Forrester and the men Vere had known at Abu Hamed. Once more, memories swamped him to revive frustration and uncertainty.

In the act of setting aside the newspaper, a minor headline caught his eye and he read with a mixture of emotions of the murder of yet another missionary in Africa. The Reverend Philip Monk Daulton and his helper, Sister Agnes Drew, had been found dead in the charred remains of their mission during a tribal war prompted by the siting of the new East African railway, which cut through tribal territories. The deaths must once more raise the question of whether or not missionaries should be permitted to penetrate far into the interior, where tribal lore was so strong as to cast doubts on their effectiveness.

Lowering the paper, Vere gazed into space imagining what the report would have contained if Philip had succeeded in taking his wife and children to that isolated spot. Dear God, it did not bear contemplation!

340

Shock brought visions of burnt villages *en route* to Omdurman and fill his ears with the screams of those massacred innocents. How would Charlotte and Sir Gilliard feel *now* about Margaret's actions? They never mentioned her, considered her beyond the pale for seizing her chance of happiness with a man who must surely love the children, too. Nicolardi's advent had been at the most propitious time to avert total disaster for a woman and two bright, beautiful children. Philip's god had smiled on his family and deserted him, it seemed.

Only then did it occur to Vere that Margaret was free to marry her lover and give the children a legal stepfather. Getting to his feet, he walked to the far window which gave a view of the slope where his sister loved to walk. Where was she? From what Charlotte had written of the affair in her letter, he deduced Nicolardi had given their whereabouts to his family in Verona. A letter enclosing the cutting from the paper, addressed to the Italians would be the best way of ensuring Margaret knew of Philip's death. She might be in a place where news reached her late, or not at all.

Acting on the decision, Vere went to his rooms and sat at the desk. He wrote swiftly, covering several pages in his eagerness to make contact with those he missed in a home which had once been so lively. He ended by expressing a hope that his dear sister would reply and tell him about her new life. Sending love to her, Timothy and Kate, he sealed the envelope and began to write the address given by Nicolardi's banker. Then, like a ray of bright sunshine penetrating the gloom, an idea hit him. Why not go in person with the letter? Why not travel to Verona?

He walked back and forth developing the notion with growing excitement. *Italy!* The land of Floria Pallini's birth, land of culture, art and ancient stones. He would see famous galleries, ruins, romantic villages. At the opera he would hear the great voices. He would soak up the sun and wander in Bohemian fashion through narrow streets where artists copied scenes people came from all over the world to see. Venice, Rome, Florence: the prospect was unbearably exciting. *This* was what he needed; *this* would surely still his yearning.

On the fourth day of the new year influenza hit the residents of Knightshill. With his blood thinned by desert heat, Vere was afflicted more seriously than anyone else and Sir Gilliard began once more to doubt the strength of his grandson's constitution. Back on his feet, Vere determinedly set about making plans for his trip to Italy. He had decided to post the letter to Margaret, so the news would be on its way while he engaged in arrangements for a lengthy trip. He said nothing of it to his family, deciding to wait until the eve of his departure.

It snowed heavily on 20 January. During after-luncheon coffee in the small sitting room, Vere and Charlotte discussed the prospects of relatives arriving for the Khartoum Dinner, while their grandfather read the newspaper.

'Ned heard the line is blocked near Winklesham,' Charlotte said. 'The Carlton-Jays are unlikely to get through.'

'If they've any sense, they won't set out,' Vere commented. 'They're liable to be stranded here for days if it continues as it did two years ago.'

'When Miss Bourneville was here,' put in his sister tartly.

'When Val was jumped on by the whole family for saying he wanted to join the cavalry,' he replied just as tartly.

Before Charlotte could respond further, they were interrupted by the entry of Winters with the mail.

'Ha, at last!' declared Sir Gilliard, putting aside the newspaper with energy. 'Is the *Military Quarterly* there, man? Want to see if anyone has dared respond to my letter concerning Nugent's abortive attack in 'Fifty-eight.'

The butler laid out the letters and packets addressed to the old general, then placed several before Vere and Charlotte. When he made no move to leave, Vere glanced up from sorting his letters. The man looked upset.

'What is it, Winters?'

'There is a communication addressed to Mrs Daulton, sir . . . in Master Valentine's handwriting.'

The room grew unnaturally quiet. Vere looked across at his grandfather and met a stony expression. The same from his sister. He stood up, took the letter from the tray, and nodded dismissal to Winters. His companions were still silent and grim as he slit the envelope and began to read the contents aloud in determined fashion.

My dear Aunt Meg
When you receive this I shall be in South Africa. Don't be angry with me for not writing sooner. I waited until I could show I am attempting to redeem myself. I joined the ranks of the 57th Lancers in April. The life suits me very well. I have a fine horse called Samson, who is almost as splendid as Merlin. Apart from a frightful silly ass called Pickering, the officers are very dedicated. The men are second to none. A Troop, to which I belong, is the best in the regiment. Max Beecham is the finest colonel anyone could want. After an incident concerning a fire in the stables, he was good enough to offer me a commission. I had to confess my identity and waited for his condemnation, but it seems Julia Grieves had never approached him about my hope of joining the regiment. That affair at Chartfield

342

was a pretty rotten trick on her part, don't you think? Sandhurst is out of the question because of my false enlistment. Fortunately, there is trouble afoot in Pretoria and other areas of South Africa, so we're likely to see action before long. Colonel Beecham has promised to commission me in the field if I earn the honour. I'll do my very best. For the moment, I'm Corporal Martin Havelock. I hope Grandfather won't consider the rank too lowly, because I'm learning my profession in the most thorough manner possible.

Saw the pictures in the magazine. Good old Vere! Can't understand why he didn't do one of Khartoum and Kitchener's memorial service, though. Perhaps they're saving it for a special edition.

I missed you all at Christmas. It was quiet in barracks despite preparations for the voyage being under way. Most men went home. I thought of coming to have a look at Knightshill from the village, then realised it was a pretty idiotic idea. When I come, it will be as an officer with an honourable record which will wipe out that awful affair.

Give the children my love, also Lottie, Vere and Grandfather. To you I send the very warmest affection, because you've been more than a sister to me. I can never repay you for that, but I swear I'll earn your trust and devotion one day.

Val

Vere finished reading and looked up, clearing his throat before saying, 'This was posted in Sierra Leone *en route* to Cape Town. I hope *no one* in this house will again say he has let us all down badly.'

Only a small number gathered at Knightshill for the Khartoum Dinner. No family members had reached Wiltshire due to a severe blizzard overnight. The colonel and eight officers of the West Wiltshire Regiment had battled through from Salisbury to honour their hero. As there were no female guests Charlotte remained in her room, and Vere stood with Sir Gilliard to offer sherry before the meal. This year, he wore a scarlet jacket like the others. Knowing the evening would prove a severe test, he was nevertheless soon in conversation with men who bombarded him with questions on the campaign in which he had fought. He had no hesitation in speaking of every aspect of it and his descriptive powers created avid listeners. Only when Khartoum was mentioned did he produce the lie that a wound had prevented him from crossing the Nile for the memorial service.

Tonight, he was supremely at ease with those who had formerly been alienated by the scarlet jacket. Tonight, he spoke as they did and recalled anecdotes to relate to an amused audience. Tonight, he enjoyed being with men who had experienced the desert and understood his inability to forget it.

Was he, after all, a true Ashleigh who would never settle to a country life? Would desert sunsets continue to haunt him when twilight came? Would he lie in bed in the peace of this county imagining distant bugles, and sigh? Would he for ever catch the echo of a thousand marching feet in the beat of rain on a window, or hear in the calls of sheep the quiet laughter of men bivouacking beneath the midday sun? And when darkness fell, would his seeking eyes create an image of glowing camp-fires beneath a spread of stars in dark equatorial skies? Would Second Lieutenant V. P. R. Ashleigh ever die now he had come alive?

'So, you defied your doctor to follow family tradition,' said a voice beside him, breaking into his trance. 'You took a great risk with your life.'

Vere turned to find at his side Gerard Dunwoody, colonel of the West Wiltshire Regiment. 'A worthwhile risk, as it turned out, sir.'

'Medical opinion in error, eh?'

'More probably a case of acceptance of past diagnoses. My youth was dogged by fever.'

Dunwoody's long face lit in a smile. 'You're now an old man?'

'Older in wisdom and experience, certainly.'

'When do you rejoin your regiment?'

Vere had not yet penned his resignation to Colonel Winterton. 'I'm not certain I shall.'

Dunwoody's smile broadened. 'We understand each other perfectly.'

Baffled, Vere asked, 'We do?'

'While it was understandable that you should join another regiment in order to avenge the death of our hero, you can now transfer with honour. There's no more propitious time for you to join us, Ashleigh. I understand you're well informed on oriental history.'

What had that to do with his transferring to the West Wilts, a move which had never occurred to him? Completely out of his depth, Vere murmured, 'Only in the context of cultural art.'

'And you sketch very well. Did some valuable field work for Reggie Forrester, I heard, apart from those impressive studies of the campaign. That's the kind of thing *we* need. Photographs are all very well, but they don't have the emotive quality you expressed in those drawings. Must admit they moved me. Takes a lot to do that, these days, but they revived the smell, the feel, the sounds of the Sudan so very strongly. I even experienced the anger we all felt on withdrawing from Metemma, knowing we had failed. If your brother had managed to reach us with that communiqué, if we had sent him in to Khartoum earlier . . . but that's history.' He sipped his sherry, watching Vere speculatively. 'There's no man I'd sooner welcome to our Mess, Ashleigh. As I hinted a moment ago, that's not wholly due to sentiment. We received orders this morning to embark for the China Station at the beginning of March. The damned Boxers are becoming more than a mere nuisance. A show of strength is needed before they gain a hold on the country.' His smile accepted Vere as his subordinate already. 'I think we're the best regiment for the task, don't you?'

If Vere answered, it could have been no more than a murmured affirmative. His mind was racing. *China!* An opportunity to see a fabled land peopled by a race which could be unbelievably barbaric, yet which could create exquisite beauty of every form. A chance to widen his knowledge further, to deepen personal experiences and understanding of the world. It was an irresistible lure for any artist eager to capture with pen and brush the unique quality of one of the oldest civilisations.

Throughout the meal Vere grappled with indecision. Italy or China? Dunwoody believed the matter resolved, but it was not. Even so, the man must be given some answer when he left at the end of the evening. Italy offered a multitude of pleasures, but would they be enough to quieten the restlessness within him? China beckoned, but transferring to the West Wilts would burden him with the achievements of his ancestors. He would simply become Sir Gilliard's grandson, or Roland's second son, or the brother of . . . Could he accept that last and remain silent? Allowing an old man his dream was one thing; serving with men who mistakenly lionised a young scoundrel was another. Yet should he allow a plaster hero to dominate his life further by preventing the enrichment of it with a trip to the Orient? Had he not shrugged off Vorne's ghost at Omdurman? Memories of those wretched prisoners made him think again of Floria. In Italy he might find the answer to *that* problem. Which was he: artist or soldier? Could he continue to be both?

He had still not reached an answer to that question when Sir Gilliard rose to make his customary speech. Then, as his grandfather began to recount the story fabricated from conjecture into a gallant myth, which in turn had been accepted as the thrilling truth, Vere found the answer to his uneasiness. It was not a man but a *concept* they were here to honour. Vorne Ashleigh represented ideal manhood: courage, endeavour, strength, devotion, patriotism; an upholder of right and freedom, defender of the weak and oppressed. During the past eighteen months Vere had witnessed these virtues around him. Every man possessed *one* of them.

Civilisation had always needed heroes for inspiration. Others had performed deeds of greater daring than the supposed heroic crawl of a man determined to deliver a vital message. It was not the actual doing of them, but the belief that they had been done which was important. That belief had driven him to seek richer experiences and deeper understanding of his own personality; it had caused Val to fight back after adversity. The West

Wilts needed its hero of Khartoum as much as England needed its martyr, Charles Gordon. The faults and blemishes of the men themselves were immaterial, it was what they inspired which was vital. The family regiment might soon have a hero of Peking, or Shanghai, or Canton because of that inspiration. Long live heroes!

When Vere rose to his feet glass in hand, along with the other scarlet-jacketed warriors, his silent toast was for all those lying beneath the lone and level sands of the desert who had died with honour, for they were the true heroes.